Ann Cleeves is the author behind ITV's *Vera* and BBC One's *Shetland*. She has written over 30 novels, and is the creator of detectives Vera Stanhope and Jimmy Perez — characters loved both on screen and in print. She is a multimillion-copy bestselling author, and her books are sold worldwide. Ann worked as a probation officer, bird observatory cook and auxiliary coastguard before she started writing. She is a member of 'Murder Squad', working with other British northern writers to promote crime fiction. In 2006 Ann was awarded the Duncan Lawrie Dagger (CWA Gold Dagger) for Best Crime Novel, for *Raven Black*, the first book in her Shetland series. In 2012 she was inducted into the CWA Crime Thriller Awards Hall of Fame, and in 2017 awarded the CWA Diamond Dagger. She lives in North Tyneside.

You can visit the author's website at www.anncleeves.com

THE LONG CALL

In North Devon, Detective Inspector Matthew Venn stands outside the crematorium as his father's funeral takes place. The day Matthew turned his back on the strict Christian sect in which he grew up, he lost his family too. Now he's back, not just to mourn his father at a distance, but to take charge of his first major case in the Two Rivers region: a complex place not quite as idyllic as tourists suppose. A body has been found on the beach at Crow Point: a man, stabbed to death, with a tattoo of an albatross on his neck. The investigation will take Matthew straight back into the community he left behind, and the deadly secrets that lurk there.

ANN CLEEVES

THE LONG CALL

Complete and Unabridged

CHARNWOOD
Leicester

First published in Great Britain in 2019 by
Macmillan
an imprint of Pan Macmillan
London

First Charnwood Edition
published 2020
by arrangement with
Pan Macmillan
London

A catalogue record for this book is available
from the British Library.

ISBN 978–1–4448–4449–8

Published by
Ulverscroft Limited
Anstey, Leicestershire
Set by Words & Graphics Ltd.
Anstey, Leicestershire
Printed and bound in Great Britain by
T. J. International Ltd., Padstow, Cornwall

This book is printed on acid-free paper

For Issy, Martin, Paul and Sue,
without whom this book would never
have been written.

Acknowledgements

I do the easy bit: the sitting-at-the-kitchen-table-telling-stories bit. The hard work of getting the book to readers is done by a magnificent team on both sides of the Atlantic and beyond. So huge thanks to Pan Mac in London, especially Vicki, Charlotte, Natalie and Anna and to the reps who slog up and down the motorways building relationships with booksellers. The same goes to the Minotaur team in New York, especially to Catherine, Sarah and Martin. My agents Sara and Moses are always there to support me with advice and good humour — I'm not entirely sure when they sleep. Maura has been, as always, amazing, though I'll probably never forgive her for leaving me! Thanks to the libraries and booksellers who keep me reading and writing. And finally, a special thanks to a reader, Jacquie White, who gave me the courage to tackle this subject.

Dear Reader

This is a new character and a new series. Having worked with Vera Stanhope and Jimmy Perez for so long, I feel nervous introducing Matthew Venn to you, almost like a teenager bringing a new girlfriend or boyfriend home for the first time. I hope that you'll like him, despite his lack of confidence and his awkwardness in company.

The Long Call takes me back to North Devon, where I spent much of my childhood. It grew out of a visit to a schoolfriend, walks round old haunts, discussions about the people we knew. I'd forgotten quite how beautiful the place is, but sometimes beauty is skin deep, and it's that contrast which interests me most. As with Shetland and Northumberland, there's so much to reveal about the area and the people who live there.

Creating a new character and a new setting is always challenging and I hope that you will come to love Matthew and North Devon as much I have enjoyed creating them.

Thanks and all best wishes,

Ann

1

The day they found the body on the shore, Matthew Venn was already haunted by thoughts of death and dying. He stood outside the North Devon Crematorium on the outskirts of Barnstaple, a bed of purple crocus spread like a pool at his feet, and he watched from a distance as the hearse carried his father to the chapel of rest. When the small group of mourners went inside, he moved closer. Nobody questioned his right to be there. He looked like a respectable man, a wearer of suits and sober ties, prematurely grey-haired and staid. Not a risk-taker or a rule-breaker. Matthew thought he could have been the celebrant, arriving a little late for the service. Or a diffident mourner, sheepish and apologetic, with his soft skin and sad eyes. A stranger seeing him for the first time would expect sympathy and comfortable words. In reality, Matthew was angry, but he'd learned long ago how to hide his emotions.

He checked his feet to make sure that no flowers had been crushed, then walked between the headstones towards the path. The door to the chapel of rest had been left open — it was a warm day for so early in the year — and he could hear the service underway inside. The rich and passionate tone of a voice he'd have known anywhere: Dennis Salter, rousing his troops, persuading them that Andrew Venn was in

1

heaven and they might be sad for themselves, but they should not be for their brother. Then came the heavy breathing of an electric organ and the slow and deliberate notes of a hymn that Matthew recognized but couldn't name. He pictured Alice Wozencroft bent double over the keys, dressed entirely in black, hands like claws, a nose like a beak. As close to a crow as a woman could be. She'd been old even when he was a boy. Then he'd been a member of the Barum Brethren by birth and by commitment. His parents' joy and hope for the future. Now he was cast out. This was his father's funeral but he wasn't welcome.

The hymn ground to a dreary close and he turned away. Soon the service would be over. His father's coffin would slide behind the curtain and be turned to ash. The small group of mostly elderly women would gather in the sunshine to talk, then they might move on to his mother's house for tea and home-baked cakes. Tiny glasses of sweet sherry. His name might be mentioned in passing. These people would understand that a bereaved woman would be missing her only son at a time like this, though, despite their sympathy, there would be no question that he should have been invited. It had been his choice to leave the Brethren. Matthew stood for a moment, thinking that lack of faith had little to do with choice. Doubt was a cancer that grew unbidden. He pushed away the guilt that still lurked somewhere in his body, physical, like toothache. The root of his anger. And the tattered remnant of belief that made him think that his father, the spirit or soul of his father, might be somewhere watching him, still disappointed in his son. Then he walked quickly back to his car.

The call came when he was nearly there. He leaned against the perimeter wall of the cemetery, his face to the light. It was Ross May, his colleague, his constable. Ross's energy exhausted him. Matthew could feel it fizzing through the ether and into his ear. Ross was a pacer and a shouter, a pumper of iron. A member of the local running club and a rugby player. A team player except, it seemed, when he was at work.

'Boss. Where are you?'

'Out and about.' Matthew was in no mood to discuss his whereabouts with Ross May.

'Can you get back here? Someone's found a body on the beach at Crow Point. Your neck of the woods.'

Matthew thought about that. 'Accident?' It happened, even in still weather. The tides there were treacherous. 'Someone out in a small boat and washed ashore?'

'No. The clothes are dry and they found him above the tideline. And there's a stab wound.' Matthew had only heard Ross this excited before in the run up to an important match.

'Where are you?'

'On my way. Jen's with me. The news has only just come through. There's a plod there who went out to the first call. Like you, HQ thought it would be an accident.'

Plod. Matthew bit back a criticism about the

3

lack of respect for a colleague. *You speak about a fellow officer like that and you'll end up back in uniform yourself.* This wasn't the time. Matthew was still new to the team. He'd save the comment for the next appraisal. Besides, Ross was the DCI's golden boy and it paid to go carefully. 'I'll meet you at the scene. Park at the end of the toll road and we'll walk from there.' The last thing they needed was a car stuck in the sand on the track to the point.

This early in the season there was little tourist traffic. In the middle of the summer it could take him more than an hour to drive home from the police station in Barnstaple, nose to tail behind big cars that blocked the narrow lanes and would have been ridiculous even in the London suburbs where they were registered. Today he sailed over the new bridge across the River Taw; upstream, he glimpsed Rock Park and the school where he'd been a student. He'd been a dreamer then, escaping into stories, losing himself on long, lonely walks. Imagining himself as a poet in the making. No one else had seen him that way. He'd been anonymous, one of those kids easily forgotten by teachers and the other pupils. When he'd turned up at a reunion a few years ago, he'd realized he'd had few real friends. He'd been too much of a conformer, too pious for his own good. His parents had told him he'd be a great preacher and he'd believed them.

He was jolted back to the present when he hit Braunton. A village when he'd been growing up but it felt like a small town now, not quite on the coast, but the gateway to it. The kids were

4

coming out of school, and he tried to control his impatience at the lights in the village centre. Then a left turn towards the mouth of the estuary, where the Taw met the Torridge and flowed into the Atlantic. In the distance to the north stood the shoulder of Baggy Point, with the white block of a grand hotel just below the horizon. Monumental, but at the same time insubstantial because of the distance and the light.

This, as Ross had said, was home territory, but because he was approaching a crime scene, Matthew took in the details. The small industrial park, where they made surfboards and smart country clothes; the strip fields, brought back to life to feed incomers and posh grockles organic vegetables. The road narrowed; on each side a dry-stone wall, the stones laid edge on, with a hedge at the top. There were already catkins and soon there would be primroses. In sheltered parts of their garden they were already in bloom.

When Matthew hit the marsh, the sky widened and his mood lifted, just as it always did. If he still believed in the Almighty, he'd have thought his response to the space and the light a religious experience. It had been a wet winter and the ditches and the pools were full, pulling in gulls and wading birds. The flatland still had the colours of winter: grey, brown and olive. No sight of the sea here, but if he got out of the car, he'd be able to smell it, and in a storm he'd hear it too, the breakers on the long beach that ran for miles towards the village of Saunton.

He got to the toll road that led to the river and

saw a uniformed officer standing there, and a patrol car, pulled onto the verge opposite the toll keeper's cottage. The officer had been about to turn Matthew back, but he recognized him and lifted the barrier. Matthew drove through then stopped, pushed a button so his window was lowered.

'Were you first on the scene?'

'Yes, it came in as an accident.' The man was young and still looked slightly queasy. Matthew didn't ask if it was his first body; it would certainly be his first murder. 'Your colleagues are already there. They sent me up to keep people away.'

'Quite right. Who found him?'

'A woman dog-walker. Lives in one of those new houses in Chivenor. She's arranged for a neighbour to pick up her kid from school, but she wanted to be home for him. So I checked her ID, took her address and phone number and then I let her go. I hope that was okay.'

'Perfect. No point having her hanging around.' Matthew paused. 'Are there any other cars down there?'

'Not any more. An elderly couple turned up to their Volvo just as I was arriving. I got their names and addresses and took the car reg, but they'd been walking in the other direction and said they hadn't seen anything. Then I still thought it was an accident so I didn't really ask them much and let them drive off.'

'I don't know how long you'll be here,' Matthew said. 'I'll get someone to relieve you as soon as possible.'

6

'No worries.' The man nodded towards the cottage. 'I had to explain to them what was happening and they've already been out to offer tea. They say they'll keep an eye if I need to use their loo.'

'I'll be back to chat to them. Can you ask them to stick around until I get to them?'

'Oh, they wouldn't miss it for the world.'

Matthew nodded and drove on. He'd left the window down and now he *could* hear the surf on the beach and the cry of a herring gull, the sound naturalists named *the long call*, the cry which always sounded to him like an inarticulate howl of pain. These were the noises of home. There was a bend in the road and he could see the house. Their house. White and low and sheltered from the worst of the wind by a row of bent sycamores and hawthorns. A family home though they had no family yet. It was something they'd talked about and then left in the air. Perhaps they were both too selfish. They'd got the place cheap because it was prone to flooding. They'd never have been able to afford it otherwise. If there was a high tide and a westerly gale, the protective bank would be breached and the water from the Taw would flood the marsh. Then they'd be surrounded like an island. But the view and the space made it worth the risk.

He didn't stop and open the gate to the garden, but drove on until he saw Ross's car. Then he parked up and climbed the narrow line of dunes until he was looking down at the shore. Here, the river was wide and it was hard to tell where the Taw ended and the Atlantic began.

Ahead of him the other North Devon river, the Torridge, fed into the sea at Instow. Crow Point jutted into the water from his side of the estuary, fragile now, eaten away by weather and water, and only accessible on foot. The sun was low, turning the sea to gold, throwing long shadows, and he squinted to make out the figures in the distance. Tiny Lowry figures, almost lost in the vast space of sand, sea and sky. He slid down the dune to the beach and walked towards them just below the tideline.

They stood at a distance from the body, waiting for the pathologist to arrive and the crime scene investigators to come with their protective tent. Matthew thought they were lucky that it was a still day and the man had been found on the dry sand away from the water. Exposed here, a gale would have the tent halfway to America and a high tide would have him washed away. There was no time pressure, apart from the walkers and the dog-owners who'd want their beach back. And the usual pressure of needing to inform relatives that a loved one had died, to get the investigation moving.

Jen and Ross had been looking out for him and Jen waved as soon as he hit the shore. The Puritan in Matthew disapproved of Jen, his sergeant. She'd had her kids too young, had bailed out of an abusive marriage and left behind her Northern roots to get a post with Devon and Cornwall Police. Now her kids were teens and she was enjoying the life that she'd missed out on in her twenties. Hard partying and hard drinking; if she'd been a man, you'd have called her predatory. She was red-haired and fiery. Fit and gorgeous and she liked her men the same way. But despite himself, Matthew admired her guts and her spirit. She brought fun and laughter to the office and she was the best detective he'd ever worked with.

'So, what have we got?'

'Hard to tell until we can get in to look at him properly.' Ross turned to face the victim.

Matthew looked at the man. He lay on his back on the sand, and Matthew could see the stab wound in the chest, the bloodstained clothing.

'How did anyone think this was an accident?'

'When the woman found him, he was lying face down,' Ross said. 'The uniform turned him over.' He rolled his eyes, but Matthew could understand how that might happen. From the back it *would* look like an accident, and community officers wouldn't have much experience of dealing with unexplained death.

The man wore faded jeans, a short denim jacket over a black sweatshirt, boots that had seen better days, the tread gone, worn almost to a hole at the heel. His hair so covered in sand that it was hard to tell the colour. On his neck a tattoo of a bird. Matthew was no expert, but the bird had long wings. A gannet perhaps or an albatross, subtly drawn in shades of grey. The victim was slight, not an old man, Matthew thought, but beyond that it was impossible to guess from this distance. Ross was fidgeting like a hyperactive child. He found inactivity torture. *Tough*, Matthew thought. *It's about time you learned to live with it*. There was something of the indulged schoolboy about Ross. It was the gelled hair and designer shirts, the inability to understand a different world view. He seemed a man of certainty. His marriage to Melanie, whom Jen had once described as the perfect fashion accessory, hadn't changed him. If anything, Melanie's admiration only confirmed his inflated opinion of himself.

'I'm going to talk to the people who live in the toll keeper's cottage. The gate's automatic these days — you just throw money into the basket — but they'll know the regulars and might have seen something unusual.' Matthew had already turned to walk back along the shore to his car and threw the next comment over his shoulder. 'Jen, you're with me. Ross, you wait for the pathologist. Give me a shout when she arrives.'

Glancing to see the disappointment in Ross's face, he felt a ridiculous, childish moment of glee.

2

Maurice Braddick was worried about his daughter. The social worker at the day centre had come up with this notion to make Luce more independent. *Let her get the bus back from town by herself. We'll make sure she's at the stop on time and you live at the end of the route. No danger of Lucy missing her stop. She can walk up the street to the house. She knows the way.*

Maurice knew what that was all about. Lucy was thirty now and he was eighty. Getting on. Lucy had been a late child; a bit of a miracle, Maggie had said. But now Maggie was dead and he wasn't as strong as he once was. He'd always thought he'd go first, because he'd been ten years older. It had never occurred to him that he'd be the one left behind, having to make decisions, holding things together. The social worker thought he wouldn't be able to cope much longer with his lovely great lump of a daughter, because she had a learning disability. The social worker thought Maurice should be making arrangements for after he was gone. That might be sensible enough but *he* thought they were less concerned about Lucy's independence than saving the council the taxi fare.

Every day since the new regime, he'd waited at his window to watch for his daughter walking up the lane. They lived in a little house on the edge

11

of Lovacott village. He and Maggie had been there since they were married. It had been council then, but they'd bought it when the rules changed, thought it'd be a bit of an investment for Lucy. It was a semi at the end of a row of eight, curved around a patch of grass, where kids sometimes kicked a ball about. There was a long garden at the back looking out on a valley, with a view of Exmoor in the distance. These days, Maurice spent most of his time in the garden; he grew all their own veg and they had a run with half a dozen hens. He'd grown up on a farm and worked as a butcher in a shop in Barnstaple, knew about livestock dead and alive. Lucy wasn't much into healthy eating, but she could sometimes be persuaded if she picked a few salad leaves herself or fetched the eggs. He paused for a moment to regret the passing of Barnstaple as he'd known it. Butchers' Row had been full of butchers' shops then. Now the little shops facing the pannier market were smart delis and places that sold pixie-shittery to the tourists. There wasn't one real butcher left.

He was standing by the living room window because that had the best view of the road from the village. As soon as he glimpsed her coming around the corner he'd move away, so she wouldn't know he was looking out for her, worrying. On the windowsill there was a photo of Lucy, one of his favourites. She was standing between two friends with her arms around them: Chrissie Shapland, who had Down's Syndrome too, and young Rosa Holsworthy. They were all beaming straight into the camera. He looked

12

outside again, but there was still no sign of Lucy walking down the road.

The afternoons it was raining Maurice was pleased, because that gave him the excuse to drive up and wait for the bus. Lucy didn't like getting wet. If it was sunny like today, he waited. He'd always found it best to do what he was told and besides, he loved to see Lucy's triumphant smile as she rounded the corner, her bag slung across her shoulder, proud because she'd made it home on her own. His mood lifted, just to see her. Today she was a little later than he would have expected. The bus should have been in twenty minutes ago and it was only a ten-minute walk to the house. He was just thinking that he'd walk up to the main road to check that all was well when there she was, dressed in the yellow dress that she loved so much, plump as a berry.

She gave him a wave as she approached but there was no wide smile. Perhaps the walk had become routine, even a bit of a chore. Luce had never been one for exercise. That was something else the social worker nagged about. *We've noticed she's been putting on a bit of weight, Mr Braddick. You should be careful what she's eating, cut out all the fat and the sugar. No more chocolate! And what about taking her swimming? She loves it when they go from the centre. Or you could both get out for a walk when the weather's better.* Maurice thought it was easy for them. They didn't have to deal with the sulks when she couldn't get her way. And really, if she liked a piece of cake after her tea, what was the harm? He wasn't one for walking much either

13

and he'd never learned to swim.

He walked around to the front door to greet her as she came in. 'All right, maid? I'll put the kettle on, shall I, and you can tell me all about your day?' Because she had a better social life than he did since he'd retired and he liked to hear her chatting about what she'd been up to. It made a change from the telly. Maggie had been the one who made friends and most of her pals from the village had stopped trying to get in touch with him. Some of them had turned up when she'd first died but he hadn't known what to say to them. He'd just wanted to be on his own then; now, he thought, he might welcome their company.

Lucy pulled the strap of her bag over her head and took off the purple woollen cardigan she'd been wearing over the yellow dress.

'The man wasn't on the bus today.'

'Oh?' He was in the kitchen now, kettle switched on, not giving her his full attention. He opened the biscuit tin and set it on the table. 'What man might that be?'

'My friend. Most days he sits next to me. He makes me laugh.' She'd followed Maurice through to the kitchen and stood leaning against the door frame. Her voice was troubled and now he did listen to her properly. He'd known, he thought, watching her walk towards the house, no smile, that something was wrong. 'I waited when I got off the bus in case he came to see me there.'

'Do you know him from the Woodyard?' Lucy wasn't the only person from the day centre who'd been encouraged to be more independent.

She shook her head. 'He doesn't go to the day centre. I've seen him before, though. On the bus. He tells me secrets.' She frowned again. Her accent was pure North Devon, just like his. Warm and thick like the cream his mother used to make. Not always very clear to strangers, but he was tuned into it, tuned into her moods.

'Where's he from, maid?' Maurice didn't like this. Lucy was a trusting soul. Anyone who showed her kindness was a potential friend. Or a boyfriend. Maggie had tried to talk to her about it, about the people she could hug and the people she should keep at a bit of a distance, but he couldn't find the right words.

'I dunno.' She looked away. 'I just seen him around.' Making it clear she didn't want to answer the question. She could be stubborn as a mule when she chose.

Maurice turned back to face her. 'Did he ever do anything? Say something to upset you?'

She shook her head and sat down heavily. 'No!' As if the idea was ridiculous. 'He's my friend.' Her face was still red with the exertion of walking.

'And he didn't do anything he shouldn't? He didn't touch you?' Maurice tried to keep the worry out of his voice. Luce picked up the tone of a person's voice better than she understood the words.

'No, Dad. He was always nice to me.' And there was that wonderful smile again that lit up the room and made the world seem better.

Maurice felt a rush of relief. He didn't know

how he'd manage if someone hurt his daughter. He'd promised Maggie at the end that he'd always look after her. He had a brief picture of the overheated room in the hospice. Maggie, thin and bony with hair so fine he could see her pink scalp through it, gripping his arm. Fierce. Making him swear. She should have known him better than that, known he loved Lucy as much as she did. And perhaps she *had* known, because afterwards, she'd smiled and said sorry, she'd lifted his hand to her lips and kissed it. He chased the image away.

'He gave me sweets,' Lucy said. 'Every day on the bus he gave me sweets.'

That made Maurice worried again. He thought he'd phone the social worker and tell her it wasn't safe for Lucy to travel on her own on the bus. If he had to, he'd scrape together the money and pay for a taxi himself.

'Where did he usually get off the bus, this man?' Maurice set the mug of tea in front of Lucy. She liked it milky and weak.

'Here,' she said. 'With me. That's why I was late. I waited in case he'd got another bus and he'd come back to see me.'

'Maybe you'll have seen him in the village then.'

She reached out and took a biscuit from the tin. She nodded but Maurice could tell that he'd lost her attention. Now she was here with her dad and her tea and a biscuit, the man seemed forgotten. Any memory that might have troubled her had disappeared.

16

3

The woman had the door of the toll keeper's cottage open almost before they'd got out of the car. There was something hungry, desperate, about her need for information.

'I'm DI Venn,' Matthew said. 'This is DS Rafferty.'

'Hilary and Colin Marston. You're here about the body.' She looked them up and down. 'You're detectives. Unexpected death, your chap out there said, but this isn't natural causes, is it? Not just a heart attack or an accident. There wouldn't be all this fuss for an accident.'

'Perhaps we could come in and ask you a few questions?'

'Of course.' She backed away and they were let into a hall. A pair of wellingtons stood at the foot of the stairs and a waxed jacket hung on a peg next to a smart black coat, which seemed out of place in the cottage.

It was hard to age her. The hair had been dyed almost black and she was wearing make-up. Late fifties? Matthew wondered. Early sixties? She was big-boned and strong, taller than the man who stood behind her in the passage. She wore black trousers and a black jacket over a white top, office wear for a middle-manager, Matthew thought. The coat must belong to her. Again, out of place, here on the edge of the marsh.

Her husband seemed more at home. He was short and round, a woollen jersey stretched over his stomach. Matthew thought they must have moved in recently; there was a hint of a Midlands accent and he'd seen the previous residents — an elderly couple who'd come out to collect the toll and have a chat — at Christmas. Perhaps the automatic barrier had been installed because the couple had retired. Or one of them had died. It seemed all he was thinking about today was death. The woman led them into a living room and the man followed. The room was cluttered, a little untidy. Uncared for. It was as if they were camping out here. Matthew wondered what had brought them to the house. They all sat awkwardly for a moment, staring at each other across an orange pine coffee table.

It was Jen Rafferty who spoke first while he was still taking in the surroundings. 'If you could just repeat your names for our notes.'

'Hilary,' the woman said. 'Hilary Marston, and this is my husband Colin.' Then she started speaking again and Matthew's curiosity about the couple's background was answered without need for any questions. 'Colin took early retirement, redundancy really. He worked in the legal team for a car manufacturer; that's all changed of course. Everything's outsourced these days, nobody has any pride in British industry now. And our area had changed — people from outside moving in. One time, you knew all your neighbours. Not any more.'

Matthew broke in. Jen leaned so far to the left that she'd only recently become reconciled to the

18

Labour Party. She couldn't cope with intolerance, and he could tell that she was already a bit prickly. 'What brought you to North Devon?'

'We'd been here on holiday,' Hilary Marston said. 'Loads of times. We thought: *That's the place for us to end our days.* We never had any kids to think about and we loved it to bits. So quiet and so clean.' A pause. 'No foreigners.'

'Well, it's certainly very quiet *here*.' Jen had an edge to her voice that only Matthew picked up.

'Yeah, well,' Hilary said. She shot a look at her husband. 'Sometimes you can have too much of a good thing. We're only renting here — it certainly wouldn't be our choice of furniture — and it wasn't the best decision we ever made. Maybe we saw the cottage through rose-coloured glasses when we viewed it in the summer. Colin's a birdwatcher. The marsh is his idea of heaven. It's not mine. We won't be staying. We've put an offer in on a house in Barnstaple, where there's a bit more life.' She paused. 'A bit more culture. And it'll be closer to work for me.'

'What is your work?'

'I'm a mortgage advisor with a bank in town. I was planning to retire too, but this job came up. Only part-time, but the extra cash is always useful.'

Matthew turned to Colin Marston. 'Were you out on the marsh birdwatching today?'

The woman, her resentment palpable, didn't give her husband the chance to answer. 'He's out there every day.'

Colin Marston ignored her. Perhaps her sniping was so common that it had become no

19

more than background noise for him. 'I do a daily census.' He spoke with a quiet pride. 'Real ornithological research is about regular counts of common birds. I'm not just a lister, interested in rarities.' The last sentence was spoken with a sneer.

'Does your research take you onto the beach too?'

'That's part of my census walk. I end up there. I count the gulls on the shore and come inland at Spindrift, then back along the toll road home.'

Spindrift. Our house. Matthew thought now he might have seen the man walking past, anonymous in the waxed jacket and wellingtons they'd seen in the hall, binoculars round his neck. Out in all weathers.

'What time were you there today?' Jen asked.

Colin Marston left the room. Through the open door, Matthew saw him take a soft-back notebook from an inside pocket of the jacket. He sat down again and opened it.

'Twelve thirty-five.' He looked up. 'I note the time at every watch point. My own way of working. Citizen science in action.'

In an armchair in the corner Hilary rolled her eyes. Matthew thought it must be a strange marriage if they had so little in common, if she could be so dismissive of her husband's passion.

'Did you see anything unusual while you were walking today?' He was aware of a silence and stillness in the room. An awareness of danger or, more likely, excitement. Perhaps it was a shared passive voyeurism that kept the couple together.

'I didn't see a body on the beach,' Marston

said. 'I asked your constable where it was and I know that I'd walked that way. I would have seen it.'

'But did you notice any strangers? You'd know the regulars if you're out every day.'

There was another silence, broken by the sound of a car pulling up outside. Matthew recognized it as belonging to Sally Pengelly, the pathologist. The barrier was raised and the car drove on.

'Who was that?' Hilary was on her feet.

'Just one of the team.' Matthew turned back to the husband. 'So, Mr Marston, any strangers?'

'There are always one or two people I don't recognize. Even at this time of year, there are visitors. And I don't take much notice unless they've got a dog that disturbs the birds while I'm counting.'

'But today.' Matthew was a patient man. 'You must be a good observer, used to registering detail.'

The flattery appeared to have worked. Marston looked back at the notebook and seemed to be reliving his walk on the shore. 'There was a couple, a man and a woman. He was in a suit, not really dressed for the beach. She was a bit younger and she was wearing jeans.' He paused. 'I was watching something I thought might be a little gull and they flushed it.'

Matthew was thinking the man in the suit seen by Marston couldn't be their victim because the clothes didn't tally, but Marston was still speaking.

'They were walking hand in hand and they

21

stopped once to kiss. Not just a peck, if you know what I mean. As if they'd not been together for a long time.' He stared out of the window. 'I wondered if they might be having an affair, because they came in two cars and there was a sense that they were doing something dangerous. Exciting.' His voice was wistful.

'You saw the cars?'

'Yes. They climbed the dunes and after a bit I followed them. I wanted a better view of the birds near the tideline.'

Jen shot Matthew an amused glance. *Yeah right! Not that you were hoping to catch them making out.*

'I saw them getting into their cars. I didn't get the reg of either of them, though. Pity, they might have been useful for you.'

'But you do remember the make of the vehicles? The colour?'

'Of course!' Marston almost sounded offended that the question had been asked. 'As Hilary said, I used to work in the car industry. Behind the scenes, working on contracts, but it's still in my blood. One was a red Fiesta. A few years old. That was the woman's. And a black Passat.'

'You saw them drive off?'

Marston paused for a moment. 'I saw the man drive off. The woman was still in her car, looking at her phone, when I dropped down onto the beach.'

'Did you see anyone else?' The low sun must have been streaming in through the window all afternoon and the heat had been trapped in the small room. It seemed airless.

'One guy in the distance.' A man, it seemed, held less interest for Colin Marston than a couple.

'Could you describe him?'

'He was a long way off, close to Crow Point.' Colin set his notebook on the table in front of him.

'And he was on his own?'

'Yeah. Though maybe he was waiting for someone. He didn't seem to move while I was there. He was still on the beach when I headed back towards Spindrift.' The man looked up sharply. 'You live in the house there, don't you? I thought I knew you. I've seen you in the garden and going through the toll.'

Matthew didn't answer. Instead he asked another question of his own. 'How many cars were parked there when you made your way inland?'

'Just a Volvo. They're regulars. An older couple.'

Matthew nodded to show he understood. Those would be the people seen by the constable on duty outside. It was so warm in the room that it was an effort to move. He stood up and thanked the couple for their help.

'What happens now?' Hilary was on her feet too, leaning forward, desperate for more information.

'We continue with our enquiries,' Matthew said. 'Someone will be in touch if we need to speak to you again.'

As he stopped to unlock the car he saw both the Marstons at the window, staring out at them.

23

★　★　★

The CSIs' vehicle passed them as they were getting into Matthew's car, and they must have worked quickly because by the time he and Jen arrived at the scene, the tent had been erected and a white-suited team were doing a finger-touch search of the surrounding sand. Ross was standing well away, still pacing.

'Any ID?' Matthew was hoping they could inform relatives before the press got hold of the story. He was surprised they hadn't already arrived. He could imagine the Marstons spreading the news. They'd enjoy their fifteen minutes of fame. Perhaps the long walk from the toll gate had put the journos off, or perhaps the couple hadn't known who to contact with the story.

'No wallet or credit cards,' Ross said.

'You're not thinking a mugging gone wrong? Not all the way out here?'

Ross continued. 'There was this in the back jeans pocket.' He held out a scrap of paper: a pulled apart envelope with a shopping list on the blank side. *Tomatoes, eggs, rice, bin bags.* On the other a printed address. No name. *The Occupier, 20 Hope Street, Ilfracombe.* Some form of junk mail. The name of the street rang a faint bell for Matthew, but he couldn't picture it. 'Should we check it out?' Ross was bouncing on the balls of his feet, eager for any form of action.

Matthew relented. 'Both of you go.' There might be a wife, kids or an elderly mother and Jen was brilliant with families. 'Give me a ring

24

when you've got something.' He looked at his watch. It was gone six and the light was already fading. A buoy in the estuary was flashing. 'Let's meet at the station at eight thirty this evening and we'll pull together all we know.'

★   ★   ★

He stood outside the gate to Spindrift and waited for a moment. The curtains hadn't been closed and he could see the kitchen, fully lit, like a stage set. An orange pan was on the stove and a jug of daffodils stood on the green oilskin cloth that covered the table. Matthew had bought them the day before as buds and they were nearly open. And as if this was a piece of theatre, a single actor stood back-on in front of a chopping board. Hair so blond it was nearly white. A T-shirt with a logo that urged support for whales or dolphins or the entire planet. There was a chest of drawers full of the shirts and Matthew was too far away to make out the detail of the design. Jonathan, his husband and love of his life, the endless optimist, who had lifted him from depression and brought him to what felt like home. He still wasn't sure what Jonathan had seen in him, how they could be so happy.

Matthew lifted the latch on the gate and walked into the garden. Perhaps Jon heard the noise, because he turned and he must have seen Matthew's shadow, or a movement at least, because he waved. Inside there was the smell of good soup and new wood. Jon was replacing rotten window frames. The house was his project

25

and once the day job was over, he spent his spare time working on it. Unlike Matthew, he had boundless energy, the build of labourer. There was sawdust in his hair and on his shoulders.

'Good timing. I was just about to have a beer.' Jon approached, the knife still in his hand, to kiss him.

'I can't. I have to go out later. Work.' Matthew explained about the body on the beach and thought he hated work coming so close to home. 'Weren't you stopped at the toll gate on your way in?'

'I took this afternoon off to get on with the window in the bedroom. Lieu time. I was home not long after midday. There was nobody on the gate then.'

'Did you see anything unusual?'

'Am I a suspect?' A big grin. The question was intended to lighten the mood. He could sense Matthew's stress.

'A witness, maybe.' He wasn't in the mood for jokes. A pause.

'Oh fuck, I'm sorry. I'd forgotten. It was your dad's funeral. Did they let you in?'

'I didn't try.'

'Oh, Matt. I knew I should have gone with you.'

Jon was brave. He would have faced out the relatives and the Brethren. He would have stood at the front, singing his heart out, and then charmed the old ladies afterwards. Matthew was a coward, more scared of embarrassment than breaking up a fight in a bar or facing an addict with a knife.

'Dad would have hated a scene,' Matthew said. 'Staying away was the least I could do for him.'

'They would have been the ones causing the scene. Not you.' But he gave Matthew a hug to show this wasn't something they'd fall out over.

They shared a meal — soup and freshly baked bread, cheese and a salad. Jon's competence astounded him. How could one man be so good at so much? Where had his confidence come from? In contrast, he felt endlessly incompetent.

'I should go,' Matthew said. He'd loaded the plates into the dishwasher. At least he could do that much. 'I've sent Ross and Jen to track down the relatives. We still don't have a name for the man.' He pulled on a jacket. Outside it was clear and still, with a slice of moon and stars sharp in the night sky. The only lights came from Instow and Appledore on the far shore. 'Don't wait up. It could be an all-nighter.'

And Jonathan wouldn't wait up. He'd potter with his projects and go to bed when he was tired. Matthew, however, couldn't settle when Jonathan was out. He'd fret, watching out for the headlights sweeping past the bedroom curtain. Sometimes Jon would go to the folk club in the pub in the village, drink too much and walk home, arriving almost as it was getting light. Then Matthew would pretend to be asleep and say nothing. His mother had nagged and his father had hated it.

4

Jen let Ross drive the few miles to Ilfracombe. He took it for granted that he'd be behind the wheel and sometimes she couldn't be arsed to make a fuss. Besides, it meant she was free to text the kids and check they were both in, doing homework, and that they'd foraged for something to eat. They were old enough to fend for themselves now and they'd always been resilient and self-contained; they'd had to be.

She still got anxious, though. Guilty because she wasn't there, cooking something nutritious, making intelligent conversation as they ate together. But they weren't the perfect family you saw in TV sitcoms and they never would be. She'd tried doing the selfless wife and mother thing when they lived in Merseyside and it had nearly killed her. Literally. That didn't mean that she didn't wish she could be better at it, more organized, there more for them. It wasn't that she liked work better than she liked Ella and Ben. Not exactly. But work gave her life structure and meaning and she needed it. Without it she'd go crazy.

They texted her back. Yes, they were both in. Yes, they'd found pizza in the freezer. No, they weren't planning to go out again. When they'd first moved to Devon and they were younger, Jen had found a string of childminders for them, but the women she'd employed had been used to polite kids and parents with regular hours. Despite their professional smiles, they'd struggled with Jen's rackety Scousers, their bad language and their independence. In the end, Jen had made do with Adam, a sixth-form lad, who was happy to babysit for pocket money as and when needed. It wasn't ideal. Often, Jen had come home to chaos, Adam on the sofa, engrossed in his phone, while the kids ran riot upstairs. Or the three of them squabbling over the controls of a computer game. They'd survived. Adam had headed off to university and still came back to see them when he was home, though the kids were independent now. Occasionally she had sexy dreams about Adam, who'd turned into a very fit young man.

She was still thinking about Adam, the tight bum in the skinny jeans, when they crossed the roundabout on the high ground at Mullacott Cross. It felt like a bit of Exmoor up here, even though they were so close to the town and the descent into Ilfracombe. There were hedges, bent by the westerly wind, and lambs. Once Ilfracombe had been a grand seaside resort, with elaborate gardens and hotels and a paddle steamer that carried passengers along the Bristol Channel to Somerset and South Wales. With cheap flights to the Mediterranean available so readily, it had faded, lost its purpose. The tourists had fled to Spain and the Greek islands instead. Now, the place was trying to find a new role.

The town was surrounded by hills and the lights of the place seemed held in a deep bowl directly below them. They drove past big villas, which had been turned into guest houses called *Sea View* or *Golden Sands*. Most had 'No Vacancies' boards, not because they were full but because this early in the season their owners had decided it wasn't worth opening. Ross followed his satnav into the town centre, stopped at the top of a long, steep street of three-storey terraced houses, beautifully proportioned but decaying now and turned into flats and bedsits. Some had boarded-up windows. An empty can, which had once held strong lager, rolled down the pavement.

'Hope Street,' Ross said. 'Otherwise known as addicts' avenue. I thought I recognized the address.'

Jen liked Ilfracombe, the mix and edginess of it. A few of her friends lived here and she'd considered moving herself because the houses were cheaper, the parties wilder and more her style. But the kids were settled at school now and the drive to work would be a bit of a drag. Like other former holiday towns, it pulled in transients and misfits, people lured by the prospect of seasonal work in the big hotels. When the trippers went home the workers stayed, because they'd found friends, or out of inertia, or because they had nothing left to return to. Some of the guest houses had been turned into hostels or bedsits, others rented out rooms for the winter, not caring that they had no real facilities for a long-term let. Hope Street contained those sorts of premises but there were signs of gentrification too; some houses had bright new paint and coloured blinds, window boxes and shrubs in tubs in the tiny front gardens. At the bottom of the street, Jen saw the silhouettes of two men, hunched together in conversation.

They found number twenty halfway down the hill. A black door, freshly painted. No sign that it was a place of multiple occupancy, no separate doorbells or letter boxes. No doorbell at all, so Ross knocked. Jen thought she heard someone moving inside. Ross knocked again and the door was opened to reveal a generous front hall, the floorboards stripped and patchily varnished, and a young woman who wore jeans and a long sweater in kingfisher blue, a slash of red lipstick.

'Hiya.' She looked them up and down with interest. 'Sorry, if you're selling something, I'm skint. And if you're selling religion, I'm an atheist. The resident God-botherer is out. So, there's nothing for you here.'

Jen thought she'd remember that next time she got cold callers at the door. 'We're not selling anything. We're police officers.'

'Is it about my bike?' Her face lit up. Expressions flew across her features like the shadows of clouds on a windy day. The face was never still. 'Don't tell me you've found it after all this time. We've got a new lock on the door into the back alley so we haven't had anything nicked since.'

'Not the bike,' Ross said. 'Perhaps we could come in.'

The woman led them into a large room at the back of the house. Jen, who was an expert on these things, thought all the furniture had been

31

upcycled or freecycled. Seating was a huge squashy sofa in purple velvet, cushions on the floor, a couple of armchairs that looked as if they'd been newly upholstered, but not quite finished. It seemed the craftsperson had become bored with the project. A long, low table had been formed from a plank door. On the walls posters and original paintings. A small black wood burner, dirty and unlit, and a wicker basket full of logs. A single patio door led out into a tiny yard, where huge ceramic pots provided a garden. Daffodils were already coming into bloom. There was a high wall with a rickety doorway, through which, Jen assumed, the stolen bicycle had been taken.

'Could we have your name?' Jen had chosen one of the armchairs. Ross was still standing.

'Gaby. Gaby Henry.'

'Do you own the house?'

'No, that's Caroline. Caz. Well, theoretically she owns it. It's mortgaged to the hilt. And of course, she was helped out with a deposit from the bank of mum and dad. Or just dad actually, because her mum died years ago. Helped too by the rent from her lodger. That's me.' A flash of a smile and a pause, as if she was a stand-up comedian waiting for applause after the punchline of a joke. Her voice was southern but not local. London maybe.

Jen leaned forward. 'A man was found dead on the beach at Crow Point this afternoon. There was something on his person to connect him to this address.' She paused. There was no response from the woman. For a moment Gaby stood very still. Jen looked at her, then continued. 'Do you have a husband? A partner?'

Now Gaby did speak. 'I'm fancy free. Caz has Edward. A curate. But he's not here at the moment. He doesn't live in. They don't believe in that sort of thing. No sex before marriage. They're Christians of the happy-clappy arm-waving variety.'

'Any male lodgers?'

There was a pause before she answered. 'Simon Walden. He's been here since October. Caz brought him in. He's one of her lost sheep.'

Jen thought that might be important; she'd come back to it. 'Could you describe Mr Walden?'

'He's a bit older than us. Pushing forty. We're planning a party for him in a few weeks' time. If he decides to behave himself.'

Jen was intrigued, but again refused to allow herself to be distracted. 'Weight? Height? Any distinguishing marks?'

'A bit taller than him.' Gaby nodded towards Ross. 'But about the same build. He has the tattoo of a bird on his neck. An albatross. He says he carried guilt round with him like the Ancient Mariner, so he had the tat done to remind him.'

Now Jen allowed herself to be distracted. 'Do you know what he meant by that?'

Gaby shook her head. 'After a few drinks he can get like that. Maudlin. Or angry.'

'But you let him stay?' This was Ross. He lived with his perfect wife in a tidy little house on an estate on the edge of Barnstaple. He must be

33

hating this place, the muck and the clutter. He certainly wouldn't share his home with strangers.

Gaby shrugged. 'He doesn't often lose it. Caz can manage him. Besides, he cooks like a dream.' She stopped speaking and stared at them. 'Are you telling me Simon's dead?'

'We don't know yet. It's possible.'

Gaby turned away from them. Jen thought she might be crying but when she looked back, she was quite composed and when she spoke her tone was still light, brittle. 'Shit, if he's dead, there'll be no more amazing Friday night feasts.'

'Have you got a photo?'

'Just a minute. We took a joint selfie a couple of weeks ago. I put it on Facebook, but I'll still have it on my phone.' Gaby flicked through her phone and then passed it across to Jen. There were three faces crammed into the image. Two women — Gaby and a short, round woman with big specs — then in the centre of the picture a man. Simon Walden. The body on the beach. In the photo his head was turned slightly and Jen could see the tattoo.

'I'm afraid that's him,' Jen said. She passed the phone to Ross, so he could see for himself that they had an ID for their victim.

'Did he kill himself?' Still the tough, flip shell didn't crack.

'Why? Would that surprise you? Had he talked about suicide?'

'He had really dark moods sometimes. That's how Caz met him. She works for a mental health charity. And she's too bloody soft for her own good.'

'Is this Caroline?' Jen took the phone back from Ross and pointed to the short woman with the glasses.

'Yeah, that's her. My landlady. My mate now too. We're as different from each other as chalk and cheese, but I love her to bits. I'm not sure she can quite cope with the chaos I've brought into her house . . . ' She waved her arm at the recycled furniture and art. 'She knows she'd be bored without me, though. And it's a bit cheerier than the place where she works: an ancient church hall filled with suicidal addicts and depressives.'

'What about you?' Jen asked. 'What do you do?'

'I'm the artist in residence at the Woodyard. I help horrible adolescents with behavioural problems to find themselves through art. And teach bored middle-aged women who want to dabble in watercolour. They got funding for me for three years.' She looked at Jen to check that she didn't have to explain the Woodyard Centre. Jen nodded to show she recognized the name. 'That's the day job. But mostly I paint. Painting's my true love. I went to art college when I left school and the Woodyard gives me my own studio space.'

'You must be very talented.' Jen sensed a slight sneer in her own voice. Jealousy perhaps. She'd have loved to be able to paint. 'How do you and Caroline know each other?'

'Through her father, Christopher. He's on the board of the Woodyard and he was one of the people who interviewed me for the residency.

I'm not local and when they appointed me, I needed somewhere to live. He put me in touch with Caz, who'd just bought this place and was looking for someone to share. Then Simon came along.' There was a sudden edge to her voice.

'You didn't get on with him?' Jen said.

'We were getting on fine without him. I suppose it changed the dynamics. I'm sad he's dead of course. But honestly? I won't be sorry to go back to the way it was before he turned up.'

Jen stared at the photograph again. For the remainder of the investigation this would be how she would remember the residents of Hope Street: Gaby, the arty one with the dark eyes and red lipstick, Caroline, the religious one with the big specs.

'Does Simon have any family? We need to inform them.'

'There's a wife,' Gaby said. 'She threw him out. I think she lives in Bristol but I don't have a name or address.'

'Work?'

'He spent last summer as a chef at the Kingsley House Hotel, here in Ilfracombe. When the season ended he lost his accommodation too of course. That's the gig economy for you.'

Jen nodded.

'Since then he's done a bit of volunteering at the Woodyard — he works in the cafe there, Caz or her dad got him in — but he's had no paid work.'

'How does he pay his rent?' Ross was less sympathetic to the troubles of seasonal workers. He thought they should get a proper job.

'I don't know,' Gaby said, 'but according to Caz, it landed up in her bank account every month. I hope she doesn't struggle without it.' A pause. 'Her father's loaded, though. I expect she'll survive.'

'Could we have a look at Mr Walden's room? It'll need to be sealed for a proper search, but we'd like a quick look now.'

Gaby nodded and got to her feet. They followed her to the first-floor landing, where she stopped. 'Simon's room is on the top floor at the back. I'll leave you to it, if that's okay.'

Jen thought Simon Walden had been given the smallest and darkest room, the one that nobody else had chosen. He was a lodger, a charity case and not a real friend. It was in the roof and faced up the hill looking over the yard and other houses, not to the sea. It was bare and impersonal. There was a single bed under the small dormer window. A white-painted wardrobe held a sparse number of clothes. No TV and no computer. A radio on the bedside table. No photos.

'He's someone who travelled light,' Jen said. 'It could be a monk's room.'

Ross was standing beside her, his back against the closed door. 'Or a prison cell.'

⋆　⋆　⋆

They found Gaby in the kitchen. An old-fashioned airing rack hung from the ceiling and she was taking towels and pillowcases from it and folding them on the table, smoothing the

37

pillowcases so they wouldn't need ironing. Jen recognized the technique. The woman stopped what she was doing when they came in. An opened bottle of wine and a half-full glass stood on the scrubbed pine table.

'What time are you expecting Caroline back?' Jen could have fancied a glass of wine herself. God knew when she'd get home to have one.

'Not until nine. I think I explained: she's a social worker for a mental health charity, attached to the church where her boyfriend's a curate. This is one of her nights for an evening session. She's passionate about it.' A pause. 'Her mother committed suicide. Maybe that's why she's so dedicated to the cause.'

'And Mr Walden was one of her clients?'

'Yeah,' Gaby said. 'Like I told you, one of her lost sheep.'

'Isn't it a bit unusual, inviting a client into your home?' Jen thought social workers were trained to keep their distance. All the professionals she'd ever met had been detached to the point of not caring.

'Well, I didn't think it was a good idea.' Gaby paused. 'When I first met him, I thought he was odd, creepy. I wanted him out. Caz said if I knew more about him, I'd be more supportive.'

'Did you find out any more about him?'

Gaby shook her head. 'Caz said she couldn't tell me any more because of confidentiality, so that didn't help much.' A pause. 'In the end, it's her house. I guess she can have whoever she wants to stay.'

'We'll need to come back tomorrow to speak

38

to your friend.' Jen looked at her watch. The briefing would start in half an hour and she didn't want to miss that. 'When would be a good time to catch you both before work?'

'About eight thirty? Neither of us start early.' She walked them to the front door. Jen thought she could be an actor as well as an artist. She gave nothing of herself away.

★ ★ ★

The police station in Barnstaple was concrete, ugly, built next to the civic centre that was already empty and earmarked for demolition. It looked out on the green space of Castle Hill. There was no castle now, and the hill, round as an upturned cup, was all that was left of the earthworks that had supported it. It was grassed over and covered with trees and bushes. Barnstaple stood inland from Ilfracombe. Once it had been a small market town, and the centre still felt like that, with its pannier market and busy high street, but the town had spread, sprawled. It had council estates and retail parks on the outskirts. Tourists coming for the first time might be disappointed by the initial impression it gave. It could have been any other English town. Apart from the river. The river, tidal still at this point, changing with the moon and the weather, made the place wilder, hardly a town at all. In good weather, Jen ate her lunchtime sandwiches on the green and sometimes walked to the top of the hill. Even from there you could smell the salt of the estuary

39

and there was the special light you only find close to the sea. She'd always loved the sea.

She knew she was lucky to be here. There were colleagues who would have given their right arm for a posting to Devon; she'd jumped to the top of the queue because she'd been daft enough to marry a bastard who'd knocked her around. She was grateful for the transfer and she loved the place, but sometimes she missed the buzz and challenge of city policing. And it felt like an escape, a cop-out. Why should she be the one who'd had to move? And why had the CPS cocked up the prosecution of her smooth-talking, brown-nosing accountant husband? He was still there, living it large in *her* patch, telling the world that she was a psycho, that the police had moved her to Devon because she couldn't cope with the stress of real policing. She'd been in Barnstaple for five years, but it still rankled.

On her way up the stairs she phoned Ella. Jen knew Ben would have headphones on and he wouldn't hear his phone. 'All okay?'

'Yeah.' Ella was a swot. She'd be lost in an equation. Or a chemical compound. Jen could tell she was distracted.

'I should be home by ten. Get yourselves to bed if you're tired, though.' Matthew Venn despised meetings that dragged on. He said there was nothing that couldn't be decided and achieved in an hour.

'Cool.' And the line went dead.

The room was full; there were volunteers who'd stayed on after their shift. Murder wasn't common in North Devon and Jen sensed affront

40

as well as excitement. She wondered if the team would be so keen on justice when they knew that the victim was an incomer from upcountry and not one of their own. Ross had bounded up the stairs ahead of her. He'd bagged the desk with the fastest computer and was obviously checking out the name they'd been given by Gaby Henry in Ilfracombe, digging the dirt on Simon Walden. Jen heard the whir of the printer. Ross would want to present any information he could find about the victim to the team. He'd probably take the credit for the ID too. Sometimes, Jen thought, she found him tricky to work with because he reminded her of her former husband. Competitive. Controlling.

Matthew called the room to order, but before he could speak, the DCI appeared. Joe Oldham was a big, lumbering man, but none of them had heard him coming. He had the ability to walk silently; Jen had looked up from her desk on several occasions to find him there, looking down at her, listening to her chatting to a colleague. Now she took care that he was nowhere around before she passed on any gossip that she wouldn't want him to hear. He'd moved to Devon as a constable but he was still a proud Yorkshireman, a sports fanatic, chair of the local rugby club. As different from Matthew as it was possible to be.

Oldham nodded to the group. 'I won't keep you. I know you've work to do.' He was wearing a sports jacket that had seen much better days and his shirt wasn't quite tucked into his belt. That was his image: the rugged old-fashioned copper who'd have nothing to do with media types. In contrast, Matthew looked as if he never left his office, smart, suited, closely shaved. His skin was pale as if it never saw sunlight. He could be a banker. Or an undertaker.

Oldham looked around the room. Jen thought she saw him wink at Ross. The son he'd never had. 'I just wanted to let you know I'm with you on this. Matthew here will report to me and you'll have all the resources you'll need.'

Then he disappeared as quietly as he'd arrived. To get in a couple of pints at the club before closing, Jen suspected. Ross, who was the rugby club's star fly half, would probably join him later and fill him in with all the details of the evening. Oldham didn't need to eavesdrop when he had a mole like Ross in the ranks. Once, Oldham would have wanted to take over the investigation, but he was on the long slide to retirement and his red face and big belly were signs that he was getting in practice for when the day finally arrived. Ross gave him the confidence that he still had a finger on the pulse.

Matthew took Oldham's place and waited until the DCI had left the room before speaking. He gave a brief summary of the discovery of the body and stuck photos of the locus on the board. 'Dr Pengelly has confirmed cause of death as a stab wound to the chest. The killer was facing his victim. No weapon was found at the scene.'

Ross stuck up his hand. 'Time of death?'

'Impossible to say with any accuracy. Some-time today. We might have a little more information after the post-mortem tomorrow.'

Matthew paused. 'There was no ID on our victim, but we found an address in his pocket and I hope that Ross and Jen can shed a little light. You've been to Ilfracombe to track it down?'

Ross was on his feet before Jen had a chance to answer. He'd printed out a photo and pinned it to the board. 'Simon Andrew Walden. Date of birth thirty-first of May 1979.' It was a classic mug-shot photo. Walden was looking directly at the camera. 'Joined the forces straight from school. Left the army in 2010 and ran his own business — a restaurant in Bristol — until 2013 when he was convicted of causing death by careless driving. He drove from a junction straight into the side of a passing car and a child was killed. Alcohol in his system, but just under the legal limit.'

Jen stared at the face and understood the albatross, the guilt.

'He served three months in prison. No contact with the police since that date as far as I can tell.'

'And we are sure this is our man?' Matthew looked at Jen and she answered immediately.

'We saw a photo and the tattoo is clearly visible.'

'Any more information?'

'The house is owned by a young woman, Caroline Preece. She lets out rooms to cover the rent. To a friend of hers and to Walden. The remaining tenant is Gaby Henry. She works as something arty at the Woodyard.' Jen paused because she understood that might be a complication for Matthew. Jonathan worked at

43

the Woodyard; he ran the place. Maybe it would be seen as a conflict of interest. 'No details but it seems Walden had mental health problems and Preece was his social worker. He also volunteered in the Woodyard.'

'Have we checked out Henry and Preece? Either of them known to us?'

Jen shook her head. 'Not even a parking ticket. Caroline Preece wasn't there so I'm going back in the morning.'

Matthew nodded, but said nothing. Jen thought that was classic Matthew Venn. He was a man who never opened his mouth unless he had something useful to say.

5

When the police left, Gaby went back to the kitchen and poured herself another glass of wine. She needed to pull herself together, to get her story straight before Caroline came in. It was one thing talking to the police, who didn't know her, quite another talking to Caroline, who knew her as well as anyone in the world, who behaved quite often as if she was Gaby's big sister, her protector: indulgent, but somehow in charge of Gaby's morals.

Gaby's mother had never cared about her in that way. Linda, her mum, had been occasionally wayward herself. There'd never been a father on the scene. The two of them had lived in a council flat in north London and Gaby had often been left to fend for herself. Linda had always been a grafter, cleaning offices, stacking supermarket shelves, just to put food on the table. But as soon as Gaby had got to secondary school, she hadn't been around much. She'd had Gaby while she was still a teenager and felt she'd missed out on life. Once Gaby was halfway independent, her mum had started making up for lost time. There'd been so many boyfriends that Gaby had lost count. Gaby had just got on with things, had felt her way through life without, it seemed, any rules.

She'd discovered art even before school, scribbling on scraps of paper, losing herself in the designs to block out the chaos of the flat; her mother's constant exhaustion from work had meant there was little energy to keep on top of things at home. In class she'd doodled instead of listening to teachers. It had been a rough school in a poor area and they'd just been grateful that she was quiet, not disruptive. She still had a maths book decorated with cartoon dragons, strange imaginary landscapes. An art teacher had been her salvation, praising her creations, sending her out at weekends to look at galleries, showing her a different world.

Gaby had come into her own at art college, made friends, become the joker in the pack, still living at home and including Linda's exploits in stories to entertain the other students. They'd been mostly middle-class kids, with an eye to making it in advertising or film. Her passion had always been painting. A year after college, she'd been doing the same sort of work as her mother — bar work, cleaning — putting off the inevitable slide into teaching, when she saw the advert in the *Guardian* for an artist in residence at the Woodyard Centre in North Devon. She'd skipped most of the details, just seen there was a salary she could live on. And the words *studio space* had jumped out at her.

Sitting on the little train easing its way down the Taw Valley from Exeter to Barnstaple, she'd seen paintings in the dense trees, the water and the watchful heron, and decided she wanted this job more than anything else in the world. She'd been interviewed by two men: Jonathan Church, who managed the whole of the Woodyard

46

Centre, and Christopher Preece, who was chair of trustees. Jonathan had already shown her around the centre, describing its philosophy. 'This is a space where everyone should feel comfortable — the A-level students attending specialist masterclasses and the guys in the day centre who have a learning disability. We very much believe in art for everyone.' She hadn't said she only cared about *her* art. She'd seen the big empty room in the roof and imagined herself there, painting. She'd have promised the earth to get the gig.

The interview had gone well. She'd always been good at telling people what they wanted to hear. And then Christopher Preece had asked her if she'd need somewhere to stay. 'I could put you in touch with my daughter. She's looking for a lodger.' They'd met that evening and Caroline had showed her the house, the room. The place had been pretty boring then, magnolia paint, hardly any furniture.

'I need so much stuff,' Caroline had said. 'But the budget's pretty tight and I don't want to ask my dad.'

So, Gaby had introduced her to the joys of charity shopping, freecycling and eBay. As the house filled with Gaby's purchases and creations, they'd become close friends. Very different — Caroline was so earnest, reliable and punctual and Gaby was none of those things — but strangely interdependent. Gaby cared what Caroline thought and didn't want to upset or offend her. She thought she'd lightened Caroline, made her more fun. Now, hearing the

47

key in the door, she wondered how she would break the news of Simon Walden's death to her.

Gaby must have been sitting almost in the dark with her daydreaming because when Caroline flicked the switch as she came into the room, the sudden light came as a shock.

'What are you doing?' Caroline disapproved of drinking too much in the week, though she didn't mind letting her hair down if the mood took her.

'It's Simon.' Gaby turned around in the low sofa and looked at Caroline.

'What about him?'

'The police were here earlier. He's dead.'

She saw that Caroline was as thrown by the news as she had been. They both had their own reasons for mourning Simon. Caroline dropped onto the sofa beside her. 'Did he kill himself?' The question seemed loaded with guilt. 'I didn't notice he was depressed. If anything, a bit manic, I thought.' A pause. 'Oh, I should have realized!'

'He was murdered,' Gaby said. 'On the beach at Crow Point.' She thought she'd hit just the right tone. Not cold, but not too upset either. Caroline would never believe upset.

6

When Matthew got back to the house, Jonathan had lit a fire and was sitting on the floor of the living room, the curtains open to let in the moonlight, a glass on the low table beside him. He'd been reading but he set down the book when he heard Matthew.

'A drink? Something to eat?'

'I might have to hand over this murder investigation.' It had been on Matthew's mind since he'd left the station. He followed Jonathan through to the kitchen. 'The victim was a volunteer at the Woodyard. And one of the people he shared a house with has a residency there.'

'Who was killed?'

'A man called Simon Walden. Did you know him?'

'I recognize the name. He worked in the cafe with Bob.' Jonathan took an opened bottle of Chablis out of the fridge.

'Walden had mental health problems,' Matthew said, 'and it seems one of your trustees pulled strings to get him the placement.'

Jon frowned. 'Whoever it was didn't go through me.'

'Christopher Preece? His daughter runs the project at St Cuthbert's. She was Walden's landlady.'

'They must have organized it directly with

Bob. He runs his own show there.' Jonathan handed a glass of wine to Matthew. 'They can't take the case off you just because I manage the place. That's crazy. It's the first major investigation since you took over the team. Besides, Joe Oldham's an idle bastard. He won't want to run a case like that. He couldn't do it! He has the sensitivity of a gnat. Imagine him stomping through the Woodyard, upsetting people.'

'Joe doesn't stomp.' But Matthew could understand Jonathan's point and he smiled.

The Woodyard was Jonathan's pride and joy, his baby. The site was on the south side of the Taw and had once belonged to a timber firm, that had long since stopped operating. There'd been the carcass of a huge warehouse built of old brick, full of rusting machinery. There'd been plans to demolish the buildings, flatten the site and put up a retail park. At the same time the council was contemplating closing the day centre for adults with a learning disability where Jonathan worked. He'd made the imaginative leap to connect the two. Matthew had been living and working in Bristol then, but he'd been swept up by Jonathan's enthusiasm. Most of their phone calls had included his plans for the site, his passion for bringing together different groups of people in one place — artists and adults with a learning disability — so it seemed to Matthew that the project almost embodied their love affair, the reckless, unimaginable possibilities of two alien individuals becoming one.

'Don't we have enough stores already in

Barnstaple?' Jonathan would rant. 'The high street's already all charity shops, hairdressers and estate agents. Why not use the timber yard as a community hub? Let's have an arts centre, a cafe, a place for people to meet and explore ideas. And my people from the day centre can be there too, right at the heart of things instead of being hidden away from view as if we're somehow ashamed of them.'

Jonathan had formed a committee, pushed through the plans, persuaded the Lottery Fund to give them cash and had raised match funding. Now the Woodyard was just as he'd imagined. There was a theatre and studio space, a bar and a cafe. The day centre for adults with a learning disability was there too, in a space converted from one of the smaller buildings. And he managed the whole place. Matthew couldn't have been more proud.

Today, though, Jonathan's involvement with the Woodyard might provide complications. 'I might have to hand the case over,' Matthew repeated. 'My choice, not Oldham's.'

'Well, don't do anything until he forces your hand! You want to work this, don't you?'

Matthew thought for a moment. 'Yes. I definitely want to work it.' A pause. 'I'm just not sure it would be right.'

'I love you to bits, you know that.' Jonathan had an accent that Matthew had struggled to define when they first met. Jon had been brought up on Exmoor, a farmer's son. No university for him. He'd left school at sixteen and travelled. There'd been no real explanation when Matthew

51

had asked why. Just: *Things weren't brilliant at home. It was for the best.* He'd worked in vineyards in France, picked strawberries in Spain, and he'd cooked for rich sailing types on smart yachts out of ports throughout Europe. Romantic stuff that had turned Matthew's head, made his mind spin. Wherever he'd stayed, Jonathan had picked up odd accents. When he was serious, though, his voice became rural North Devon again. Now he was definitely serious.

'You keep me real and rooted.' Jonathan put his hand on Matthew's arm. 'But you do have far too many principles. Sometimes I think you hide behind them. Just have the balls to take this on. Just this once, Matthew. Fight for it.'

★   ★   ★

When Matthew woke the next day, it was already light and he had a moment of panic, convinced he'd be late. He never overslept, but he'd been awake until the early hours, restless. He'd arranged to go to the victim's home with Jen this morning — he needed to get a feel for the place and the people who had known Walden best — and he had a brief rush of horror when he thought he'd missed the appointment. The other side of the bed was empty. But when he checked his phone he saw that it was still early and he had plenty of time.

All night, he'd been aware of Jonathan sleeping beside him, motionless, the gentle breaths not moving his body. Jonathan had a gift for sleep that Matthew envied more than anything. More than his husband's easy confidence, his courage, his ability to laugh off hurt and insults. Now Matthew was alone in bed and that rarely happened. Usually he was the first up.

Jonathan was in the kitchen and there was the smell of coffee and toast. For years this had seemed unattainable: a companion, a shared home, love. Matthew thought he was the most fortunate man in the world and the anxiety and insomnia of the night before seemed like an indulgence.

But your father died less than two weeks ago and you only found out because of a notice in the North Devon Journal. His funeral was yesterday. Cut yourself a bit of slack, Matthew. You're going through a tough time. Dump the guilt.

Then Matthew felt himself smiling because he could hear Jonathan's voice speaking the words.

They stood together in the kitchen drinking the coffee. Jonathan had already eaten the toast; he knew Matthew didn't do breakfast. Outside everything was clear and sharp-edged, sparkling. A breeze blew the river into tight little waves and scattered the light. There were new daffodils on the edge of the grass.

Walden's body had already been moved to the mortuary and the CSIs had finished their work, so there was nobody on the toll gate to stop cars coming through. The barrier lifted automatically, as it always did on exit. As he pulled out onto the road that led towards the sea, Matthew saw Colin Marston standing on the verge, scanning the flat land leading towards Braunton Burrows, the extensive area of dunes that stretched between the marsh and the shore.

On impulse, Matthew turned the car left at the junction, away from the village and the main road and towards the coast. This way to Ilfracombe was longer but he had time to spare and there would be less traffic. And the route brought back memories. His father had worked for an agricultural supply business and occasionally, during school holidays, Matthew would be allowed to go with him on business calls to farms along the coast. His father had converted to the Brethren to marry, and away from the house he'd seemed more relaxed, younger. Not like the rest of the sect. They'd chatted about trivial things — football, fishing — and his dad would describe the customers they'd be visiting:

Geoff Brend would be a good enough farmer if he didn't take to the bottle whenever he hit a bad patch.

And then when they'd driven into the sunset towards a whitewashed farmhouse at the head of a valley leading down to the sea:

Mary Brownscombe's a grand woman. She kept the business going while her Nigel was ill with cancer and she's still making a go of it now.

The woman had been out in the yard when they'd arrived. Everything had been flooded with the red glow from the sun setting over the sea at the bottom of the Brownscombe land. Matthew had thought it the most beautiful place in the world, magical. It was a picture-book farm with ducks on a small pond by the side of the house and bales of hay in the barn.

All the young Matthew had seen of the woman when he'd first got out of his dad's vehicle was her outline. She'd come up to them and given his dad a little hug and that was when Matthew had first seen her face, the grey eyes and the dark hair tied back with a bit of bailer twine.

'Good to see you, Andrew.'

Matthew had been expecting an old woman. Then, he'd thought all widows were old. But she'd been about the same age as his mother, dressed in jeans and wellies and a sleeveless vest top. His mother never wore jeans. He'd followed the adults into the house, which had a collie in the kitchen and books. Books on shelves and piled in heaps in corners.

Mary had made tea and put an open packet of chocolate biscuits on the table for Matthew to help himself. There were never biscuits in the Venn house unless his mother made them herself. She said God wanted his children to care for their bodies as well as their souls, and they weren't going to eat fried food or processed junk while she had the time and the strength to cook for her family.

The grown-ups had talked about business while Matthew played with the collie. But once the order had been placed, his father had still sat there, long after his cup was empty. There'd been some conversation, but Matthew had stopped listening. After a while, the man had got to his feet.

'I'll be back next week. And the boy'll be at school then so I'll be on my own.'

Mary had stood up too. 'You'll be very welcome.' A pause. 'Always.'

Out in the yard, the colours had been fading into dusk. Matthew had climbed into the car, waiting for his father to say goodbye. The adults hugged again and then they were driving away. Usually his dad talked about the meetings that had just taken place, chatted and gossiped about the customers, but that night, he'd remained silent all the way home.

Now, driving along the narrow lanes to investigate the murder of an apparently lonely man, Matthew thought for the first time that his father had loved Mary Brownscombe. There might not have been an affair, but there'd been a tenderness in the encounter that had seemed unusual even to a boy. Matthew wondered if Mary was still at Broom Farm and if she'd been to his father's funeral. He imagined her sitting at the back of the chapel of rest, weeping, incongruous.

⋆ ⋆ ⋆

He'd arranged to meet Jen Rafferty in the car park at the top of Hope Street, and she was already there, sitting in her vehicle, looking at her phone. She seemed to spend her life on her phone. They walked together down the hill to twenty Hope Street and Jen filled him in on overnight actions.

'We released a photo of Walden to the press, as you agreed. It'll be on the television news this morning. We were too late to get it in this morning's newspapers, but I'm guessing it'll be

56

all over social media. Ross was going to monitor that. And there are a few more details of him.'

'The victim's wife has been notified?'

'Yes, someone from Avon and Somerset went to see her last night. I haven't talked to them yet.'

'Do they have any children?' Matthew wondered how it would be to have a father who'd run away only to meet a violent death. Would they turn him into a hero or a martyr? Blame the mother? Or carry resentment around like a burden for the rest of their lives?

'No, no kids. Apparently, she's in another relationship now. She doesn't live in their old home any more. There's a different address.'

They'd arrived at the house. Jen paused on the pavement. At the bottom of the street a homeless man in a shabby sleeping bag with the stuffing seeping out stirred and raised himself onto one elbow. She knocked at the black door. They heard footsteps and the door opened.

A young woman stood there. She was stylish in an art student sort of way: model skinny, very short hair and a slash of red lipstick, a sweater dress over black tights and heavy boots. Long black earrings. The tights had a hole at the back of one leg. She grinned at Jen. 'You're a bit early. I'm the only one up.'

Jen went through the door first. 'Hi, Gaby. This is my boss. Inspector Matthew Venn.'

'Well, you'd better come in. I'll give Caz a shout.'

Matthew followed her into the kitchen. He thought Jonathan would have felt at home here;

he would have loved the clutter of pans and jars, the mismatched furniture, the little pieces of art. A large painted wooden parrot hung from the ceiling and sticks of pussy willow had been stuck in a brown earthenware pot. Brightly coloured towels were draped from an overhead rack like a string of flags, but they stopped halfway. Matthew found the effect of the room disturbing, overwhelming. He would need to concentrate to think straight here.

'Take a seat. There's coffee in the pot.' Then Gaby was gone. It seemed to Matthew that her mouth, scarlet with lipstick, remained in the room like the Cheshire Cat's smile. He heard her call from the bottom of the stairs: 'Hey, Caz. The cops are here. They want to speak to you.'

Jen had wandered over to the coffee pot and waved it in his direction. He nodded and watched her take a mug from a dusty cupboard, was ridiculously pleased when she rinsed it under the tap before filling it for him.

There was the sound of footsteps on bare floorboards, doors closing and a young woman appeared. Gaby followed her, shepherding her like a dog or a mother, then presented her with a flourish. It seemed everything was a performance for her.

'This is Caroline, known to her friends as Caz. She's the kind one who landed us with Simon. My landlady.'

Caroline was small and round with a button nose and huge spectacles. 'Give it a rest, Gaby. Show a bit of respect. Simon's only been dead for a day.'

Matthew felt that the interview was already slipping out of control. 'Do you know that? Did you see Simon yesterday?' He needed facts to hang on to.

Caroline shifted a pile of *Guardians* and *Observer Magazines* and sat on what looked like an old church pew next to the table.

'He was here first thing, wasn't he, Gaby? I left before you, but I heard him in the bathroom and we had a shouted conversation. Did you see him at breakfast?'

There was a moment of silence. 'Briefly,' Gaby said. 'And I can assure you that he was still alive when I left.' Another silence. 'Shall I make toast for everyone?' Now there was a hint of desperation in her voice. 'Or would that be seen as a form of bribery and corruption?'

'You can make toast for yourself and your friend,' Jen said. 'But we'd like to ask you both some more questions.'

Jen would do the talking. That had been Matthew's decision. She was engaging and he'd decided the women might find her less threatening. Now, he thought that these women would be hard to intimidate.

'Just sit down, Gabs.' This was Caroline. 'This is serious and we can have breakfast later.'

'Yes, miss.' But Gaby sat.

Jen looked around the table. 'I'm very sorry that your friend died yesterday.'

'No friend of mine.' The words were muttered, barely audible, followed by a shocked silence. 'Well, I'm sorry . . . ' Gaby fixed her eyes on the parrot. 'I'm not glad he's dead. Of course I'm

59

not. But I'm glad he's not living here any more.'

'Why do you say that?' Jen put down her coffee mug on a coaster that could have been made from elaborately knotted rope.

Gaby took a while to answer. 'We were happy here before he moved in. We were close. It was fun. Then suddenly having this stranger in the mix, a bloke we scarcely knew, seemed to spoil everything. He was so tense, you know. Uptight. And that was contagious. The whole house felt different, unsettled.'

'It was only temporary,' Caroline said. 'He already had plans for moving on. He was going back to Kingsley House, the hotel where he worked until the autumn, as soon as the season started. Besides, his rent made a difference. He wasn't here out of charity. And he was a wonderful cook. All those amazing Friday night meals. You never complained about those.'

'I was thinking of moving out.' Gaby was muttering again. 'I couldn't stand it. I was looking for a place of my own.'

'You never said!'

'I'd complained about Simon enough, about the way he made me feel, but you wouldn't listen, Caz. It was as if you cared more about him than me.' Matthew thought she sounded petulant and spoiled like a child in the playground, dropped for another 'best friend'. Perhaps such a beautiful woman was used to getting her own way. It must have been hard, though, having a stranger about the place when the friends had been so close. Hard, too, for Walden to live with the resentment.

60

'When did *you* last see him?' Jen directed the question towards Caroline.

'As I said, I heard him yesterday morning but I didn't see him. Sometimes I gave him a lift into Barnstaple, but not yesterday. I shouted up to ask him, but he said he wasn't ready and he'd make his own way in. Something important had turned up. I wondered if he had a meeting at the hotel to discuss starting work there again at the beginning of the season.'

'Did he volunteer at the Woodyard every day?'

'Most days,' Caroline said. 'He enjoyed it.'

'Who organized the placement?'

'I did.' Caroline paused. 'My father's on the board of trustees, so I know the place. I thought it would be great for Simon's confidence; it would help him to prepare for paid work again.'

'Simon Walden had psychiatric problems?' Jen asked it as a question but it was clear that she knew the answer.

'He'd suffered from depression and alcohol dependence, but there'd been a huge improvement since he started living here.' The reply was almost defensive.

'You were his social worker?'

Caroline hesitated. 'His project worker. My father set up a small charity at St Cuthbert's in memory of my mother, a place where people in crisis would be made welcome. She suffered depression and committed suicide when I was a teenager. It changed my life. Neither of us wanted any other family to go through that loss. I trained as a psychiatric social worker and took over the running of the project once I'd had a few years' experience in the field. We run it as a safe space for people with mental health problems during the day and organize evening group sessions a couple of times a week.'

Caroline seemed young, in her early thirties at most. Matthew wondered how she could spend her day in such emotionally intense situations, working with people who must remind her of her mother. He found the notion horrific. But then, he thought, he was spending his working day investigating murder. The sensory overload in this room made him feel suddenly ill, as if he'd overdosed on sugar, and besides, they shouldn't be having this conversation in front of a witness.

'Look,' he said. 'I suggest Miss Henry heads off to work. Let's leave Miss Preece and Sergeant Rafferty here to chat in private.' He turned to Gaby. 'I'll catch up with you at the Woodyard later if I need to.'

Gaby stood up. He followed her out of the house. She lingered on the step, but he turned away and walked briskly up the hill to his car.

7

Maurice Braddick had got into the habit of watching television at breakfast time. When he was working there'd been no time for anything but a quick cup of tea and then he'd be out of the house, driving into Barnstaple to Butchers' Row, often arriving before the others even though he had furthest to go. He'd pick up something to eat when he got to the shop — Pam, the owner's wife, made bacon sandwiches to sell to the stallholders in the pannier market — or he'd hang on until lunchtime and have a pasty. He didn't think much about work now, because it was too painful to remember the companionship and the jokes, what he was missing.

After his retirement, he and Maggie would sit together for a few moments in the kitchen once the taxi had come for Luce and they were on their own. They'd have another cup of tea and chat over their plans for the day. Maggie had never been a great one for TV, because she hadn't been able to stay still for long enough to watch it. She'd be on her feet and out into the garden. Or up to the village to organize the over-sixties club or chivvying him to drive her out with the meals-on-wheels. He'd never minded. He liked being told what to do.

Now, he and Lucy watched the small television in the kitchen while they ate their breakfast. Lucy had her favourite presenters and it made her day if one of them was on. There was a woman with short hair and a Northern accent, whose voice made her giggle. Maurice was delighted if he switched on the set and that woman appeared on the screen. He loved to see his daughter laugh.

He was always up first. He set out the bowls and the boxes of cereal, got the milk from the fridge, stuck a couple of slices of bread in the toaster. He'd put Lucy's clothes out the night before and she came in, dressed and ready, and heaved herself onto the stool by the breakfast bar. She'd always liked going to the day centre. Some of her friends had found it hard to settle in the Woodyard. Rosa had stopped going soon after they moved into the new premises. Her mother hadn't caused a fuss about it, though when Maurice had asked her, she'd said she didn't think it was right, all the different groups in the same building. Lucy had loved the buzz of the new place and had seemed at home there right from the start. Maurice was very proud of her, of how confident she was.

Before the Woodyard had opened the year before, there'd been talk of closing most of the learning disability services in the county, because the council didn't have enough money to keep them going. That had been just after Maggie's death and it had been a dreadful time. The thought of having Lucy at home all day, bored and frustrated, had kept Maurice awake at night. Now the day centre had moved into the Woodyard and he could relax again.

It was eight o'clock and the TV changed to local news. The bus was at nine so there was no rush. Maurice walked Lucy to the stop in the mornings to get a bit of exercise and to make sure she got off all right. It was another lovely day, and the soil would be warm enough to start planting. In his head he was already in the garden, that earthy smell in his nostrils and the sun on his neck. He was pulled back to the present when Lucy pointed at the screen and started shouting, so upset that the words spilled out and he couldn't understand what she was saying. There was the photo of a man, staring out at them, and it was gone before Maurice could get a proper look.

He waved at Lucy to be quiet for a moment so he could hear what the presenter was saying.

'Anyone with information about Simon Walden, whose body was found on the beach near Braunton yesterday afternoon, should contact Devon and Cornwall Police.'

Then it turned to the weather.

'What is it, maid?'

'That's my friend,' Lucy said. 'My friend from the bus. The man with the sweets.'

★   ★   ★

Maurice drove Lucy to the day centre in Barnstaple. He wanted to talk to the staff there before calling the police. It wasn't that he didn't trust Lucy — she seemed so certain about the man on the TV — but he didn't want to be on his own with her if an officer turned up at the house. Not everyone was sympathetic. They didn't take his daughter seriously; they ignored her or they stared. Just because she had Down's syndrome and you could tell she was different. Lucy's friend Rosa hadn't looked different at all — she was a pretty little thing — and he and Maggie had never been sure if that was good or not. People might expect too much from her, not realize she saw the world differently from other people. Today, Maurice wasn't sure how he'd cope if somebody ignorant came to do the interview. Lucy was sharp as a tack about most things and it was easy to patronize her.

Inside the main door of the Woodyard, there was a big space with paintings hanging on the wall. This week there was an exhibition about ships and sailing and he was drawn to one picture of the quay in Bideford, with an old boat tied up. It was all browns and greys, as if there'd just been rain. Maurice thought Maggie would have loved it. It was sudden thoughts about the things Maggie would have liked or pieces of gossip that he'd like to pass on that made grief come back and bite him on the bum. He felt tears welling in his eyes and blinked them away, told himself not to be a soppy old git.

He left Lucy with her mates in the day centre and went to the main office. Jonathan was there. He was in charge of the place. Maurice recognized him from outside the door, even though the man had his back to him. He had hair that was so blond it was almost white and he wore shorts and sandals whatever the weather. Maurice hadn't known what to make of him when they'd first met. Now, he saw him as some sort of hero, because he'd been the energy behind the Woodyard, and Lucy was so happy here. Today the shorts were khaki and came below the knee and there was a T-shirt with a sheep on it. He was having problems with a printer and was swearing, words that Maurice would never say out loud, not even if he was on his own.

Maurice tapped at the door and Jonathan turned around.

'Maurice, are you any good at technology?'

Maurice shook his head. 'Sorry.'

'Ah, bugger! Never mind, Lorraine will be in soon and she's brilliant.' He moved so he was closer to Maurice and leaned against the desk. 'How can I help? I saw Lucy yesterday and she seemed very well. I know that some of the chaps had problems moving out to the Woodyard, but I hear from the workers at the centre that she's thriving here. Gaining in independence and confidence every day, I hear. And a great asset in the cafe.'

'I know.' Maurice wasn't sure how to start explaining. There was an awkward silence. He felt himself blushing, wished Maggie was here, because she'd know what to say.

'Is this about where Lucy might live when you can't look after her any more? I know the social worker's asked you to think about that.'

'No!' Maurice knew he *should* think about that, but he wasn't ready. He couldn't imagine life at home without her.

'Because there are options, you know, and it

probably is time to talk them through. You and Lucy. I think she'd be fine on her own with a bit of support.'

Maurice thought he would come and talk to Jonathan sometime about Lucy's future, though he'd hate living on his own. He shouldn't be such a coward. 'I know,' he said, 'but there's something more important I need to tell you now.'

'I could do with a coffee. Why don't we go to the cafe and you can tell me what's worrying you?' Jonathan moved towards the door. Maurice thought he was pleased to be leaving the office and his work there.

They sat in the cafe, by the big windows that looked down the river towards Anchor Woods. The tide was out and there was an expanse of mud, the skeletons of rowing boats left to rot. Here, Maurice found it easier to start talking. He told Jonathan about the man on the bus and how worried he'd been about him approaching Lucy in that way.

'He might just have been friendly, but it seems odd. Luce said he got off at her stop each evening, but when I saw his picture on the telly, I knew he wasn't someone I recognize from the village. I don't know everyone there; sometimes there are incomers. But it's weird, don't you think? As if he was stalking her. You hear of people taking advantage of vulnerable people. Bullying. Sexual assault. There was something in the newspaper only last week.' Maurice stopped for a moment. He wanted to say that if this Walden had plans to harm his daughter he didn't

68

mind if someone had killed him, but Jonathan might take it the wrong way. If the police were involved, you had to be careful what you said.

'And Lucy definitely identified the man on the TV as the person who was chatting to her on the bus?'

'Yes.' Maurice sipped his coffee. It was stronger than he liked, but it would have been rude not to drink it. 'She was certain it was him. And she's good at remembering pictures.'

Jonathan nodded. 'You do know you'll have to talk to the police. If he's been going out to Lovacott each day on the bus, they'll want to know what he was doing there, who he might have been meeting. It's hardly the centre of the universe, Lovacott, is it? Only six miles from town but it feels like the back of beyond and I can't think why he'd be making the regular trip.'

Maurice nodded. 'I wanted to make sure they sent someone who'd understand to talk to Lucy. Someone patient, who wouldn't get her flustered or upset. And I hoped you would be there with her. I know there are other people working in the centre now you're running this place, but you still know her best.' Maurice was tempted to talk about his feelings about the new people, with their notions of independence and making Lucy get the bus, but maybe this wasn't the right time. And deep down, he knew Jonathan would think it was good for Lucy to learn to do more on her own.

'Of course. I can do that. I'll make sure it's all carefully handled.' Jonathan gave a quick grin. 'My husband's a cop. I should be able to pull a few strings. I'll give him a ring, shall I?'

Maurice blinked at that. He'd heard that Jonathan had married a man, but he wouldn't have thought he'd be the sort to take up with a policeman. He was too much of a free spirit. Then he thought times had changed, and all that mattered now was that Lucy would be well looked after.

'There's one other thing.'

'Yes?' Jonathan had taken his phone out of his pocket to ring the police, but he set it on the table and gave Maurice his full attention. Maurice went on: 'Lucy thought she'd seen the man before. I'd have recognized him if he'd been knocking around the village, so I think the Woodyard is the only other place she could have met him.'

Jonathan nodded as if this was something he'd already suspected.

★ ★ ★

In the end, Maurice spent all morning at the Woodyard. Jonathan's man was there sooner than either of them had expected, and the three of them talked together before Lucy joined them. Matthew Venn was serious, sober, dressed in a suit. When he reached out to shake hands, Maurice saw that his fingernails were round and clean, like little pink shells. It was impossible to imagine him in shorts and a T-shirt. But the man's formality inspired confidence; he wouldn't be one for cutting corners and there was nothing flashy about him. Maurice had always been suspicious of flashy.

They were in the day centre, which was part of the Woodyard, enclosed by the perimeter fence, but separate from the tall main building. It was light and pleasant, with exposed wooden beams. Only single-storey so there wasn't much of a view, but perfect for Lucy and her chums. Safe. It was linked to the Woodyard arts centre by a short glass corridor, but the door was shut once everyone got in. They walked past the kitchen on their way to the meeting room, where they talked before bringing Lucy in. Through the open door, he saw there was a cookery lesson going on. Lucy was chopping onions with the sort of knife he'd never let her use at home, but she seemed to be managing fine. Another woman with Down's syndrome was peeling potatoes at the sink. Maurice recognized her but she was too engrossed in her task to turn round and say hello.

When he'd first visited the old day centre, Maurice had found it disturbing. Not everyone there was like Lucy, who was independent, bright. Lucy had been to mainstream school until she was in Year Nine — Maggie had fought for that — and she could read and write. She was better at working the TV than he was and she was always watching some rubbish on her phone.

Some of the other people had more severe learning disabilities. They were cared for in a different group. Some couldn't talk, but made odd noises, squeaks and squeals. There was a man with a head too small for his body, people

71

with twisted limbs, who couldn't walk and used wheelchairs. Maurice was embarrassed now at his reaction, his horror, his feeling that this was some kind of freak show and that his Lucy didn't belong there. Now, he knew the regulars by name and was impressed by the kindness and patience of the staff. As he followed Jonathan through the building, he nodded to the people he knew.

The detective had brought a photo of the dead man, the one they'd shown on the television, and he set it on the coffee table in front of them. The room was very small. It looked out to the wooden fence and Maurice felt trapped there, too hot. It reminded him of the rooms in the hospice where Maggie had spent her last days. Pleasant but airless. Lifeless.

'Do either of you know him?' the detective asked. 'He lived in Ilfracombe with a couple of young women. One of them, Gaby Henry, is the artist in residence here. He worked as a volunteer here too, in the cafe kitchen. I presume that's how Lucy recognized him when he sat beside her on the bus.'

Maurice shook his head. 'I've never seen him. Lovacott's a small village. No school any more and no post office. Only the pub and that's more for visitors now than locals. I don't think he lives there. I can ask around if you like, when I get back. Take it into The Fleece and see if anyone knows him.'

As soon as he'd spoken Maurice wondered if he'd done the right thing. Perhaps the police didn't like people interfering. But Venn nodded.

'Thanks, that would be very helpful.'

Jonathan turned to Maurice. 'Shall we get Lucy in now? Is that okay with you, Maurice?'

Maurice couldn't help feeling proud of Lucy when she came in, chin up, and that bit of a swagger she had when she wasn't quite at ease but didn't want people to know. That smile that made everyone smile back. She took the seat between Maurice and Jonathan. The photo was still on the table.

'That's him,' she said. 'The man on the bus with the sweets. I'm not making it up.'

'We don't think that for a minute,' Venn said. He was listening properly and could make out her words. 'I'm impressed that you recognized him. Lots of people wouldn't.' He paused. 'I don't suppose you remember what he was wearing when you saw him last?'

Lucy screwed up her eyes. 'Jeans and a denim jacket. Boots.'

'That's what he was wearing when he was found. Is there anything else you can think of?'

'He had a tattoo on his neck. A big bird.'

'That's right. Brilliant.' A pause. 'Tell me about the sweets.'

Maurice couldn't understand why that might be important, but Lucy answered straight away. 'Sherbet lemons and eclairs, fruit salads.'

'All in the same bag?'

She nodded.

'A paper bag?'

She nodded again.

'That's useful, you see, because it means Simon Walden went to a proper sweet shop to buy them. Not a supermarket where they'd all be ready packaged. And there aren't many old-fashioned sweet shops left.' Venn paused. 'You told your dad that you'd seen the man before. Can you remember where that might have been?'

Lucy shut her eyes again. It seemed a bit showy to Maurice, as if she was only pretending to take them all seriously. But when she opened them again she shook her head. 'I'm sorry. I tried to think.'

'It doesn't matter. We'll sort that out.' Venn paused again and smiled. 'Just one last question. Did the man get *on* the bus at the same time as you? You walked to the stop with your friends and one of the workers from the Woodyard. Was he with you then?'

'No,' she said. 'He got on at the next stop, the one just coming out of town at the bottom of the hill.' She paused, a little shame-faced. 'I looked out for him. I was pleased to see him.'

'What did you talk about?'

For the first time she hesitated and seemed unsure how to answer. In the end she gave a little shake of her head. 'Nothing much. Nothing important.'

'And was he on his own when he got on the bus?'

Lucy thought about that. 'Yes,' she said. 'But he always sat with me.'

8

Jen Rafferty ate breakfast with Caroline Preece. She wondered what Matthew would say if he knew — he was such a stickler for rules that taking food from a witness and potential suspect might be disapproved of — but she decided she was so hungry, she didn't give a shit. Caroline set out the table, tidily, and even put milk in a jug and the toast in a rack.

'Homemade marmalade. My grandmother's a good cook.' Setting a jar with a gingham cover fixed with an elastic band in front of Jen.

They watched each other across the table as they ate. Caroline was tidy too, dressed not quite in twinset and pearls but in the contemporary equivalent: a neat little white blouse and black trousers, with a cardigan on top. Jen wouldn't be seen dead in anything so boring. Round Caroline's neck a chain and crucifix. Small, tasteful and tucked inside her blouse. Jen thought she must be the God-botherer Gaby had mentioned when they'd first turned up at the house. Jen was comfortable with that. She'd been brought up in a family of botherers and been taught by nuns.

'Tell me about the work you do.'

Caroline didn't answer directly. It seemed she wanted to tell the story in her own words. 'Mum killed herself when I was still at school. Dad had been a businessman — he ran a number of holiday parks and hotels along the coast — but after her death he really didn't have the heart for the work. He staggered on for about five years then he sold up; I think making money just didn't seem so important any more. He'd already started fundraising for the drop-in centre at St Cuthbert's and when I qualified, I took it over, made it more professional. Before then it had been run by a few well-meaning amateurs.'

'And your father got involved with the Woodyard too?'

'Oh yes. He helps wherever he can. He's become almost saintly.' There was an edge of bitterness to Caroline's voice, but she continued talking before Jen could follow that up. 'There's a real need for the service we provide. North Devon isn't just about public-school kids coming for the surfing or families turning up for perfect beach holidays. We attract transients, homeless people, drifters. And local people can suffer from depression too. Not everyone has a family to provide support.'

'Is the church directly involved?'

'Well, I'm a member of the congregation there and the clergy and congregation have been terrifically supportive. Originally, we just used their hall, but we've extended the premises.' Another pause and a shy Princess Diana glance through dipped eyelashes. 'I'm going out with Edward Craven, the curate.'

Something about the simper made Jen feel like throwing up. Or telling the woman to wise up. She'd been besotted once and look where that had got her.

'We run as a partnership project now, not just with the church but with a GP practice and the local authority. Groundbreaking.' Caroline had obviously given this pitch before, but the passion hadn't left her.

'How did you first meet Simon Walden?'

'He turned up at St Cuthbert's in the middle of some sort of crisis. Very drunk. Acutely depressed.' Caroline leaned back in her chair. The eyes behind the large glasses were very bright. 'I made him an appointment with a GP and persuaded him to join the programme at the centre. He responded to medication and to our talking therapies very quickly. A few weeks later I suggested that he move in here. It was clear that he needed support.'

'Wasn't that a bit risky?'

Jen thought there was something of the fanatic about her. Caroline had fallen for the idea of saving Walden. She liked him because he'd followed her advice, and that seemed the worst kind of pride.

'Well, it certainly wasn't policy and I got a bit of stick about it from my father. He said I shouldn't have become so emotionally involved. I didn't think so. I thought Simon needed a more personal approach.'

So, she needed to show what a good woman she was. Who was she trying to impress? Her friends or her colleagues? Edward the curate? Or her father?

'What kind of treatment was Simon getting?'

Caroline hesitated.

'Come on,' Jen said, 'that's hardly confidential.

His doctor will be able to tell me.'

'I've already told you. He received antidepressants from his GP and took part in a weekly group-therapy session. As well as that, we encouraged him to do yoga and meditation. Once his mood started to steady, he began volunteering in the cafe kitchen at the Woodyard.'

Very right-on.

'The group therapy. Was it for recovering addicts?' Jen thought Hope Street wasn't the best place for a druggie to live. As Ross had said, the street was known as a place where dealers hung out. Though it was more likely, because there'd been alcohol in his system when he'd killed the child in the road traffic incident, that booze had been Walden's poison.

Another long pause before Caroline spoke. 'When he first came to St Cuthbert's, Simon was so drunk he could hardly stand. That's not breaking a confidence; anyone who was there would tell you that. We filled him full of coffee and let him sleep at the back of the church for the night. A few days later he came along to the centre there. It was a few weeks before I found out he was sleeping rough. By then, he was much more stable.'

'And you offered him a bed here? You must work with a lot of homeless people. What was it about Walden that made him so special?'

There was a moment of silence. 'I'm not sure. There was something about him that made me think he was worth the effort, I suppose. A kind of intensity. A charisma. I probably should have asked Gaby first, but it *is* my house.'

'He moved in, but he hadn't stopped drinking?'

'He hasn't been drunk like that first time. Besides, I'm not the booze police. I can't take responsibility for all the people I work with.

'How did he pay the rent? If he was volunteering so much, he wouldn't be eligible for job-seekers allowance.'

Caroline shook her head. 'I don't know. He said he could pay. And he did pay, every month.'

'So, if he had access to cash, why was he homeless?'

'Accommodation's not that easy to find round here. Not reasonably priced accommodation.' But the woman sounded uneasy, defensive, as if she too had been worried about the source of Walden's money. She looked at her watch. 'Is there anything else? I should be going soon.'

'Was Simon close to anyone? Friends he might have made at work in the hotel? Any of the other service users?'

Caroline answered immediately. 'No. He was a loner.'

'Did you know that he'd killed a child?'

'You know about that?' Caroline's eyes looked very large behind the glasses. 'It was an accident. It haunted him. Really haunted him. He still had nightmares about it and it ruined his marriage.'

'Did Gaby know about that? Your father?'

'Dad wasn't at St Cuthbert's the night Simon turned up. I told you: he's not hands-on these days. He gives more of his time and energy to the Woodyard. He even dragged Edward along there to help at one time.' Her mouth snapped shut. Again, Jen thought her relationship with her father was more complicated than she was letting on. 'That night, it was just me and Ed. That was when Simon let it all spill out, about the child and his guilt. Simon spoke about it in group therapy, but Dad never attended those sessions. And I don't think Simon ever talked to Gaby about anything important.'

'We'll need your fingerprints,' Jen said. 'The CSIs will organize that. Can you let Gaby know?'

'You think one of us might have killed him?'

'From what you've said, Simon Walden didn't know anyone else.' Jen realized she'd been too sharp. She couldn't understand why she found the woman so hard to like. Caroline was compassionate, doing good work. They believed in the same causes: social justice, equality. 'But no, it's about elimination. We'll try to trace any stranger who might have visited the house.'

'The house is often full of people — musicians, artists. Gaby sings too and she's always bringing people back.'

'All the same,' Jen said, 'we'll be asking for your fingerprints. Do you have any problem with that?' There seemed something odd about the woman's reluctance to co-operate.

'Of course not.' Caroline marched towards the door, expecting Jen to follow her.

9

The Woodyard was a monument to Jonathan's confidence and competence and Matthew regarded it with a mixture of pride and envy. He was a good detective, but he'd never achieved anything quite as great as this. This place would still be a derelict timber yard with a decaying warehouse at its heart if it weren't for his husband. After his travels, Jonathan had returned home to Exmoor, taken a low-paid job as carer of a man with learning disabilities and loved it. He had the right mix of humour and compassion and worked his way through the system, without really meaning to, no end goal in sight, until he was managing a day centre. He'd loved that too and that was when Matthew had met him.

Matthew had been policing in Bristol then, the big city, only two hours from where he'd grown up but a world away: culturally diverse, buzzing, alive. He'd felt as alien there as he had in Barnstaple, but anonymous. Nobody cared that his family were religious bigots who'd disowned him because he could no longer believe in their God, or that he'd dropped out of university, because the academic pressure had stressed him almost to madness. He was good at his job and that was all that counted. He'd met Jonathan at a conference about working with vulnerable adults. There'd been a three-line whip from management that someone should attend and nobody else in Matthew's team had been interested. It had been his fortieth birthday and Jonathan had been his present.

They'd kept in touch, spent weekends together, mostly in Barnstaple, quietly, under the radar. Not a real couple, Matthew had told himself. He couldn't be that lucky. This was a phase that would pass. Jonathan would set off on his travels again or find someone more interesting. Instead, he'd found a new project. The Woodyard. It had been a time of local authority cuts and the day centre where he'd worked had been under threat. Jonathan had been transformed from a laid-back guy, who moaned about the restraints of his work but left it behind at the end of the day, to an activist, passionate, consumed, organized. Matthew would arrive from Bristol to Jonathan's tiny flat in the oldest part of the town, tired at the end of a busy week, to find it full of people. Earnest people talking money, funding applications and lobbying, and arty people like Gaby from Hope Street, painting posters and planning social media campaigns. Businessmen in suits and radical activists all in the same place. Matthew had been intimidated and retreated into work. He'd been certain that Jonathan would find someone more interesting to spend his life with.

Matthew had been thrown by the change in Jonathan, the fact that he could be so serious. Until then *he'd* been the serious one, the worrier. Jonathan had drunk beer and sat in the sun. He'd always slept at night. In those days of planning and activism, every waking hour had been spent thinking about the Woodyard project.

And he'd made it happen. Here it was, just as the planning committee had hoped. A glorious community hub bringing people together. Jonathan was general manager of the place. It was overseen by a board of trustees, but he was the man on the ground. With his assistant, Lorraine, he ran the centre.

Matthew had feared that once the Woodyard was up and running, Jonathan would become bored and restless again. That he'd run away. So, Matthew had kept his distance. No point getting too close. No point setting himself up to be hurt. Then, one Sunday afternoon in early autumn, Jonathan had taken him to meet his parents. The first time and Jonathan had been nervous, jittery. Not at all his usual self. They'd sat around a kitchen table scattered with farm accounts, wary dogs at their feet. Matthew had been reminded of the visits he'd made with his father to the customers who had never been able to pay on time. There'd been the same shabbiness, a sense in the air that was almost desperation. This couple, Matthew could tell, might live in a beautiful place, but they were poor. Like the dogs, the family had been wary. He'd had no real idea of what Jonathan's parents made of him.

On the way back to Barnstaple, where Matthew would pack his bag before returning to Bristol, Jonathan had pulled into a layby near a little stone bridge. It was at the edge of the moor where the landscape became gentler. They'd got out and stared into the water. The trees on either side were changing colour and were reflected in the stream.

'What did you make of them?'

Matthew hadn't known what to say.

'They're not my parents. Not really.' This wasn't the confident Jonathan. The hand on the stone parapet was shaking. 'I'm adopted. They didn't tell me, though. I found out by chance when I was sixteen.'

'That's why you left home?'

Jonathan had paused for a moment. 'Among other things. I got angry. A bit wild. Got thrown out of school.' He'd been looking out at the hills, but turned back to Matthew. 'Will you marry me?'

It had been the last thing Matthew had been expecting and it had taken him a while to realize this wasn't a joke. Even then it had occurred to him that Jonathan wanted a father as much as a husband — although there wasn't so much difference in their ages — but he hadn't cared. He'd have agreed whatever the terms.

'Yes!' He'd shouted it so loud that they'd have heard it back at the farm, so loud that they were both shocked by the sound. He was, by nature, a quiet man. 'Of course I will.'

The next day he'd asked for a transfer to the Devon force. Miraculously there was a vacancy and they were desperate for someone to start quickly. The following weekend, they'd gone to look at the house by the estuary, and they'd bought it, despite the danger of flooding. Matthew, so cautious and risk-averse, had decided it was time to be reckless.

★ ★ ★

84

Now they were in the Woodyard garden, eating lunch. It was odd to be here in his own right. Matthew had been to the Woodyard before, with Jonathan, to see plays and to attend exhibition openings. But only occasionally and only after he'd moved to Barnstaple permanently. They still weren't much recognized as a couple in the town. Their worlds were very different. At first it had been an ordeal, presenting himself in public as Jonathan's partner, smiling and shaking hands. After all, what did he know about art or theatre? Sometimes the anxiety that he would say the wrong thing or express an opinion that was foolish swallowed him up, made him want to run away or lock himself in the lavatory. Now he was here as Inspector Matthew Venn, investigating a murder, and he had to take centre stage.

They'd bought coffee and sandwiches in the cafe and were sitting on one of the benches outside the building. There was a view of the river and the tide coming in, that distinctive smell of salt, mud and decay. A group of older volunteers was tidying, sweeping up debris that had gathered on the grass over the winter, but nobody was near enough to overhear.

Matthew spoke first. They were close enough to hold hands, but he was here as a police officer and not as a husband and his words sounded oddly formal. 'You think Lucy Braddick is a reliable witness?'

'Absolutely. I've known her for ages. Since when the old day centre was still going.'

'Jen's just phoned with confirmation that Walden worked in the kitchen here. That *must* be where Lucy first saw him.' Matthew paused. 'How well do you know Christopher Preece? I didn't like to ask in front of Maurice.'

'He's on the Woodyard board and without a donation from him, we probably wouldn't have got match funding to renovate the place. You must have heard me talk about him and you've met him a few times. He was there at the beginning, at those first meetings in the flat.' Jonathan paused. 'He was behind the mental health project at St Cuthbert's too. There's something of the passion of the convert about him. The ruthless businessman who suddenly found a social conscience. Sometimes he can come across a bit arrogant. As if he has all the answers.'

'I met Christopher's daughter, Caroline, this morning. She seems pretty driven too. She shares a house with one of your workers. Gaby Henry?'

'Gaby's amazing. We appointed her as artist in residence, but she's brought the whole place to life. Her work's stunning. One day it'll put this place on the map.'

'You, this, it's all too close.' Matthew felt the words come out as a cry. 'You do see now that I'll have to declare an interest?'

'Of course you should. But don't withdraw from the case just yet. You're better at your work than anyone I know and your investigation might lead you in an altogether different direction. Surely the answer is more likely to lie in St Cuthbert's than here?'

Matthew could understand the sense in that, but he thought this case was complicated, twisted, the threads unlikely to be quickly untied.

★ ★ ★

Gaby Henry had arranged to meet him in one of the meeting rooms. She'd been running an art appreciation class and had obviously been showing a series of images on a screen. The group reminded him of the friends Jonathan sometimes brought home — they had intelligent, earnest faces. The women wore loose floral dresses, the men jeans and sweaters. Informal but at the same time a uniform. Matthew watched through the glass door as Gaby wrapped up the meeting. 'That was fabulous,' she said. 'Thanks so much for your attention.' She stood at the door as they drifted out and waited until they were out of earshot before speaking to Matthew.

'Thank God that's over for the week,' she said. 'I've never met such a boring, pretentious bunch!'

He couldn't help smiling. He often thought the same about Jonathan's arty friends.

Gaby led him back into the room. 'Do you know what happened to Simon yet?'

'Not yet.' Matthew paused for a moment. 'We have discovered that for the last week or so he'd been taking a bus to Lovacott every afternoon. Did he have friends there?'

Gaby shook her head. 'I don't think he had friends anywhere. I realized he'd been home late a few times, but often we were back late too, so we didn't notice. We just assumed he was in.' She seemed to be thinking. 'We didn't see him much, poor bastard. Only Friday nights when he cooked for us both. Other evenings he disappeared into his room. Caz might know if he had pals in Lovacott. She sometimes gave him a lift into Barnstaple.'

'He never had any visitors?'

'I never saw anyone.' She paused. 'Someone phoned for him once. We've got a landline but we hardly ever use it. We've got our mobiles. One day, I decided to check the landline messages and one had been left for Simon.'

'Can you remember any details? The name of the caller? A number?'

'Nothing like that. It was as if the guy on the other end of the phone assumed Simon would know who he was. *Hi, Si! How's this as a blast from the past. But I tracked you down in the end. I told you I would. You can't escape your old buddies after all.*' She turned sharply, so she was facing him. 'It sounds a bit sinister now, doesn't it? But the tone wasn't like that. It was friendly. As if they were old mates.'

'When was the call made?'

'I picked it up a couple of weeks ago. It could have been made a few days before that, though. Like I told you, we don't use the landline much.'

'Did you save the message?' Matthew thought they needed to trace the caller whether he was a friend or an enemy. They knew so little about Walden's past.

'Of course! Because I told Simon it was there so he could hear it. He might have deleted it afterwards, though.'

'Were you there while he listened to it?'

'No!' Gaby was firm. 'None of my business.'

There was a moment of silence. Matthew texted Ross to get a trace on the phone and to pass a message to Jen to listen to the call. She might still be on the coast. He'd asked her to go to the hotel where Walden had worked once she'd finished with Caroline and he'd send her back to the house. Gaby had given them a spare key the night before. He felt a bubble of excitement rising in his stomach. The phone call might be an important factor in the investigation. This was why he loved the work.

'Where were you yesterday afternoon?'

'I was out on the coast,' she said. 'Making sketches for a painting I was doing.'

'Where exactly on the coast?'

There was another moment of silence. 'Not far from where his body was found. I wasn't there to kill him, though. He bugged me, but it wasn't as if he planned to stay in Hope Street indefinitely. According to Caz, he was starting back at the hotel once the season had started. He'd be living in.' She stared at Matthew. 'Come with me!' Her voice was insistent and demanding. 'I can prove what I was doing on the shore.' She stood up. Without comment, he followed her.

She led him up two flights of stone steps to the top of the building without speaking. Refurbishment had ended at the lower floors and the steps were bare and uneven. When she threw open the door to a large room, he saw stained floorboards, crumbling plaster and old brick. It was flooded with light through sash windows on two sides. There was a filter coffee machine on a window ledge with a few dirty mugs, an easel, a pile of canvases leaning against one wall. Otherwise the space was empty, echoing. She nodded to the coffee machine. 'Do you want one? I made it this morning, though, and it'll be stewed by now.'

'I'm caffeined out, thanks.'

She seemed a different woman in this space. The flip, easy-going Gaby of Hope Street was gone. She showed him the painting on the easel. A seascape, with a shimmering promontory of land. Crow Point, not where they'd found Walden, but seen from the other side of the marsh. There were bare patches of canvas.

'It wasn't going well,' she said, 'so I went back to do some sketches. I didn't go through the toll road. I parked by the marsh and walked from there.' She got out her sketchbook and held it out for him to see. Rapid pencil drawings that captured the movement of waves, the wingbeat of gulls. He recognized the shape of Crow Point in the distance.

'These are very good.' The words came out without thought.

'That's why I'm at the Woodyard. Because it gives me the time and the space to paint. The work is mostly mind-numbingly dull, like the class you just saw. A bunch of bored middle-aged and middle-class people, who think they have talent or that they understand art.'

'Why did you accept the residency if you feel like that?'

'Because it pays.' She spoke as if the answer

was obvious. 'I don't have a rich daddy like Caz — my mother brought me up on her own — and I don't make any money from my painting yet, so I do this. It's better than stacking supermarket shelves or pulling pints. Just.'

He nodded back at the sketches. 'Of course, this doesn't prove anything. You could have done them anytime.'

'But I didn't.' Her frustration was obvious.

'Why did you dislike Simon Walden so much?'

'I didn't dislike him.' She turned away. 'I just didn't see the point of him. If you don't mind stepping over the needles in the morning or being harassed by the neighbourhood drunk, Hope Street is a pretty cool place to be. It's the best house I've ever lived in. And I don't mind those things. I didn't need a man to protect me.'

'Did Caroline?' Matthew was surprised. He'd had them both down as strong, independent women.

'Nah, but that was one of the excuses she gave for letting him stay. That we'd be safer with a man in the house. Which was pretty daft. We could have been letting in a maniac.'

'Was he a maniac?'

Gaby didn't answer immediately. 'He was pretty screwed up. Especially at first. Depressed, I suppose, but no, I didn't think he was dangerous. I just found him unsettling.' She looked away for a moment and when she turned back the words sounded like a confession. 'I painted him.'

'Can I see?'

She shrugged and pulled a canvas from the

stack by the wall and propped it on the easel. Matthew looked. He thought he should say something intelligent but he was embarrassed again. What did he know about art? The embarrassment got in the way of an honest response this time, but he couldn't take his eyes off the painting. It was just of Walden's head. The likeness was there at first glance, then everything seemed to shift under Matthew's gaze. There were blocks of colour that he had never seen in human skin. Matthew took a few steps back and looked again. Walden was staring into the distance, frowning.

'Did you do this from a sketch too?' Again, Matthew felt the ignorance seep into his face like a blush. Growing up with the Brethren, he'd learned so little of the world that his brief time at university had been an act, a performance. He'd pretended to understand the references to bands he'd never heard of and films he'd never seen. At school, he'd considered himself an intellectual, but every day since there'd been the fear of being found out as a fraud. It had taken him a while to be open with Jonathan. There were still times when he felt the need to pretend.

Gaby didn't seem to think this was a stupid question. 'No, I did this from a photograph.'

'Why? I mean, why did you want to paint him? Did he have an unusual face?'

'No, not at first glance, at least. You wouldn't look at him twice in the street. I suppose I wanted to understand why he'd got under my skin.'

'Did you find him attractive?' Matthew thought this was one of the oddest interviews he'd ever conducted. Gaby had pushed to have Walden excluded from the house but there was something about her obsession that felt like a teenage passion.

He'd expected an angry response to the question. *No, of course not. He was a creep.* But she was thinking about it, deciding how much she wanted to tell him.

'Perhaps,' she said at last. 'Perhaps I did. There was something about him, despite the moodiness and the occasional bouts of anger when he'd had too much to drink. Something compelling. I'd never thought about it until I started painting him.' She stared at Matthew. 'Crazy, huh?'

'Did he ever talk to you about his life before he ended up at the hotel in Ilfracombe?'

There was a pause and again he thought she was choosing how much to say. 'Once. Indirectly. It was after one of the Friday meals. Simon always cooked for us on Fridays. He said he was keeping his hand in. He'd throw us out of the kitchen early in the evening and tell us only to come back when he was ready. Usually we went to the pub. It was the one night of the week that Caz was prepared to let her hair down. Sometimes Ed was there, though I was always glad when he wasn't. I can be a bit of a potty mouth and I could sense disapproval oozing from every pore whenever I spoke. We'd rock back to number twenty after a couple of beers and the table would be laid and there'd be the most amazing food. It was what Simon was born for, cooking. Like painting is what I was born for.'

She stopped for a moment. The coffee must have been cold but she sipped it to provide a pause in the story, a beat. 'That night it was paella. The most amazing seafood. We were drinking something light and white that slipped down like lemonade. Caz and Ed decamped to the sitting room. Usually Simon did all the clearing up himself, but I'd had enough of playing gooseberry and I stayed behind to help. We'd both had a lot to drink and we started to talk.'

She stopped again, but Matthew didn't prompt her. He sensed this was worth waiting for.

'He asked out of the blue if I wanted kids. I said I was too selfish. Nothing mattered more than my work. I made some crap joke, like *That's why I'm still single*. He said he'd always wanted to be a dad, but that would never happen now. He didn't deserve a happy family. He'd had a wife that he'd loved but he'd let her go. By that point we'd loaded the dishwasher and he was washing the pans that were too big to go in. He turned away from the sink with a scourer in his hand. *Sometimes I think I'd be much better dead.* I said something crap again. Something like *But you can't kill yourself. We'd miss the Friday night feasts.* He said suicide wasn't an option. Not yet. He still had work to do.'

'What sort of work?'

'I don't know. I was pretty pissed by then, but he was seriously weirding me out. Like he had

94

some kind of Messiah complex. Like there was something he was meant to achieve and nobody else could do it. I left him to the pans and went to bed. The living room door was open and I could tell Caz and Ed were having a deep and meaningful and I didn't want to intrude.' She set down her mug. 'But I could almost believe it, you know. That he was special. He had a kind of charisma, a lack of bullshit and compromise. I could imagine him as one of those gurus that gullible people follow without question. I could really believe that he had a mission in life and he didn't care what other people thought; nobody was going to get in the way.'

Matthew suddenly pictured Walden as a very different man from the helpless, hopeless rough sleeper described by Caroline Preece. He wondered which view was the more accurate. 'I don't suppose you saw Simon at all on your travels yesterday afternoon?' His voice was light.

There was a brief hesitation, hardly noticeable. 'Of course not. I think I might have mentioned it, don't you, if I'd seen him just before he died?' She'd turned away before speaking to look out of the long window, so he couldn't see her face.

10

When Jen left Hope Street, she tried phoning Matthew but there was no reply. The sharp sunshine and the daffs blowing in the little garden next to the car park made her think of new beginnings. Spring. They also made her remember that time was passing and she wanted a man in her life before it was too late. Sometimes Ella brought a lad home and although the pair were well behaved when Jen was around, she sensed their adolescent lust. The touching and the easy intimacy provoked an envy that shocked her. She thought she could kill for that: a good man to hold her hand when they were out walking, to stroke her neck when she'd had a bad day, to lie next to her at night and screw her senseless as the dawn came. She knew she tried too hard with the men she met, was too desperate and she scared them off. And she still hadn't met a good man, at least not one who was right for her, who could keep her interest after a couple of nights.

She sighed and phoned Ross. 'I've just finished with Caroline Preece.'

'Anything?'

'Only that Walden liked yoga and meditation. He volunteered in the caff at the Woodyard. In Caroline's eyes that made him next best thing to a saint.' Jen hoped that Matthew Venn had made better progress in Barnstaple than she had here in Ilfracombe. 'But it also seems that he liked a pint or five to keep him going. What about you? I've tried phoning the boss, but he's not answering.'

'Seems Walden took a bus trip to Lovacott, that village up the Taw Valley, every afternoon for the couple of weeks before he was killed. Something, at least.' Ross paused. 'I've been digging around a bit. I'm trying to prise Walden's army records out of the MOD.' Jen heard the trace of a whine in his voice. Sitting in the office and working the phone wasn't his idea of fun.

'Perhaps the boss will let you out to play tomorrow.' *Or you could go to your best mate Joe Oldham and pull a few strings.*

'You could come back now and take over, at least help shift some of the calls that came through after the broadcast on breakfast TV.'

Ross would think that was women's work, sifting through the recorded messages, phoning back the callers. And she *would* be better at it than him, more patient, more sympathetic, but she knew better than to start giving in to a man's blackmail or flattery. She'd been caught that way before.

'Sorry,' she said. Sharp and tight. She needed to keep her temper. 'I'm off to the Kingsley House Hotel to talk to Walden's former employer. I'll see you at the briefing tonight.' She clicked the phone off before he could answer, before she allowed herself to be persuaded.

She sat for a moment in the car and told herself she shouldn't let Ross bug her. He was young and brash and it wasn't his fault that he reminded her of her bastard ex-husband. As far as she knew, he'd never punched a pregnant woman in the stomach. It probably wasn't *even* his fault that he was the son of Oldham's best buddy and the DCI had taken him under his wing.

Kingsley House was on the edge of the town, a grand Victorian pile, with gothic turrets and steep terraced gardens leading down to a small private beach. Jen drove down a shingle drive through trees just coming into leaf. In the distance, the island of Lundy looked improbably large on the horizon. The sun was high and the sea glittered. If you were forced to move away from your family and friends, Jen thought, there were worst places to be exiled.

The hotel had a reputation for understated luxury and the best food on the coast. Once it had been the holiday home of a minor royal and its marketing talked of its still having the atmosphere of a country house party. The entrance hall seemed dark and cool after the sunlight. There was a stag's head on one wall and three huge leather armchairs were gathered around a low mahogany table. No reception desk, but a grey-haired woman in black appeared as if by magic through a door. No name badge and no uniform. Nothing as tasteless as a credit card machine in sight.

'Yes? Can I help you?' A flash of a smile. She wasn't rude, because Jen *could* have been an eccentric guest. Most people staying here didn't look like Jen, but the hotel might entertain a few ageing rock chicks. Wealthy ageing rock chicks.

Jen dropped her bag on the marble floor. 'Could I speak to someone in HR, please?'

'If you're applying for employment, we ask you to enter your contact details and CV online.' The woman's voice was still kind but a little patronizing; her judgement had been spot-on. This was some chancer looking for work.

'I already have a job, thank you.' Jen dipped into her bag, opened her warrant card and laid it on the table.

The woman only lost her poise for a moment and Jen couldn't blame her for the brief lapse. Police officers weren't supposed to look as she did. 'Just a moment, Sergeant, I'll fetch Mr Sutherland.' She went back through the door and returned almost immediately with a tall young man in a suit.

'Please.' He held out his hand for her to shake. 'Peter Sutherland. I look after staffing here. Come into my office.' The voice was educated Brummie, the accent well-hidden. A young fogie with pretensions.

She thought of the sunshine, the smell of newly cut grass that had followed her in on her walk from the car. 'Perhaps we could talk in the garden.'

He seemed surprised but maybe he'd been inside all day too. Or perhaps he'd been trained to please. 'Of course. That's a splendid idea.' Out in the light she realized he was even younger than she'd thought.

He led her away from the building down a narrow path to one of the terraces and a pond, sheltered by laurels and rhododendrons. The shiny leaves reflected the light, but the water was in shadow. They sat on a white wrought-iron bench with their backs to the sun, looking down at the sea. This was miles away from the grey houses in Hope Street, youths lurking at the end of the road, the *Big Issue* sellers and the homeless guy blank-eyed in his tatty sleeping bag. This was like a secret paradise.

'How we can help?'

'Have you seen the local TV news today?'

He shook his head. 'We're gearing up for the new season. I'm afraid I haven't stopped since I came on shift at seven.'

'A former employee of the hotel was found dead yesterday afternoon. We're treating his death as suspicious.' Jen couldn't believe that word hadn't got out through social media, through other colleagues.

'Oh God! Who was it?'

'A man called Simon Walden. He worked in the kitchen.' She turned towards him but couldn't read anything from his face. 'Do you remember him?'

'Simon. Yes.'

'Well? Can you tell me anything about him? Like why someone might have wanted to kill him.'

He didn't speak for a moment. Jen could hear waves breaking on the sand below them.

When he did speak, the old-fashioned politeness and gentility had disappeared. 'There were times when I would have gladly killed him myself.'

'Why?'

'He was moody and people took against him.' Another pause. 'Managing the guests here is easy compared to managing the staff. When we took Walden on, I thought he'd fit in well. He'd been in the forces and people are thrown together in the army, aren't they? It's all about being part of a team.'

'But Walden wasn't a team player?'

Sutherland gave her a brief smile. 'Unfortunately not. Some days he'd never speak. He seemed to suck the energy out of the kitchen.' A pause. 'And he was a drinker. That's not unusual in this business. Your body clock gets thrown by the strange shifts, so it doesn't seem wrong to keep drinking when everyone else is just about to wake up. He functioned, still turned up for work every day, but there was no attempt to get on with his colleagues.'

'Did anyone specific take against him?' In the distance, Jen heard a child laughing. She thought next time she had a free weekend she'd drag the kids away from their screens and their school work and bring them down here for a picnic.

Sutherland didn't speak for a moment. He'd be reluctant to point suspicion towards an individual employee. She didn't blame him. He was relatively young to hold a position of such responsibility. Some of the kitchen staff would be older, intimidating. Not the sort you'd want to offend when the hotel's reputation depended largely on the quality of the food.

'I could come in, demand to see all your staff records.' She kept her voice reasonable. 'That would be time-consuming just as you're

101

preparing for the season. Or I could check through Revenue and Customs . . . That would go down well with your employees.'

Sutherland shrugged. He knew when resistance was no longer an option. 'It's the chef. Danny Clarkson.' He paused as if Jen should know the name. 'He's a celebrity if you know anything about this business; gets reviews that some people would die for. He's the reason the restaurant is fully booked, even in the winter when we have fewer guests. Walden wound him up. Clarkson's got a temper. He's one of those quiet men who suddenly lose control if things aren't right or what they expect. A genius but close to the edge. It's Clarkson's kitchen and he's boss there. Maybe they were too similar to work together happily.' Sutherland got to his feet. 'I'll take you through.'

'Just one more question first. If Walden was such a nightmare, why did you agree to employ him again this season?'

Sutherland shuddered as if the idea was anathema. 'But we didn't. There was no way we would have had him back.'

★   ★   ★

Clarkson was small, wiry, a head shaved so closely that he looked almost bald, the skull obvious beneath the stubbled skin, gingery eyelashes. Chef's whites that seemed as crisp as when they'd come out of the laundry. He was bent over a pan, intense as a priest at communion. The kitchen was all stainless steel

102

and gleaming, unexpectedly quiet. The lunch-time service had yet to begin. In the background, acolytes moved swiftly and silently about their work.

Sutherland approached him warily. 'This is a detective, chef. She'd like a few words.'

'Not now.'

'Yes,' Jen said. 'Now.'

The man looked up. His eyes were blue and hard. He took the pan off the heat. 'What do you want?'

'Simon Walden,' she said. 'He's dead. He was murdered.'

'He stopped working here in the autumn.' The voice was unexpectedly pleasant, a light tenor.

'I know that.'

'So why are you bothering me?'

'You worked with him all season. I was hoping you'd be able to tell me something about him. Something that might help us find his killer.'

'We weren't friends. I didn't know anything about him and I wasn't interested. He was a decent baker. Reliable enough, but no real attention to detail or presentation. And he couldn't take instruction.'

'He didn't like being bossed around.' Jen thought she'd struggle to take instruction from this man.

'He had an attitude problem. Passive aggres-sive. He thought I didn't trust him. This is my kitchen. I don't trust anyone. It caused a negative atmosphere and it affected my work. I couldn't have that.' Clarkson's attention was pulled back to the pan. 'When did he die?'

'Yesterday. Sometime in the afternoon.'

'I was here all day. From mid-morning. We were catering for a wedding. You'll have to look elsewhere for your killer.' He moved the pan onto the heat again and turned his back to Jen.

⋆ ⋆ ⋆

Jen stood outside the hotel. In a large conservatory with a view of the sea, well-dressed women sat drinking coffee. Through the glass she couldn't hear what they were saying, but the painted nails and occasional flashes of silver as the sunlight caught bangles and earrings made them seem exotic, glamorous. Brightly coloured birds in an aviary. It was hard to imagine Simon Walden working here. She thought he'd probably hated it, and wouldn't have come back, even if he'd been offered the chance again.

So, who had lied? Simon or Caroline? Caroline had said that his stay was temporary and soon he'd be moving out of Hope Street. It was one thing to have a strange lodger for a few months, quite another to have him lurking there indefinitely, a reminder that not everyone was as lucky as they'd been. Haunting them, like the albatross he'd had tattooed on his neck.

Jen thought he'd been unlucky at the hotel. The chef was obviously a sociopath. She couldn't imagine getting on with him either; she'd have clashed with him as Walden had done. She was beginning to feel some sympathy for the man. She walked back to her car.

She phoned Matthew again. There was still no answer, but there was a voicemail from Ross asking her to go back to Hope Street to check the recorded messages on the landline there. By the time she arrived at number twenty, it was mid-afternoon and school chucking out time. Groups of school kids wandered down the high street at the bottom of the road. She let herself into the house with the spare key she'd been given. The CSIs were still working in Walden's bedroom, and she shouted up to them to let them know she was there. She could tell by the powder on the handset that the phone had already been fingerprinted; she lifted it and dialled 1571 to pick up the message.

It seemed the messages hadn't been checked recently. There was a list of cold calls: charities seeking donations, insurance companies, one from a dentist reminding Ms Preece that her appointment with the hygienist was due. Nothing personal. The women at number twenty were of the generation when texts were more common than phone calls, certainly more common than phone calls to landlines.

Then there came the message that Matthew had been most interested in. It had been left fifteen days before. First the usual pause that came once the caller realized he wasn't speaking to a real person. Then a male voice, jaunty, friendly. Jen thought she could catch an undertone of threat, but that could be her imagination; after all, she was looking out for it.

'How's this as a blast from the past? Bet you never thought I'd track you down. I told you I

would, didn't I? You can't escape your old buddies after all.'

She got out her phone and set it to record, then replayed the message. The boss would be eager to hear the recording. They should be able to trace the originating number from the phone company. She played it again and tried to place the accent. It was southern and she found southern voices hard to pin down. Walden had come from Bristol, so perhaps that was it.

Out on the pavement she hesitated for a moment then walked to the corner of the high street. Although the rough sleeper had moved away, a different man stood almost in the same place. He waved a copy of *The Big Issue* in front of her and she felt in her pocket for change.

'This your regular spot?'

He nodded.

'Do you know the people who live at number twenty? Two lasses and a bloke?'

'You a Scouser?'

'Yeah, you?' She'd been able to tell just from those three words and wondered what his story was.

'Birkenhead,' he said.

'What brought you here?'

'A woman,' he replied. 'It's always a woman, isn't it?'

She didn't know what to say to that. 'I was asking about the people at number twenty.'

'You a cop? You don't look like a cop, but I can smell them.' He touched the side of his nose. Not hostile, just telling it like it was.

She gave a brief nod up the hill towards

Caroline Preece's house. 'Investigating the murder of the guy who lived there.' She thought he'd know about that, even if he didn't have access to morning television. 'I heard he'd been having a rough time before he moved in there.'

'What was his name?'

Jen thought the man was buying time, planning his response. He knew already. 'Simon Walden.'

'Yeah, I'd seen him around. Bit of a boozer. Seemed to have landed on his feet. Nice place.'

'Not landed on his feet now, though, has he?'

There was no reply.

'Any reason why he should have been killed? Had he made any enemies round here? Owe any money?'

'He wasn't dealing.'

'Using?' Though they'd find out soon enough once they got the post-mortem toxicology report.

The man shook his head. 'The drink was his poison. He drank in The Anchor at the other end of the high street.'

'Anything else you can tell me?'

'I don't know that he'd ever been sleeping rough. He was one sad bastard, though. I never saw him smile.'

★   ★   ★

The Anchor was a locals' pub, small and dark. There was nothing to attract tourists. No food, no fancy ciders. If strangers did walk in, they'd be stared at, a matter of interest and curiosity

107

rather than resentment. Most visitors found the attention off-putting and left after one drink. At a table in a corner a middle-aged couple were holding hands. They looked as if they'd been there since lunchtime. Behind the bar a little man, thin as a whippet, was cleaning glasses.

Jen held out the photo of Simon Walden. 'I hear he used to drink in here.' When the man didn't answer immediately. 'I'm a police officer. We're investigating his murder.'

'I'd heard he was dead.'

'Killed,' she said. 'Stabbed on the beach at Crow Point. Sounds as if he'd upset someone. Any idea who that might have been?'

The man shook his head. 'He wasn't a social drinker. He always turned up early and on his own. Five-ish. Not every night and I hadn't seen him the last few weeks. I thought he'd moved on. Most of the people who come in at that time are here for the company. A game of dominos, a chat. Older people or guys stopping for a quick pint on their way home from work. He would come with a paper, sit with his back to the room, drink solidly for an hour and then go away. I never even knew his name until I saw his picture on the telly.'

11

In the Woodyard kitchen, the working day was nearly over, the pans clean, the stainless-steel surfaces scrubbed. It was open to the cafe, separated by a counter, tiny with an oven and a hob on one side and a sink on the other. Matthew had been to the cafe often with Jonathan. The coffee was good and the cakes were better. A few lingering visitors were finishing tea. They passed Matthew on their way out as he was taking a seat at the table nearest to the counter. The chef, Bob, was a large man but nimble on his feet. Jonathan had once said that watching him at work was like seeing an elephant dancing. Miraculous. Bob hung a tea towel over the hob and looked at Matthew. 'I expect you could use a coffee. I'm ready for one myself.'

Once the coffee was made, they moved to a table looking out over the river. 'Is this about Simon?'

'You heard?' Matthew wasn't surprised. Of course, the news would have spread through the place by now.

'Saw it on the telly this morning.'

'He worked with you?'

The big man nodded. 'As a volunteer. He was a lovely baker. They taught him that in the army. Apparently, he did a couple of tours to Afghanistan. Soldiers have to eat like the rest of us.'

'Of course.' Again, Matthew's perspective on Simon Walden shifted. Had the man been suffering from PTSD? Would that account for the mood swings and obsessions? 'How did he come to be working with you?'

'Caroline Preece asked me to take him on. Her dad's on the board of trustees of this place and it's not wise to upset Christopher.'

'Why?'

Bob shrugged. 'He's a wealthy man and he's used to getting his own way. He runs the board. And he dotes on that daughter of his. But Simon was okay. Not like most of the volunteers, who are pains in the arse. Chatty bloody women. He just did what was needed. I could leave him to get on with it. Some days he'd come in early — no fun on the bus from Ilfracombe — to start the bread. We do all our own baking. It would pretty well be ready when I got here. Saved me a bit of work.'

'He didn't drive?'

The cook shook his head. 'He killed a child once. He never got behind a wheel again. You can understand it.'

Matthew thought Walden had confided in Bob more than he had the women with whom he was living. That made sense. They were men together, closer in age. 'Lucy Braddick works here too?'

'Only a day a week at the moment.' Bob showed no curiosity in why Matthew was asking. 'Her group at the day centre take it in turns. Not in the kitchen but waitressing, clearing tables. She's one of the good ones, Lucy. A great little

110

worker. And sunny. Always smiling. The customers love her.' He paused. 'I'm thinking of taking her on properly, paying her a living wage if the day centre is up for it. It only seems fair; she's every bit as good as the regular staff.'

'Would she have met Simon Walden?'

'Well, we keep the day centre chaps this side of the counter. Health and safety. You know how it is. Anyway, no room to swing a cat back there. But yeah, they chatted to each other. Simon was brilliant with all the regulars from the centre. I think Lucy was a favourite.'

Matthew nodded and thought that was one mystery cleared up. Lucy had recognized Walden from the kitchen. It didn't explain, though, why she'd seemed so vague about where they'd met or why he'd made the trek to Lovacott on the days before he'd died, making a point of sitting next to her on the bus.

* * *

By the time Matthew had finished talking in the cafe, it was late afternoon. Outside, there was still a bit of heat to the sun. Matthew could feel it on the back of his neck as he walked to his car. He crossed the bridge and drove into the town, planning to get to his desk at last, to catch up with what had been going on at the station, to put Ross out of his misery by allowing him to show off what he'd achieved during the day. But at the last minute he changed his mind and headed towards his old school and the big houses that looked out over Rock Park. He'd

111

been given Christopher Preece's address by Jonathan. He was interested to meet Caroline's father, the man whose money had given birth to the Woodyard.

The house was detached, built in the arts and crafts style, with mellow brick and mullioned windows, small dormer windows to break the roof-line, not very old but traditional. A row of trees marked the border of the garden; there was a small pond and a terrace. A pleasant garden, slightly left to run wild. Wrought-iron gates stood open but Matthew parked outside in the street. He rang the bell and the door was opened almost immediately by a middle-aged man, tall, attractive, healthy-looking, in jeans. Matthew realized he *had* seen him a few times before: in their old flat in Barnstaple and at Woodyard social events. He and Jonathan usually kept their working lives separate, but occasionally he was dragged along to meet the great and the good, councillors and potential donors.

'Hello?' It was clear that Preece wasn't accustomed to strangers turning up on the doorstep, but this was a smart stranger so he didn't just close the door. And perhaps there was a brief moment of recognition too. He smiled, like a politician, anxious not to alienate a voter whom he might have met before.

'Matthew Venn. Devon Police.' Matthew held out a card. 'I'm here about Simon Walden. He was murdered yesterday. He was living in the same house as your daughter and her friends.'

'Of course. I heard about it. And I'm sorry, of course I should have recognized you. You're

112

Jonathan's partner. Do come in.' A serious frown, followed by the same politician's smile and a good firm handshake. Preece led him into a back room. A long window looked out onto a lawn, shrubs. Inside, there was an upright piano, comfortable chairs gathered around an open grate. Lots of photos of Caroline, framed music exam certificates, pony club rosettes. It seemed it had been a comfortable childhood. Until her mother had died. Matthew looked for a picture of the mother, but there was just a wedding photograph, formal. Preece and a fair, willowy woman standing on church steps. She wore traditional white and carried flowers. Nothing more recent. 'Can I get you something? Coffee?'

Matthew shook his head. 'Did you know Simon Walden?'

'I met him a couple of times,' Preece said. 'Caroline asked me not to interfere, but I wanted to judge him for myself.'

'Did you see him at the house in Ilfracombe?'

'Not the first occasion. I saw him in the house a few times later when I'd calmed down.' Preece paused. 'I'm afraid I lost my temper when I heard she'd invited him to stay there. It seemed such a very reckless thing to do. But Caroline made it clear that her tenants were none of my business. I might have helped provide the deposit for the place but she said it was *her* house, her decision who lives there.' Another of the smiles, self-deprecating, confiding. 'You see, Inspector, it seems that I'm only welcome if I'm invited. And perhaps that's as it should be. I still think of her as my little girl, but I do understand that she needs to be independent.'

'So, where did you meet him first?'

Preece took a while to answer. 'I asked him to come here. I was worried about a stranger with apparent mental health problems moving into my daughter's home.' Matthew wondered what Preece made of Caroline's career choice — after all, she spent every day working with people with mental health problems — but he was still speaking. 'As I told you, at the very least, I wanted to make my own assessment of the man.'

Preece stared into the garden. 'I didn't want to see Walden in the Woodyard where he was a volunteer. That would have been too formal, too complicated. I've always tried to leave the practical business there to the professionals. I wouldn't want them to think I was meddling. In this case, I was, of course, but in my daughter's affairs, not the Woodyard's.'

'You did get him the place in the Woodyard cafe.' Surely, Matthew thought, that was interference of a sort.

'The volunteering was Caroline's idea, Inspector. Nothing to do with me.'

Matthew imagined Walden here, summoned to this calm and comfortable house. Surely it must have been an intimidating encounter. 'What did you make of him?'

Preece thought about that. 'He wasn't quite what I expected. I liked him.' He paused for a moment. 'He told me he'd killed a child. A road traffic accident. He'd been drinking. Not enough to be over the limit but enough to lose concentration for a moment. I was impressed by

114

his honesty. He told me he'd carried the guilt around with him ever since. We had that in common. The guilt. Survivors' guilt. If you've been to the Woodyard, you'll have heard about my wife.'

'As you said, Jonathan Church is my husband. He explained that she'd taken her own life. I'm very sorry.'

'Becca had suffered depression on and off since soon after we met. It was much worse in the last five years of her life. I didn't understand it. I wanted to help but I couldn't see how and that was a nightmare for me. I'm a control freak. I make things right. But I couldn't make *her* right. And there was nowhere to go for help. The medical profession was completely useless. I think I took out my frustration and irritation on her. We had a row the night that she died. My last words to her were that she was selfish. I said if she cared at all about Caroline, she'd pull herself together and give more time to her daughter.' He stopped and turned away. 'That was unforgiveable and I've been punished ever since because that conversation is the last memory I have of her.' He turned back to Matthew. 'I went out to calm down, walked along the river for an hour. When I got back she'd hanged herself.'

'And that happened in this house?' Matthew didn't think he'd be able to stay here with such dreadful memories. He wasn't sure what to make of Preece. The story seemed to come easily. Was this something he'd repeated many times before so he'd become distanced from it, or was he

115

confiding in Matthew because he was a stranger?

'Caroline wasn't here when her mother died,' Preece said. 'It was a weekend and she was at a festival. Something for young Christians. She'd developed a strong faith even before her mother's death. Afterwards, she didn't want to move, so I didn't think I had the right to make her.' He was still for a moment, lost in thought. Matthew could tell there was more to come. 'I hadn't expected the guilt when Becca died. I expected the grief. Missing her, missing the woman I'd loved and married. But, you see, part of me was glad she was dead. I walked into the house and saw her there, hanging from the bannister in the hall, and there was a brief moment of relief. It had been such a strain living with her, the moods and the anger, the days of total withdrawal, the helplessness because I couldn't help her or make her well. And it was that moment that caused the guilt. That was what prompted me to get involved in St Cuthbert's and in setting up the Woodyard.'

There was the same smile, implying that Matthew was easy to talk to, that just in those moments the two had become friends: the politician's knack of making a person feel special. Dennis Salter, the Brethren elder who'd preached at his father's funeral, had the same ability, the same warmth.

Matthew understood what Preece meant about guilt, though. Perhaps because of the memory that had conjured up Salter, his childhood mentor, he found himself back in the cemetery. He was watching the service to mark

116

the death of his father from a safe distance. The crocus at his feet and the drone of the organ in his ears. He wondered if he'd felt a moment of relief too when he'd heard his dad had died? Perhaps. Because any decision about whether or not he should visit the hospital had been taken away. It made things cleaner, easier. And now he was feeling guilty again, because he hadn't had the courage to visit, to make things right. Because he hadn't walked round the pool of crocus to stand with his mother in the chapel of rest.

In the silence that followed there was the sound of birdsong, loud and clear, from the garden.

'I'd grown a number of businesses in this area,' Preece said. 'Becca was a local girl, but I grew up in London. We met when I was here on holiday with some friends. I only moved down when we married, and perhaps, as an outsider, I could see the potential for development better than the locals.' He was still standing, his back to the long window, the new green of the garden behind him. 'And I've always been a risk-taker. I didn't think the British love affair with cheap package holidays would continue. Not for the discerning young middle classes. I built an estate of luxury holiday flats in Westward Ho! and took on a run-down caravan park in Croyde, turned it into an upmarket chalet and glamping site. Later I diversified into bars and restaurants.'

Matthew nodded to show he was listening. Let the man explain in his own way.

Preece continued. 'When Becca died, I'd

already been thinking of selling the businesses on. I enjoyed the start-up phase, the planning, the negotiations, but found myself rather bored once they were up and running. I'm not really a details man and I was ready for a new challenge. So, being active in the charity sector wasn't as altruistic as it might have seemed. I started the drop-in centre at St Cuthbert's soon after Becca died, but we needed something more professional and Caroline has made that happen. The project has developed beyond my wildest dreams. Then I was ready for something more demanding and I got behind the Woodyard. I got a buzz out of being part of a completely new organization, finding my way round charity laws and the way NGOs operate, helping to recruit a set of trustees. We've got a good team there now with a mix of skills: an accountant, a lawyer, a couple of senior social workers and a former building society chief. It fended off the guilt and the grief, at least for a while. And it made Caroline proud of me. That was important.' He paused. 'I know it's an old-fashioned thing to say, but my reputation is important to me, and I see the whole of the Woodyard as my baby now. My legacy. I'll always be associated with it.'

This, Matthew thought, was the politician talking again. 'You say you liked Walden. Was there anything about him that made you anxious about the fact that he'd be sharing the house with your daughter and her friends?'

'There was an intensity about him that I found a bit unnerving. As if he didn't have a protective skin of any description. Perhaps he was too

118

honest for his own good.' A pause again. 'Actually, after meeting him, I was more worried about how he'd fare in that house with two confident young women than whether he'd be any kind of danger to them. Gaby Henry has a sharp tongue and I'm not sure I'd be able to live with her. She's entertaining for an evening but I know she'd exhaust me after a while.'

'When did you last see Walden?'

'About ten days ago. Caroline invited me to have dinner with them.'

'Ah,' Matthew said. 'One of the famous Friday feasts?'

'You know about them?' Preece smiled. 'Yes, Simon was a great cook. If I'd still been working in hospitality, I'd have employed him like a shot as a chef.'

'So, it was a good evening?'

Preece took a while to answer. 'It was a strange evening. Tense. Simon cooked the meal but then he was reluctant to eat with us. Caroline persuaded him. She has a knack of getting her own way. It was clear that he didn't want to be there, though. Perhaps I was being paranoid but I felt that his resentment was directed at me. I can't think of anything I'd done to upset him. As I told you, I'd never seen him at the Woodyard.'

'Was Walden drinking that evening?' Gaby had spoken of Walden getting maudlin drunk on occasions.

'No, and perhaps that was all it was. He was trying to clean up his act and maybe he found it hard to be social without alcohol, especially when everyone else was drinking.' Preece paused and gave a little wry smile. 'Caroline's friend, Edward Craven, was there too, and he makes rather awkward company. I know she's very fond of him, but I find it hard to be entirely natural with a cleric in the room.'

Matthew could understand the awkwardness — he'd spent his life surrounded by people of religion — but he wasn't going to confide in Christopher Preece. He stood up. 'Thank you for your time.'

After leaving the house, he sat in the car for a moment, wondering if he'd gained a clearer sense of the man who'd died. But all that remained from the conversation was the notion of guilt hanging over Walden, clouding his judgement, taking over his life.

★ ★ ★

The sun was still shining. Matthew thought Lucy Braddick would be finishing at the Woodyard. Her father had decided to spend the afternoon in Barnstaple and would give her a lift home. There would be no need for her to take the bus that had carried Simon Walden to Lovacott every day in the week before he'd died.

Perhaps it was the sunshine or the uneasiness the interview with Preece had provoked, but Matthew couldn't face the grey box of the police station yet, or Ross's repressed energy. He'd have to be there for the evening briefing, but that would be soon enough. So instead, he drove into the town centre and left his car there, then he walked towards the bus station. If he was quick, he'd get to it just in time for the Lovacott bus.

In the end, he was there with five minutes to spare and he waited until a line of elderly women laden with shopping bags and a couple of mothers and babies had boarded. He showed the driver his warrant card and a photo of Walden. 'Do you recognize him? He took this bus every afternoon last week.'

The woman shook her head. 'I've been off on maternity leave. This is my first day back. You'll need to talk to the depot.'

Matthew hesitated, but instead of jumping back down to talk to a supervisor, he pulled his wallet out of his pocket and bought a ticket to Lovacott. He'd follow the route Simon Walden had taken and see what happened. The front seat was vacant and he sat there. He'd never bunked off school, but he thought it would have felt like this. He sent a message to Jen and Ross saying he probably wouldn't be back at the police station until the evening briefing.

The bus went back across the bridge to the stop where Lucy would usually get on. A middle-aged woman boarded. They were just across the road from the Woodyard and Matthew had a good view of the tall, red-brick building. Life there would be continuing, Jonathan would be holding things together with good humour and efficiency. Nobody was waiting at the stop where Walden always joined the bus. Why had he walked the little way up the bank to catch it? So he couldn't be seen from the Woodyard? Matthew wondered why he'd felt the need to keep his visits to Lovacott and his encounters with Lucy Braddick secret.

Looking back on Barnstaple, Matthew saw the curve of the river widening towards the estuary, the town sprawling away from it. The bus circled the suburb of Sticklepath, called at the Further Education College at the top of the hill and picked up a handful of students, before heading inland on roads that scarcely seemed wide enough for a vehicle of this size.

Matthew thought he should be canvassing the passengers, showing Walden's photo, but what would they say? 'Yes, a guy looking like that got on. He sat next to a woman with Down's syndrome and he offered her some sweets. They chatted.'

Because Lucy had said that nothing else happened and her father had believed her. But the man who had made Lucy happy, had made her giggle and stand by the bus stop in her village the day before, waiting in case he should turn up, sounded nothing like the dour and angry Simon Walden described by the women in the house in Ilfracombe. So, what had been going on here? What motive might Walden have had for this trip into the countryside, for gaining Lucy Braddick's confidence? Why had he wanted her to trust him?

The bus stopped less frequently now and only to drop off passengers. It was overheated and Matthew found himself struggling to stay awake, in almost a dream-like state. He hadn't travelled by bus since his father had taught him to drive while he was still at school and he'd forgotten how much better the view was. He was high enough to see into the upstairs window of a cottage standing next to the road. A bed with a yellow candlewick cover and a heavy mahogany wardrobe. A woman with her back to them. They moved on before Matthew could make out what she was doing. Over the hedge, there was a glimpse of water, a pool or a lake; two grand pillars formed the entrance to an overgrown track that disappeared into nothing but woodland and a buttery patch of celandines. The bus stopped, apparently in the middle of nowhere, to let off an elderly couple.

The road climbed steeply and then they were looking down at the village of Lovacott: a group of houses clustered around a small square, which was hardly more than the main street widened. A shop that seemed to sell everything, a pub. There was nothing picturesque here. No thatch. It would never have featured in an episode of *Midsomer Murders*. The houses were sturdy and pleasant enough, but unremarkable, unlikely to pull in tourists. Beyond the square the road wound on to the row of 1950s council houses where the Braddicks lived. The bus stopped and the passengers climbed out. The driver stayed in her seat and pulled out a paperback book. This was the end of the route. There was sprayed graffiti on the shelter. A group of the students who'd got on in Sticklepath lingered on the pavement, smoking and chatting. Matthew pulled out the photo of Walden.

'Have you seen this guy on the bus?'

'Yeah.' This was a slender girl with dyed yellow hair and dark roots, wearing a white print dress and canvas tennis shoes. A pretty face, huge dark eyes. She looked like a character in a Japanese cartoon. 'He sat next to Lucy Braddick. It seemed a bit odd. She's a sweetie and we've all grown up knowing her, but most strangers avoid her.'

'Was the man a stranger? He never stayed in Lovacott?'

'Why do you want to know?' The boy had lurid acne and wore a hoodie. A wannabe baddie. Suspicion in his voice and the way he held his body.

'He's dead. Murdered. I'm a police officer investigating.'

There was a shocked silence. A thrill of excitement. Matthew thought the police presence in Lovacott would be all over social media as soon as his back was turned. If they'd had the nerve, they'd have taken a photo of him on their phones.

'I've never seen him,' the girl said. 'Except on the bus.' She turned to her friends. They all nodded in agreement.

Matthew left them and walked into The Golden Fleece. It stood proud and imposing at the head of the square. An attempt was being made to bring it back to its former grandeur, to attract tourists passing through on their way to the coast. There were pictures on a board in the entrance hall: refurbished bedrooms, a dining room gleaming with polished wood and glasses, wedding guests gathered on the lawn at the back of the hotel. The bar smelled of fresh paint and varnish. Most of the tables were laid for meals with cutlery wrapped in paper napkins, small vases of flowers and there were menus on the counter. This was a pub with aspiration.

A leather sofa and a couple of easy chairs had been placed near to the fireplace. A woman sat there with a latte looking at her laptop. This didn't seem Simon Walden's natural habitat. Behind the bar stood a middle-aged woman, in a simple black dress, the sort of make-up that made her look as if she wasn't wearing any, neat silver earrings. She smiled. 'What can I get you?' She liked the fact that he was wearing a suit.

'Coffee, please.'

'Americano?'

Of course, there would be a choice of coffees. 'Yes please.'

There was a fancy machine behind the bar, a little homemade biscuit on the saucer when it arrived. Matthew showed her the photo of Walden.

'Do you know him?'

'Why do you want to know?' Now she seemed less impressed.

'He's dead. I'm a police officer.'

'I think I heard about it on the radio this morning. He was stabbed at Crow Point?'

'Yes. Has he been in here?'

'Yes. Most days last week. He never stayed long, though. It seemed to me that he was waiting for someone. When it's quiet here, I make up stories in my head about the customers. It passes the time. I thought he might be waiting for a woman, but she never turned up. Each night he'd come in, just off the bus like you.

He'd sit by the window and he'd wait. But whoever he was hoping to meet never appeared.'

Matthew thought about that. 'Do you work in the bar every day?'

'My husband and I own the hotel. I'm usually here in the afternoons when it's quiet.'

'And he never talked to anyone?'

She shook her head. 'Not while I was here. The last time I saw him he just seemed to disappear. I'd gone to the kitchen to order sandwiches for a customer and when I got back he'd gone. It was earlier than usual. I hoped that his woman had finally turned up.'

'What was he drinking?'

She paused for a moment as if the question had surprised her but she seemed sure enough of the answer. 'Diet Coke. Two pints, each time.'

Outside on the square, he stopped to get the feel for the place. It was dusk now and there was a chill in the air. In the houses grouped around the square, lights were being switched on. Matthew saw children doing homework at kitchen tables, meals being prepared. The teenagers had gone. There was more traffic, commuters on their way home from Barnstaple, Bideford and Torrington, but there were no longer pedestrians on the pavement. Matthew made his way through the square and down the road towards the cul-de-sac of houses where Lucy and Maurice Braddick lived. He wasn't planning to call on them, but he was interested. Beyond the necklace of house lights, there was nothing, a black expanse of open countryside. This was only six miles inland from Barnstaple, but it could have been the edge of the world.

If a woman had arrived here, as the landlady had imagined, surely someone would have noticed. She hadn't come with Walden on the bus. The mysterious lover was all speculation, of course, but if Walden hadn't been here to meet a woman, what had brought him to Lovacott? Why had he wanted to stay completely sober and in control?

Matthew took out his phone to call Ross for a lift. Without the stops and detours, it would only take fifteen minutes to drive into Barnstaple. Suddenly the bus's headlights went on and it revved into life. Of course, it must go back to the depot, it wouldn't stay here all night. Matthew waved at the driver and climbed aboard.

12

Jen had a chance to get home to check on the kids before the evening briefing. They lived in the district of Newport, on the edge of Barnstaple and close to the school where Matthew Venn had been a pupil. Her place was squashed into a terrace of mismatched cottages, three storeys so it was bigger than most of the houses in the street, but very narrow and too small for a woman with a hoarding problem and two growing teenagers. She parked in the alley at the back and walked down the strip of garden. It thrived despite months of neglect. The daffodils were just coming out and soon there would be tulips. The first nice weekend she had off she'd tidy it, get rid of the dead leaves. She didn't care if her house was a mess, but she loved being out in the garden.

The door led straight into a tiny kitchen. Ella must have loaded the dishwasher and she felt a glow of gratitude because she wasn't walking in to the usual chaos. The living room was dark and cold. The room looked out onto the street and the window was so small that it scarcely got any sunlight. She'd tried to brighten it with throws and pictures, and it was cosy enough in winter with the fire lit, but now it just seemed dusty and cluttered. The stairs led up from a corner of the kitchen. She shouted up.

'Kids. I'm home!' Her voice was very loud

because their rooms were in the attic. It seemed to echo. There were footsteps on the stairs. Ella appeared, still in her school uniform sweatshirt, a ballpoint pen tucked behind one ear.

'What's for tea?'

Jen couldn't answer that. 'Where's Ben?'

'At Max's. His mum said he can eat there.' Ella walked on down and sat on the bottom step. 'I can't find *any* food in this house.'

'Oh God, I'm sorry. I meant to do a shop yesterday on my way home from work and then there was that murder. Do you fancy a takeaway?' Jen looked at her watch. 'If I go now, I should have time to eat it with you before I need to go out again.'

'You're out again?'

'Yeah. Final briefing of the day. Shouldn't be late back, though.' Jen thought that these days her life was all about compromise and never doing anything well. She was guilty that she couldn't put all her energy into work because she was distracted by what might be going on at home, and guilty that her kids might be turning into tearaways because she gave them so little attention. Ben was feral, seldom at home, and Ella seemed perpetually stressed and anxious. Sometimes she worried that Ella, after being a monstrous pre-teen, was becoming *too* conscientious, too straight and boring. She'd been hanging around with the same lad for months and their idea of a good night was watching the telly in the front room. The last thing Jen wanted was for her daughter to marry early without experiencing any kind of life. *She'd* made that mistake, fallen for the dream of the perfect man and the perfect life, and look what had happened.

'No worries. I can work better in an empty house anyway.' Ella stood up. 'Look. I'll go and get the food. You grab a shower, sort yourself out. Want your usual?'

'Yeah, fab, thanks.' Jen's head was so filled with ideas about Walden and the women in Hope Street that she couldn't even begin to think about what she might want to eat.

⋆   ⋆   ⋆

The room was already full when Jen arrived at the police station and she'd made an effort to get in early so she could catch up with Ross before they started. She'd felt a flutter of excitement as she climbed the stone steps to the door. A relief at escaping the house and the demands of the family. Matthew Venn was there at the front, chatting to the crime scene manager. Ross was hovering beside them, obviously trying to get a word in, not realizing that he'd just piss them both off by interrupting. He had the social skills of a worm, but because he was Oldham's favourite nobody had the nerve to tell him. Jen went up and tapped him on the shoulder, got him to turn around so he wouldn't seem to be hassling them.

'Any news on the phone call?'

'Yeah, it's just come through. I was going to tell the boss.' He shot a glance over his shoulder.

'Well, now you can tell me.'

Ross was just about to speak when Venn called everyone to order. The room fell silent so quickly that the inspector seemed a little shocked, as if he was surprised by the authority he had. Jen loved that about him: his lack of macho bullshit, his courtesy.

He stood in front of them and spoke just loud enough for them all to hear. He knew there was no need to shout. They'd all be listening. 'Let's get through this as quickly as we can, shall we? We've all had a long day. Ross, I know you've been doing the detailed work here in the station. Anything worthwhile from the callers after this morning's media?'

'We managed to phone everyone back. I've left a report with the contact list on your desk.'

'Anyone been in touch admitting to owning one of the cars Colin Marston saw parked by the dunes the afternoon of the murder?'

Jen thought that interview with the Marstons in the toll keeper's cottage felt like weeks ago. That was how it was at the beginning of a case: so many people and ideas crammed into just a couple of days, time seeming elastic.

'Two,' Ross said. 'The elderly couple with the Volvo. But it doesn't sound hopeful — they said they were walking the other way, down the river and away from the point. They've left contact details and I said someone will be in touch.'

'Anything else?'

'A few possible leads. A woman called Bale claims to have seen Walden in conversation with a woman in a cafe in Braunton yesterday.'

'That could be significant and needs following

131

up,' Jen said. 'According to Caroline Preece, Walden didn't need a lift into Barnstaple yesterday morning because he was skipping his group therapy session. He'd told her there were things he needed to sort out. She thought he was going to Kingsley House to discuss his return to work, but we know now that couldn't have been true. They weren't prepared to have him back.'

'And he'd have had to go through Braunton to get to Crow Point,' Matthew nodded, agreeing it could be important. 'We know he doesn't drive any more, but he could have walked it from there, just about. So that's an action for tomorrow: get the witness in to make a statement. She can give us a description of the woman Walden was with and if we're lucky, she'll have overheard them talking.' He paused. 'There was also a phone message left for Walden. Jen, you heard it on the landline voicemail at the house in Ilfracombe.'

'I took a recording.' She got out her phone and played it. The male voice sounded thin and tinny in the big room. 'It could just be an old friend, trying to get in touch, but I don't know . . . ' She looked around the room. 'It might be my imagination, but I think I can hear a threat in there.'

Nobody spoke; they were unwilling to commit themselves.

'Do we know who it is?' Matthew asked.

Ross stuck his hand up, too eager, too desperate to impress. Jen wondered if she'd ever been like that.

'It came from a mobile phone registered to a

guy named Springer. Alan Springer. He lives in Bristol.'

'That makes sense — after all, it's where Walden comes from. Of course, it *could* just be an old friend, but it would have taken an effort to track Walden down at the Ilfracombe address. He must really have wanted to speak to him. I think you're right, Jen. There's something a bit odd about it.' Venn looked at Ross. 'Do we know anything about Mr Alan Springer?'

'No police record. I haven't got much beyond that. The phone company only got back to us half an hour ago.'

'That's something else for tomorrow then. Let's see what there is to know about him. Find out if he can account for his movements. And even if we can rule him out as a suspect, he might be able to give us some information about Walden. I'm still curious about how a married man, running his own restaurant, ended up sleeping rough and throwing himself on the mercy of the Church.'

'He killed a child,' Jen said. 'That would do terrible things to you.'

'You're right. Of course it would.' A moment of silence. 'How did the child's parents react at the time of the accident? Did they swear revenge? Demand compensation? It might be a possible motive.'

'No,' said Ross. 'I've looked the story up online.' He paused. 'They said they forgave him. The papers made a big deal of it.'

'Perhaps that was their reaction immediately after the child's death,' Matthew said, 'but things change over time. Families break up under the stress of bereavement. Resentment grows. I'd like to know if the family is still together.' He looked sharply at Ross. 'I suppose their name wasn't Springer?'

'No!' He looked at his notes. 'Sally and James Thorne. I think we can dismiss them from our enquiries. They emigrated, moved to Australia to be close to her family. She grew up there. I've checked and they're at home in Adelaide.'

'You spoke to them?'

'They were at work. I spoke to Sally's mother. She was going to tell them about Walden's death, but she seemed unfazed by the news, as if somehow it wasn't a big deal for them. She said they'd all moved on.'

Jen thought that was a weird thing to say. How could you move on so easily after the death of a child? But perhaps people survived in different ways.

Venn considered this for a moment, then he nodded. It was dark outside now. One of the strip lights in the room was faulty and flickered, but nobody moved to switch it off. 'Jen, fill in the rest of the team on Walden's housemates. We know a bit more about them now and about how he fitted in there.'

Jen stood up again. She'd never minded being the centre of attention; she just didn't crave it like Ross. She tried to capture the atmosphere of the house in Ilfracombe, described the two close friends who'd found a way of living together despite their differences. 'They're bright women, confident, good at what they do. Then Walden came in and threw the household out of balance. They thought he'd be leaving at Easter, but his boss at Kingsley House told me there'd be no way they'd have him back. So, unless he'd found another job, they were stuck with him.'

'Why wouldn't the hotel employ Walden again?'

'The chef didn't like him. I don't think there was any more to it than that. And Walden was a moody bastard, not prepared to play their games.'

'He got on well enough with the chef at the Woodyard,' Matthew said. 'They seem to have confided in each other. And I spoke to Christopher Preece, Caroline's dad and one of the trustees at the Woodyard. He used to work in hospitality and said he'd have employed him.'

'There'd be less pressure at the Woodyard, perhaps. It's high-end dining at the Kingsley. The sort of place where they charge you an arm and a leg and you still come out starving.'

The room was quiet for a moment. They were waiting for Venn to speak. 'Our Mr Walden seems a complicated character,' he said at last. 'Moody and aggressive, according to some witnesses, yet when he travelled to Lovacott he sat next to Lucy Braddick on the bus and made her laugh. Made her day. Even Gaby Henry, who took against him, admits there was something about him that attracted her. She painted him in the hope of understanding him better.'

'Any idea what he was doing in Lovacott, boss?' The question bordered on rudeness. Ross wanted to make it clear that he didn't see the point in the character analysis, couldn't understand how it could help them to find the killer. He wanted them to move on and to stick to the facts.

'According to the landlady of The Golden Fleece, he was waiting for a woman,' Matthew said. 'But that was just guesswork. It sounds as if he was waiting for *someone* who didn't show up, though.'

He leaned back against a desk. 'We'll continue the enquiries in Braunton and Ilfracombe. Let's track Walden's movements from the moment he left the house that morning. How did he get to Braunton? Did he take the bus, or did the person he was meeting there give him a lift? There's CCTV in Ilfracombe high street and at the bus station and we might find something in Braunton too. But I want to know more about our victim and to do that we need to speak to the people close to him.' He paused and looked at Jen. 'How would you be fixed for a trip to Bristol tomorrow? I'd like you to speak to Walden's wife. And while you're there, to arrange a meeting with Alan Springer, the chap who left the message on the landline in Hope Street.'

'Yeah, sure.' As she answered, she was thinking that it would be another early start and late finish, that the kids would have to get themselves to school again, but there was no hesitation.

'Take Ross with you,' Matthew said. 'It'd be useful to have two perspectives.'

Oh great, she thought. *Bloody great.*

13

Matthew was in his office early the next morning. The sun was shining again on the mound of Castle Hill, making the grass look new and impossibly green. He'd woken to a high tide; the sound of the water outside the bedroom window had invaded his dreams. Even on waking, he'd still believed for a moment that he'd been in a boat and had a brief sense of drowning, of disappearing under a black wave, high as a cliff. Then he'd realized where he was and that it was *his* turn to make the coffee. Jonathan was barely moving and only sat up in bed when Matthew came back into the room with his hands cupped round the mug. Poised in the doorway, Matthew stared at him for a moment: blond-haired, bare-chested. Beautiful.

At his desk, Matthew looked at the contact list Ross had left for him the night before. There were a few people to follow up and he'd pass them on to other members of the team. He looked at the details of the woman who'd seen Walden in the Braunton cafe on the morning of his death. Her name was Angela Bale and there was a mobile number. Matthew phoned it.

'Hello?' She sounded suspicious because she didn't recognize the number.

'Miss Bale.'

'Mrs.'

'This is Matthew Venn. I'm a police officer

working on the Simon Walden case. I wonder if you could come into the station to give us a statement. You said you saw the victim on the day he was killed. In a cafe in Braunton.'

'I can't come today,' she said quickly. 'It's not convenient. I'm working.'

'Where do you work?'

'For the Landmark Trust. In the booking office for the *Oldenburg* at Ilfracombe Harbour. The season has only just started and we're very busy.' The *Oldenburg* was the Lundy Island ferry. He and Jonathan had spent a few days in a tiny cottage on Lundy in the autumn. It had been wild and rainy. He'd been sick on the boat across but Jonathan had loved the stormy sea. They'd spent most of their stay hiding from the weather, either in bed or in the Marisco Tavern, the island pub. Or arguing to relieve the boredom and then making up.

'You'll have a lunch break, though? Perhaps we could speak to you then.'

There was silence at the end of the line. 'My husband said I shouldn't have spoken to you, that I might have made a mistake. That I shouldn't get involved.'

'What do *you* think?' Matthew asked. 'Do you think you made a mistake?'

Another silence before she spoke. 'No.'

'Then it would be very helpful if you'd make a statement.'

'Would you be the person I'd be speaking to?'

'If you'd find that easier.'

'Meet me at work then. Twelve o'clock.'

He felt a moment of joy at having an excuse to

138

leave the office. It occurred to him that he should call into Chivenor on his way to Ilfracombe. The dog-walker who'd found Walden's body still hadn't made a formal statement. He'd have to leave soon to allow himself time to speak to her, and thinking of that, he felt as if a weight had lifted from his shoulders. The claustrophobia that overwhelmed him sometimes in the office had become almost pathological. He'd need to deal with it; he couldn't spend his working life on a bus or drinking tea in witnesses' houses.

★ ★ ★

When Matthew had been growing up, Chivenor had been an RAF station and the yellow search and rescue coastguard helicopters had been based there. He remembered one Christmas, during a brisk post-lunch walk on the beach, seeing an officer dressed as Father Christmas being winched down to the sand to the delight of the other children. He'd been carrying a sack full of sweets. Matthew had been entranced. He'd wanted so much to believe that Santa was real despite his parents' telling him otherwise. His mother had been horrified and had muttered loudly about blasphemy and filling children's heads with dangerous nonsense, while other parents had glared at her for spoiling the magic.

Now, the base was still there, but much of the land had been sold off for housing. Sharon Winstone, the woman who'd discovered Walden's body, lived in a cul-de-sac of raw, red-brick properties, detached from their neighbours by barely more than six inches. He was early and when he arrived, loud music was playing. Through the living room window, he saw that she was watching a keep-fit DVD and exercising violently to pumped-up music. Although her face was red and she was sweating, her hair, which looked rather like a brown helmet, hardly moved. He rang the bell, but there was no response. He leaned on it and at last she heard the ringing over the noise. She turned, gave him a little wave, switched off the screen and came to the door. She was wearing purple floral leggings and a long T-shirt.

'Sorry, I thought I'd have time for a shower before you got here.' She seemed bothered by her appearance and he thought she was going to ask him to wait while she changed. In the end, she led him straight into the room where she'd been doing the workout. 'I saw about the poor man at Crow Point on the TV. I thought you'd be in touch.'

She offered him coffee and brought in a couple of mugs of instant, put a coaster on the pale wood table before setting it down for him. She'd told Ross she had a boy at school but there was no sign of him here. Any toys in the place had been hidden away. The house was spotless, a show home, bland. A small dog lay in a basket with a floral print cushion to match the curtains. It had lifted its head when Matthew came in, then went back to sleep.

'I know you spoke to my DC,' Matthew said, 'but could you take me through what happened on that day? I'll make some notes and ask you to sign a statement.'

'Sure.' Any upset she might have felt at coming across a dead man on the beach had long gone. He thought she was enjoying the attention, perhaps even the company.

'You don't work?'

'Not at the moment.' A tight smile. 'Taking a career break.'

He wondered what that was all about. Had she been recently sacked? Given up work because of stress? She didn't seem the anxious type, though there was something driven about the exercise. 'So, you were walking your dog on the beach at Crow Point. Had you taken your car down the toll road?'

'Yes. I parked close to the house by the shore, crossed the dunes onto the beach and walked towards the point. I was on my way back when I saw the guy lying on the sand.'

'You were on your own?'

There was a pause and he could tell she was wondering whether she'd get away with a lie.

'We're told all sorts of things during an investigation. Not all of them are relevant and not everything comes out in court. But we do need the details.'

'I was meeting a friend on the beach,' she said. 'A man.'

'I'll need his contact details.'

'Okay.' She looked up at him, a kind of challenge. 'But he's married, so can you catch him at work?'

He nodded. 'We'll try. Where did you meet

141

him that day? Did you park together?' He was thinking of the evidence Colin Marston had given.

She nodded.

'And he drives a Passat and you drive a Fiesta and he's older than you?'

'Yes!' A look of total astonishment. 'He was my boss at work and it came out that we were seeing each other. So embarrassing. I had to leave my job.'

No, you didn't have to leave. He could have been the one to go. Matthew thought he should get Jen Rafferty to bring her statement back to be signed. She might talk some sense into the woman.

Sharon looked at him. 'My husband doesn't know. He thinks I left work because I was bored in the office. He doesn't mind. He likes me at home to keep on top of things, to be around for our son.' A pause. 'Nothing happened that afternoon on the beach. We're not kids. We didn't make passionate love in the dunes.' Another moment of silence. 'But I'd been missing him. I love his company.'

'Did you see the body when you were on your way to Crow Point?'

'No, not until we were on our way back.'

'And you *would* have seen the man if he'd been there?'

'I've been thinking about that,' Sharon said. 'We were talking, catching up. We hadn't seen each other for a few weeks because Dave had been away with his family for the half-term holiday. But I think we would have seen the

142

body. It wasn't hidden in any way and we followed the same tracks back in the sand.'

If that was the case, Walden had been killed while Sharon and her lover were walking out to the Point. That had been risky. Perhaps Matthew should be looking for somebody reckless, who enjoyed danger. Or somebody desperate.

She was staring into the empty coffee mug. 'I didn't want to be left there on the beach with the dead man. Not on my own. I know I should have stayed with the body, but I just couldn't face it. So Dave walked with me back to the cars and then he drove off to work. He had a meeting. I phoned the police from there and waited.'

'Can you give me some timings?' Matthew asked. 'When you arrived, when you saw the body?' Because that would pin down a time of death much more accurately than any information the pathologist could give him.

'I was supposed to meet Dave at midday, but he was a bit late.' Matthew imagined her sitting in her car, getting more and more anxious that her lover wouldn't turn up. 'It was probably nearer half past when he got there. It was ten past two when we first saw the body. I checked my watch.'

'Did you see anyone else on the beach?'

'Nobody that I was aware of. We were talking, you know, making plans for the future, for when our kids are old enough to understand.'

Matthew nodded. He suspected the guy was stringing her along, making promises that he had no intention of keeping. Would she enjoy the affair, anyway, if it stopped being illicit and

143

exciting? But relationship counselling wasn't in his job description and it wasn't his place to give advice. He stood up and told her how helpful she'd been and left the house. As he unlocked the car, he heard the music again, compulsive and manic, and thought she was trying to dance away her boredom and her demons.

★ ★ ★

In Ilfracombe the breeze was stronger and eddied through the narrow streets. He knew it was a westerly, because he'd heard the shipping forecast that morning, but whichever way he walked it was in his face. He was early here too — punctuality was a curse, inherited from his mother who thought it was a sin to be late — so he left his car at the top of Hope Street and walked down the hill, along the high street, then on towards the harbour. There was a smell of fried fish. A couple of optimistic cafes had opened early in the season. A gift shop owner had stacked all his goods to one side and was mopping the floor.

Verity, Damien Hirst's sculpture, stood at the end of the pier. A huge pregnant woman. Triumphant, one arm raised. From one side all her internal organs were showing and Matthew was reminded of a body on the pathologist's table, the skin peeled back. In the Lundy Island ferry offices, there was a short queue of people booking tickets. A woman sat in the waiting room, her coat wrapped round her for protection, looking out of the window.

'Mrs Bale?' But he knew it was her without asking. She looked so nervous, so mousy, so scared of the world.

She jumped to her feet. 'I've only got half an hour.'

'That's okay. It won't take longer than that. Perhaps I could buy you lunch.'

'Oh no. I always bring my own sandwiches. I'll eat them at my desk later.'

In the end, they sat on a bench, looking out over the water, wrapped up in their coats. Angela Bale seemed happier outside where they couldn't be overheard.

'What were you doing in Braunton when you saw Mr Walden?'

'It was my day off,' she said. 'I always meet my mother on my day off. She lives in Braunton, so I get the bus. Then she buys me coffee. The least she can do, she says, because I've made the trip over to see her. That place we went to, the cafe by the stream where I saw your man, is our favourite.'

Matthew nodded and saw that this trip to Braunton to see her mother was the highlight of her week. She was still talking.

'Then I do a bit of supermarket shopping for her and carry it home. She's got arthritis in her hands and she can't manage heavy bags these days.'

'What time do you usually get to the cafe?' Matthew thought it would be the same time each week. There would be an element of ritual in her days out.

'The bus gets in at ten forty-five and I walk

145

straight there. Eleven o'clock? Mum was there before me and she'd bagged our favourite table.'

'You'd caught the bus from Ilfracombe?'

Angela Bale nodded.

'I don't suppose you noticed Mr Walden on the bus? We think he came from Ilfracombe too, you see.'

'No,' she said, certain now. She'd lost her shyness. 'He was there before me. Sitting at the table next to ours.'

'What was he wearing?'

'Jeans. A denim jacket.' She shut her eyes for a moment. 'He was eating a bacon sandwich. I thought it looked very good, but Mum and I always go for a milky coffee and a scone.'

'And the woman next to him?'

'I didn't see her so clearly because she had her back to me.'

'What sort of age?' Matthew was careful not to prompt, not to let his disappointment show.

'Young. Well, everyone seems young to me these days.' Angela appeared more confident now. 'Dark hair. A green coat. I don't think I saw her face at all.' A pause. Matthew could tell she was trying her best to remember. She wanted to please him. 'She was drinking that herby tea. I could smell it. I've never seen the point. And she wasn't eating anything. Not even a bit of toast or a biscuit. It always seems a waste to me, going out to a cafe, if all you choose is something you could have for much less money at home.'

'That's really helpful. Who left first? Them or you?'

She didn't have to think about that. 'Oh,

them. We don't rush, Mum and me. We like to take our time.'

'Did you see who paid? The man or the woman?'

This time she took a while to answer. 'They didn't pay at the table. They paid at the counter on their way out. I think it was her.'

'I don't suppose you noticed whether she paid with cash or a card.' Matthew kept his voice light. He didn't want to put her under any pressure. But under the table he was crossing his fingers. If the woman had paid with a card, they'd have a name for her.

Angela shook her head. 'Sorry. I didn't see.' She looked at her watch. 'I should probably go.'

Matthew stood up. 'You've been very helpful.' That was true because it was *possible* the woman had paid by card. Most younger people did.

Outside on the pavement, Angela Bale hurried away back to the ferry offices. Matthew stood for a moment. He was trying to remember if he'd seen either of the women from Hope Street in a green coat.

He stopped at the cafe in Braunton where Angela Bale had seen Walden on his way back to Barnstaple. He and Jonathan were regulars; the place did a terrific weekend brunch and on a Saturday morning you had to queue for a table. It was quieter now. A couple of women were taking an early afternoon tea and a businessman engrossed in a laptop was eating a sandwich. Lizzie was at the counter. She owned the place and did most of the front of house.

'Hi there, Matt! What can I get you?'

He was tempted to order another coffee, but he'd been out of the office for long enough. 'Sorry, Liz, this is official.' He put Walden's photo on the counter. 'Do you recognize this man?'

She squinted. She wore specs for making up the bills but was too vain to put them on for serving. 'He's not a regular.'

'He's the guy that was killed on Crow Point on Monday afternoon. We think he had coffee in here on Monday morning.'

Now she did take her glasses from a pocket in her apron to look more carefully. 'What time?'

'About ten thirty. Maybe a bit later. We think he was with a woman wearing a green coat.'

'I don't remember. You know what it's like here in the mornings. Pretty manic and people move through really quickly.'

'He had coffee and a bacon sandwich and she had herbal tea, nothing to eat.'

'Yeah, I do remember them.' She was triumphant. 'At least not them, but the order. I can't give you any more than you've already got, though. I can't describe them.' She took off the glasses. 'You know what I'm like without these.'

'Did they pay by card or cash?'

'I'm not sure. Want me to check?' Without waiting for an answer, she went to the machine and stuck her specs on her nose again. 'Sorry, it must have been a cash transaction.'

'No worries. Can you ask the other staff? They might remember something useful.' He pushed across his card. 'Give me a shout if you remember anything.'

* ★ * ★ * ★

In his office at the station, someone had left a note on his desk. The writing was rather beautiful and he spent a moment wondering which of his team might have written it. Then he read the contents: *Your mother rang. Can you visit her at home? She says it's urgent.*

14

His mother lived in a neat little bungalow on a tidy estate of seventies houses at the edge of the town. It was set on a hill and there was a view all the way down to the estuary. The bungalow looked as if it belonged to an older person, but the family had lived there even when Matthew was a boy. His parents had bought it when they were first married. Matthew wouldn't have been surprised if his mother hadn't already been planning ahead for the time when they might not be able to manage the stairs. She'd never discovered the knack of living in the present.

Matthew sat outside in the car for a moment, worrying. His mother had said it was urgent that she see him, but if there had been some medical emergency, she would have called a friend from the Brethren and not him. He'd only found out that his father was ill through a third person. Now he was nervous, wondering how he would react to her if she let rip again, if that was why she had phoned him: to accuse him again of killing his father.

He wondered how it had come to this, replayed again the moment when faith had been replaced by a different kind of certainty and his life had fractured. It had been his first year at university and he'd come home for the Easter holidays. His parents had taken him to a meeting on his second night home, wanting to show him off. The bright boy who'd got into Bristol University, who was a credit to them all. But things had already started falling apart, his confidence unravelling, anxiety taking hold. He might have been considered bright in a comprehensive school in Barnstaple, but there'd been gaps in his knowledge and understanding. He'd struggled to make friends in Bristol, knew people laughed at him behind his back, felt ill at ease, not right in his own skin. And he'd been forced to think for himself, to challenge the belief system he'd grown up with.

The meeting had been held in a hired village hall, somewhere on the edge of Exmoor. It had felt damp and dusty, and there was a smell of paraffin from the heaters. There'd been quite a crowd, perhaps fifty people. Brethren from all over the county were there, not to see him, but because it was one of the quarterly sessions when decisions were made. He'd sat near the back with his parents. Dennis Salter, who had conducted his father's funeral, had been taking the service. He'd been younger then, of course, but still the acknowledged leader. Dennis had welcomed them as they came into the hall, had taken Matthew into his arms and held him for a moment. 'I couldn't be more proud, son.' As if he wished Matthew really *was* his son.

Looking at the assembled group, the families and the ardent young converts, Matthew had had a sudden understanding, as the early evening sunshine shone through the dusty glass, a vision close to a religious experience: this was all a sham. The earnest elderly women in their

151

mushroom-shaped hats, the bluff good-natured men — they were all deluding themselves. They were here for their own reasons, for the power trip or because they'd grown up with the group and couldn't let go. Through cowardice or habit. With the understanding there'd come a liberation, a sense that he was now free to do what he wanted and be who he wanted to be.

Perhaps it had been youthful arrogance or perhaps he'd been suffering some stress-related minor breakdown, but he'd needed to speak about this sudden new insight, to spread the word. He'd felt different, lit-up, excited. To sit there, listening to the worship, knowing he didn't believe a word, had made him want to yell at them all; he couldn't just sit there pretending. At the end when Salter had asked if anyone wanted to share with the group, Matthew had raised his hand and got to his feet.

'None of this is true. I'm sorry, but I don't believe any of it. You must be mad if you think it's true!'

There'd been silence. He still had an image of faces turned towards him in horror and disbelief. His mother had given a little gasp. After that, he could remember little detail. There were muddled memories of confusion and embarrassment. His mother and father shepherding him out of the hall. Dennis Salter standing at the door, sad and stern-faced. 'Are you sure, boy? You're turning your back on the Brethren?'

'I can't lie.' He'd still been a little defiant then.

'You'll always be welcome back when you see the light, but until then, you're a stranger to us.'

Then the door had been shut on them and they'd driven home, his mother weeping all the way.

The next day he'd left for Bristol, seen his tutor and told him he was leaving university. The day after he'd got a job entering data for an insurance company, because he needed to earn a living. The following week he'd applied to join the police. He'd realized that he still needed rules and the idea of justice, that chaos made him panic. He'd tried to communicate with his parents, but half-heartedly, through birthday cards, a present at Christmas. There'd been no response. In the beginning, his father had phoned occasionally, begging him to reconsider his denial of faith. 'Can't you just go along with it for the sake of your mother? She's in pieces.'

But Matthew was stubborn. 'She taught me not to bear false witness.' He'd dropped them a note when he moved to Barnstaple, but they hadn't got in touch. The separation had gone on for so long that neither side had known how to bridge the gap.

When he'd heard about his father's condition from a neighbour, Matthew had called his mother immediately. She'd been almost speechless with rage.

'I don't know how you've got the nerve to speak to me. You do know it's your fault, the heart attack? We saw it in the *North Devon Journal*. Marriage to a *man*.' The last phrase explosive, as if she was spitting into the telephone. Spitting at him.

He'd wanted to visit his father in hospital, but

had never been brave enough to go, anxious that there might be some truth in her accusation, or that he might bump into her in the hospital ward. She'd never minded making a scene. But he'd longed to see his father, to chat about football and music as they had on those summer days when Matthew had gone with him visiting the coastal farms, to hold his hand.

The net curtain at the window moved. She'd seen him. He got out of the car and rang the doorbell. She wouldn't want him to know that she'd been looking out for him, so it was best to pretend he hadn't seen the twitching curtain.

He hadn't seen her for twenty years, except a couple of times by chance recently, at a distance, in the street. She hadn't changed so much. She was small, fit for her age. The obsession with healthy eating might not have saved his father, but it had worked for her. She still walked most days into town to get her own shopping. She'd never learned to drive. She stood aside to let him in quickly, so ashamed of who he was, it seemed, that she didn't want the neighbours to know he was there.

'I was expecting you earlier.'

'I've only just been given your message. I was out working.' He tried to keep the fight out of his voice and to remember the good times: her reading to him when he was very small, putting on silly voices to make him laugh, her cheering him on at sports day, telling him how well he'd done even when he came next to last. Telling him, and everyone else who would listen, that he'd grow up to be a great preacher.

154

'Susan Shapland's here,' she said. 'She's out of her mind with worry.' It sounded like an apology of sorts.

They were standing in the hall. There was the same woodchip wallpaper. His father had put on a fresh coat of paint every two years. It still looked clean and bright so perhaps he'd done it just before he became ill. His mother continued speaking in a whisper. 'She came here because she didn't know what else to do. She thought you'd be able to help.'

Susan Shapland was a widow, his mother's closest friend. She would have been by her side at the funeral, taking Matthew's place. He didn't know what to say.

'Come on through,' his mother said. 'She'll explain herself.'

He stepped into the front room and back in time. This wasn't a Proust madeleine moment. Memory here was triggered by a series of objects, not taste or smell. There was the paperweight with a dandelion seed head trapped in the glass, the wooden solitaire set on the coffee table, the beads smooth and in their place, his parents' wedding photograph on the mantelpiece, next to the picture of him in his uniform, his first day at the Park School, a mug he'd made in pottery class when he was eleven. Susan was sitting in the easy chair next to the gas fire, where his father had always sat, and Matthew felt a moment of affront. But the woman had been crying and the feeling passed quickly.

'It's Susan's Christine,' his mother said. 'She's missing.'

155

Only then did Matthew remember that Susan had a daughter, about the same age as himself. They'd played together occasionally when Brethren meetings dragged on, the members lingering to discuss esoteric points of dogma and practice. Should hats be worn or not worn at meetings? What was really meant by the virgin birth? As he recalled, both questions had been considered equally seriously.

Christine had been a quiet little thing, dark-haired, brown-eyed, with an awkward gait and slow speech. As he'd matured, started to grow up, she never had. She'd always looked different. When she was thirteen she still brought a doll with her to meetings, still sucked her thumb. His mother had explained that she'd *never* grow up, because she had Down's syndrome and had been born that way. A cross that Susan and Cecil had to bear, but a blessing too, because she'd always be innocent. As Matthew remembered, Christine had never left home.

He took the seat next to Susan's. 'Why don't you tell me what happened?'

'I didn't want Christine to be at your father's funeral. She gets bored and I was worried she'd start wandering around, upsetting people, getting in the way. My sister lives in Lovacott and she said she'd have her to stay. You remember Grace? My sister? She's not the most sociable of people and she didn't mind staying at home. She said Dennis would be there to represent them both.'

Matthew nodded. Of course he remembered Grace, but more because she was Dennis Salter's

156

wife than in her own right. She'd been kindly enough, but shy, happy to stay in Salter's shadow. Dennis Salter had a huge personality, and a warmth that held the Brethren together. Until Matthew's outburst at the meeting, he'd taken the young Matthew under his wing, encouraged him. It was not surprising perhaps that Matthew's memory of the woman was sketchy. Occasionally she'd brought sweets along to meetings for the children, secretly slipping them from her bag when she thought none of the adults were watching, but he remembered little else about her now. 'Of course.'

Susan continued:

'So, Dennis came to collect my Christine on Monday morning and the idea was that she'd stay with them until last night. I was expecting her back before bedtime. When they didn't bring her home, I assumed they'd decided to keep her an extra night. To give me a break, like. I tried phoning, but Grace don't always answer. They go to bed early. I thought if there'd been any problem they'd have let me know.' As the story continued and she became more upset again, Susan's accent grew stronger. 'I phoned first thing this morning and Grace told me Christine wasn't there.'

'When did she go missing?' Matthew thought this was the last thing they needed. A vulnerable missing person while they were working on a murder inquiry. He was making links too, wondering about coincidence, because Lucy Braddick lived in Lovacott, and she had Down's syndrome too.

'Well, we don't know that. Not exactly.'

'Perhaps you'd explain.'

'Well, she goes to the Woodyard three times a week, to the day centre. To give me a break as much as anything.'

Matthew nodded but felt his pulse racing.

'Dennis brought her in yesterday as normal. And he came back in the afternoon to wait for her, but she never came out with the others, so he just thought she'd taken the minibus home.' Her voice suddenly warmed. 'Poor soul, he's in such a state. He's blaming himself for the fact that she's missing and for not calling me to check. But he got caught up with another emergency. One of the Brethren was taken poorly that afternoon, so they went straight out again when they got back to Lovacott. They were in A&E with him when I phoned them at home last night.'

'You're saying that Christine could have gone missing anytime yesterday?' Matthew paused. 'Have you checked with the day centre?' *I was there for most of the day. She could have disappeared while I was sitting in the sun, chatting to my husband.* He remembered his walk through the day centre and thought that Christine could have been in the kitchen when he passed, peeling potatoes at the sink.

'I haven't done *anything*!' Susan said. 'I didn't know where to start. I just came here to Dorothy's, because I knew you were a detective. I thought you'd know how to find her.'

He was going to ask why she hadn't called the police as soon as she'd realized Christine was missing, but the woman felt bad enough. No point making accusations now. She was here and so was he. Back in the family home and making himself useful at last.

'Have you got a photograph of Christine?'

'Not here.' She seemed so distressed that he worried she'd start crying again. 'I never thought.'

'I'll drive you home,' Matthew said. 'Mother can come with you, keep you company. You want to be there, don't you, in case Christine finds her way back.'

'Oh yes!' She looked up, horrified. 'I never thought of that.' He saw that panic had overwhelmed her; she was drowning in it.

'In the meantime, I'll phone the station and get things started. Let's see if we can find her for you.'

★　★　★

Susan Shapland lived in a little cottage, the middle of a terrace of three on a creek running in from the Taw, on low-lying land close to Braunton Marsh. It was only a couple of miles from Matthew's house, and from the place where Walden's body had been found. Susan must have called a taxi to Matthew's mother's house as soon as she realized Christine was missing. An impulse because she knew she couldn't cope with this crisis on her own. When Matthew had been a boy, the creek had been neglected, overgrown, with remnants of its industrial past: staithes and the rusted remains of a small crane.

In the nineteenth century, boats bringing coal to the county had tied up here, and had taken away the clay, which had been dug close by. Now, it formed part of a nature reserve. Colin Marston probably walked along the bank every day while he was doing his bird census.

The Shaplands' cottage was low and damp. Susan had given up her battle with the wet that seeped in from outside, and there was mould on the window ledges and crawling across the ceiling. Matthew wondered if anyone had suggested that she and Christine should move. Some incomer would buy the place, and make it habitable, but it was barely that now. Perhaps the husband, Cecil, had been the person holding things together. He wondered too when his mother had last come here. He imagined the delight she would take in throwing open windows and spraying the place with bleach, scrubbing until it shone.

They sat in the cluttered living room while Susan hurried away to find a photograph.

'A man came to the Woodyard a couple of months ago and took the pictures.'

Christine was still recognizable as the girl he'd once played with. Short, dark-haired, a little dumpy. He thought it was the woman he'd seen helping to cook in the Woodyard. She was smiling shyly at the camera.

'That's very useful. How old is she now?'

'Forty-two,' Susan said. 'But not in her mind. In her mind she's still a little girl.'

'Has she said anything recently about someone hurting her or asking her to do something that made her feel uncomfortable?'

Jonathan had occasionally brought home anxieties about the sexual abuse of service users in his care. Allegations against relatives, carers. Matthew had never been able to proceed with a prosecution. It was one person's word against another and often the victims didn't *have* the words to explain what had happened to them. A court case was intimidating enough at the best of times and would be so much worse for someone like Christine, with a limited understanding of what was going on.

Something unusual was happening here and ideas and possibilities skittered through his mind, unformed and difficult to catch. Lucy Braddick was brave and she'd been clear that nothing untoward had gone on with Walden. But his behaviour could have been seen as grooming, stalking even, and perhaps Lucy viewed the world through an innocent's eyes. Although the man hadn't sounded like the sort of person who'd be excited by having sex with a vulnerable adult, Matthew had never met him. If he'd been close to a breakdown, perhaps he'd find something almost reassuring in being with a woman who'd be compliant, easy to dominate. Walden couldn't have abducted Christine; he was already dead when she went missing. So, what were they talking here? A circle of abuse with other people involved? And if an adult with a learning disability had been assaulted by Walden and the family had found out, wouldn't that be a motive for murder?

Susan still hadn't answered. She was staring at

161

him in horror. At last she spoke. 'My Susan's a good girl. She wouldn't do anything like that.'

'She wouldn't be responsible,' Matthew said. 'It wouldn't be her fault at all. You do see that? There are men who take advantage of vulnerable women. Has she seemed herself recently? Happy?'

There was another long silence.

'We didn't really talk,' Susan said. 'Not about things like that. Feelings. Chrissie was closer to her dad. I think they talked. With us it was practical, like. What she wanted for tea and did she have anything that needed washing. Then we watched telly together. We were used to each other. We had a routine. The only time she got upset was when the unexpected things happened. She hated that. She'll hate what's happening now. Missing the routine, her days at the Woodyard, *Coronation Street* on the television.' She looked up. 'You've got to find her.'

Matthew nodded. He said he'd get off and make sure his officers knew how important it was. He left Susan in the small, dark front room, but his mother followed him to the door to see him out.

'Would you like me to come back later?' he asked. 'I could give you a lift home.'

'No,' she said sharply. 'I might stay over and if I need to go back to Barnstaple, I can always get a taxi.' Making it quite clear that he hadn't yet done enough to be forgiven for his loss of faith, for abandoning the Brethren.

15

Maurice Braddick had decided he'd keep Lucy at home until Walden's killer was caught. The police obviously believed the Woodyard was involved in some way in the murder and he wasn't going to put his daughter in danger. No way. Maurice thought it would be good for the two of them to spend a day together in the garden. Lucy could get some of that exercise the social worker was always talking about and since the weather had improved he'd been itching to get out there, to get his hands covered in soil and some fresh air in his lungs. Then they could treat themselves to tea in The Golden Fleece. Lucy would like that; she was always glad of an excuse to dress up.

Lucy, though, had other ideas. She was up and ready just the same as usual, and she had her bag with her when she came in for breakfast.

'Morning, maid. I thought we'd give the Woodyard a miss today.' Maurice tried to sound bright, in control.

'Why?' She reached out for the box of cereal, filled her bowl to the rim, then stared at him, demanding an answer.

'We could have a day here and then go to The Fleece for our tea. A bit of a treat.'

'We could go to The Fleece when I get back from the Woodyard.' She started to eat, as if the matter was already settled. Maurice thought she

163

got that from her mother: a stubbornness, a refusal to listen to a good argument. But he knew she also loved routine. Anything different threw her.

Still, he gave it one more try. 'But that man from there was killed.'

'Not in the Woodyard, Dad. On a beach.' And he had no answer to that.

'I'll give you a lift there and back then. See you safe inside.'

Of course Lucy agreed to the lift because it would save her the walk to and from the bus stop in the square, and the bus ride was no fun any more, without Walden to chat to and feed her sweets. She gave him one of her lovely smiles.

★ ★ ★

The wind was stronger. He could see it gusting on the river as they drove down towards Barnstaple. He thought the weather was changing and though he'd lost the heart for it now, he should still spend a bit of time in the garden before the rain came. He parked at the Woodyard and walked with Lucy to the door, then followed her at a distance until she was safely through the glass tunnel and into the day centre. He knew that was ridiculous. What could happen to her here, with all these people about?

But even in the day centre, there were sometimes accidents. Perhaps Lucy's friend Rosa's parents had had the right idea taking her away and keeping her safe at home. Maurice thought this notion of giving people like Lucy more independence was going too far. Of course they shouldn't go back to the Dark Ages when folk were locked away in institutions, as if there was something shameful about them. But they needed to be protected. Properly cared for. In the past he'd seen the day centre as a place of safety. Now, he wasn't so sure.

Maurice couldn't face driving home straight away; he knew he'd be too restless to settle to anything. Instead, he went to the cafe, ordered a sausage toastie and sat there, staring out of the window, watching the scudding clouds reflected in the water, until the place filled up and they needed his table.

16

They had an early start. Jen pulled rank and insisted on driving because she'd get paid the mileage and she needed the cash. When she got to Ross's immaculate little house on a smart new estate on the edge of town, Melanie let her in.

'Come and wait for a moment. He's nearly ready. You know what he's like in the morning, he spends more time in the bathroom than me.' Melanie rolled her eyes in mock-despair, but Jen could tell she'd forgive Ross anything. Jen wished there was something to dislike about Melanie. She was as immaculate as the house, with flawless skin and hair already styled for work. But she was kind too. She worked as a manager in an old people's home, had started as a care assistant straight from school at sixteen and still took her turn at wiping bums and laying out the dead when they were short-staffed. As far as Jen could tell, her only fault was her taste in men. She and Ross had been going out together since they were teenagers, but Melanie still worshipped him.

He appeared at the bottom of the stairs, gave Jen a quick nod that might have been an apology for keeping her waiting, and hugged his wife. A real hug, full of affection but sexy too. At that moment Jen realized what she really felt for the couple was envy.

All the way up the M5 Ross was talking,

rambling about the previous weekend's rugby match against a Cornish team, about his moment of glory, saving the day with a last-minute drop goal. Jen's ex had been into football and the story didn't sound so different from the ones she'd been forced to fake interest in at home. This was different, though, because Ross was just a colleague, and *she* was different. She didn't have to pretend to care. When he paused for breath, she broke in.

'You do know I don't give a flying fuck about this sporting crap?'

He stopped, shocked and offended, and they spent the next few miles in silence. Then she thought this was ridiculous. Ross wasn't Robbie and they had work to do. She should make more of an effort to get on with him.

'So, you made appointments with Walden's wife and Alan Springer. Who are we seeing first?'

'Springer. It was hard to pin him down. He didn't want us going to his home.'

'Has he got something to hide, do you think?'

'Maybe, but I didn't think I should push it. We don't want him disappearing and all we have at the moment is that phone call. There's no record from the GPS on his mobile that he was anywhere near North Devon when Walden died.'

'So, where are we meeting him?' Jen indicated and pulled off the motorway.

'The local nick. Bedminster. I've booked an interview room. The boss knows an inspector there and pulled some strings.'

'Stringer preferred to come to the police station rather than talk to us at home?'

'Yeah.'

Jen hoped the man wasn't messing them around, buying time. She hoped he'd turn up.

★ ★ ★

In the end, Springer was there before them. He was waiting when they walked in and the officer on the counter nodded towards him. Tall and well-built, muscular, sandy hair and blue eyes. In the interview room, he sat on the other side of the table from them, apparently easy and relaxed.

'Thanks for agreeing to meet us.'

'No worries. I was sorry to hear about Simon.' A Bristol accent, the one Jen had heard on the answer machine.

'How did you know him?' They'd decided she'd take the lead on the interview.

'We were in the army together. We became friends, both from the same neck of the woods. You know. Got married at about the same time and I left the forces soon after he did. When he set up the business with Kate, his ex, I put a bit of money in.' He looked straight at Jen. 'Big mistake. Never do business with a mate.'

'Tell us about that.'

'Kate was the driving force behind it. She'd worked in hospitality. When Si left the army, she said she wanted to see a bit more of him. She hated being a forces' wife, left behind, moving every few years. So, when he came out, they bought a little restaurant. He'd be the chef and she'd do the admin and front of house. A

168

partnership.' Springer paused. 'Si wasn't so fussed about the idea. He'd have been happy working in a kitchen somewhere, finish at the end of the day. No responsibility. He wasn't ambitious and he needed time to settle back in civvy street. The last thing he needed was more stress.'

He paused, stretched his legs. 'It worked well at first, though. Si was a good cook and they built up a local following, then things started to fall apart. Maybe the business grew too quickly, maybe it was the pressure of being in charge. He started drinking. Often the way old soldiers deal with pressure.'

'He started drinking because he killed a child.'

Springer shook his head. 'The other way round. He killed a child because he'd been drinking.'

'Not over the legal limit.'

'Yeah, well, he must have been bloody lucky because I was with him that day and I wouldn't have driven home.'

Silence in the room. Someone was swearing in the corridor outside.

'What was the phone call about?' That was Ross, impatient, jumping in. Jen wanted to know about the day the two men had been drinking, but Springer had already started his answer.

'I wanted my money back. Needed it back.'

'The money you'd invested in the restaurant?'

He nodded. 'I went to see Kate, but she said they'd sold the business and the house and split the equity. She refused to pay me, said Simon had the cash, that it had been a private

169

arrangement between me and Simon.'

Jen thought that explained how Walden had been able to pay his rent for twenty Hope Street. She wondered where he'd stashed away the rest of the money, but one of the team would be already checking the bank accounts. They'd soon know.

'How did you track him down?'

'That was through Kate too. She said she'd heard from him. He'd rung from a landline and she'd made a note of the number. Worried about him, maybe, or wanting to keep track.' He paused. 'She's found another man. More her kind. Runs his own software business, big flat in Clifton. Mummy and Daddy would approve.'

'Her family didn't approve of Walden?'

Springer shrugged. 'That was the impression I got. Si always felt he had to prove himself. He was never quite good enough.'

'Did he call you back after you left the message for him?'

'Yeah. A little while later.' Springer snapped his mouth shut.

'And did you get your money back?'

Another silence. 'He promised he'd get it to me, but there was something about the way he spoke . . . I wasn't sure I believed him. He said it was tied up in a project. Something he really had to do. I'd get it back but I might have to wait.' He paused. 'I told him I couldn't wait. My wife wants a baby. I mean, we both want a baby, but she's desperate and it's just not happening. We only get one shot at IVF on the NHS. I've told her we'll go private, but she's a teaching assistant and I work in a gym and money's tight.' He looked up at them. 'We were mates, served together. He knew how much I needed that cash back. He knew what my marriage means to me.' He paused. 'He said he'd get it back. That he understood.'

'But he didn't deliver?'

Springer shook his head. 'No, he didn't deliver. At least he hadn't. Not before he died and I guess I'll never get it now.'

'Did you go and see him? Kate will have given you his address.'

He looked up. 'You think I killed him? For twenty grand?'

It was Jen's turn to shrug. 'People have killed for less.'

'But I haven't got the money.' He stood up, finally exasperated. 'I have no idea what he did with it. And now I'll never know.'

★   ★   ★

Walden's wife Kate had never taken her husband's name. The flat where she lived with her new partner was one of a number in a grand stone crescent in Clifton. She stood at the door and held out her hand.

'Kate Dickinson.' Cool and polished. Long legs in skinny jeans, a white linen shirt. Her hair looked polished too. It was hard to imagine her hooked up with the itinerant cook.

Bedminster had been busy, the pavements crowded with shoppers, pushchairs, cycles ridden illegally to avoid the busy road. Express

171

supermarkets and pound shops. Chuggers and buskers. This seemed like a different world. Calmer. Lighter. The apartment was on the first floor, and the living room spread the width of the house, with views of the Downs to the front and over the city roofscape at the back. Polished hardwood floor and classy furniture. Little colour and no clutter. The palette various shades of grey.

'You're here to talk about Simon.' She offered them coffee and Jen caught a glimpse into the kitchen, which was just as she would have expected. Granite and chrome, without a mucky pot in sight. Again, as different as it was possible to be from the arty house in Hope Street. Or her house in Barnstaple. The coffee came from a machine that hissed in a genteel, upmarket sort of way. Jen felt an overwhelming desire to scribble on the wall with wax crayon.

'When did you last hear from him?'

She and Ross were on a sofa and Kate sat in a chair opposite, legs curled under her.

'Months ago. Before Christmas, certainly.'

'Could you be more specific?'

She looked up with a little triumphant smile as she remembered. 'Yes! It was the end of October. There are Americans living in the flat next door and they'd put pumpkins outside for Halloween. I remember seeing them on my way out. I was going to the theatre with Guy, my partner. I'd not long moved in.' She paused. 'Then my mobile started ringing. It was Simon, in a dreadful state. Pissed of course. I was used to that, but he was distraught. Suicidal. I didn't know what to do or how I could help.'

'Was he genuinely suicidal?'

'I think so. He said he was weighed down with guilt and he couldn't live with himself. The only way to stop the pain was to kill himself. I tried to talk to him, but he wasn't listening. I knew I wasn't doing any good.'

And your flash new partner was waiting for you. You wouldn't want to miss the first act.

Then Jen told herself that was unreasonable. What could Kate have done? And what right did Walden have to guilt trip her?

'So that was the last time you spoke to him?'

'No!' Kate said. 'No! I should have explained. He phoned a few weeks later. I'd been trying to get in touch with him on his mobile, but he said he'd lost it that night when he was on a bender. He called me from a landline.'

'And that's the number you passed on to Alan Springer when he came to you for money?'

The question seemed to throw her. Perhaps she didn't want to be seen as mean or uncharitable. Not in this grand apartment, with its spectacular views. 'You know about that? Yes. Simon got a very good deal out of the divorce. I thought it was his responsibility to pay back *his* friend.'

'Even though he'd invested in your joint business?'

'It wasn't like that. There was nothing formal. It was a loan to a former colleague, a mate.'

'Tell me about that second phone call. The one from the Ilfracombe landline.'

She paused for a moment. 'It was as if I was

talking to a different man, the man I first fell for. He sounded well. Peaceful. He said he'd started to put his life together. No more self-pity or anger and he'd pulled back on his drinking. He'd found somewhere to live. Nowhere grand, but it would be fine until he got himself sorted. He was cooking again, volunteering in a cafe in a community centre.' Another pause. 'He said I wasn't to worry about him.'

'Quite a transformation.'

'Maybe. Though, like I said, it was almost as if he was himself again and the angry, self-loathing Simon was the man who'd changed.'

'Where did you first meet?'

'At school. We were childhood sweethearts. He was a couple of years older than me and I fell for him. Worshipped him from afar for a while and couldn't believe my luck when he noticed me.' She sipped her coffee, seemed lost in memories. 'There was something frail about him even then. Emotionally, I mean, not physically, but I thought it was attractive. That vulnerability. I felt that I was strong enough for the two of us. I thought I could look after him.' She looked up. 'The arrogance of youth, right?'

Somewhere in the distance, schoolboys were playing a ball game. It would be rugby probably, here in Clifton. Jen could hear cheering, boys' voices shouting. She waited for Kate to continue, glared at Ross so he wouldn't jump in. Sometimes people had to tell their stories in their own time.

'Simon joined the army straight after school. I couldn't understand it. I mean, he was never a macho kind of guy. But I can see now that he was probably looking for security, a family. His mum was on her own, pretty dysfunctional. She died a couple of years ago. He and I kept in touch, though, and I saw him whenever he was home on leave. I started at uni, dropped out after a year. My parents blamed Simon for that, said it was an infatuation, but it was nothing to do with him. He was encouraging me to stay and complete the course. The academic life just wasn't my thing. I got a management trainee post with a boutique hotel chain and worked my way up. Then Simon asked me to marry him. It was what I'd been dreaming of since I was sixteen. Of course I said yes.'

'But it wasn't quite what you expected?' Jen knew about marrying too young, what it was like to be caught up with the romance of the idea, to blink away the solid reality of the man.

'Not quite.' Kate gave another little smile. 'Simon was an officer in charge of catering for his regiment. He was sent to war zones, went with the men when they were away on exercise. They have to be fed wherever they are. He was often close to the front line. He might be chatting to a fellow officer one day, drinking to him the next because he was dead or invalided home. And while he was away, I wasn't there to support him. I had no role in his life. I couldn't be the dutiful army wife, staying in quarters, waiting for my man. I carried on working. It was no wonder we drifted apart.' She paused. 'We hadn't actually spent very much time together since we were at school. It's hardly surprising he seemed like a stranger when we did meet.'

'So, he decided to leave the army.' Jen thought she'd misjudged this woman when they'd first met, had her down as hard and cold because she had a smart home in a classy neighbourhood. People were always more complex than she realized and she was always too quick to jump to conclusions.

'Yes, we decided to set up in business together. A little restaurant. Simon's cooking and my admin skills. Where could we go wrong? I'd saved a bit and we found nice premises in Redland, here in Bristol. Perfect, we thought.' A pause. 'And it was at first. Bloody hard work, mind, but we were in it together. It was only when we started to get successful, the reviews and the queues at the door, that the splits started to show. Simon couldn't handle the stress. As I said, he'd always been a bit emotionally frail.'

'But this time you couldn't fix it?'

Kate looked up at her, hollow-eyed. She wouldn't be used to failure. 'No. He tried to fix it himself. He self-medicated with drink. Easy enough in our business.'

'And then he killed a child.'

'Yes!' Now there were tears in her eyes. 'I've never felt the slightest bit maternal. But a child like that. So helpless and young.' She fumbled in her pocket for a tissue. 'It was Simon's decision to leave. I would have stood by him. I went to see him in prison. But as soon as he came out, he disappeared. I don't know where he went.'

'To North Devon to work in the hotel?'

Kate shook her head. 'No. That came later.

Like I said, he disappeared for a while and I had no idea where he was. He did come back to Bristol briefly while we sorted out the separation. The restaurant had still been a going concern and we got a reasonable price for it. I didn't want to run it on my own; I'm in corporate hospitality now. My own little business. I sold our house.' She looked up. 'Then I met Guy. He hired me to run a party for his clients. He hasn't swept me off my feet, but he's kind. Reliable.'

'And you shared the profit on the house and the business with Simon?'

'Absolutely. Fifty-fifty.'

'How much would that come to?'

'Well, the house was still mortgaged, so it was just under two hundred grand.'

'Between you?' Jen wondered what on earth Simon Walden had done with his hundred thousand pounds. How was it tied up, so he couldn't give Alan Springer back the money he was owed?

'No!' the woman said, as if that was a crazy idea. 'Each.'

★ ★ ★

Jen pulled Ross across the road so they could walk on the Downs with the elderly dog-walkers and the runners. She needed fresh air before they started the drive home, and the air here *was* fresh, westerly with the smell of rain in it.

'So, what do you think?'

Ross looked at his watch. Jen thought he'd

probably promised Mel he'd be back at a reasonable time. Then she thought again that she should be more tolerant. Ross was young and keen and happy. When she spoke her voice was more joke than recrimination.

'Your attention, please, DC May. This is a murder we're investigating.'

He had the good grace to look sheepish. 'We need to find out where all his money's gone. If he really meant to pay his mate back, where has it disappeared to?'

She gave a little clap of her hands, mocking him. 'So, get on that phone of yours and call that in. Let's get someone at the station to push for an answer. Find out why they haven't already tracked it down.'

17

When Matthew left his mother and Susan in the damp little cottage by the marsh, he drove back to Barnstaple and parked outside the police station. Inside, he checked the progress the team had made in their initial attempts to trace Christine Shapland.

'It's important. She's a vulnerable adult, she has a learning disability and the mental age of a child.' He thought Christine was different from Lucy, less confident and more sheltered. 'She's been missing for at least one night. And her disappearance might be linked to the Crow Point murder.' He added the last sentence to make them take the matter more seriously. The young officers saw murder as exciting, sexy. In their eyes, a middle-aged missing woman with a learning disability certainly wouldn't be. 'She lived in one of the cottages on the marsh, not far from where Walden's body was found. She wasn't there that day — she was with her aunt in Lovacott — so perhaps that's a coincidence, but I need to find her.'

'We've checked the hospital and her GP practice. Nobody's heard from her.' This was Gary Luke, the oldest member of the team, relaxed, fatherly.

'Anyone been in touch with the Woodyard?'

'Yes, Christine was definitely there all day yesterday. Her uncle dropped her off in the

179

morning and they assumed he'd be picking her up. She wandered out with the others to the reception area of the centre and when she didn't come back, they assumed she'd been collected or gone home with the minibus as usual. The centre's trying to encourage a degree of independence, so they didn't actually accompany her to the car.' Vicki Robb was young, keen. Matthew was already impressed.

'Has anyone spoken to the aunt and uncle?'

'Not yet,' Vicki said. 'I could go if you'd like me to.'

'No, I'll do it. There's another call I need to make in Lovacott anyway.' *It would be interesting to catch up with Dennis Salter after all these years. And this was a good excuse to leave the office.* Walking back down the stairs to collect his car, he wondered if his mother would see his job differently if he managed to deliver Christine back to Susan. And if he failed to find the woman, would his mother see that as just another example of his failure as a man?

Matthew was on his way out when Oldham appeared at the top of the stairs and called him into his office. 'If you've got a moment, Matthew . . . '

Oldham's office was like its owner: shabby, untidy. Matthew had always been wary of the man. There was something about his attitude to Matthew that wasn't dislike exactly, but more akin to distaste. Something Oldham couldn't help and tried to control, but a prejudice that was always there under the surface. Matthew wasn't sure if he was a homophobe or he just

180

didn't like the idea of a new inspector on his patch. He also found the DCI an object of pity. His wife had died of cancer a couple of years before and rumour had it that he'd started to hit the bottle then, that the beer with friends in the rugby club each evening had taken priority over work. They'd had no family. Ross, the son of a good friend, was the closest thing he had.

'This Crow Point murder.' Oldham leaned back in his chair. 'I understand the victim worked at the Woodyard?'

'He was a volunteer there.'

'And your partner runs the place?'

'My husband. Yes.' A moment of silence. 'And it seems that the woman with Down's syndrome who's missing was abducted from there.' Matthew took a deep breath. 'I wondered if I should withdraw from the case. I obviously have a conflict of interest. Perhaps you should take over as SIO.'

Another silence. Oldham closed his eyes for a moment, then opened them very slowly. Matthew watched the lids slide up and was reminded of a lizard, or perhaps a crocodile. 'No need for that,' Oldham said at last. 'I trust my team. Just keep me in the loop.'

So, Jonathan had been right and idleness and a need for a quiet life had won, but as Matthew was leaving the office, Oldham spoke again:

'Just don't cock up, eh? If you cock up, we'll both be in the shit, and that's the last thing I need.'

★　★　★

Matthew carried on down the stairs, collected his car and took the same route as he'd travelled with the bus the afternoon before. The light was fading and the weather was changing. It was still warm but the air felt heavy with rain. He arrived in Lovacott more quickly than he'd expected, surprised to be suddenly there, dropping down to the village. He hadn't noticed any of the landmarks that he'd glimpsed from the bus. Christine's aunt and uncle lived in a tall, straight, confident house right on the square. Once, Matthew thought, a merchant might have stayed there, trading in wool, spreading prosperity. Now it was the home of Grace and Dennis Salter, stalwarts of the Barum Brethren. He'd known them since he was a child. Salter's rejection of Matthew, after his statement of independence at the final meeting he'd ever attended, had hurt. Before that, Matthew had liked the man. He'd been one of the few Brethren to take Matthew seriously when he was a child, to answer his questions. Grace he hardly remembered at all.

He hadn't phoned ahead, but there was a light on in the front room and he stood for a moment looking inside. He'd been in that room with his parents. Occasionally meetings had been held there. Dennis had led the worship and Alice Wozencroft, the most elderly member of the Brethren, had played a squeaky keyboard so slowly that the singing was always a few bars ahead. There was dark varnished panelling on the walls, a long, polished table. His parents had always found it a little intimidating; it was also where the elders met and decisions were taken.

As Matthew remembered, the Salters spent most of their life in a room at the back, next to the kitchen, and he'd been taken there too on more social occasions. That had been their private space, more comfortable and more welcoming. He rang the doorbell and Dennis appeared, older of course, but recognizable. A generous lion's head, made even bigger by a mane of white hair, large features.

Matthew held out his hand. 'Matthew Venn. Perhaps you remember me.'

'Of course I remember you. Come on in, man, don't stand out there on the doorstep.' The arms wide now in greeting. Matthew was astonished by the response. Did Salter think he'd returned to the fold? Or had time mellowed him? Perhaps he was less dogmatic now than Dorothy, Matthew's mother, despite his position of authority. Perhaps he welcomed sinners into his home as well as the chosen. 'You'll be here about Christine.'

'Yes, she's still not turned up and we're getting concerned.'

Of course, Dorothy would have phoned Dennis Salter and told him that she'd called the police in the form of her son. She would probably have asked his permission first. Matthew's visit wouldn't be any kind of surprise to the man.

'You were taking care of her so Susan could go to my father's funeral?'

'We were. At least Grace was. I was at the funeral of course. I couldn't miss that. Dorothy

183

wanted me to lead the service. I can't tell you how distressed we are about the confusion. I'm still not quite sure how it happened.' He showed Matthew into the dark front room; this was official, then, rather than a family matter, despite the man's apparent contrition.

'Is Mrs Salter at home? If so, it would be useful to talk to her too.'

'Do you really need to speak to Grace? She feels as dreadful about this as I do, though she wasn't responsible. Not at all. It was all my fault.' Salter paused. 'She's not a well woman, and the unexpected can throw her off balance. I'd hate this to make her ill again.'

Matthew remembered the whispers surrounding Grace Salter now. There'd been times when she hadn't been to meetings; there'd been talk about 'nerves', a spell in the psychiatric hospital at the other end of the county. Women had been glad to look after Dennis Salter, delivering food parcels and casseroles. Matthew couldn't remember anyone offering to visit Grace.

'I won't keep her for long, but I'd like to ask her a few questions. Christine's been missing for a day and a night. We're taking this extremely seriously.'

'Of course. If you think it's important to speak to her . . . We all want Christine found.'

Matthew sat on his own at the long table, while Dennis disappeared to fetch his wife. This house was very different from the little cottage on the edge of the creek and Matthew wondered how Christine had settled here on the night of his father's funeral. The Salters had never had

184

children and when Matthew knew her, Grace had never worked away from the home. Her only sense of the outside world would have come from Dennis when he returned from his office, and from the other Brethren. How would she have coped with her niece? Matthew wondered how many younger people still belonged to the community and thought Grace might not be used to dealing with people different in age from herself and her husband. He suspected members were all of his mother's generation now, slowly dying off. In twenty years, the Barum Brethren, which had seemed so powerful in his childhood, would no longer exist.

The couple returned. Grace looked like a scarecrow, tall and stick-like, very thin, with wild grey hair. Her eyes were grey too. She wore trousers and a hand-knitted jumper that swamped her. It seemed she'd been crying and she twisted a handkerchief in her hands.

'It's such a terrible thing to have happened.' Her voice was a surprise, more educated than her sister's, precise. The three of them sat at one end of the long table, as if they were part of a committee, waiting for other attendees to arrive.

'Could you talk me through the events of the last few days? I understand that Dennis picked Christine up from her mother's house before the funeral.'

'Yes, she doesn't go to the day centre on a Monday.' Dennis did the talking. 'She spent the day and the evening here.'

'And how did she seem?'

'She has a learning disability,' Dennis said,

'and I'm never quite sure how much she understands. Perhaps I'm not sufficiently patient. We didn't have any real conversation the evening after I got back from the funeral. She loves television so we put it on for her, though we don't tend to watch much ourselves. She seemed settled enough, didn't she, Grace? She knows us and she's spent time with us before.'

'You've known her since she was a baby,' Matthew said. 'You'd be able to tell, wouldn't you, if something wasn't quite right?'

'She was missing Susan,' Grace said.

'Well, of course she was missing her mother.' Dennis sounded as if he resented the line of questioning. Perhaps he'd thought he'd be able to control the conversation as he always had with Matthew in the past. Or perhaps guilt at not making sure Christine had arrived back in Lovacott safely had made him defensive. 'Since Cecil died, there's just been the two of them. They're very close. Christine hasn't stayed overnight here since she was a young child. Susan is very protective.'

'Was she happy to go to the Woodyard on Tuesday morning?'

'Oh yes,' Grace said. 'She loves the Woodyard. I thought she might not enjoy it so much when her friend Rosa stopped going, but she loves it just the same.'

'Could Christine have gone to Rosa's house?' Matthew asked. 'If she and Dennis missed each other at the Woodyard and she wasn't sure where to go?'

There was a silence while Grace thought about that. She shot a quick look at her husband before answering. 'Oh, I don't think so. Rosa lives on the other side of Barnstaple from the Woodyard. Christine would never be able to get there by herself.'

Matthew nodded but he thought he'd get Rosa's address from Jonathan and ask one of his officers to check.

'She wasn't reluctant or anxious to go to the centre that morning?'

'No.' Grace looked at her husband. 'I don't think so. You took her in, didn't you, Dennis? You didn't think she was upset?' It was as if she couldn't answer even a simple question without her husband's agreement. But that was the way it was supposed to be within the Brethren. The women always deferred to their men.

Except in our house, Matthew thought. *My mother was always the boss there.*

'She seemed perfectly fine to me.' Dennis appeared to have recovered his composure. Perhaps he no longer felt he was being accused of being responsible for Christine's disappearance. 'Really, Matthew, no different from normal.'

'And the plan was that Dennis would pick her up and bring her back here to the house until later, so that Susan would have an evening to herself?'

'Well, we *thought* that was the plan,' Grace said. 'But when she didn't come out Dennis assumed that she'd got the centre minibus back to Susan's cottage as usual.'

'You didn't go in to the Woodyard, Mr Salter? To find her.'

'Not until later.' His face was very red now. 'I lost track of time and when I went to look for her they'd all gone. The day centre was empty.' There was a silence, the bluster had gone and there was a sudden confession. 'I was listening to the cricket on the radio in the car. The test match in Barbados. But I was there, parked right outside. I don't see how she could have missed me. She knew the car. Susan doesn't drive and I go a couple of evenings a week to take them shopping. Of course I should have been more attentive. I feel terrible that she's gone missing.'

Matthew almost felt sorry for him. He could understand how that might happen.

There was a rather awkward silence, broken by Grace. 'When Dennis got home we had to go straight out. A friend, one of the Brethren, needed a lift to A&E. We were there all evening with him. That's why we didn't get my sister's phone call. We didn't realize Christine was missing until Susan rang again this morning.'

On his way out, shepherded to the door by Salter, Matthew remembered something that Christopher Preece had said. 'Weren't you a manager of the Devonshire Building Society before you retired?'

'I was.' An obvious matter of pride. 'Of the branch here in Lovacott.'

'Are you on the board of the Woodyard?'

'Yes. I knew Christopher Preece through the business community. He asked if I would join them and I was delighted that he thought my

188

skills would be of use.' He paused for a moment and then thought he should add a further explanation. 'I was rather vocal in my opposition to the development of the Woodyard at first.' He gave a wry smile. 'A useless palace for arty hippies, I think I described it as in one of my lectures. Not something the council should be supporting when there are so many other demands on their resources. I'm afraid I believed what I'd read in the local press.'

'But you changed your mind?'

'I did, once I understood the range of activities that would be going on there, and that the day centre would be a part of it. There's nothing wrong with admitting when you're wrong. I knew Christopher had a sound business sense and of course Grace and I have been a part of Christine's life since she was a baby. It seemed a very worthy cause.'

★ ★ ★

Standing outside on the pavement, Matthew could understand why Christine might have chosen not to spend another night with her relatives in Lovacott. The cottage she shared with her mother might be dusty and damp in comparison, but it was full of her things. She and Susan would watch television together and share a meal. There'd be warmth and companionship. In this house, there was a tension between husband and wife that Matthew still couldn't quite understand. The relationship seemed tight and cold. Christine might simply have decided she didn't want to spend another night there. If Dennis was sitting in his car, concentrating on the cricket, she could have walked past without his noticing and got the minibus with the other service users, making her own decision. He'd need to check with the driver. If she'd headed out towards Braunton, that would help narrow down the search area. He phoned Jonathan and explained.

'I heard.' Jonathan sounded fraught. 'If she went missing from here, it'll be a nightmare. We'll have a safe-guarding issue. Inquiries from the press and other parents. There's resistance as it is to the policy of encouraging greater independence.'

'But it was Dennis Salter's fault for not looking out for her, surely.'

'Unfortunately, I don't think the press will see it like that.'

Matthew had rarely heard him sound so tense. 'Can you text me the address of a woman called Rosa? Apparently, she and Christine were friends. It's an outside possibility but she might have gone there.'

'Yes, sure. That'll be Rosa Holsworthy. It'll still be on file.'

'And could you ask the minibus driver if he saw Christine?'

'Yeah,' Jonathan said. 'Of course.' Then: 'I do hope she's okay. Christine's a sweetie. I've known her for years.'

Matthew left his car where it was and walked down the road towards the crescent of council houses that he'd seen the evening before. The street lamps had come on.

Maurice Braddick opened the door. There was a smell of cooking. Fish fingers and chips.

'I'm sorry,' Matthew said. 'I'm interrupting your meal.'

The old man shook his head. 'You come on in. We've just finished. We always eat early. Lucy's ravenous when she comes in from the centre. I say she could put away a horse.' He moved away from the door. He was wearing slippers that had seen better days, a frayed sweater. He'd changed since getting in from Barnstaple. 'We were going to go out to The Fleece for our tea, but we thought we'd save it for the weekend.' A pause. 'There's a show Lucy likes on television tonight.'

'I was hoping to speak to her.'

'That's all right. I don't think it starts until later and she can get it on catch-up anyway. She knows how to work that machine better than I do.'

Lucy was in the small living room, on the sofa, a mug of tea on the low table by her side. Comfortable and very much at ease. The television was on but she looked up when he came in. 'Hello.' As if he was an old friend.

'Is it okay if I talk to you again?'

'Is it about the man on the bus? Have you found out who killed him?'

'No,' he said. 'This is about someone I think you know.' A pause. 'Can we switch the television off for a bit. We'll put it back on soon.'

She nodded a little reluctantly and pressed the remote.

'Do you know Christine Shapland? Dark hair.'

'Yeah. She comes to the centre. But not every day. Not today.' A pause. 'She's my best friend.'

'Did you see her at the Woodyard yesterday? That was the day that I came in and talked to you and your dad.'

Lucy thought for a while and then she nodded. 'We did cooking in the morning.'

'Christine's missing, Lucy,' Matthew said. 'We don't know where she is. She seems to have disappeared from the Woodyard yesterday afternoon when everyone was on their way out. Did you see her?'

'Couldn't they keep her safe?' Maurice's voice high-pitched with anxiety. 'We send our kids there and expect them to keep them safe. You're not going back, maid. Not until all this is sorted out.'

'Lucy?' Matthew understood Maurice's anger, but now he needed information. 'Did you see Christine when you were coming out of the Woodyard yesterday?'

'No,' she said. 'I saw my dad. He was waiting for me, just like today, and we came home in the car.'

'Christine left the centre with you, though? She walked with you through the glass corridor to the big entry hall where your dad was waiting?'

'I don't know.' Lucy seemed to be losing concentration now. Her eyes drifted back to the blank screen of the television. It seemed she just wanted Matthew to go so she could watch her programme in peace.

He persisted all the same. 'How was she

192

yesterday? If you remember, I came to the Woodyard and I talked to you about the man on the bus. You and Chrissie were cooking together. Did she tell you she'd been staying with her aunty and uncle here in Lovacott the night before?'

Lucy shook her head. Matthew sensed he'd get little more from her and turned to Maurice. 'Could we have a chat?'

They sat in the kitchen and without asking Maurice switched on the kettle, made tea in a pot.

'It's not right. That woman's parents will be going out of their minds with worry.'

'She's only got a mother. Susan Shapland. Do you know her?'

'I met her a few times. While they were in the old day centre. And at the Christmas party at the Woodyard. All the relatives were invited to that.' He'd calmed down a little, but Matthew could still sense the outrage. Because this could have happened to *his* daughter, he was shaken, horrified. But there was relief too because it was someone else's child who was missing. Lucy was safe, watching television, drinking tea. 'My wife knew her better.'

'And Christine?' Matthew asked. 'Had you met her?'

'Yes, her and Lucy have known each other for a while. Not when they were kiddies. Christine went to a special school. Her parents thought she'd be better off there. And Susan didn't have the fight in her that my Maggie had when she battled to get Luce into mainstream education.'

'You were there yesterday afternoon, waiting for Lucy, to bring her home. Did you see Christine? Or anyone waiting for her?'

Maurice Braddick thought for a moment. Matthew could tell that he was desperate to help. 'I don't know,' he said at last. 'I was just looking out for Luce, you know. I wanted her to know I was there for her. Because of all that had gone on earlier in the day. Her being so upset because the man she'd met on the bus was dead. Then speaking to you. Her day was turned upside down.' Another pause and then a kind of confession. 'I know it's daft, but I'd been worried about her. Imagining all sorts. It was wonderful when I saw her, coming out of the room, her bag over her shoulder.' He looked up at Matthew. 'I don't know what I'd do if anything happened to her. Since Maggie died, she's all I've got left.'

Matthew nodded and realized that, with those words, Maurice was making *him* responsible for Lucy. *You just make sure she's safe, boy. I'm relying on you.*

He stood up. By now Jen Rafferty and Ross May should have returned from Bristol. They should have more information. But he couldn't lose the image of Christine Shapland as a thirteen-year-old girl, clutching her doll, looking lost.

'Can you talk to Lucy again, see if she remembers anything?' Because he thought now that Lucy hadn't seemed sufficiently concerned about Christine's disappearance. They were friends after all. But surely the idea of Lucy Braddick being part of a conspiracy to hide

194

Christine Shapland was ridiculous.

'I'll try,' Maurice said. They walked together to the door. 'I'm not letting her go to the Woodyard tomorrow. Not until this is all over and I know it's safe there. Will you tell Jonathan for me?'

Matthew nodded. Outside it was very dark and mild, and a gentle rain had started to fall. He walked back to the centre of the village and his car. He stood for a moment outside the Salters' grand house. The curtains had been drawn and there was nothing to see.

18

Gaby Henry arrived in from work before the others and was glad of the time to herself. The house felt different without Simon. Empty. Quieter. It wasn't that he'd made much noise, except when he was cooking and those had only been good sounds: the rhythmic beat of a knife on the chopping board, the sizzle of searing fish in a pan, the rattle of pots. He'd given up drinking quite so much recently and so even those noises had been calmer, less frenetic. He'd been a fierce presence, though, even when he had nothing at all to say; there'd been something about him that demanded attention. She felt suddenly bereft.

It had been a weird day at the Woodyard. Jonathan had come to find her in her studio with a tale of one of the day centre clients having gone missing. Although he was the boss, he called in sometimes, not to talk about work, but to drink coffee and look at her art.

'Christine Shapland. Gentle soul. Down's. Very quiet. A bit shy. She just seemed to disappear.'

'Sorry. I haven't seen her since last week.' Gaby thought Jonathan had come to the studio to escape the panic in the rest of the building, to have a few moments of calm. He wouldn't really expect her to have seen the woman recently. Gaby had nothing to do with the day centre,

196

except for running an art class there once a week.

'There seems to have been some kind of breakdown in communication. Her uncle thought her mother had picked her up and Susan, her mother, thought the uncle was doing it. Nobody's seen her since yesterday.' Jonathan had been standing by the window, the light catching one side of his face, turning the blond hair to silver thread. 'It's a bloody nightmare. Her uncle is Dennis Salter. He's on the board of trustees and should have known better. He should have gone in for her, or at least looked out properly. It'll be the Woodyard that gets the blame, though. The press will have a field day.'

He'd turned towards Gaby then and she'd thought she'd never seen him so tense, so fraught.

'Why don't you talk to Christopher Preece? He must be good at handling the media.'

'Yeah, maybe.' But Jonathan hadn't seemed too sure. 'I just want her found safe and well. This, on top of the murder of one of our volunteers, seems like a nightmare. I always thought of the Woodyard as a kind of sanctuary. Not a place where terrible things happen to the people who belong here.'

★   ★   ★

Now, in Hope Street, she could understand Jonathan's unease. The disappearance of the woman from the day centre was unsettling. In Gaby's mind, it had become twisted together

197

with Simon's murder, two strands of the same piece of rope, though she couldn't see how there could be a connection. The only link was the Woodyard. What else might Simon Walden and a woman with a learning disability have in common?

Gaby went upstairs and collected a pile of dirty laundry from her room, picking up stray items from the floor. She considered changing the sheets on the bed but couldn't be bothered. In the utility room in the basement, the machine was already full of someone else's washing. Damp, not wet, so it had probably been done a while ago and forgotten. Gaby pulled it out into a plastic basket, not too irritated because usually *she* was the person who left her stuff there.

That was when she realized the clothes had belonged to Simon Walden. He must have put them in the machine the morning of his death or the evening before. Underpants and socks, a couple of shirts and pairs of jeans. She began to fold the damp clothes. It seemed the right thing to do, almost a mark of respect. She wondered what she should do with them next. Would the police want to see them?

She shook a shirt and something fell from the breast pocket. A Yale key on a key ring with a plastic tag shaped like a bird. Like the albatross he had tattooed on his neck. It wasn't to this house; they'd had back and front door keys cut for Simon when he moved in and they were quite a different shape. She set it on the washing machine and was staring at it when she heard footsteps on the stairs to the basement and

Caroline was there, standing right behind her. She took in the damp washing, saw immediately what it was, and then noticed the key.

'What's that?'

'It must be Simon's.' What else could she say?

'You'll have to show the police,' Caroline said. She used that bossy, big-sister voice that usually Gaby didn't mind. Today it grated on her nerves and made her want to swear. 'It could be important.'

'I suppose it could.' Gaby felt helpless standing there with the washing half folded in the basket. She'd railed against Simon and now she felt like weeping.

'I'll take it.' And Caroline tucked the key into her little black handbag before Gaby could reply.

19

After the evening's briefing in Barnstaple, Matthew was discouraged. He felt the old insecurity biting at his heels, telling him he was useless, an impostor in the role of Senior Investigating Officer in this case. Perhaps Oldham would have made a better fist at it. They had so much information now that he should have formed some idea about who might have killed Walden, some notion at least of a strong motive, but there was nothing substantial, nothing to act on. Too many stray leads that needed to be followed up. And Christine Shapland was still missing. There'd be another night of anguish for her mother. Another night of Matthew knowing he'd let *his* mother down.

On the way out of the police station, Jen Rafferty stopped him. 'I don't suppose you fancy a drink?' A pause. 'A chat. I could do with running some ideas about Walden past you. Today in Bristol, it was as if they were talking about a different man from the homeless guy who turned up pissed at the church. But I didn't want to discuss it in there.' She nodded back at the building. 'It's all too complicated and I find it impossible to think straight with an audience.'

'Okay.'

'Would you mind coming back to my house? I've hardly seen the kids since all this started. I probably won't see them tonight. By this time, they'll be holed up in their rooms. But at least I'll know I'm there. I've got wine.' Noticing his hesitation, she grinned. 'Decaf coffee, herbal tea . . . '

He looked at his watch. It was already nearly ten and he'd been looking forward to being home, to being with Jonathan. But he trusted Jen's instincts and was still weighed down by the sense of duty, drummed into him in childhood. 'Sure. Just half an hour, though. I need my beauty sleep.'

★   ★   ★

He sat in Jen's cottage. She'd lit the wood burner before running upstairs to check on her children and putting on the kettle, and the small room was already warm. She'd lit candles and switched off the big light. The edges of the space drifted into shadow. He felt himself grow drowsy and was almost asleep when she came in with a tray, mugs, a packet of biscuits. Her Scouse voice shook him awake.

'Only digestives. The bloody kids ate the chocolate ones.'

He stretched, tried to focus. 'What's been troubling you?'

'It's Walden. When we first ID'd him, I had him pegged as a rough sleeper, a drunk, who'd been scooped up by a well-meaning do-gooder and helped to put his life back together. But I don't think he was ever like that. I mean, I think he was a drinker and there must have been a moment of crisis when he turned up at the

201

church and met Caroline, but he must still have had money somewhere. He can't have drunk away two hundred thousand pounds. That's a fortune! Besides, while he was working at the Kingsley he still had an income.'

'He could have been a gambler. Reckless.'

She shook her head. 'Nobody's mentioned that. His business started falling apart because it expanded too quickly, but everyone put that down to Kate's ambition, not because Walden was spending wildly. His wife or his mate would have told me if he'd had a gambling problem.'

'What are you saying, exactly?'

'That I'm not convinced he was homeless when he landed up at the church. He might have been lonely and depressed, but at the end of the season in North Devon, it's not that hard to find a landlord prepared to let you stay in a holiday rental. Besides, that tiny room in Hope Street was almost empty when he was staying in it. He must have accumulated more stuff than that. I left home with two suitcases and a bin bag when I ran away from Robbie at an hour's notice. I know I had two kids, but *everyone* has more possessions than a couple of pairs of jeans.' She paused. 'Gaby Henry had the impression that Walden was still fond of his wife, but we didn't find a photo of her, or of his army mates in his room. I just don't see it. And there's a gap in the timeline between him leaving work at the Kingsley and moving into Hope Street. According-ing to the women, he'd been rough sleeping during that time, but I spoke to the homeless guy who hangs out at the end of the street and he only came across Walden once he'd moved into number twenty. There's a community of rough sleepers in Ilfracombe. They look out for each other. He would have come across Walden if the man had been living on the streets.'

'You think Walden had a house or a flat somewhere and that his stuff might still be there?'

'I think it's possible.'

'Nobody has come forward to say he'd rented from them.' Matthew set his mug back on the tray and took another biscuit.

'But would they recognize him? After all this time? Especially if he went through a letting agency.'

Silence. Jen opened the door of the wood burner and threw on another log. Matthew was thinking. Walden was a man who'd been described by Gaby Henry as being born to cook. If he had the money, he'd want a kitchen of his own. He'd have had his own knives, and they weren't in the Hope Street house. The women had said that he often disappeared, that he spent time on his own.

'Why would Walden pretend to be homeless? And why would he accept that depressing room in Hope Street if he had somewhere better to live?'

'I don't know,' Jen said. 'I've been thinking about that all the way back from Bristol. Do you think he needed the company? Female company? I mean in an inappropriate way — like looking through bathroom keyhole weird. Gaby described him as a bit of a creep.'

'And if we're talking inappropriate, what was he doing chatting up Lucy Braddick? Where was he going on those trips to Lovacott? Do you think he had a place there?' Matthew was still obsessing about Christine Shapland and made a strange illogical leap. If Walden had his own accommodation away from Hope Street, perhaps the missing woman was being kept there. But that wouldn't work, would it? Because Walden had been killed before she disappeared, so he couldn't be responsible for her abduction. He was clutching at straws.

'Get Ross on all the letting agencies tomorrow,' he said. 'And the estate agents, in case he bought a place. Let's see if we can trace what happened to that money.'

$$\star \quad \star \quad \star$$

It was raining again when he drove home. Braunton was empty, but there was a light in the toll keeper's cottage. Matthew wondered what the Marstons could be doing in there and thought he'd be glad when they found somewhere more to their liking and moved away. They were his nearest neighbours and, driving past, he realized he disliked them with an intensity that surprised him. Jonathan hadn't closed the curtains and must have seen the headlights of his car as he drove towards the house, because he came outside to greet him. He stood just outside the door, turning his face to the light rain.

'Is there any news?' He was talking about

Christine Shapland of course. Jonathan had never been this involved in any previous case. He'd listened in the past while Matthew had run through his anxieties about an investigation, offered the occasional piece of advice, but this was different. This was personal. He knew the woman and besides, the reputation of the Woodyard, his life's work, was at stake. Before Matthew could answer, he continued talking. 'I'm sorry. Come inside. I shouldn't have ambushed you like this.' Jonathan put his arm around Matthew's shoulder and drew him in, then clung onto him. It was as if Jonathan were drowning and needed support.

20

Early next morning, they were in the police station, fuelling up on caffeine, buzzing because there were so many things to do. Too many leads and possibilities, but this was better than the torture of waiting for something new to turn up.

Jen had slept deeply and felt well. If she'd been on her own the night before, she'd have opened a bottle of wine, called up to Ella to see if she fancied a glass, so she wasn't drinking alone, then finished most of it herself anyway. But Matthew had been there, asking for camomile tea, so the wine had been left unopened. He'd listened to her, trusted her instinct about Walden, and that was where they started this morning.

'We know now that Walden had access to a substantial sum of money. I need you to track it down. Now. I can't understand why that hasn't already happened. So, let's have one person dedicated to that. Go through our fraud experts; they have contacts in the banks. It's hard these days to open an account in a bogus name so it shouldn't be difficult to trace. I think it's highly possible that Walden was living in a flat or house of his own before moving into Hope Street. If we find his bank account, that'll give us an address for him.' Matthew was standing at the front of the room, softly spoken but demanding their attention. Jen knew a little of his background and thought there was still something of the zealot about him. She'd known nuns with the same passion, the same presence. She'd have followed them to the end of the world, believed every word they said. Until she'd grown up.

'This is even more important.' Matthew was handing out copies of Christine Shapland's photograph. 'We talked about her yesterday. She's now been missing for two nights. A woman with Down's syndrome who left her day centre, part of the Woodyard complex, on Tuesday afternoon. I spoke to her uncle yesterday.' Another photograph was handed out — Jen knew Matthew had been in early to source that, taken it from a piece in the *North Devon Journal* covering the man's retirement. 'Dennis Salter. He also happens to be on the board of trustees at the Woodyard, chosen because of his background in finance. He was supposed to have collected Christine from the Woodyard but claims to have missed her. Let's dig around a bit and see what we can find. Was his car picked up on CCTV anywhere on Tuesday late afternoon or evening?'

Matthew paused for breath. There was silence in the room. 'I think it's possible that Christine might have evaded him deliberately and tried to make her own way home. I've checked with the transport company used by the centre and they didn't deliver her back that afternoon. Home is a cottage on the edge of Braunton Marsh. Can we check the public service buses going out that way? Let's get this out to the media now, see if anyone gave her a lift. There are always people walking the footpath along the creek on their way to the shore. Ross, you head out there and talk to the people in the area. If we get an inkling that she might have got that far, we'll organize a search along the river. I'd even be prepared to get the public involved.'

Jen smiled at that. Matthew hated anything flash or showy. He didn't like media attention and photos of well-meaning people in rows walking across the saltmarsh would certainly attract the press. Now, he turned to her.

'Jen, you take the Woodyard. Catch the staff as they come in. It's a strange warren of a place. The day centre is in its own building to the back of the yard attached by a glass corridor to the rest of the complex, but the users go through the main entrance hall to come in and out. That's used by everyone: the cafe customers, school parties, people coming in for adult education classes. Someone might have seen a stranger approaching her, chatting to her. She'd be trusting. If they said her mother had asked them to give her a lift home, she'd probably go with them.'

Jen nodded, but felt a stab of resentment. She'd come up with the new theory about Simon Walden having his own place somewhere, but it felt as if she'd been side-lined, taken off the murder inquiry. Matthew was still talking and it was as if he'd read her mind. His words were directed at her.

'I'm convinced that Christine's disappearance and Walden's murder are linked somehow. I have no idea how they can be. But the Woodyard is there at the heart of the inquiry.'

208

She nodded again, wondering for a moment if she was being soft-soaped, taken for a mug, before deciding that wasn't Matthew's style.

★ ★ ★

Waiting in the reception area of the Woodyard, Jen felt right at home. Most of the staff were women of about her age, they dressed like her and looked like her: arty, dramatic. She thought that Matthew had known what he was doing sending her here. It didn't do to underestimate him. She stood at the door, showing Christine's photo, catching members of the public as they came in. There was a sympathetic response, interest, but no useful information. It was as if Christine had disappeared into thin air that afternoon. But as they drifted off to their classes, they were still discussing the missing woman. Word would get out.

In the distance Jen saw Gaby Henry approaching the building, and she was so focussed on the woman that she almost missed the man who was walking past her. He was familiar but for a moment she couldn't place him. He was small, balding, in late middle-age, dressed more for a country walk than for a visit to an arts' centre, in corduroy trousers and boots. He carried a clipboard. In the end it was the binoculars strung around his neck that gave him away. This was Colin Marston, who lived with his wife in the toll keeper's cottage on the way to Crow Point. Jen turned her head away, hoping he'd not see her, that he'd put her down as just another woman with untidy hair and eccentric clothes. She wanted to find out more about his connection to the Woodyard before talking to him. He walked past her and into the body of the building.

Jen brought her attention back to Gaby. Today the woman was dressed in black — a long black dress, black tights and black bikers' boots. Slung across her body like a holster, a red leather bag. The signature red lipstick. Jen waved to her as soon as she came into the building.

Gaby waved back and looked as if she was about to approach her, but seemed to think better of it and disappeared into the crowd. Before Jen could follow her, her phone rang. A number she didn't recognize. 'Jen Rafferty.'

'Sergeant Rafferty, it's Caroline Preece. You gave us your card, said to call you if we had anything useful to tell you.'

'Yes.'

'Well, there's something I'd like to show you. I can't leave St Cuthbert's. Is there any way you could come here?'

★　★　★

St Cuthbert's was right in the middle of Barnstaple on a cobbled lane that ran on to a series of alms houses, black and white timbered, ancient but still used for their original purpose of caring for the elderly. It was too narrow for cars, though pedestrians used the lane to cross between two busy streets. The church itself was newer, Victorian, rather too grand for its setting, and it backed onto the road, shutting out the traffic noise. Beside it, and surrounded by grass holding a couple of mature oaks, stood a former dame's school, of the same age as the alms houses. It had been used for many years as the church hall, but recently it had been renovated and it housed the charity where Caroline Preece worked. Jen had always loved this part of the town. She'd felt she was stepping back in time. It was an oasis of peace.

A skinny young man with bad skin stood outside the old school, smoking a roll-up cigarette. He took no notice of Jen. The doors were arched and locked. There was no bell. The young man finally looked up. 'You'll need to go around the back.'

The building had been extended at the back, and was connected to the church by a new, open cloister of stone and wood. The extension was beautifully done, but Jen wondered how it had slid past planning rules. Surely the old school was listed. Perhaps Christopher Preece had influence with the council, or perhaps, because it wasn't immediately visible from the lane, it had been allowed through anyway. As Jen approached the door that led into the newer part of the building, a young man in a clerical collar emerged. He nodded to her and walked down the cloister and into the church. Jen supposed this was Edward, Caroline's curate.

Inside, there was a reception space with a desk and a middle-aged woman staring at a computer screen. She looked up and smiled. 'Can I help you?'

'I'm here to see Caroline Preece. It's Jen Rafferty.'

'Of course. I'll let her know you're here.'

Caroline led her past rooms where it seemed various forms of group therapy were taking place. In one, women lay on the floor. Yoga or some form of meditation. Jen liked the idea of yoga, but didn't have the patience for it. The building was deceptively spacious and light. There were posters on the walls, semi-religious imagery of rainbows and doves, slogans about taking power, and loving the inner you. Here it seemed hope and the possibility of redemption abounded. It made Jen feel like punching someone.

Caroline's office was in the old school. It might once have been a small classroom, but her desk and the shelves and filing system were bright and new. It looked out over the courtyard and had a view of the trees. Two easy chairs faced a small coffee table on one side of the desk and Caroline sat there and waited for Jen to join her. Jen supposed this was where she talked to her clients, to the desperate suicidal, the ill.

'You wanted to see me.' Jen had planned to talk to Caroline anyway, but let her think Jen was doing her a favour by coming to *her*.

Caroline brought out a Yale key on a ring attached to a plastic bird and set it on the table. 'We found this yesterday. At least Gaby found it in some laundry Simon had left in the washing machine. I thought it might be important.'

It lay on the table between them. A vindication of Jen's theory that Walden had a hideaway somewhere. She thought of it as a secret place, because he'd never mentioned it, had he? They'd all thought he'd been homeless, and they'd taken him in as a charity case. But it was worth checking again. 'You've no idea what it might be for? He never mentioned another place?'

Caroline shook her head. 'This bird. It's an albatross, isn't it? Like the tattoo on his neck. It must belong to Simon.'

'Perhaps it's to his former home, his wife's house,' Jen said, though she didn't believe for a moment that was true. 'He could have kept it for sentimental reasons.'

'I don't think so.' Caroline shook her head again. 'He always said he'd left his old life behind.'

Jen thought they'd get a photo of the key and the ring off to Kate just to check.

'I was planning to see you,' Jen said. 'We need to talk again about Simon Walden.'

'Sure.' Caroline blinked behind the big round specs. 'Of course. Anything I can do to help.'

'When he turned up at the church that night, drunk, desperate, you had the impression that he was homeless?'

'Yes.' Caroline was unsure now, though. Jen could tell. Outside in the corridor, footsteps came and went as somebody paced.

'Did he tell you he had nowhere to live?'

'That night he was so confused and distressed that he didn't say much at all. Nothing that made sense.' Caroline closed her eyes again as if she were trying to remember. 'We put him up in St Cuthbert's because he wasn't safe to let out

213

on his own. He was so full of self-disgust. He was clearly having suicidal thoughts. He said he'd be better dead.'

'That was the end of October. Halloween.'

'As a church, we don't recognize that as a festival.' She pulled a face to show her distaste. 'But yes, I remember there were kids trick or treating in Hope Street before I went out to the meeting.' A pause. 'Gaby encouraged them by dressing up as a witch, jumping out at them when they knocked at the door, trying to scare them.' Another pause. 'I suppose I assumed that he was homeless. He left the next morning with the worst kind of hangover, but the following week he came here again. He was waiting outside the door when I arrived at nine o'clock. I brought him into my office for an assessment. I needed to get a medical history. He said he hadn't seen a doctor since he'd left the army.' She looked up at Jen. 'That was when I asked for his address. I told him I'd need it for the records.'

'And what did he say?'

'He didn't answer,' Caroline said. 'Not really. I thought at the time he was embarrassed because he didn't have a place of his own. He didn't look as if he'd been rough sleeping for a long time, but I thought maybe he'd been sofa-surfing. Or he had a certain pride so he'd found somewhere for a shower. Some guys go to the sports centre. He told me he'd left the hotel at the end of September and that his accommodation there had gone with the job. The implication was that he hadn't found anywhere permanent since. I should have pushed him, perhaps, found out where he'd been staying in the meantime.'

'It seems he had money. And we think he could have been renting somewhere. Can you explain why he accepted a room in Hope Street when he already had his own place?'

There was silence except for the screeching of a gull outside the window, the relentless pacing of the person in the corridor.

'Perhaps he was lonely,' Caroline said. 'Perhaps he was worried he might do something foolish if he was living on his own. He settled well here at St Cuthbert's, but we only run during the day. The nights must have seemed very long and very lonely.'

Jen nodded. That made sense. And it was possible that Walden had believed he wouldn't be made welcome in Hope Street if they thought he already had a home. Gaby was already unsympathetic. She'd have been glad of an excuse to force him out.

'A woman with learning disabilities, who attends the Woodyard day centre three days a week, has gone missing.' A breeze was moving the new leaves on the tree outside the window. 'Her name's Christine Shapland. Does that mean anything to you? Did Simon ever mention her? We know he'd become friendly with Lucy Braddick, another woman who attended the day centre.'

Caroline shook her head. Jen thought she was still digesting the news that Walden might already have had his own home when he accepted her charity. Was she feeling betrayed

215

because he hadn't trusted her enough to confide in her? She'd thought she'd saved him with her offer of a room, companionship. Now it seemed he hadn't needed her quite as much as she'd believed.

'It could be a coincidence of course,' Jen went on, 'but it seems odd. Two dramas connected to the Woodyard within a few days.'

She waited for Caroline to comment, but she said nothing and Jen continued:

'In the last couple of weeks before he died, Simon travelled back to Lovacott on the same bus as Lucy and sat beside her. Can you explain that?'

'No!' Now Caroline seemed distraught. Her perfect client, the man she'd thought she'd fixed, made whole again, had kept secrets from her and had followed a woman with a learning disability home. Perhaps he'd been a predator, a stalker, and quite different from the man she'd believed him to be.

Jen wondered if that would undermine Caroline's faith in the work she was doing. And if she might be more forthcoming about Walden now she knew he hadn't been entirely honest with her. Because sins of omission were still sins. 'Why do you think Simon might have wanted to keep all this secret from you?'

'I don't think it was about secrets,' Caroline said. 'He was a private person, that's all. He could just have been protecting his privacy.'

Jen was about to say that was rubbish, that he'd created a story about himself that was nowhere near the truth, when her phone rang.

216

Ross. 'Sorry, I'll need to take this.' She left the office and stood in the corridor.

She could tell Ross was excited. She knew he was out at the marsh, talking to the reserve volunteers and regular dog-walkers, showing them Christine Shapland's photo.

'Has someone seen the missing woman?'

'No,' he said. 'No, it's a dead end here. A complete waste of time. But I've just had a call from Barnstaple. They've found it.'

She thought she knew what he meant but she asked just the same. 'What have they found?'

'Simon Walden's place.'

'So, I was right.'

But Ross wasn't listening and certainly wasn't prepared to give her a moment of glory. 'It's in Braunton. A flat over a betting shop. One of the streets off the main road. I'm heading out there now.'

'I know where you mean.'

'We can't get in yet. The letting agent is the only person with a key and he's out all day. Matthew said to meet up there as soon as we can; we might be able to find a way in. He reckons the workers in the betting shop might have a key.'

'No need for that.' She paused, savouring the moment. 'I think I've got a key myself.'

217

21

Matthew was visiting Rosa Holsworthy and her parents when news came through that Jen had been right about Simon having another home of his own. He'd gone to visit the Holsworthys on impulse, because he'd forgotten to ask anyone else to do it the night before. Besides, it was close to the police station, in the terrace of houses that had once looked out towards the cattle market that had long gone, and he was glad of the chance for a walk.

Rosa was younger than Lucy Braddick, thinner, dark-haired. Less mature. Matthew wouldn't have known she had a learning disability apart from a vague look of anxiety in her eyes, the sense that the world was a mystery to her and not somewhere she felt at ease. Her legs jiggled as if she found it impossible to keep still. She flashed him a grin when she was introduced to him. 'Are you all right?' As if she needed to make sure that everyone around her was settled, comfortable. As if she wanted to please them. Or it could have been a verbal tic. Her parents were both at home with her. Ron Holsworthy walked with a stick.

'Arthritis,' his wife said. 'He's had it since he was a young man. He had to give up his job and he's in terrible pain. The social took his benefit away; they say he could work if he tried. I do nights in an old folks' home.'

'It must be a struggle.'

They were wary of him and had only asked him in when he insisted. Matthew thought their whole life had been a struggle: against bureaucracy, doctors, social workers. They would have been suspicious of anyone in authority turning up on the doorstep.

'You took Rosa out of the Woodyard.'

'She never really liked it,' Ron said. 'Not in that big old place. It wasn't the same as the centre they had before.'

'Nothing happened? To make you take her away?'

'No, there was nothing like that,' Janet, the mother, said. 'We'd just rather have her at home. She's company for Ron when I'm working and she's a good girl. She looks after him, makes him a cup of tea, helps him to the bathroom when he needs to go.'

Matthew nodded. He could understand why the couple had decided to keep their daughter at home. She was as much a carer as someone who needed to be looked after. 'She was a friend of Christine Shapland, in the old day centre. Christine's gone missing. I wonder if you have any idea where she might be.'

The couple looked at each other in horror. And vindication perhaps that they'd made the right decision in keeping their daughter at home.

'No,' Ron said. 'We haven't seen Christine since Rosa stopped going to the Woodyard. We keep ourselves to ourselves mostly. I hear from Maurice Braddick occasionally and he's been over for tea with his daughter. But that's once in a blue moon. Usually I go days without seeing a soul. Janet has to catch up on her sleep. There's only Rosa. I'd be lost without her.'

Matthew was thinking again that the Holsworthys had their own reasons for keeping Rosa at home when the call came through that they'd tracked down Walden's secret accommodation.

★ ★ ★

Now, Matthew stood with Ross outside the betting shop, looking out for Jen. Ross had picked Matthew up at the police station and they'd travelled to Braunton together. They must have looked like reluctant punters, hanging around on the pavement. Ross was all for going inside and asking if the bookies' manager had a key to the flat above, but Matthew decided to wait for a while — he wanted to get a feel for the neighbourhood first — and moved them down the street a little so they wouldn't draw attention to themselves. This was still a place for locals and they were already attracting attention. There was a convenience store on the corner and a hardware shop, a bakery selling cakes with brightly coloured icing. Nothing healthy. Nothing here for the tourists. The breeze was still westerly and mild. Matthew imagined Walden living in the flat, letting himself out occasionally to buy food and booze. Because he'd been troubled here. Depressed and guilty, drinking heavily. Otherwise, why would he have turned up at the church in Barnstaple looking for salvation? Why would he have moved into the house in Hope Street?

He walked into the convenience store, leaving Ross outside. The place was almost empty; it was too late for schoolkids buying sweets on their way to school, too early for people looking for lunchtime snacks. On the shelves behind the counter were jars of old-fashioned confectionery: sherbet lemons, rhubarb and custard chews, humbugs. This must have been where Walden had bought the sweets he'd given to Lucy. Matthew showed the man behind the counter Walden's photo.

'Do you recognize him?'

The shopkeeper was of South Asian heritage, shiny-haired, handsome. He looked up from his phone and considered the picture. 'Yeah. He was a regular for a bit, then he didn't come in for a while. I thought he'd moved away from the area. But he's been back again a few times more recently.'

'He's the guy that was killed out at Crow Point. We think he used to live round here.'

The man shook his head, as if this meant nothing to him. There was a pile of *North Devon Journals* on the counter, the headline — *Man killed at local beauty spot* — was large and dramatic. But it seemed that he sold the papers; he didn't read them.

'Can you tell me anything about him? Did he have any friends round here?'

'I'm sorry.' The shopkeeper sounded genuine. He was giving Matthew his full attention now. 'When I first met him, he came into the shop

221

every couple of days, that's all I can tell you.'

'What did he buy?'

The man could answer that. 'Tea, milk, bread. And booze. Always booze.' A pause. 'I think he must have given up drinking, though, because he's been back a few times recently and now he's just buying sweets. Perhaps it helps. Like when people give up the fags.'

Through the glass door, Matthew saw Jen walking down the street towards them. She was wearing a long raincoat, reaching almost to her ankles, and pulled it round her to keep off the drizzle. Her head was bare and the red hair was a blast of colour in the greyness. She stepped off the pavement to let an elderly woman with a shopping trolley walk past. Matthew thanked the shopkeeper and went outside.

'Sorry to keep you waiting. I'd been talking to Caroline at St Cuthbert's and I couldn't just dash away without saying goodbye.' Jen pulled the key from her pocket, like a conjuror lifting a rabbit from a hat, with a flourish and a grin. 'I hope it works after all this. I'll look a right twat otherwise.' She held it out so they could see the albatross key ring. 'Gaby Henry found it in a pile of washing Walden had left in their machine.'

It did work. The key turned easily and smoothly in the lock. The door to the flat went straight from the pavement and was right next to the entrance to the betting shop. Inside, a narrow, bare staircase. They stood just inside the door to pull on scene suits, away from public view, struggling in the cramped hallway. The space was lit by a bare bulb that swung above them.

'Hello!' Matthew shouted up the stairs. He still had the irrational idea that they might find Christine Shapland here, and he didn't want to scare her. Three police officers looking like something from a horror film in suits and masks would look like aliens, hardly human. There was no response and he went up.

He'd been expecting a bare, clear, organized space, like Walden's bedroom in Ilfracombe. The man had been in the army. Even at times of distress it would be his habit to be tidy. But they walked into chaos. The stairs led straight into the living area, a kitchen and living room separated by a breakfast bar. The floor was scattered with cutlery and broken crockery, drawers had been turned upside down, dry food had been emptied from packets and there was a blue snow of washing powder on the grey lino. Beyond the breakfast bar there was a small sofa and a cupboard on which a television stood. The cushions had been pulled from their covers, the base of the sofa had been slashed and the contents of the cupboard now lay on the floor. The detectives stood where they were.

'What do you think?' Ross said. 'Did Walden lose it? Have some sort of psychotic episode and trash the place?'

'I don't think Walden did this.' Because although it seemed like random mayhem, Matthew thought this was a search. Someone in too much of a hurry, or too desperate to be careful and quiet had been through the place.

They'd been thorough. If they'd been looking for something specific, it would have been found. It would be unlikely that a police search would find anything now. He tried to keep his thinking slow and methodical, but the senseless mess jangled his nerves and made it hard for him to think straight.

He walked through to the bedroom, aware of Ross and Jen following. It suddenly hit Matthew that Walden would have hated this. The intrusion. The disorder. He hoped the man hadn't seen it before he was killed. That led on to the question of *when* the place had been ransacked. Surely after Walden's death, Matthew thought. There'd been no sign of a break-in. Perhaps the key found in Walden's laundry had been a spare and one had been stolen from his body, along with the phone, wallet and credit cards they'd never found. Unless the women in number twenty had been involved and were very, very clever, and Gaby had pretended to find the key in the washing machine after they'd already used it.

Walden had kept all his photographs in his bedroom, but they'd been left untouched. It seemed the searcher had been looking for something bigger than a slip of paper that could be hidden behind an image. The glass hadn't been smashed. Another indication, Matthew decided, that this was a search, not an act of revenge or hatred. There were pictures of a woman, in various stages of maturity, growing from a schoolgirl to a smart businesswoman, standing proudly in front of a restaurant. 'His wife?'

Jen nodded. 'Yeah, that's her. Seems as if he was still a little bit in love.'

There were only two other photographs: one of an older couple and another of Walden in uniform surrounded by a group of soldier friends. They had their arms around each other's shoulders and they were laughing.

Jen pointed to one of the men in the picture. 'That's Alan Springer, the guy we spoke to in Bristol. The one who claims Walden owed him money.'

The rest of the room was a heap of clothing and bedding. In the small bathroom, the bath panel had been ripped off and the lid of the cistern had been removed. There wasn't much else to damage there.

'We'll lock it again and get the CSIs in.' Matthew thought there was little point adding to the confusion by doing a search of their own. 'I doubt that the person who did this left their fingerprints behind, but it would be interesting to see if anyone else involved in the investigation has been in here.'

They stood outside while Ross called it in. It was proper rain now, not a downpour but deceptive, insidious. Matthew felt it seeping into his skin down the neck of his shirt. He pushed open the door of the bookmaker's and went inside. A middle-aged woman was behind the counter. A couple of men stood in front of the machines and another was glued to a television showing a horse race. All glanced at him briefly then turned back to what they were doing. Except the woman at the counter. She turned towards him. 'Hiya!'

He felt as if he'd wandered into a different and seductive world. Of course the Brethren had been hot on the sin of gambling, a vice on a par with adultery, sodomy. And not wearing hats to meetings. It was warm in here and welcoming. As a child, he'd scuttled past the doors of betting shops, anxious that he might be drawn into temptation. Even now, he experienced something of the thrill of a guilty pleasure, just by being inside.

The manager had a badge that named her as Marion. He introduced himself but didn't explain his true interest in the flat. The last thing he needed was her talking to the press. 'It looks as if there's been a break-in upstairs. I wonder if you heard anything.'

'No!' She was interested but he thought she hadn't linked the tenant to the dead man at Crow Point. 'You're not safe anywhere these days, are you? Did they take much?'

'It's hard to say.' He paused while the horse race came to an end and the punter tore up his slip in disgust. 'So, you didn't hear anything?'

She shook her head. 'I wasn't even sure if anyone was still renting. You never see anyone going up. I just thought they must be out at work all day.'

'And no one hanging around outside?'

She laughed. 'Anyone hanging around outside would be my punters having a fag.'

He smiled back and was about to leave when she called him back. 'Hang on, there was a letter for him. It arrived a couple of days ago. It was too big for the letter box and it had to be signed for, so the postie brought it in here. One of the juniors was on and took it. If I'd been around, I'd have told them there was no point because we never saw the tenant and we didn't have a key.'

Another question answered.

She disappeared into a room at the back and emerged with a large white envelope. He took it from her and left the warm, comfortable room. Ross and Jen were still on the pavement, miserable now. He put his hands on both of their shoulders, felt that their coats were sodden. 'Come on! What are we waiting for?'

★   ★   ★

They sat in his office. He made them coffee, because he'd never wanted to be the kind of boss who demanded that his minions wait on him, and anyway, he knew he'd never get a decent brew if he left it to them. He'd sent Ross and Jen ahead of him in her car, and had sat in the one Ross had been using in the car park at the end of the lane until he got the text from the CSIs saying they were there and needed to be let in. Now he set the envelope, still unopened, on the desk between them.

'This was left for Walden in the bookie's. I've checked the post mark. It was sent just over a week ago.'

He took a paper knife and slit it across the top of the envelope rather than pulling it open at the flap. These days most envelopes were self-sealing, but if it had needed licking there could be DNA in the saliva on the gum.

The bulky content was an A4 brochure, glossy, explaining the services provided by a firm of solicitors called Morrish and Sandford based in Exeter. With it was a letter on thick, cream paper, written by Justin Cramer, one of the solicitors in the firm.

I write to confirm the appointment made today by telephone and enclose some details of our services. I look forward to discussing your concerns and to seeing you on March 11th at 10.30 in our offices.

The date of the appointment was less than a week away. There was no explanation of the concerns that had prompted Walden to contact the lawyer. Matthew was wondering why Walden would have needed a solicitor. Perhaps Walden had decided to buy a property with all his money. But why would he choose a solicitor in Exeter, at least an hour's drive away? Part of a fancy firm who provided potential clients with glossy brochures? Matthew was about to phone the number on the letter to find out, when Vicki, the young PC, who'd taken responsibility for the search for Christine Shapland, knocked on the office door. She looked flushed, excited.

'I thought you'd like to know. There's been a sighting. A passenger on the Lovacott bus thinks he saw Christine. Might be nothing. He said it was just a glimpse as the bus went past. There's a patch of woodland near a pool. There was a big

228

house there once but it burned down years ago and nothing much is left. Someone was sitting there, next to the water. It was too far away to see the face but he recognized the clothes, described them exactly.'

22

The rain stopped as they drove towards Lovacott. The clouds ripped apart to let through shafts of sunlight when they climbed out of the vehicle. It was wet underfoot, though, water dripped from the trees and Jen's coat was still damp after she'd stood outside Walden's flat in Braunton. She was starving, couldn't remember the last time she'd eaten. She'd wanted to stop to pick up some chocolate or a sandwich from the canteen, but the boss had said there was no time. Jen thought he cared about this missing woman in a way that was personal for him.

They'd parked by the side of the road, pulling the car right into the verge on the long grass so traffic could still pass. Matthew had got her to drive and sat beside her, an OS map on his knee, shouting directions. He was old-fashioned that way and never trusted the satnav. They'd left Ross back at the station to phone the solicitors' in Exeter and they'd all been pleased with that arrangement. Matthew had said they shouldn't go mob-handed; if Christine Shapland was really there, she'd be terrified enough as it was.

Now they were outside and everything was glistening and strange; the sunlight through the holes in the cloud seemed brighter than usual, more focussed, features of the landscape seemed spot-lit. They climbed a five-bar gate and walked down an avenue of trees to the pool. Once this would have been parkland, an artificial setting to provide a bucolic view from a grand house. Now, it seemed pointless, a bit crazy. Surreal.

Jen thought as soon as they'd pulled up that this would be a wild goose chase. How would a woman like Christine Shapland make her way all the way out here? It was miles from her home. And if she'd been brought out here, no good would have come of it. There were people who took pleasure in humiliating those who were different, trusting. They were easy prey. If Christine had been targeted by a man who needed to dominate, who got off on cruelty, they could be looking for a body not the woman, alive and hungry and grateful to be found. Jen realized with a jolt that this search was personal for her too. It had been hard enough for *her* to fight back against a controlling man with such a pathetic ego that he needed to hit a woman to prove his strength. It'd be worse for a woman like Christine, confused and already accustomed to being diminished and patronized.

Matthew was striding ahead and had already reached the pool. The avenue continued into an area of untended woodland and a blanket of celandines, startling, almost unpleasant, in the yellow light. The pool had been created to please the eye, though. At one end there was a stone bridge across the narrowest stretch of water. It served no purpose. The lake was fringed with iris and there was a small wooden jetty, with a rowing boat still attached. It was only as they got closer that they saw that the planks of the jetty were rotting and that the water itself was clogged with weed, green with algae.

'Christine was seen by the bridge,' Matthew said. 'I can't see how the witness could have made it up. He described it perfectly. I came past on the bus myself on Tuesday and there was a good enough view.'

Jen could tell he was trying to convince himself, not her. 'Let's walk round there then, shall we?' she suggested. 'Even if she's not still here, there might be some trace of her.'

'Well, someone's certainly been here recently.' Once there'd been a path around the water, but it was overgrown, grass pushing through the paving stones. In places the grass had been crushed.

'Could be anyone. It *is* a bit special here. You can see how it would attract walkers, locals.' She didn't want him to build up his hopes, then be disappointed.

Jen saw her first. There was a bench just beyond the bridge, hidden by the stone walls that flanked it. The bench was wrought-iron; it had once been black, but it was rusting now and the paint was flaking off. The woman was lying back in the seat, her face turned towards the sun, as if she was enjoying its heat. She was wearing the clothes that had appeared in all the descriptions that had been sent to the press: navy blue trousers, purple knitted cardigan, black anorak. On her feet, blue socks and white trainers. The trousers were a little short for her and they could see six inches of white leg. Everything wet, the shoes and the trousers spattered with mud.

Matthew had run ahead and was crouching

beside her, holding her hand, feeling for a pulse. 'She's still alive.' He stroked the damp hair away from her face. 'Christine. It's Matthew Venn. Do you remember me? We used to go to meetings together.'

Jen got out her phone and punched in 999 to call an ambulance. 'No reception. I'll go back to the road, see if there's anything there.'

Christine opened her eyes and slowly pushed herself up into an upright position. Not frightened at all, it seemed, but frail, shaky.

'You came,' she said. 'They said that you would.' Then she shut her eyes again and they couldn't tell if she was asleep or unconscious.

In the end Jen stayed where she was and they carried Christine to the car between them. She seemed so cold and confused and the pulse was so weak that Matthew was worried she wouldn't survive the wait for an ambulance. 'There's no guarantee that you'll get phone reception even at the road and if she was out here all night, she could get hypothermia.'

They laid her on the back seat, covered her with their jackets, switched on the heater and blasted out hot air. Jen drove again back to Barnstaple, very fast, while Matthew called 999 and asked for instructions. 'We're to take her to A&E at the North Devon District Hospital,' he said. 'They'll be waiting for us.'

Jen wanted to ask him what Christine could have meant. *You came. They said that you would.* Who could she have been waiting for? But there was no chance because Matthew was turning away from her, checking on their

233

passenger, making sure she was still breathing. Then he was on the phone again. 'Mother? Is that you?'

Jen knew this was a big deal because Matthew *never* spoke to his family, who belonged to a weird sect and had cast him out as an unbeliever. Matthew had told her that in a joking manner once, when she'd asked him about them. Flip, as if he hadn't cared. But she knew that he *had* cared, by the way he always asked about *her* family, the looks of anxiety when she came into work hungover or with tales of a new, unsuitable man. He'd been thinking that wasn't the way a good mother should behave; she should always put her children first. *Wait until you've got kids,* she'd wanted to say. *They drain your energy and personality and sometimes you need time for yourself. I feel bad enough without you doing the guilt-trip thing.*

Now she was driving like a maniac down these twisting, overgrown lanes, trying to listen in to the exchange between the boss and his mum, but pretending not to. Just as well she was a woman and good at multitasking. And just as well that Matthew's mother came from the generation who thought you had to shout into a phone to make herself heard, because Jen could make out every word, both sides of the conversation.

'We've found Christine,' Matthew said. 'I wanted to let you know.' As if it really wasn't a big deal, as if he hadn't been haunted by the search since he'd realized the woman was missing.

'Alive?' One word. A demand and an

234

accusation. The woman couldn't believe that her son had succeeded in this.

'Yes. But she's very cold and a little confused. We're taking her to A&E.'

'At last!' He wasn't to be congratulated for finding Christine then, just blamed for not finding her sooner.

'I thought you'd like to let Susan know.' There was no resentment in his voice. 'Tell her that we've found her daughter and she'll be at the hospital.'

'Yes, I can do that.'

Of course you can. You'll get the gratitude, the vicarious praise. This was a huge gift he was giving.

Matthew's mother was still speaking. 'I'll call one of the Brethren. They'll pick her up and take her to the hospital. I can meet her there.'

There was a moment's pause. Jen could tell that Matthew was choosing his words. 'Don't ask Dennis Salter to collect Susan. I don't think that would be a very good idea. He's too close to my investigation.'

A silence at the other end of the phone. Jen could sense that Matthew was tense, that he was expecting his mother to question his request. The hand holding the mobile was shaking slightly. But when Dorothy Venn spoke, it was to agree with him. 'Yes,' she said. 'I can see that would probably be best.' Another pause. 'I'm sure we can find someone who lives closer than Lovacott to go out to Braunton to fetch Susan.'

'I'm sure that you can.'

It seemed that the conversation was over.

They'd reached the outskirts of the town. Matthew was about to switch off the phone when his mother spoke again. Two words, sharp, almost curt. 'Thank you.'

23

Matthew left Jen in the hospital with Christine and started back to the police station. He would have liked to stay with the woman himself, but he didn't think Christine would remember him after all this time. She hadn't seen him since he was a teenager and he'd just be a stranger now. A strange man, invading her predominantly female world. Jen would interact better with Susan Shapland too; her manner was easy, unthreatening. And she'd cope better with his mother. He had too much baggage to be relaxed in her presence. He'd been tempted to wait to see Dorothy; surely now she'd feel the need to be gracious, to thaw a little in her attitude to him. He was worried, though, that he'd be disappointed and that she'd still be cold and disapproving. That she'd still blame him for his father's illness and death.

He looked at his watch. It was later than he'd expected, only an hour until the evening briefing. Matthew thought he'd go home, shower, change into clean, dry clothes. He'd feel more ready afterwards to face the team. Then he remembered that Jonathan was working late. He'd still be in the Woodyard and the trip home didn't seem quite so attractive. It would be a rush and Matthew hated rushing. Instead, he headed to the Woodyard and found his husband in the familiar office, head bent over a pile of paper.

Even from the corridor outside, Matthew could tell he was hating every minute of the work he was doing. Jonathan was great at practical stuff, unafraid of tackling wiring or plumbing, cooking an elaborate meal for friends. He had a blind spot for admin. He'd worry at it for days and in the end Lorraine, his assistant, would sort it for him. She always did. Matthew had once offered to help him and it was one of the very rare occasions when Jonathan had lost his temper. 'Are you saying that I can't do my job? That I'm incompetent?' His voice raised and his face red.

Now Matthew pushed open the door. 'You heard that we found Christine? I asked Ross to let you know.'

'Yes!' Jonathan got up and put his arms around Matthew, squeezed him. 'I don't know how to thank you. I was starting to think that we'd never get her back.' He was still beaming when he returned to his seat. 'Have you worked out what happened?'

'Not yet.' Matthew sat in one of the easy chairs facing the desk. Outside, the lights were coming on in the town. The tide was high in the river and the street lights along the opposite bank were reflected in the water. 'Christine's okay, but she can't explain what happened. What she was doing there. She got cold and wet and she's dehydrated. It seems as if she was waiting for someone. Perhaps she misunderstood what Dennis Salter told her, tried to make her own way back to Lovacott, got off the bus too early.'

'But you don't think that's what happened.' Not a question.

238

Matthew shrugged. 'It's too soon to say. I checked the bus that Lucy usually takes. The bus driver didn't recognize Christine, and she probably would stand out.'

The following silence was broken by a wailing sax, the sound floating up from the yard. The cafe was holding its regular jazz night. Matthew thought they should be there, sitting in the half-light, a bottle of wine on the table in front of them, not agonizing over a dead man and a woman who had mysteriously disappeared.

'Would you like me to talk to her?' Jonathan asked. 'Not tonight, but tomorrow if they let her home. I've known Christine and her mum for years. Since the old day centre days. Chrissie's not confident like Lucy, not very used to strangers.'

Matthew nodded. 'Yeah, that would be kind.' Something positive at least had come of his need to touch base with Jonathan. 'I've got to go. Evening briefing.'

'And I have to finish this sodding paperwork. I can't even make the simple figures add up. I'll see you at home. At this rate you'll be back before me.'

'Don't be too late.' This was the closest Matthew could ever get to being demanding, and even that felt like a risk.

★   ★   ★

The police station conference room again. White board and pin board. Officers slumped in chairs waiting for this to be over so they could go home

239

and sleep. Oldham had left ages before, but nobody commented on that. The rest of the team had all put in extra hours in the search for Christine Shapland. Matthew wondered if they resented the fact that *he'd* found her, apparently without any effort. They'd think he'd been sitting in his office and responding to a phone call from a member of the public. They'd been out in the drizzle all day, knocking on doors, searching the footpaths around the marsh and the creek.

'Huge congratulations on finding Christine Shapland. If you hadn't got word out so speedily or so accurately, we'd never have got that witness call. I've just checked with the hospital and she'll be fine. A big thanks to everyone from her very grateful mother.' He looked at the room. No appreciative difference in attitude, but he'd done his best. And he'd meant it.

'We're not sure yet if Christine's disappearance is linked in any way to the Walden murder. It seems a coincidence, especially as Walden had been seen making overtures to another learning-disabled woman, Lucy, who lives in Lovacott, in the days before his death. And that Christine's home is very close to where his body was found. But there's no evidence that Walden knew Christine so we should keep an open mind. We've moved forward considerably today, though, so let's sum up what we've learned so far and plan out actions for tomorrow. Then we can finish in time at least for you to get the last hour before closing in the pub.'

A weak cheer from the back row.

'We've discovered that Walden had a place to

240

live other than twenty Hope Street. A flat in Braunton. We have Jen Rafferty to thank for this. She's not here so I can tell you that, without the danger of making her feel she's indispensable.' A pause and another little cheer. 'So, I'd be very interested to know *why* he moved into the house in Ilfracombe with the two women.'

Vicki Robb, sitting at the back, stuck up her hand. 'Could he just have been feeling lonely and desperate? Maybe having suicidal thoughts and thinking he needed company to keep himself safe.'

Matthew thought about that. He'd been viewing this from his own perspective. He needed solitude far more than he needed company, but not everyone was like him. He nodded. 'Yeah,' he said. 'Good point. Yes, that makes sense.'

The woman coloured with pleasure and Matthew continued. 'Someone has been in the flat and trashed the place. It looks more like a search to me than an act of vandalism. A search by someone in a hurry. There would have been a lot of noise — glass and crockery got smashed — so it could have happened at night when the bookie's shop below is shut. Or very early in the morning. Can we get some canvassers into Braunton tomorrow to do a house-to-house? Find out if anyone saw or heard anything unusual? There was no break-in so they would have used a key. It's possible that the killer stole one from Walden after his death. So, we're talking an evening between Monday and Wednesday inclusive. It seems likely that the person who was in Walden's flat was implicated in his death, so this is important.'

Ross stuck up a hand. 'They could have used the same key we used to get in. The one Walden had left in Hope Street.'

'They could, Ross, and that would implicate one of the women living there. Let's get the canvassers to show photographs of Preece and Henry and ask specifically if any of the women were in Braunton on that night.'

It occurred to Matthew that they could be close to tying up the investigation. It could be that easy: they'd get a description of someone lurking outside Walden's Braunton flat and they'd have their culprit. In his mind he explored a variety of scenarios that might fit. Could Walden have been murdered simply for access to the flat? Perhaps by one of the men Walden had met through St Cuthbert's? An addict raging for a fix, desperate enough to commit murder. Maybe Matthew was overthinking this, looking for complex motives that didn't exist. It was possible that word had got out about Walden's wealth and he'd been killed just for his money. Greed often provided motive enough. But the man wouldn't have been daft enough to keep cash in his flat, would he?

He turned back to the room. 'Have we tracked down Walden's bank accounts?'

Ross shook his head. 'Sorry, there doesn't seem to be any account in his name.'

'The hotel must have paid him through his bank. Nobody gets paid by cash any more.'

'I'll check with them tomorrow.'

'That has to be a priority.' Matthew tried to hide his irritation. He thought that even if Walden hadn't hidden cash in the Braunton flat, there might be information there that would have allowed the intruder access to the money: passwords, the e-reader that allowed transfer of funds, building society pass books. It seemed even more likely now that greed had been the main motive in the case; Walden's attachment to Lucy Braddick and the disappearance of Christine Shapland could be nothing but distracting coincidences.

He continued: 'We were given a letter that had been delivered to Walden and left at the bookmaker's shop below his flat. It was from a firm of solicitors in Exeter. Ross, you were going to check that out.'

Ross stood up. Matthew hadn't had a chance to discuss this with him beforehand, so he waited with interest like the others.

'Walden first contacted the lawyers to make a will,' Ross said, 'but apparently he got in touch again wanting advice about something else. They wouldn't give me the details over the phone but apparently one of the partners will be in North Devon tomorrow and is prepared to 'fit us in'.' He waved his fingers in the air to indicate the quotation marks. 'Honestly, they're the most pompous bunch of arses I've ever dealt with. It took me more than an hour to get past the receptionist.'

'What time can he see us?'

'He's coming here to the station at three.' Ross paused. 'You'd better see him, boss. I doubt he'll be prepared to talk to a lowly constable.'

Matthew nodded in agreement, not because he was prepared to pander to the lawyer's prejudices, but because he wanted to hear what the man had to say. 'So tomorrow we need to focus on the financial aspect of Walden's life. We'll go back to St Cuthbert's and see if one of their clients has suddenly come into money. Ross, you need to really have a go at the banks and see what was going on there. And we'll leave Jen to work with Christine Shapland. There might still have been a crime committed: abduction or abuse. I can't believe she'd been wandering around that pool for three days. It's much more likely that she was being held somewhere and then dumped in a place where she'd be unlikely to be found for a while. We'll meet again the same time tomorrow evening.'

They moved away to their homes and families; a group of younger, single officers got together to go to the pub. They asked Matthew if he'd like to go along, but he knew they weren't really expecting him to say yes. They found him a little upright and proper and they couldn't quite relax when he was there.

When he arrived home, he was pleased to see that Jonathan's car was already parked outside the house. Matthew doubted his prompting had made a difference, but he liked to think that it had. The rain of earlier in the day had quite gone and there was moonlight on the river. Inside, Jonathan seemed restless. He wasn't good at sitting still all day; the pile of papers and accounts and the anxiety about Christine

Shapland had taken its toll. Matthew knew how it would be. The man would stay up late switching TV channels, drinking too much whisky.

'Do you fancy a walk? It's light enough.' Matthew thought that might help and he wasn't fit for bed yet either. And anyway, he wouldn't sleep until Jonathan did.

They went through the gate in the wall at the edge of the garden and that took them straight onto the beach. It was impossible here to tell where the river ended and the sea began. Arm in arm they walked, the shadow thrown by the moonlight turning them into one person, misshapen and weird.

24

Gaby was working in her studio when she heard that Christine Shapland had been found. Jonathan Church had come all the way up to her eyrie to tell her. She resented the interruption briefly; she'd been entirely focussed on one piece of sky in the Crow Point painting and it was always hard to get back the concentration once she was pulled away from her work. But he seemed so joyful, so sure that she would share his excitement that it was impossible not to smile.

'How is she?' Gaby cleaned her brush. The moment was lost and anyway, it was probably time to finish. She sang in an amateur kind of way — at one point in her life she'd dreamed of performing, of wealth and celebrity — but art had always come first. Each month there was an evening of jazz in the Woodyard cafe and she'd been invited to sing with a band she admired. She needed to change, to chat to the musicians. It wasn't a big deal, but most of her friends were coming along to watch. Caz and Ed would be there. Even Simon had said that he'd come; she hadn't quite known what to make of that. Now, she wondered for a moment if she should pull out, if it would be disrespectful to perform so soon after the man's murder. But it was an honour to have been asked and besides, it was a paying gig. She could use the cash.

'Christine's fine. Dehydrated and cold and they're keeping her in hospital overnight, but no lasting damage, physically at least. It'll have affected her mother, though. She's always been a bit nervous and this won't help.'

'Do the police know what happened?'

'No. They found Christine by a pond out towards Lovacott. Nobody knows how she got there.'

'Not even your husband?' Gaby had known that Jonathan's Matthew was a detective, because of gossip around the centre, but had only linked him with the inspector in charge of the investigation into Simon's death when she'd seen the two of them eating lunch outside the Woodyard cafe.

'Not even him.' Jonathan paused. 'Are you okay? It must be hard to lose a housemate, even if you weren't very close. You know you can always take a few days off.'

He was so sympathetic that she was almost tempted to confide in him. To confess. But she'd grown up thinking that secrets were sometimes all she had, so she just shook her head. 'Nah. I'll be fine. I want to finish this.' She stood aside so he could see the painting.

He didn't speak for a moment and when he did his tone was unexpectedly serious. 'You do know this is terrific. I think we should talk about holding an exhibition of your work, see if we can get some of the London press down. Christopher Preece has contacts in the media and he's always keen on anything that would put this place on the map.'

She looked up at him to see if he was just being kind, but he was still staring at her work.

★ ★ ★

When she got to the cafe Caz and Edward were already there. She hadn't thought this would be quite Ed's thing, but perhaps Caz was working her magic on him, making him more mellow. He drank a couple of glasses of wine and slid his arm around his girlfriend's shoulder. Gaby thought he seemed even more adolescent and needy than usual. Caz had untied her hair and was wearing a little red dress and silver earrings.

Gaby gave her a hug. 'You look gorgeous.'

'Well, I had to make a bit of an effort for your first public performance.'

Gaby could tell the compliment had pleased her. The room was transformed for the evening with candles and fairy lights and the music had already begun. They were sitting at the back, furthest from the stage, around a small table, and there was a bottle of cava in a bucket of ice. Everything, apparently, as normal.

When the piece finished, there was a chance to talk for a while.

'Did you hear that the missing woman was found?' Gaby said. 'Jonathan came up to the studio to tell me.'

'Yes.' Caroline's face was in shadow so it was hard to tell what she was thinking. 'Dad phoned me. He thought I'd want to know.'

'He must be pleased.'

Caroline didn't answer that. 'The detective

who talked to us in Hope Street, Jen Rafferty, came to St Cuthbert's today. I gave her the key you found in Simon's laundry. She seemed pleased to have it.'

'Oh.' Gaby wasn't sure what to make of that. 'Did your dad know anything about the investigation? Do they think Christine's abduction was linked to Simon's murder? I didn't ask Jonathan. He's married to the officer in charge of the case, so he wasn't going to tell me anything even if they believe there's a link.'

'Oh, Dad wouldn't know about any of that. Why would he?'

Gaby didn't think that was necessarily true. She saw Christopher Preece as a powerful man, with fingers in lots of pies.

Caroline was still talking. 'Jen Rafferty thought Simon might not have been homeless when he came to us. She thought he might have had his own place. I don't think he would have kept that sort of secret. In the meetings at St Cuthbert's he was very open about other aspects of his life.'

Gaby reached out for the bottle and poured more cava into her glass. 'You don't know that. Just because he sat round in a circle listening to other depressed people baring their souls, it doesn't mean he was prepared to spew out every detail of his personal life. We all need secrets, just to keep sane, to feel that the world doesn't own us.' She felt that her hand holding the glass was shaking a little. She drank and then set it back on the table.

Caz didn't say anything. Perhaps she was remembering secrets of her own.

When it was her turn to perform, Gaby got to her feet and walked through the shadowy room. She was suddenly so nervous that she wasn't sure her legs would carry her to the low stage. She'd changed in the studio before coming to the cafe and was still in black, but in a slinky dress and heels. She took the proffered microphone and stood for a moment looking out at them. The audience's faces were lit by candle flame from below, and they looked like masks, barely human. The band started the intro and soon she was captured by the music, or escaping into it, singing of loss and love. As she finished, she looked to the back of the room where her group had been sitting. With surprise, she saw that Christopher Preece was there, standing behind his daughter. Gaby was touched that he'd come along to show his support. Caz and Ed were holding hands, staring at each other, their faces caught in the candlelight, in a way that Gaby suddenly found very moving. She handed back the microphone and began to make her way back to her seat. Only then did she realize that there were tears streaming down her face.

25

Jen Rafferty was in the hospital. It was evening and the lights had been switched down. Christine had had a barrage of tests. She was fine but the consultant had decided to keep her in overnight. The nurses at their station spoke in whispers. Jen was keeping vigil with Christine's mother and Matthew's mother, Dorothy Venn. Christine herself was deeply asleep, troubled only by an occasional loud snore, which startled her for a moment but never really woke her.

The two older women sat on one side of the bed on the easy chairs provided for patients and visitors and Jen was on the other side on the hard, orange plastic seat she'd dragged from the corridor. The curtains had been drawn around them. Despite the discomfort, Jen found herself drowsing. Matthew had said she should leave if it seemed that Christine would be unlikely to pass on any useful information — she could always come back in the morning — but Jen stayed out of inertia. And because she was earwigging on Susan and Dorothy's conversation. They seemed to have forgotten that she was on the other side of the bed.

'I don't understand what Chrissie was doing all the way out there,' Susan said.

'It's not so far from your Grace and Dennis's place.' Dorothy Venn was furthest away from Jen and her face was in shadow, but her voice was

251

clear. 'Not as the crow flies. We used to walk from Lovacott up to the pond when we were children for the summer picnic with the Brethren. You remember those picnics, Susan. What wonderful times we had! There was the three-legged race and hide-and-seek and our mothers had all baked, the fields were covered in buttercups and clover, all pink and yellow.' She paused as if lost in her memory, before continuing more sharply: 'It's hardly any distance, even the little ones kept up.'

'What are you saying? That Dennis did take her back to their house after all, and Chrissie ran off? That would make him a liar.'

There was a silence that dragged on so long that it became uncomfortable. In the end it was broken again by Susan.

'Grace won't hear a word said against him.'

'Grace is a loyal wife,' Dorothy agreed. There was another pause before she continued. 'Matthew says you shouldn't let Chrissie back there. Not until the investigation into the dead man is over.'

'I won't,' Susan said. There was no hesitation this time and her voice was fierce. 'I won't be letting her out of my sight, whoever wants to care for her. She'll be staying with me from now on.'

That was when Jen decided she could leave the women to it. Susan would be there for Christine in the unlikely event that she needed protecting. She could talk to Christine tomorrow, when the woman had had a good night's sleep and when she was back in her own home.

She'd have more to tell them then. She said her goodbyes and left. It wasn't until she got home that she remembered seeing Colin Marston marching into the Woodyard when she was there that morning handing out the flyers about the missing woman. It was midnight, too late to call Matthew Venn now. It would save until the morning.

26

Another morning and Matthew was preparing for another briefing. It was grey outside and not long past seven, so he'd had to switch on the lights. He stood in the empty room trying to order his thoughts, planning for the day. The priority was to find out what had happened to Christine Shapland. At the moment, they couldn't eliminate her disappearance from the murder investigation because of the Woodyard connection. That was distracting, so it was important to know if the woman had wandered away or had been taken, and if she'd had any real involvement with Walden. He felt the weight of responsibility for all that was going on and worried again that he might be the wrong man for the job. The stress was growing; tension made his muscles ache and shortened his temper. Soon it would be an effort to keep it under control.

The team started to arrive, early. Keen. Sniffing the possibility of a result. Matthew wasn't so sure. Optimism had never been his default setting. Ross was laughing and joking with a colleague. Jen slipped in at the back at the last minute. She looked tired, a bit dishevelled. Matthew wondered if she'd been hitting the wine when she got in from the hospital the night before. He wouldn't have blamed her.

'Christine Shapland.' He leaned back against the desk at the front of the room and thought he must look like one of the older teachers at his school, jaded, a bit of a joke. 'We need to find out what happened to her as a priority. Even if there were no murder inquiry involved, she's a vulnerable adult and if there *was* an abduction, we need to find the perpetrator. I've just phoned the hospital and she's fine. She's going to be allowed home this morning. Jen, I'd like you to wait until she's home and go to see her. Jonathan's offered to go with you. He's known the woman for years and the mother trusts him too. She wants him there for the interview. You met Susan at the hospital and I don't want to introduce someone new at this stage.'

Jen nodded. Matthew thought she'd rather be a part of the main Walden inquiry but she could see the sense in what he'd asked. He turned back to the room and raised his voice a notch. After all this time he allowed himself to show his impatience. 'Ross, where are we on Walden's finances? That missing two hundred grand? It can't just have vanished into thin air.'

'I've already left a message for the human resources guy at the Kingsley Hotel. I'll try again now, find out how Walden was paid when he was working there.'

'I'm sure you find this kind of detail tedious, Ross. Not as exciting as you'd like, but it's important and I have asked you to treat it as a priority.'

There was a shocked silence in the room. Matthew never criticized a colleague in public. Ross blushed and shifted in his seat, but Matthew was running out of patience with the man; this inability to find Walden's money was becoming ridiculous. 'The solicitor who dealt with Walden's will is coming in this afternoon. If all else fails, he might have some idea about the finances.'

'I'll sort it out.' Ross sounded moody, resentful.

'Please do.' Matthew turned his attention back to Jen. 'Once you've spoken to Susan, I'd like you to go back to St Cuthbert's. Have any of Caroline's clients suddenly come into money? Or dropped out of the programme unexpectedly? Let's see if we can find the person who searched Walden's flat.'

Matthew was about to send them on their way when Jen raised her hand. 'When I was canvassing the Woodyard service users yesterday, Colin Marston from the toll keeper's cottage came in. He looked as if he might be there in an official capacity. I didn't speak to him and I don't think he recognized me, but it seemed an odd coincidence.'

★　★　★

Matthew drove to the Marstons' house immediately after the meeting. From the beginning he'd had a niggle of suspicion about the couple who lived on the edge of the marsh; their interest in the case had seemed disproportionate and they lived not far from the Shaplands' cottage. There was no reply at the door and their car had gone. He stood, uncertain what to do next, thinking he might just call into his own house for a snatched cup of good coffee and a moment's peace, when he saw Marston in the distance on the ridge of the bank that separated the marsh from the river. It was a still day, misty and overcast, and the man was little more than a silhouette from here. Marston was staring out towards the estuary, not moving, with his back to where Matthew was standing. Matthew pulled his car further down the track and parked close to his house. There was a moment of panic when the man disappeared out of his sightline, hidden by one of their outbuildings, a crumbling boathouse. Matthew worried that Marston might have moved on. He could have walked away towards the point. Matthew thought it would be ridiculously undignified to chase after the man, to arrive breathless and sweating to ask his questions.

When he got out of the car, however, he saw that Marston was still there, still staring out over the water. The outline of the opposite bank was blurred by drizzle. Any birds that flew out of the mist would only be silhouettes. The man turned when he heard Matthew climbing the bank towards him.

'I'm glad I saw you,' Matthew said. 'I went to your house but nobody was in.'

'Hilary's at work.' His focus was still on the shore.

'That's okay. It was you I wanted to talk to.'

'Oh?' Now the man gave Matthew his full attention.

'You were at the Woodyard centre yesterday morning.'

'Yes, that's right. I'm there every Thursday. Unless we decide to do a field trip, but those are only once a month.'

'What is it you do there?'

'I teach a course for the U3A, the University of the Third Age. Natural history. Mostly ornithology, but I've become more interested in botany recently, so I can cover that too.' Marston paused. 'I'm rather enjoying it. Sharing my knowledge, you know, to interested beginners. I only started at Christmas. The original tutor was taken ill and I was asked to take over.'

Matthew could picture him at the front of a class, showing his images of birds, explaining plumage details and distribution, a little pompous, getting the validation for his hobby that he never received at home.

'Did you ever see Simon Walden at the Woodyard? He's the man who was killed here on Monday afternoon.'

'We've been watching the news of course. It's of special interest because it happened so close to home. But I didn't know him. He certainly wasn't a member of our group.' Marston paused. 'We're all over fifty in the U3A and most of my students are considerably older.'

'You didn't see him elsewhere in the centre? Mr Walden was a regular. He volunteered in the cafe kitchen. You never saw him there?'

There was a moment's hesitation before Marston shook his head. 'I seldom use the cafe. It always seems noisy and a little overpriced. I take my own coffee in a thermos flask.'

It was the sort of thing Matthew's mother

might have said. Thrift came very close to godliness in her book. Matthew wondered if that was why he found Marston so tricky. He was a man who'd turned his personal likes and dislikes into a moral code; because he didn't enjoy spending money in the Woodyard cafe, there was something morally suspect about the people who did. The Brethren had been much the same. Matthew thought they'd created a God in their own image, hard, cold and inflexible.

'And that was your only contact with the Woodyard? You just ran the natural history course?' Matthew was looking out over the estuary. It was low tide and the mist was clearing a little to show the far shore, the ridged wave patterns on the sand. He couldn't see what possible motive Marston might have for killing Walden, but this seemed another coincidence, one too far.

'For the time being. I have given some informal legal advice to the trustees and I hope to become more involved when we move to Barnstaple.' Away from his wife, he seemed more confident, and Matthew decided he liked the man less because of it. Pity had turned to active antipathy. 'I think they could possibly use my organizational skills and Hilary's always telling me to find more useful ways of spending my time than birding.' He turned towards Matthew Venn. 'Really, the administration there is a total shambles at the moment. If anyone came to do a proper audit, the place would probably be shut down.'

'And you think you'd be able to help with that?'

'Well, yes. Actually, it would be a challenge to sort out their systems. Their invoicing at the moment is a nightmare. All those different organizations renting rooms, employing staff. Different pots of money coming from social services and a variety of arts and welfare charities. I'm sure that the Woodyard itself is missing out. The whole thing needs to be simplified.'

Matthew wasn't quite sure how to respond to that. He thought Marston was probably right, but it seemed like a betrayal to Jonathan to agree.

Marston must have picked up on the ambivalence. 'Oh, I'm sorry. That was tactless, wasn't it? I'd forgotten that your . . . ' he hesitated, looking to find the right word '. . . partner runs the show.'

He didn't sound sorry and Matthew thought it unlikely that there had been a lapse of memory. There had been something snide, accusatory about the comments. Matthew wondered if the whole conversation had been a second-hand pitch for the role of administrator. Perhaps Marston was missing the status he'd had when he was working or the couple had run out of money and he was looking for employment again. Matthew could understand the man wanting an escape from Hilary.

'My husband. Yes. But he just runs the centre day to day, tries to keep all the different organizations happy. A board of trustees manages the show, as you call it.' He forced a smile. 'I'm sure they'd be delighted if you

260

volunteered your services on the administration front, and they're always looking for board members with specific skills.'

'Well, that has been mentioned.' But still, the man seemed pleased. He looked at his watch. 'I have to move on. It's time for the next census point.'

'Just a moment.'

Marston paused, turned back. 'Yes?' Impatient now.

'Do you know the Shaplands? They live in one of the cottages on the creek close to the nature reserve. You must pass it most days while you're out birding. Christine is a woman with Down's syndrome. She goes to the day centre at the Woodyard.'

'She's the person who went missing?' Marston said.

'Yes.'

'I'm sorry, Inspector, Hilary and I keep ourselves to ourselves. As you'll have realized, we don't have a lot to do with our neighbours. I'm afraid I can't help you.' He was already moving away along the bank. 'Do get in touch again if you have any more questions.' He slid down the bank to the beach and walked off towards Crow Point. Soon, he was no more than a shadow in the mist. Matthew stood for a moment looking out at the water.

In the car again, he checked his phone. There'd been a call from Maurice Braddick. An awkward message, as the man stumbled over his words. 'I wonder if you'd mind calling to see me. There's something I should have told you when you were here the other night. It's been troubling me.'

Matthew called him back. 'I got your phone message. How can I help?'

'It's not something I feel I can talk about on the phone. I wanted Lucy to stay at home until all this has been cleared up, but she's as stubborn as her mother was and made sure I took her over. I dropped her at the Woodyard and I'm home now, but I could come back to Barnstaple if you like.'

'No,' Matthew said. 'I'll come to you.' Because he thought Maurice would speak more easily in his own home, and besides, when he was on the move he felt he was making progress, on his way at least to achieving a result.

⋆   ⋆   ⋆

They sat as they had before in the kitchen, looking out on the long back garden, with its neat vegetable plot and the chicken run at the end. The hens had been let out to forage. Tea was made and poured, before Maurice started speaking.

'You were asking about Dennis and Grace Salter.'

'Yes. The night before she went missing, Christine Shapland was staying with them. Do you have something to tell me about them?'

Maurice was clearly anxious, but Matthew saw something else on his face. Discomfort? Fear? It could simply be prejudice triggered by members of a small religious community, who kept

262

themselves apart, who held views that seemed odd and outdated. Matthew had experienced fear and ridicule from his peers when he was growing up. He knew how that felt. But it seemed that Maurice's antipathy was based on more than the distrust of the other.

'Can you tell me anything about them?' Matthew repeated. 'Anything that might us help find out who took Christine?'

'This is difficult,' Maurice said. 'And I hate gossip. Everyone in Lovacott says that Salter is a fine man. He has that way about him that makes you believe in him. Whenever he speaks, people listen. If I meet him in the street, he greets me as if I'm an old friend, as if I'm special.'

Matthew nodded. 'I knew him when I was a child. He always did have that skill. A kind of warmth. An empathy.'

'I think that he hits his wife.' Maurice looked up, challenging Matthew to believe him. 'I know he hit her at least once.'

Matthew tried to make sense of that, to match it with the Salter he knew, the man who greeted everyone with an embrace, arms wide open. The man who'd made him laugh and given him confidence as a teenager. The man who'd rejected him when he could no longer believe in Salter's version of God. 'Tell me about it.'

Maurice was staring at him, still troubled, still reluctant to speak. 'Grace Salter turned up here one night when my Maggie was still alive. Tears running down her face. No coat, though it was the middle of winter. Maggie sent me out. *Why don't you have a drink in The Fleece, Mo?*

263

Don't come back until closing. So out I went.'
He flashed a quick smile at Matthew. 'I always
did as I was told where Maggie was concerned.
She knew best.'

'And what *had* happened?'

'I don't know,' Maurice said. 'Not in any
detail. But the bruise was already coming out on
her eye when I left the house and there was dry
blood on her nose. Maggie had promised Grace
she wouldn't tell anyone and she never did. I feel
awkward talking about it to you now. As if I'm
letting Maggie down. That's why I didn't say
anything when you were here before.' He
paused. 'And because of Salter's reputation as a
kind man, a good man. I wasn't sure I'd be
believed.'

'I do need to know as much as you can tell
me.' Matthew thought Maggie was still a part of
the man's life, a voice in his ear, a hand on his
shoulder. Although Matthew had lost his faith
years before, he'd been brought up with a belief
in the afterlife. Perhaps this was as near as it got,
influence beyond the grave.

'When I got back from the pub, Grace had
gone. Maggie was as sad as I've ever seen her. I
think she tried to persuade her to leave her
husband, but it would have been hard for the
woman. They belong to this odd religious group.
Strict. Maybe, if she'd left her man, she might
have been forced to leave that too. And all her
family.'

Oh yes, I know how that feels.

'And nobody else in Lovacott knows about
that night?' Matthew thought in a place like this,

there'd surely be rumours.

Maurice shook his head. 'I don't think anyone knew that Grace Salter ran away from her husband and came here. It was dark so there wouldn't have been many people about. And I've never heard any gossip about him being cruel to his wife. Grace always seems a shy sort of woman. Quiet. But Dennis has such a big personality, you can see that she might be overshadowed. I wonder if she's scared of him, though, and if she's so quiet because she doesn't dare speak.'

'You did the right thing,' Matthew said, 'telling me what you know.' He thought this was all getting too complicated. There was too much coincidence. Too many people circling round each other, without quite touching. They had no evidence that Simon Walden had known either Christine Shapland or Dennis Salter. The only connection was the Woodyard, and again that was too close to home.

27

Jen Rafferty sat in the Shaplands' small, dark cottage, which seemed to have grown out of the marsh, listening to her boss's husband talking to Christine. She'd met Jonathan a few times before — at a work's Christmas do and once at their house when she'd picked Matthew up for an early shout — but Matthew liked to keep home and work life separate and she'd never really got to know the man. Dorothy Venn, who'd stuck with Susan Shapland throughout the hospital visit, wasn't there. Matthew had said that he'd been rejected by his family long before his marriage, but Jen thought a gay relationship would be hard for a fundamental Christian to swallow. Perhaps the woman couldn't even bear to be in the same room as her son's husband.

Outside, the mist was lying low over the creek and damp seemed to ooze through the walls and into the room. There was a coal fire in the grate and Jen felt she'd slipped back more than fifty years to when Susan Shapland was a young woman and North Devon was a very different place. There was a pot of tea on a lace mat and a plate of scones already buttered.

Jonathan and Christine sat in chairs closest to the fire and the man's voice was so low that at times Jen struggled to make out what they were saying. Christine was wearing jogging bottoms and a tracksuit top, grey with pink edging. Her cheeks were flushed from the flames. Despite the chill outside, Jonathan was still in his signature shorts and T-shirt. Jen wondered if he'd worn shorts to his wedding, and thought they made an odd pair, Matthew always suited and smart, Jonathan looking as if he'd just wandered in from the beach. She was sitting at the table, phone and notebook in front of her. She'd record the conversation and take notes too, because her impressions would be as useful as Christine's words.

'The main thing to say is that you're not in any trouble at all.' Jonathan's voice was warm and easy. Reassuring. 'You did nothing wrong. Nothing at all. We just want to find out what happened. That's what this chat is about. And because it's nice for me to escape from the Woodyard for a bit and eat your mother's scones.'

Christine looked up at him, but there was no answer. She couldn't tell where this was leading.

'So, let's start at the beginning. You thought your uncle Dennis was going to pick you up from the Woodyard on Tuesday night. You'd stayed with him and your auntie Grace on Monday and he'd dropped you off that morning.'

Christine nodded.

'But when you left the Woodyard on Tuesday afternoon, you didn't see him?'

Christine looked at her mother, who was sitting at the table next to Jen, crumbling a scone on her plate.

'You can tell him the truth,' Susan said. 'The

Brethren will never find out.' Jen saw that it mattered even now what the Brethren thought of her. 'It'll just be you and me now, girl.'

'Someone came up in a car,' Christine said. 'They told me they'd give me a lift back to Lovacott. That it had all been organized.'

'Was that a man or a woman, Chrissie?' Jonathan asked.

'A man.'

'Can you tell me what he was like?'

She seemed thrown by that.

'Well, was he dressed like me? Shorts and T-shirt?'

That made her laugh. 'No! He was smart, like Uncle Dennis at meetings.'

Susan jumped in. 'She means a jacket and tie.'

'Did you know the man? Had you seen him before? If he was a friend of your uncle's, he might have been at meetings with you.'

Christine shook her head. 'I'd never seen him before.'

'That's okay. You got into the car with the man. Were you in the front or the back?'

'In the back.'

'So, it was like you were in a taxi?'

Christine nodded.

'What happened then, Christine? Just tell us as if it was a story. Your story.' Jonathan leaned back in the moth-eaten armchair as if he had all the time in the world. Outside, the mist still lay over the water. It could have been a winter's evening. There was the white flash of a swan taking off from the creek, the sound of wingbeats.

'We got to a house,' Christine said. Her speech

268

wasn't quite clear and Jen struggled to make out the words, but Jonathan knew exactly what she was saying.

'Your uncle and auntie's house?'

'No! Not a big house like that.'

'A cottage then, like this? All the rooms on one floor?' Jonathan asked. Jen thought he had the patience of a saint. No way would she have been able to prise this information from the woman. She was fine in interviews where she could get inside the head of the witness and see the world through their eyes, but this was a very special skill.

'All the rooms were on one floor,' Christine said, 'but we had to go up some stairs to get there.'

'So, it was a flat?'

A nod.

'Was it a big building with lots of floors, lots of flats?'

'No! Just one flat over a shop.'

Walden's flat, Jen thought. *They took her to Walden's flat. They knew he wouldn't be there because he was already dead. We could have arrived there soon after he took her to the pond.* She couldn't help interrupting. 'Do you know what kind of shop was under the flat?'

But Christine just shook her head.

'What did you do in the flat, Christine?' Jonathan took up the questions again.

'I watched the telly.' A pause. 'I like the telly.'

'With the man who'd driven you there?'

'He stayed for a bit. He gave me some crisps and a bar of chocolate. A can of pop.' She shot a look at her mother. Perhaps she didn't get fizzy drinks at home.

'Did you ask why *he'd* picked you up?'

'He didn't say anything.'

Jonathan leaned forward and took Christine's hand. 'Did the man hurt you in any way? Touch you?'

'No,' she said. 'He asked me lots of questions. It was like a test. I couldn't answer anything.'

'What sort of questions?'

'I don't know!' She was close to tears. 'I didn't understand what he wanted. I said I wanted to come home. Back to my mum's house. I didn't want to stay in the flat and I didn't want to go to Uncle Dennis and Auntie Grace's place. I just wanted to come home.'

Jen could hear Susan muttering beside her. Some sort of apology or prayer. She turned and saw that the woman was weeping. Jen pulled out a tissue and passed it across.

Christine was speaking again. 'The man said he couldn't take me to Mum's because he had to leave. He had important things to do. I could make myself at home until my uncle came. There was a bedroom if I wanted to go to sleep. More chocolate and more pop in the kitchen.'

'And did your uncle come?' Jonathan asked.

'Nobody came.' Christine was upset again now, reliving the panic, pleating the fabric of her top with trembling fingers. 'I was on my own and I didn't know what to do. I thought I'd go out and find someone, but I couldn't get out.' She looked up. 'He'd locked me in. The man had locked me in.'

'That must have been very scary,' Jonathan said. 'I'm so sorry you had to go through that.'

'I didn't know what would happen. I just wanted to be home with my mum.'

'How many nights did you stay there, Christine?'

She screwed up her face with the effort of trying to work that out. But panic was taking over again and she was struggling to concentrate.

'Did it get dark twice?'

'I was there for a very long time.' Jen thought she didn't really know. She'd been terrified and confused. Christine looked at them and her words came out as a wail of pain. 'Nobody came!'

'We were looking for you, really we were.' Now Jonathan seemed as upset as she was. 'We just couldn't find you.'

'I ran out of chocolate and pop and there was nothing to eat. There were people in the street below. Men smoking and laughing and I shouted to them, but I couldn't get the window open so they didn't hear me.'

'What happened next?'

'The man came back.' She was staring out at them, wanting them to understand now what she had been through.

'Were there people in the street when he came?'

'No,' she said. 'The street was quiet. Empty. It was still dark.'

'So, it was probably early in the morning . . . ' Now Jonathan seemed to be speaking to himself. 'And what did he do?'

271

'He took me into the car and we went driving again, and then we went for a walk.'

'What could you see on your walk? Could you see anything?'

'Cows,' she said. 'I don't like cows.'

'What else?'

'There were flowers. Yellow flowers. Then we came to some water and he said I should wait there. Somebody would come for me.' She looked over to Jen. 'And you did come for me.'

But not for hours, Jen thought. *If it was early morning when you left the flat and late afternoon when we arrived. It was drizzling and you didn't have a proper coat. You must have been desperate.* Jen turned to Jonathan. 'Can I just ask a question?'

He gave a little frown. 'Just one. She's been through so much.'

'The flat where you stayed, what sort of state was it in? Was it tidy? Or very messy?'

'It was quite messy after I'd been there,' Christine said. 'I didn't know where to put all my rubbish. But it was tidy when I got there.'

So, if Christine had been taken to the Braunton flat, it must have been trashed soon before Jen, Matthew and Ross had got there, between the man in the suit leaving with Christine and the detectives turning up to search it. Had they hoped Christine could provide them with the information that they ended up looking for in such a panic? Was that what all the questions had been about?

Jen would have liked to ask more about the questions, but she could see that Jonathan was right and Christine had been through enough. She wouldn't be able to focus on any further questions. Susan moved over and sat on the arm of her chair and put her arms around her daughter. 'Don't you worry, my lover. Nothing like that will ever happen to you again. You'll stay here with me and I'll keep you safe.'

★   ★   ★

Jen left Jonathan at the Shaplands' cottage and drove back to Barnstaple. Looking out over the river to the estuary she had a brief pang of homesickness for another river and another estuary. For Liverpool and the Mersey. A city full of life and action. But she knew it was too late for regrets. She parked at the police station and walked through the town to the cobbled alley at the back of St Cuthbert's church. The noise of traffic and voices faded. She made her way to the back of the old school and found the same woman sitting in reception.

'I need to speak to Caroline Preece.'

'I'm afraid she's with a group at the moment.'

'I'm a police officer. The police officer who spoke to her before.'

Two women sat on easy chairs in the lobby, chatting; they looked up when Jen said who she was. Curious and a little wary.

'Could you let Caroline know that I'm here?'

'I'm not sure.' The young receptionist looked anxious. 'She's running a session for women at the moment and she doesn't like to be disturbed when she's with a group.'

'One of her group was murdered. I think she'll see me. I'd like to speak to the rest of them too.'

Now the chatting women stared at Jen. She pulled round another chair so she was facing them, half blocking the corridor. The receptionist squeezed past and disappeared into a room. 'Did you know Simon Walden?' Jen asked one of the women.

'Yeah.' She was very thin. Lank blonde hair and a white top framed a colourless face. 'He was in my meditation class.'

'What did you make of him?'

She shrugged. 'You don't get much chance to talk if you're lying on your back with your eyes shut.'

'What about you?' Jen turned to the other woman, who was older, dressed like a Tory councillor. 'Did you know him?'

'Not really. I just bumped into him here. And a gang of us often go to the Woodyard cafe for lunch when we're finished and sometimes he'd be cooking.' A pause. 'You could tell he was happy there, in the kitchen.'

The receptionist emerged, a little flustered. 'Caroline's just finished her session. She's holding the group for you.'

'Terrific.' Jen was already on her feet. She took out two cards, handed them to the women. 'If you think of anything that might help, give me a ring.'

In the room, about a dozen women sat in a circle. Caroline stood up when Jen walked in. 'This is Detective Sergeant Rafferty, everyone. She'd like a word.'

This wasn't quite the approach Jen had been planning. She'd hoped to meet clients individually, get the gossip, ask if anyone had suddenly come into cash. These women were hardly likely to talk to her in front of their mates with a social worker listening in. But they were already fidgeting, wanting to leave for a fag or a coffee, so she'd have to go for it, or she'd lose their attention altogether.

'You'll have heard by now that Simon Walden, who was part of this community, was murdered on Monday afternoon.'

'You think one of us is a killer?' A tall, intense young woman. 'Just because we come to this place. Just because we've got mental health problems.'

'No. But Simon was a bit of a loner. You probably knew him as well as anyone.'

Silence and a wall of resentment. Jen knew when she was fighting a losing battle. 'Look, just think about it, will you? If anyone remembers anything unusual, even if it seems trivial, just give me a ring. I'm especially interested if you've noticed that any of your number has suddenly come into money. My name's Jen Rafferty and this is my direct number and email address.' She pinned her card onto a cork board next to the sort of motivational messages that her more hippy-dippy friends posted on Facebook. 'Please get in touch.'

The women filed out, leaving Caroline and Jen in the room.

'I'm sorry if they seemed rude,' Caroline said. 'Some of them haven't had good experiences with the police. And they have so little confidence. Aggression is often the only way they know to assert themselves.'

Jen nodded. She supposed that made sense. She'd been thought a moody, angry cow when she worked in Merseyside. Work had been the only place she could fight back.

'Was Simon's wallet stolen when he was killed?' Caroline asked. 'Is that why you asked about the money?'

'We think he had another source of income and it's possible that he was a victim of theft. Have you noticed any of your clients suddenly flashing the cash? New clothes? Suddenly moving into new accommodation?'

Caroline shook her head. 'Sorry.' She got to her feet and led Jen from the room. She was wearing smart black shoes with a small heel and they clicked on the wooden floor, marking a rhythm, as Jen followed. Outside in the corridor they paused. The chatting women had gone. Jen had the sense that there was something Caroline wanted to say. She waited.

'I was wondering about the funeral,' Caroline said. 'I'd like to do that for him, if there's nobody else. Organize it, I mean. Ed would help. Unless Simon's wife . . . '

Jen remembered her conversation with Kate in the big flat overlooking the Downs. The woman's memories of Simon as a schoolboy and a soldier. 'I'm not sure. Would you like me to ask?'

'Yes!' Caroline sounded pleased, grateful. 'I feel that I let Simon down in life. At least I could do something to help now.'

28

Matthew arrived back at the station from Lovacott just in time to grab a sandwich before Jason Cramer, the solicitor from Exeter, turned up. All the way back in the car, the detective had been thinking about Maurice's account of Grace Salter landing at the Braddick house, desperate, bruised and bleeding. He'd been trying to work out if there could be another explanation for what might have happened. He still found it hard to reconcile his memories of the upright, principled man he'd admired when he was a boy with this new image of a bully and a wife-beater.

Cramer arrived right on time. He was red-faced, jovial and had spent the morning golfing and his lunchtime in the clubhouse. Matthew hoped he hadn't driven from the golf course into Barnstaple after a liquid lunch. When they sat across his desk and started talking, however, he discovered that Cramer was quite sober and very sharp. Matthew decided that the jolly demeanour was a professional front, a ploy to make his opponents underestimate him.

'I saw that a man had been killed on the coast, but I didn't relate that incident to my client. Though perhaps I should have done, in the circumstance. How did you find out about my involvement with Mr Walden?'

'You'd sent a letter to one of his addresses.'

'So I did, arranging an appointment.'

'Can you tell me what he was consulting you about?'

'Not in any detail.' Cramer leaned back in his seat. 'Not because I'm being difficult, but because I wasn't clear in my own mind exactly what he wanted.'

'Had you met him?'

'No. We had two telephone conversations and then I wrote to confirm an appointment for him to come into the office in Exeter.'

'That was the letter we saw.' Matthew took the letter, still in its plastic transparent envelope, and placed it on the desk.

Cramer glanced at it. 'Yes.'

'Did he give you any idea why he'd chosen to come to you, rather than a more local solicitor?' This had been troubling Matthew since he'd first seen the letter. Walden didn't drive and the train journey along the Taw Valley between Barnstaple and Exeter was pretty but very slow.

Cramer shrugged. 'Word of mouth probably. That's how most people choose their lawyers.' He gave a little chortle. 'And we are very good.'

Matthew wasn't sure that Walden mixed with many people who would recommend a lawyer based in the county town. 'You must have some idea why he needed your advice, if you spoke twice on the phone.'

'Really, I'm not sure that I do. He came across as rather a strange chap. A bit intense. At first it seemed a straightforward matter of writing his will. He had no living relatives and he was considering a charitable donation.'

'Do you know where he thought he might leave his money?'

'To the Woodyard centre. I looked it up. It's run by a charitable trust. You're quite right, if he didn't have huge assets, it would have made more sense for him to consult a firm of local solicitors. I did suggest that and thought he'd taken my advice, because I didn't hear from him for a while. Then he called back and asked if he could come to see me. He was insistent and told me it was urgent. He said that he was having second thoughts about the will. And that there was another, related matter that he thought I could help with.' Cramer looked up and smiled. 'I explained our fee structure, thinking that might put him off. We do tend to charge a bit above the going rate. I suppose at that stage I had him down as a bit of a fantasist. North Devon seems to attract the weirdos, don't you think? Present company excluded of course.'

'What kind of fantasist?'

'There was nothing specific, but I sensed a paranoia. He came across as the sort who might be into odd conspiracy theories.' Cramer looked up sharply. 'But just because one's paranoid it doesn't mean they're not out to get you. Isn't that the saying, Inspector? It seems that I misjudged the man. Because somebody was certainly out to get him. And they clearly succeeded.'

There was a moment of silence. The image Matthew had created of Simon Walden seemed even more insubstantial, slippery, shifting with

279

every conversation about him. 'There's nothing else you can tell me about your conversation? Nothing that might help me to understand why he was so anxious to see you? What had made him paranoid? Any detail would be useful.'

'I'm sorry, Inspector. Nothing about the conversation. I was rather irritated that he'd demanded to speak directly to me without making the appointment through my secretary. It seemed that the paranoia had spread to his being reluctant to speak frankly on the telephone. Or perhaps Mr Walden was phoning in a place where he might be overheard or interrupted. There was some background noise.'

'What kind of background noise?'

Cramer shook his head, an indication of frustration. He would like to have helped. 'I'm sorry, Inspector. A murmur of voices. He could have been in the street or in a room. Beyond that, I couldn't tell.'

Matthew was about to let the man go, to thank him for his time and let him get back to his friends in the golf club, to catch up with them for gin and professional gossip, when Cramer put an envelope on the table. He had a sly grin, as if he was hoping to astonish and please.

'There is this, though. It arrived at the office on Tuesday morning.'

The day after Walden's body was found on the beach at Crow Point. He must have posted it on the morning of his death.

It had already been opened. Inside was a handwritten note and a building society cheque for £200,000 made payable to the solicitors' business name, Sandford and Marsh. The note read:

Please keep this safe for me. I'll explain when I see you.

'It's been a busy week,' Cramer said. 'I didn't get around to asking my secretary to put it into the clients' account. You do understand why I found Walden rather an unusual chap? Usually we have to fight to get money from our customers. They don't send us large cheques in the post.'

Matthew looked again at the cheque. It had been made out by the Devonshire Building Society.

★ ★ ★

When Cramer had left, Matthew sat for a moment at his desk. It was clear that Walden had experienced some sort of crisis in the weeks leading up to his death. Something that had led him to take the bus to Lovacott with Lucy Braddick and go back to Cramer to firm up an appointment. And to send a large cheque to the lawyer. Matthew wondered what might have triggered the strange behaviour. Was it possible that Walden could have experienced some kind of psychotic episode as the lawyer had implied? But the women in the Ilfracombe house hadn't mentioned that Walden had been less stable or rational in that time and Caroline was a professional. She would certainly have picked up on anything unusual or dangerous.

There was a knock on the office door and

Ross came in. He started speaking before he'd got into the room, eager, it seemed, to redeem himself in the eyes of his boss.

'I've found out where Walden kept his money.'

Well, about time! But I think I know that now already. Matthew said nothing. There was no need to rain on the man's parade and anyway, Ross wasn't in listening mode.

'Have you got the details there?'

'Of course.' Ross laid printed sheets on the desk between them and pulled up a chair. He was so close to Matthew that he could smell the gel on the slicked-up hair. 'He actually had two accounts, a current account with NatWest, where his wages from the Kingsley Hotel were paid and a savings account with — '

Now Matthew couldn't help himself. 'The Devonshire Building Society.'

'Yes! How did you know?' Ross looked so disappointed that Matthew almost felt sorry for him.

'I found out from Cramer, the solicitor.' Matthew hardly noticed Ross's reaction to the news. He was too busy asking questions of his own in his head. Why had Walden felt the need to send Cramer all that money? Was it just a coincidence that Walden had deposited the cash redeemed from his Bristol home and business in the building society where Dennis Salter had once been manager? Why had he decided to withdraw the whole amount? And what had happened to make him change his mind about leaving all his money to the Woodyard centre in his will?

29

Gaby had agreed to spend the afternoon with Caz and her father, Christopher Preece. Gaby still wasn't quite sure how she'd allowed herself to be talked into it. Caz had taken her aside after her appearance at the jazz cafe the night before.

'What are you doing tomorrow afternoon?'

'Nothing much. I don't work on Friday afternoons.'

'Will you come out with Dad and me?' Her voice had been strangely pleading and Gaby had thought Caz didn't ask many favours, so she'd go along with it, but it had seemed an odd request. 'He's suggesting a walk,' Caz said. 'A bar meal afterwards.'

'Don't you want some time on your own with him?' They'd looked across at Christopher who was standing at the bar, buying drinks for them all. Gaby had thought she wouldn't mind the man as a father.

'It's the anniversary of my mother's death,' Caz had said. 'I couldn't bear it if he got sentimental about her. He won't if you're there.'

Gaby had been made receptive by the response to her singing, and several glasses of cava. 'Okay,' she'd said. 'Why not?' She'd thought that at the very least she'd get a free meal.

Now, in the quiet house, drinking coffee together before leaving to meet the man, Caz started talking about her mother's death for the first time in any detail. Gaby just listened.

'I was away from home,' Caz said. 'A retreat for the weekend with the church youth group. We'd all left our phones behind. It was part of the deal. The guy running the centre came to my room and told me my mother was dead. No other details. Not how she'd died. A friend drove me home, but I told her not to come in. Dad was there, waiting for me. He told me my mother had killed herself, she'd hanged herself.' Caz paused for a moment. 'I lost it. Started yelling. Blaming him.'

Gaby found it hard to imagine Caz, usually so controlled and contained, losing it, but her friend was still talking.

'I said some hateful stuff: *I thought we were in this together. Working to keep Mum safe. How could you let this happen?* He'd tried to take me into his arms but I pushed him away. I know I should forgive him, but part of me can't quite.' She looked up at Gaby, her eyes very big behind her glasses. 'It's ten years, so perhaps we should make our peace. But I don't want to be on my own with him. Not on this particular day. Do you understand?'

Gaby wasn't quite sure that she *did* understand — weren't Christians supposed to forgive? — but she nodded anyway.

They met Christopher in the National Trust car park, with a view of the sea and the cliffs, as they'd arranged. Because it was so early in the season there were very few people, only a scattering of cars. There was a footpath leading

284

down the cliff to the beach and the air seemed very thin and light.

'This was my mother's favourite place,' Caz said.

Christopher was there before them, and was already out of his car, staring out towards the island of Lundy, apparently lost in thought. He seemed surprised to see Gaby; Caz couldn't have told him she'd be there and Gaby thought that was unkind. But Christopher covered his shock well.

'What do you both fancy?' he said. 'A walk over the headland? Then a pub supper?' He was dressed like a country gent in a checked shirt and round-necked jersey.

'Sure. Cool,' Caz said. Gaby thought she seemed cool too. To the point of iciness. Gaby still wasn't sure why Caz had wanted her there. As a witness to their reconciliation? To keep matters civil? Whatever the reason, she felt that, somehow, she was being used.

The cloud and fog had lifted and spring had returned again. The low sun turned everything warm and gold. Caz started talking as soon as they took the path onto the point. There was the honey smell of gorse.

'I have such wonderful memories of my mum here. She was well then, easy, relaxed. We came to the beach together while you were working, Dad.' Caz turned to Gaby. 'Dad was in full business mode then, doing his deals, developing his plans.' Christopher walked on in silence and Caz continued. 'I loved exploring the rock pools, and do you remember when she bought me a

285

little surfboard? I was so excited.'

'I do remember.'

'Do you, Dad? I wasn't sure you took much notice of what we were doing those days. You seemed to have other things on your mind.'

Again, Gaby wondered why Caz was being so cruel, and why she'd felt the need for an audience. 'Perhaps I should go back,' she said. 'Leave you two to it.'

'No!' Now Caz was being the bossy big sister again. 'Please, Gaby, I need you here for this.' They walked on for a while in silence. 'I have this picture of my mother,' Caz went on. 'I was in the sea on the beach down there and Mum was watching. She had bare feet and her trousers were rolled up to her knees, a loose white shirt and brown arms, and sunglasses hiding most of her face. She was laughing.'

Gaby looked at Christopher, waiting for him to respond, but his face was impassive, almost quizzical, as if he wasn't quite sure what was going on either. She felt so uncomfortable that it almost made her feel faint. There was something dizzying about the sound of the water way below them and the wheeling gulls.

When Christopher did speak to Caz at last, it was about Simon Walden.

'Have the police spoken to you again? Do you know if they're any closer to finding the killer?'

'I saw the red-haired woman, Sergeant Rafferty, at St Cuthbert's,' Caz said. 'She was asking if any of our clients had come into money. She didn't explain why.'

Gaby wondered if Caz would mention the key

she'd found in Simon's washing but she said nothing about that. In fact, Caz didn't have the chance to say anything else at all, because Christopher Preece stopped suddenly and turned towards his daughter, blocking her way along the path.

'You do know that everything I do is for you. That you matter more to me than anything in the world.' A pause. 'I'd do anything for you.'

Gaby watched with a mixture of fascination and extreme embarrassment. What was going on here? That sounded almost like a confession.

Christopher moved away from the footpath and sat on the grass. Gaby, who had never seen Preece as anything other than immaculately turned out, thought he'd get stains on his trousers. He turned to his daughter.

'I did love your mother. You do know that.'

'I know that you loved her at first,' Caz said. 'Before she was ill. Before it got hard.'

Another silence, broken by the sound of waves and the long call of gulls.

'Did you love her at the end then?' Christopher turned towards Caz and it sounded like genuine interest, not any kind of accusation. 'When she was so angry, and unpredictable?'

'She was my mother! Of course I loved her!' The words came out as a cry at the same pitch as the gulls' screech.

'Really? Is that true? Did you love Becca when she turned up at your school? What did she tell your teachers? That she needed to take you with her because it was the end of the world and you both needed to be here at the beach to be safe from the disaster? It didn't seem as if you loved her when I turned up to take her home. You looked horrified. Because she looked truly crazy, didn't she? With that wild hair and the velvet dress that she always wore when she was going through a crisis, weeping in the corner of the headmaster's office?'

Caz didn't answer. Neither of them was taking any notice of Gaby now. It was as if she wasn't there.

'I did try to help her, to understand what she was going through,' Christopher said at last. 'But you're right, it was too hard in the end. I escaped into my work. I told myself I needed to earn enough money to look after you both, to provide care for your mother.'

'And with other women?' Caz shouted at him. 'Was that how you escaped too?'

He looked as if he'd been slapped, but still he kept his voice even, so quiet that Gaby struggled to hear it above the sound of the gulls and the waves.

'What about you, Caroline? Didn't you have your own means of escape? At first it was the pony club and then it was the church. You always liked your form of entertainment to be organized. A hierarchy. A ritual so you didn't have to think too hard for yourself.'

Caroline seemed on the verge of tears, but Gaby couldn't bring herself to intervene. She felt a horrible fascination watching the encounter unfold.

'I'm sorry,' Christopher said. 'That was unfair. You were young and of course you wanted some structure in your life. There wasn't much at home and it wasn't your responsibility to look after Becca. That was down to me.' He paused. 'She would have been proud of what we've both achieved at St Cuthbert's, wouldn't she? And she'd have adored the Woodyard. All the terrific work that goes on there. The music and the theatre. The art. Don't you remember how she used to dance?'

'Yes, yes, she would.' Caz turned to face him. 'Is that why you got so involved in it?'

'Of course. You must have realized that.'

'We've never discussed it,' Caz said.

'I've tried to talk to you.'

'I suppose that's true. But I was always busy. A levels and then university.'

'I wondered why you came back to North Devon after university,' he said. 'You could have lived anywhere. It must have such dreadful memories for you.'

'Happy ones too, and this is where I remembered Mum best. Besides, I missed it when I was away from home.' Caz seemed suddenly to make up her mind about something. She turned to her father. She was still standing and looked down at him, accusing.

'Did you kill her?'

Gaby thought that was why she was here. As some kind of witness, in case Christopher was forced to admit to a ten-year-old crime.

'No! Of course not!' There was shock and immediate denial. 'Is that what you've been thinking? All these years?'

'I saw you,' Caz said, 'with a woman. You were

289

all over each other. In a bar in Barnstaple when you believed I was at home. I'd sneaked out to meet my friends.' A pause. More honesty. Gaby thought this was like one of the truth games she'd played as a student. 'You thought I was there keeping an eye on Mum, but she was sleeping and I couldn't face another night in.'

There was a moment of silence. 'She was called Sophie.' Christopher Preece spoke very quietly. 'I thought she was beautiful. She worked with me. She had a law degree and dealt with all our contracts. She was very bright, full of ideas.'

'You fell in love with her mind,' Caz said. Gaby thought that sounded like a cheap sneer.

'I fell in love. But there's no way I would have killed your mother to be with her.'

'Did Mum know? You weren't exactly discreet.'

He shook his head. 'I don't think so. She wasn't seeing any of her friends by then. Who would have told her? And I was very careful at home.' He turned to his daughter. 'I didn't want to hurt her.'

'It was convenient, though, with Mum suddenly off the scene. What happened? You were free to be with Sophie. Do you still see her? Do you hide her in the attic when I come to visit?'

'I think for Sophie, I was just a bit of fun. She didn't want a long-term relationship and she certainly wasn't ready for a teenage stepchild. Besides, I didn't think I deserved to be happy. I didn't kill your mother, but she died because of me.' He'd found a stray piece of long grass and was pulling the dead seeds off one by one. 'I tried to lose myself in the businesses again, to get the same buzz about the developments, but it didn't work. So, after a few years I got rid of them and set up St Cuthbert's, then I joined the campaign to found the Woodyard. I put all my money and my energy into that. Into providing a space where people who suffered like your mother could be safe.' He looked at her. 'I wanted you to be proud of me.'

There was a moment of silence.

'I am proud,' Caz said. 'Of course I am.'

Her father scrambled to his feet and started walking again. Caz joined him. Gaby hung back, then followed them. Her attention was caught by the light on a piece of the cliff face. There was lichen and some kind of prickly bush. Sea buckthorn? She was thinking how she might paint it. Then she realized that the couple ahead of her had started talking again.

'I met Simon Walden,' he said.

'I know you met him. You came to a couple of the Friday feasts.'

'Before that.' Again, it sounded as if he was about to confess to something. This whole conversation had the air of a confession. 'I wanted to meet him, before he moved in to number twenty. I asked him to the house.'

'Your house?'

Christopher nodded. 'I wanted to check that he was all right. He could have been a murderer. A madman.'

'Oh Dad, I'm grown-up. You didn't need to do that.'

'No, I realize that now.' A pause and there was another moment of apparent honesty. 'But I couldn't bear to lose you too.'

★ ★ ★

Later, they were in a thatched pub in a village just inland from the coast. There was a small campsite in an orchard across the road and in the summer, it would be heaving. Because it was still cheap, it attracted young people marking the end of exams, graduation, freedom. Gaby had brought a group of art school friends here soon after she'd started at the Woodyard. They'd all come from London and she'd basked in their admiration. 'But it's so *cool* here. And this is really where you're going to be working for the next three years?' How surprised they'd be to hear that she'd been caught up in a murder inquiry. They'd thought this was a place different from the city, a place where violence would never happen.

It was Friday night and Gaby thought it should just be she and Caz in Hope Street, cooking a meal, remembering the other Friday nights with Simon. She shouldn't be here making small talk with her boss. She felt trapped; she didn't have her car and they were miles from home. Even if she'd felt brave enough to opt out, she didn't have the cash for a taxi.

In the end, it was Caz who opted out. 'Do you mind if we don't eat here, Dad? Gaby and I would probably rather be alone this evening.'

Christopher seemed almost relieved. 'Sure,' he

said. But they made no move to leave and continued talking. Not about Caz's mother now, but about the Woodyard and Christopher's plans for the place. Gaby's attention strayed. She thought again of the sunlight on the cliff face, the colour of the lichen and the sharp, clear spikes of the buckthorn. She'd taken a photo and would have looked at the image on her phone but knew it would seem rude.

A couple of regulars, old men, sat in one corner. They'd been here when Gaby's friends from London had camped in the village. She'd wondered then if they were actors, employed by the landlord to provide a touch of authenticity for the visitors. Now, she thought they were just staking their claim to the place. It was still early and the pub was quiet and Christopher's voice provided a background white noise to her thoughts.

'I just want the police investigation to be over,' he was saying, 'so that the team can get back to work. We can't stand still. We're achieving so much there and the press will find out Walden's connection with the Woodyard soon. Reputation matters so much. It can make or break a project.'

Gaby shifted in her seat and caught her friend's eye. Caz got the message. 'Look, do you mind if we go, Dad? It's been quite a week.'

If he was disappointed, he didn't show it. He stood up. 'Of course. Keep in touch, though. Anytime.'

Caz stood too. 'Thanks. And I'm glad we had that talk.'

He nodded. 'And I meant what I said. I'd do

anything for you.' He put cash on the table and although he'd just ordered coffee, he left it, and walked with them out to the car park.

30

By the time Matthew left the police station, it was six o'clock. Jonathan might already be home, opening a beer, preparing a meal. Matthew had a vague memory that friends had been invited for dinner and thought perhaps he should put off seeing Dennis Salter until the following day. Jonathan was tolerant and understood the demands of his work, but this might be one step too far. Then he remembered Maurice Braddick's description of Grace Salter, battered and humiliated, and he texted Jonathan to say he'd probably be late and they should eat without him. As he started the car and began the now familiar drive to Lovacott, Matthew was honest enough to recognize that he probably wouldn't have enjoyed the dinner anyway. Meryl and Jo were Jonathan's friends, people he'd known for years. Matthew was only just being introduced to his husband's circle. These women were potters who worked in a craft collective on the edge of Exmoor. They were political activists, with a deep distrust of the police.

When he parked outside the house on the square, it was dark. In The Golden Fleece opposite, people were gathering for some sort of celebration. Young women in tight, skimpy dresses and older ones in long, sequinned frocks. Men in various forms of formal wear; one unexpectedly in a kilt. There was a lot of laughter. Someone walked in carrying a bunch of silver balloons with the number 60 printed on them. A birthday party then. The sort of party he would hate.

He knew he was allowing himself to be distracted because he didn't want to face the Salters, but he got out and rang the doorbell. A hall light was switched on; Matthew saw it through the long sash window next to the door, which was half opened by Grace. Her back-lit face was gaunt, all angles and planes. The grey eyes stared out at him.

'Yes?'

'It's Matthew Venn. I was hoping to speak to you.'

'Is it about Christine? We were so pleased she'd been found.' She didn't move to allow him inside, and there wasn't much expression in her voice, no real sense of pleasure. Matthew thought there was something of the robot about her.

'Is Dennis there?'

'No,' she said. 'He's away at a meeting. He's on the board of governors of the primary school here.'

'Perhaps I could come in and speak to you.'

'I'm not sure. He might be a while.' She stood her ground, pale, thin and angular, in the doorway.

'What is it, Grace? Does Dennis not like you to speak to people when he's not here? What is it he's frightened of?'

At that, she did let him in. They sat again in the large, formal room at the front of the house.

There was no heating and he felt a chill as he walked inside. From the kitchen there came the sound of canned laughter; she'd been listening to a comedy on the radio.

'Should I make you some tea?' She couldn't settle and was on her feet again.

'That would be lovely.' He felt cruel, because he seemed to be causing her such distress.

She stayed in the kitchen for such a long time that he thought she must be hiding from him. The radio was switched off and the house was suddenly silent. Then he heard muffled words and wondered if she was calling her husband on his mobile, leaving a message for him perhaps, asking him to come home. Covering her back in case Dennis was angry that she'd let Matthew in.

At last she came back with a tray. She poured tea and offered milk. He thought how different she was from Susan. They made unlikely sisters. All they had in common was their membership of the Brethren. He wasn't sure how he'd persuade Grace to talk. It had seemed easy in advance, driving down the narrow lanes from Barnstaple.

'Are you very close to your sister? As I remember, you were great friends when you were young.'

'We were. Great friends.' Grace shut her eyes for a moment.

'And now?'

'Things change,' she said, but she didn't look at him and she didn't explain.

'Do you often have Christine to stay with you?'

297

Now her eyes were open and she watched him, wary. 'Not as often as we used to.'

'Why is that?'

'We're older now. It's not so easy. Perhaps we like our own routines and rituals.'

'Whose idea was it that she should come to stay with you while my father's funeral was taking place?' Matthew paused. 'I would have thought you would both have wanted to be there. Dennis was a good friend to him.'

'Dennis was there,' Grace said. 'I was happy to stay with Christine. It wasn't one of her Woodyard days. I knew Susan would want to be with Dorothy.'

'So, it was your idea to invite her here?'

She didn't answer immediately. 'Really? I can't remember.' She looked across the table at him. 'I'm not sure that it does any good, asking all these questions. Christine is safe and nothing else matters.'

They stared at each other. Matthew wondered if her statement was a coded plea for him not to interfere. Perhaps she worried that Dennis would take out his fury at Matthew's intrusion on her. From across the square in The Golden Fleece came the bass thump of a disco beat.

'I need to ask about Dennis.' Matthew thought he should talk about this now, before the man returned from his meeting. 'I've heard rumours that he can't manage his anger, that, in the past, he hit you.'

'You know Dennis.' Her voice was flat and completely without emotion. 'He wouldn't do anything like that. He's a good man.'

'A good man, who allowed his learning-disabled niece to be kidnapped and held against her will for two nights.'

'He was distracted. Listening to the cricket. Then he got a call from one of the Brethren who needed him.'

'Are you sure?' Outside in the square, there was a high-pitched squeal of laughter. 'Are you sure he wasn't behind the kidnap? That he didn't know about it, at least?'

'Don't be ridiculous!'

Matthew remembered that Grace had taught before her marriage. His mother, very impressed, had told him that she'd ended up as a head teacher of an infants' school. She had spoken those words as if he was a silly four-year-old, with a mixture of sharp exasperation and amusement.

'Does he hit you, Grace? We can help you, find you somewhere else to live.'

'Don't be ridiculous!' she said again. 'You might have broken your mother's heart by leaving the Brethren, by setting up home with a man, but you must still know how things work. Some things aren't possible. I'm lucky to be married to Dennis. He needs me.' She looked directly at him and her voice was firm and strong. 'I want to stay married to Dennis.'

Matthew saw that she was telling the truth. She wanted to stay married. In her small world, being Dennis's wife gave her status, security, a sense of purpose that she'd relinquished when she'd stopped working. She'd probably convinced herself that she would reform him, or that his outbursts of temper were her fault. Or Dennis had convinced *her*, brainwashed her into submission. Matthew found it hard to believe that the night she'd turned up at the Braddicks' house, beaten and desperate, had been an isolated incident.

There was the sound of a key being turned in the lock and Dennis was there, already the centre of attention in the room, with his big lion's head and his mane of white hair. His arms once more wide open in welcome. A ritual that seemed meaningless now, a form of affectation. Matthew could tell that his own presence was no surprise. He'd been right; Grace had been on the phone to her husband to warn him.

'Matthew! How good to see you! What wonderful news that our niece is safely returned to her mother! A blessing and a joy.'

'She was locked up for two nights,' Matthew said. 'Imprisoned, we think, in a flat in Braunton. That's a very serious offence. Of course, we're still investigating.'

There was no immediate response to the mention of Braunton, but by now Matthew was thinking that the man wouldn't respond spontaneously to anything. His life was a performance and his face nothing but a mask. Now, he threw his arms wide again. 'Of course, you must!'

'She was released not very far from here, close to Lovacott pond,' Matthew went on. 'According to my mother, you used to have the Brethren summer picnics up there. You'll know the place.'

'Of course we do. Very well. What happy days

300

they were! Perhaps we should consider running those picnics again, Grace. Though I worry that so many of our community are elderly now that we might struggle to get everyone there.' Dennis gave a little laugh. 'And I'm not sure many of us could manage the three-legged race.'

'Oh, I don't think it's so far,' Matthew said, 'as the crow flies. If you have a map, I could show you.'

Dennis just smiled, as if he knew it wasn't a genuine offer.

Grace stood up and put the tea things on the tray. 'I'll leave you gentlemen to talk. If there's nothing else I can help you with, Matthew?' Now that her husband had returned she seemed more relaxed, almost girlish.

Matthew wondered if he'd got the relationship wrong, if Braddick had exaggerated the incident when she'd arrived at his house to speak to Maggie or misinterpreted it in some way. But at the door Grace stopped, because she couldn't turn the handle while she was carrying the tray, and he got up to open it for her. He saw that the hands clutching the tray were white and trembling. Perhaps she'd learned the art of disguise too.

Dennis Salter started talking as soon as Matthew returned to the table. 'Can I help you with anything, Matthew? Of course, we want the matter cleared up as soon as possible. The press sniffing round the Woodyard will affect the running of the place and our funding.'

'Simon Walden had a savings account with the Devonshire Building Society.' Matthew knew he was feeling his way now. He wasn't sure where these questions might lead.

'Did he? That's not unusual, you know. Not round here. It's a local institution and our customers are very loyal.'

'Walden wasn't local. Besides, he didn't seem to think his cash was safe there. He sent a cheque to his solicitor before he died.'

'Oh, it's as safe as houses, the Devonshire. No worries on that score. I keep my own savings there.'

'The Woodyard uses it too, I believe.' There was no answer and Matthew looked up. 'How long is it since you retired?'

'A couple of years. It's the best decision I made, leaving a bit early. Grace and I can spend some time together now.'

'And you're on the Woodyard board.' Matthew felt as if he was groping through a thick fog, without any destination in mind. 'You said you knew Christopher Preece.'

'Yes, though I'd come across him before of course. It's a small business community here in North Devon.' He looked up, gave one of his smiles. 'Jonathan Church knew all about Christopher's decision to invite me to join the board and he introduced me to the other members. He's the power behind the throne in that place. But of course, you'll know that. You know him well.'

The words had an edge that sounded almost like a threat. Perhaps it was just a snide dig about a relationship he considered abhorrent, but to Matthew it sounded more aggressive than that. An accusation.

'Where were you yesterday morning?' Matthew knew this was a ridiculous question, Salter couldn't have been the man driving Christine out to Lovacott pond — the woman would have recognized her own uncle — but it occurred to him that Dennis *could* have been the person who'd searched Walden's flat in Braunton.

For the first time, Salter seemed a little bothered. 'Why do you want to know?'

'We're following a number of enquiries. Just routine. I'm sure you understand. We have to ask everyone involved with Mr Walden the same questions.'

'But I wasn't involved with Mr Walden. As far as I know, I'd never even met him.' Salter had lost the easy, jovial tone and seemed almost rattled. 'And besides, wasn't he killed on Monday? You know I was at your father's funeral that day.'

'You are, however, linked to Christine Shapland and we believe the two crimes are connected.'

A silence followed, again broken by the sounds of the party across the square, the same relentless beat.

'I was here,' Salter said. 'Grace can confirm that. Shall I fetch her so you can ask her?'

'No need for that.' Because of course Grace would confirm it. She'd confirm anything that her husband said.

★ ★ ★

303

When Matthew arrived back at the coast, Jonathan's guests were still there. They were in the living room, one woman lounging on the sofa, the other on the floor, her elbow on a cushion. Jonathan was stretched in an armchair. They'd already eaten and the plates were still on the big table in the kitchen, the pans left to soak. The unwashed dishes irritated Matthew more than they should have done. The three had started on the whisky.

'I've asked Meryl and Jo to stay the night,' Jonathan said from the chair. 'It's such a trek home for them and it's the weekend.'

But not for me. I'll still be working. Matthew felt churlish. He'd hoped to have Jonathan to himself. He still wasn't used to sharing him, to being sociable. Matthew had few friends in the town and Jonathan's could have filled the Queen's Theatre in Barnstaple.

'We saved you some food,' Jonathan said. He slid from the chair and made his way, a little unsteadily, into the kitchen. Matthew followed him and watched as he lifted a casserole from the bottom of the oven and spooned food onto a plate. 'You must be starving.'

Matthew wanted to ask him about Salter and Preece, because Jonathan was an inside source. He'd know them better than anyone else attached to the investigation. But the doors had been left open and the women were still having a shouted conversation with Jonathan about some film that they were planning to see.

'Bring that in on a tray,' Jonathan said. 'Come and join us. I'll pour you some wine.'

Matthew had planned to stay where he was, to eat in peace in the kitchen with the door firmly shut, but he followed Jonathan back into the living room and sat in a chair by the fire. 'Yeah,' he said. 'Why not?'

31

On Saturday morning Matthew woke early. He'd gone to bed before the others and, wandering into the kitchen, he saw that they must have stayed up to load the dishwasher, clean the surfaces. Everything was tidy. He felt a ridiculous fizz of resentment, because there was no longer any excuse for his lingering anger. He made coffee and was just about to take a cup through to Jonathan when his husband came in, bare foot, wearing a short dressing gown.

'I'm sorry about last night,' Jonathan said. 'I should have realized the last thing you needed in the middle of an investigation was surprise sleepover guests, but you know how I get carried away when I've had a few glasses. And it was Friday. I hate spending Friday night on my own. It seems blasphemous somehow. Fridays should be shared and celebrated and I wasn't sure how long you'd be.' He nodded towards the bedroom where the women were sleeping. 'They won't be here for long. They need to be back home this morning. I promised to make them breakfast. Why don't you try to get back for lunch? They'll be gone by then.' He reached into the fridge for eggs and a bag of mushrooms.

'I doubt if I'll be able to get away.' Matthew realized that sounded churlish. 'But I'll try. It's a lovely idea.'

'So I'm forgiven then?' He sounded anxious,

as though these were more than trite words. The adopted boy, worried about being disowned, searching for a real place to belong.

'Of course.' Because Matthew always forgave him. He thought he'd forgive Jonathan anything.

★ ★ ★

The police station was quiet. Ross was already in and staring at his computer screen. Matthew had just settled at his desk when there was a phone call from Jen asking if it would be okay if she came in a bit later.

'I really need to spend a bit of time with the kids. Ella and Ben will forget what I look like soon and if I don't do some food shopping, they'll start eating each other.'

'Yeah, sure.' Matthew hoped this wasn't an excuse, that she hadn't had a wild night out and just staggered home, too rough to work.

'You got my message about Jonathan's conversation with Christine Shapland and the meeting with Caroline and the St Cuthbert's clients? I didn't get anything useful. Sorry.' Jen sounded sober enough.

'Yes.' Matthew had hoped to discuss Woodyard affairs with Jonathan the night before, to ask his opinion and share ideas. Matthew thought he should have done that instead of rushing out to Lovacott to talk to the Salters. Now he saw that had been a wasted trip. He hadn't thought it through sufficiently before challenging Grace and it had left him only frustrated and angry. And Salter had been warned that Matthew knew about his domestic life. He'd become even more closed and secretive.

'Thanks,' Jen said. 'I'll be in later. If anything important turns up, just give me a ring.'

Matthew replaced the receiver and wandered over to Ross's desk. 'Have we got anything from the CSIs after the sweep on Walden's flat in Braunton?'

If there were fingerprints not on the system, he'd be interested to know if there were any not yet identified. He'd love to find evidence that Salter had been in the flat. He pictured asking the man in to the station to have his prints taken, the powder on his fingers like a mark of shame. Salter wasn't a stupid man, though. If *he'd* carried out the search of the flat, he would surely have worn gloves. And Matthew needed to be careful — his antipathy towards the man was clouding his judgement. He had no real evidence that Salter had been abusive or that he was involved in any way in Walden's death.

'I was just about to chase it up.'

Matthew left it at that. He still felt guilty about losing patience with Ross in front of other officers; he hated losing control. Feeling trapped and restless, he went back to his glass corner of the open-plan space. He wished he could find a more tangible link between Dennis Salter and Simon Walden. There was no evidence even that the men had met. Salter's sly insinuation that Jonathan might be involved somehow with the investigation, that Matthew was in a position to protect his husband, made him think again that he should withdraw from the case. But it also made him angry. He knew, with a certainty that was almost religious, that Jonathan could not be involved in murder or kidnap.

I'll give it until the end of the weekend. If we haven't cracked it by then, I'll take it upstairs. I'll tell Joe Oldham that Jen Rafferty is perfectly able to manage this on her own.

Through the glass partition, he watched Ross making his phone calls. There was a sudden, silent mime of excitement, a fist in the air. Ross waved over to him and once more, Matthew paced across the space between the desks and computer terminals.

'What is it? Have you won the lottery?'

'Better than that!'

'Go on then, tell me.' Matthew wasn't a violent man but there were times when Ross provoked him so much that he wanted to slap him, and he was in a mood to lash out.

'The CSIs have come back with their first report on Walden's Braunton flat and they've found a couple of fingerprint matches. We have confirmation that Christine Shapland was there.'

'Ah, I think we already guessed that was the case.'

'There was another match, though.'

'Give me a name, Ross. Stop messing about.'

'You know they took the prints of the women from Hope Street for elimination?'

'I didn't know that but it makes sense. A good decision.'

'It seems that Gaby Henry had been in the Braunton flat. There's no mistake. They found her prints in the bathroom and on the chest of drawers in the bedroom.'

Matthew thought about that and wondered why he wasn't more surprised.

Back in his cubby hole, he phoned the landline in Hope Street. He thought nobody was in, or they were all in bed, and it would just go to answerphone but it was picked up. 'Caroline Preece.' She sounded tired and unwell.

'This is Matthew Venn. Could I speak to Gaby?'

'She's not here, Inspector. Gaby runs a watercolour class for the U3A in the Woodyard at lunchtime on a Saturday. Not her favourite thing but needs must. She left half an hour ago. She said she wanted to do some of her own work — there's a painting she was hoping to finish — before the students turned up.'

* * *

Matthew found Gaby alone in her studio at the Woodyard. She was working on the painting of Crow Point. 'Is it almost finished?' He couldn't see how she could make it any better. It had a luminous quality. Light behind cloud. He lost himself in the image for a moment.

'Yes.' She lowered her brush, but she couldn't stop looking at the painting. He still didn't have her full attention.

'You met Simon for coffee that morning, didn't you? At least, he had coffee and a bacon sandwich and you had herbal tea.'

She set her brush on the shelf at the bottom of the easel and now she did turn to face him.

310

'How did you find out?'

He shrugged. 'Routine policing.' Only then did he see the green jacket, hanging on a hook on the back of the door. 'A witness saw you together in the cafe in Braunton and described what you were wearing.' She didn't reply and he continued: 'Were you in a relationship?'

'I'm not sure that's what you'd call it.'

'But you visited his flat in Braunton. You knew he had somewhere else to live.'

She didn't answer.

'We know that you went there,' he said. 'We found your fingerprints.'

Still she stared back at Matthew in silence.

'Did you kill him?'

'No!' she said, provoked at last to respond. 'No! Of course not!'

'Well, you've done a pretty good job of hindering our investigation, and you admit to being in the area at the time.' A pause. 'You must see how it looks, Gaby. You lied.'

'No,' she said. 'I didn't lie. But I didn't tell you everything I knew.'

They stood, still staring at each other. 'I should take you to the police station,' he said, 'caution you, question you with a solicitor present.'

She pushed her hair away from her face. He saw she had a small smudge of paint on her cheek. It was green, the same shade as her coat.

'Please don't. I need this residency. I know I whine about it, but without it I'd never survive.'

'They can't sack you for helping the police with their enquiries.'

311

'We're not talking about Jonathan here! He's cool. We're talking the board of trustees. Local business people, mostly men, and politicians, again mostly men. They don't see the point of art. They'd rather rent out this space as a craft workshop to someone who wants to make cheap tat for the tourists. That way they could charge a fee. They're just looking for an excuse to get rid of me. They have been since I first arrived.'

Matthew pulled out a chair and took a seat. 'How long have you got before your students turn up?'

'An hour.'

'Make me some coffee then and we'll talk.'

They sat, the smell of the coffee overlaid with the smell of paint, turps and chalk dust.

'Why did you lie about Walden? Why pretend that you disliked him?'

'I told you, I didn't lie. I did dislike him at first. That wasn't a pretence. I hated him in the house. His disturbing presence. His brooding.' She rubbed paint-stained fingers around the rim of her mug.

'But you found him attractive? You admitted that the last time we talked.'

'I found him interesting,' she conceded.

'Why hide your relationship from me? From your friends?'

She took a while to find the words. 'I was embarrassed. I'd been so opposed to him staying in the house and then, there I was, dreaming about him. Thinking about him. A former soldier and alcoholic, who knew nothing about art.' She paused again. 'And it was exciting, you know,

312

keeping it secret.' Matthew understood embarrassment. The fear of looking foolish had haunted him all his adult life. It had taken Jonathan to start curing him of that.

'All the same, you should have told us. This is a murder inquiry. Your embarrassment isn't important. Finding the killer is.'

'Once I started lying, I couldn't stop. I was worried you'd think I'd murdered him.'

Matthew looked at her over the rim of his mug. 'Did you?'

'No! I just kept the relationship secret. From you and from my friends.'

'What did Simon think about that? It might have seemed as if you were ashamed of getting together with him.' Surely, Matthew thought, that would make a man resentful.

'Nah.' She gave a fond smile. 'Simon preferred it that way. He said he had so many secrets, what was one more?'

'What do you think he meant by that?'

'I don't know.' Gaby paused for a moment and seemed lost in thought. 'One day, when we were in the Braunton flat a couple of weeks ago, he started talking about secrets. I already knew he'd been married, but this was something else, something different. He seemed preoccupied and I could tell something was troubling him. I asked what was wrong. I thought for a moment that he was going to tell me; I had the sense that he wanted to share whatever was on his mind. But then he just laughed. He said if he told me everything, there would be no secrets any more. And he didn't know what that would feel like. It

313

was the secrets which defined him. He wouldn't feel the same man. It would be like having no guilt.'

Matthew thought about that. 'And he gave you no idea at all what was troubling him?'

'No. He said he'd have to sort it out. He seemed almost pleased about that. He said it was his responsibility. His chance to make amends.'

Matthew drank the rest of his coffee. It was clear that there'd been some drama in the last weeks of Simon Walden's life. He'd made a discovery that would lead to his death. In that time, he'd started travelling to Lovacott, he'd sent his money to the solicitor in Exeter and pressed for a meeting with him. Walden's life at the time had been centred around St Cuthbert's, the Woodyard and the Ilfracombe house. It seemed as if he only used the Braunton flat to meet Gaby.

'And you have no idea what he meant by that?'

Gaby shook her head. 'I confided a lot in him, but he still wasn't ready to share personal stuff with me. Or perhaps he liked being mysterious.'

'How did the relationship start?' Matthew still couldn't quite imagine these two individuals as lovers. But then, who would have ever imagined him and Jonathan together?

'It was that night that I told you about, the Friday when he'd been cooking. When Caz went to bed I knocked at his bedroom door and went into his room. I'd been drinking. I wanted to run my fingers over his cheekbones, the muscles in his back.' She looked up at him and grinned. 'That was what I told myself. That it was all about understanding the bone structure, for my art, to inform the painting I was making.'

'You became lovers.'

'Not that night. That night we just lay on his bed and talked.'

'But he didn't share his secrets?' Matthew could picture them on the narrow bed, whispering, until noises in the street told them it was nearly morning and that Gaby should leave for her own room.

'No. Like I said, I did most of the talking. About the places I'd lived in London, about my mother and her bullying, bastard men, about never feeling I quite belonged. Simon listened. He was a brilliant listener.'

'When did he take you to his flat in Braunton?'

'Not until recently. About three weeks ago. Then we went a few times.' Gaby smiled, challenging him to disapprove. 'Making love in the afternoon when he didn't have a session at the Woodyard and I wasn't teaching.'

'Did Simon explain why he had the place, why he'd felt the need to keep it secret from the rest of you, from the people, like Caroline at St Cuthbert's, who'd helped him?'

'No, though I did ask him why he'd come to live with us when he had his own place.' Gaby seemed pleased to talk now. It must have been hard, Matthew thought, to grieve for Walden in private. In secret. Even if she'd been the one to stab him in a rage of jealousy or rejection. Because though Matthew liked the woman, he couldn't rule her out as the killer.

She continued:

'He said that isolation had been killing him. He brooded. Felt as if he was drowning in guilt. If he'd stayed on his own much longer, he'd have drunk himself to death. He needed the support of the St Cuthbert's group therapy and he didn't think Caroline would be so sympathetic if he had his own place and a bit of money behind him.' She gave another crooked smile. 'I told him *I* wouldn't have been very sympathetic either.'

'Did he ever talk about his finances? We've discovered that he had considerable savings, but he seems to have distrusted the building society where he kept his cash. Or it's possible that he had plans for it.'

She shook her head. 'We weren't on those sorts of terms. We were never going to be sharing bank accounts or dragging each other round IKEA. It was fleeting, intense and we both knew it wouldn't last. Neither of us would have suited domestic bliss. Soon, it would burn itself out.'

'Do you know why he took the bus to Lovacott the last couple of weeks before he died? We think he was planning to meet someone there. Was that you?'

'No! Are you saying he had another woman?'

'There's no evidence of that. Would you have been surprised?'

She gave a sad, little laugh. 'I'd have been hurt, jealous, but no, not surprised. I don't think anything he did would have surprised me.'

'Can you talk me through the day of his death?'

She leaned back in her chair, so the light from the long window caught her face and he saw how tired she looked, how much older. 'As you said, we met for coffee. I was free that morning and I knew he wasn't planning to go in to the Woodyard, so I thought we'd go back to his flat and I'd get to spend some more time with him.'

Matthew interrupted. 'Did you travel together to Braunton?'

She shook her head. 'No, he got an early bus and I came in later. He said he had things to see to. Besides . . . ' Her voice tailed away.

He completed the sentence. 'Besides, you had to keep up the pretence that you hated each other. It was all part of the drama.'

'Yeah, something like that. Now, it seems like a kind of madness. Pointless. We wasted time we could have had together.'

'So, what happened that day after you met for coffee?' Matthew was aware of time passing. Soon eager middle-aged students would be knocking on the studio door demanding Gaby's time.

'I drove out to the coast and spent time looking for the right landscape to paint. I did some drawings and took photos, lost track of time. I had a group at the Woodyard in the evening and only just got back in time to meet Caz in the cafe for an early supper before the students turned up.' She looked up. 'I didn't see Simon again after that meeting in the cafe. I didn't drive with him to Crow Point and I didn't kill him.'

Matthew wanted to believe her. He thought Marston would have seen her car if she'd driven Walden to the point. Which didn't mean she hadn't parked elsewhere and walked around the shore to meet her lover. She could have killed him then. 'What about Simon? What were his plans?'

'Oh, he was going to save the world. That was the impression he gave. At last the big project, the stuff that had been troubling him, was coming to a climax. *Perhaps at last I'll be able to get rid of this albatross round my neck, Gabs. At last, I'll be able to face the world again.* But he didn't say anything specific. Nothing useful.'

There was a silence, and when she spoke, her words came out as a confession. 'I loved him, you know. It was crazy and it would never have worked, but I really loved him.'

32

Maurice Braddick liked Saturdays. Often, he and Lucy went into Barnstaple and did a bit of shopping, had coffee in one of the cafes that had sprung up all over the place, and sometimes they walked along the river to the park. They'd sit in the sun there, eating ice cream, watching the kiddies in the playground. They'd done the same when Maggie was alive, but Maggie had always been more energetic than him and sometimes she'd taken Lucy swimming. Maurice would sit on the raked seats, watching the pool, breathing in the heat and the chlorine, while the two women splashed. It had been their time and they'd loved it.

Lucy was in her bedroom getting ready and he went to call her, to tell her it was time to go. He stood on the landing and heard her chuntering to herself. Sometimes she did that. The social worker called it self-talk, but Lucy just said she was speaking to her pretend friends, making up a story. This sounded like an exciting story and Maurice could tell that Luce had made herself the centre of the action. She always liked a bit of drama; she'd loved being in the school plays when she was a kiddie. He and Maggie had sat in the front row cheering, not caring what the other parents made of it.

In the car on the way into town, he tried to talk to Lucy about Christine Shapland. 'You see, maid, you've got to be careful. She was lucky. They found her just in time. But there are bad people out there. So, you know all the rules, don't you? You don't go with anyone, even if it's someone you know. You stick close to me.'

But he could tell that Lucy wasn't really listening. She was nodding away to the music on the car radio. She loved Radio 2.

It was sunny again, breezy. He'd washed both their sheets before they set off. Maggie had changed sheets every week but he didn't bother so often. Today, though, had been a perfect drying day, and Lucy had helped him hang them out. They'd struggled to pin them on the line; the wind had caught the wet cotton, twisting it out of shape, almost wrapping around Lucy like a shroud, before they could get the pegs fixed.

'Look at us, Luce. What are we like? Two crocks.' Because he didn't like to admit it, but his arthritis was playing up, pulling at his shoulder and causing pain in his hip. His doctor had said they could put him on the list for a new hip, but Maurice had said it wasn't worth it. Who'd look after Lucy if he was in hospital?

He parked in one of the little side streets he knew and they walked together towards the town centre, slowly, because Lucy never walked quickly and because he was still getting that stabbing pain.

They went for coffee first. They'd drive to the big supermarket on the edge of the town for the main shop on their way home. There was a cafe that looked out over the river, where the bus station had been before it had moved, and they sat there, at their favourite table. Maurice wondered if all old people did this: if they saw the shadows of the past wherever they went. Past places and past people. He still thought of Lucy as a teenager. Then he thought he'd rather dream about the past than the future, because he didn't know what would happen to Lucy when he died. He'd need to sort it out — he'd promised Maggie that he would — but he didn't know where to start. When all this business at the Woodyard was over, he'd talk to Jonathan and see what he suggested.

Lucy's eye was caught by the chocolate cake in the glass cabinet and he bought her a slice. He thought she deserved it, her friend going missing, the man she knew from the bus having been murdered. And anyway, he could deny her nothing. The cafe was getting busy; Lucy smiled and waved at everyone as they came in as if they were old friends.

Back out in the street, they wandered past the shops. Lucy liked looking at the clothes; Maurice thought she was like one of those birds that were attracted by bright and shiny things. She loved deep colours and wild patterns. Occasionally they bumped into people they knew and stopped to chat.

They were near the end of the high street on their way back to the car when Maurice saw Pam, the woman who used to work in the butcher's shop where he'd spent his working life. Again, he found himself slipping back into the past, sharing memories and anecdotes. Pam was elderly now, a widow, but just as fierce and funny. She'd kept in touch with most of his colleagues and brought him up to date; some had died, some were in care homes, some were fighting fit and full of life.

'It's just a lottery, what happens to us, isn't it?' she said. 'Look at your Maggie. She was always the healthy one, you'd have thought she'd go on forever.'

That was when he realized that Lucy was missing. He turned, expecting to see her staring into nearby shop windows, thinking that she'd come back to him with a wish list, that wheedling voice. *Dad, look at that scarf, those shoes.*

But there was no sign of her. She must have wandered farther away, bored listening to the two friends talking about people she'd never met. Maurice had lost track of time.

'Where's Lucy?' It was hard not to blame Pam for distracting him, though he knew he was really the one to blame. 'Did you see where she went?'

Pam shook her head. She'd been as much caught up in the conversation as him, as lonely, perhaps, as he was.

Maurice felt himself breathless with panic. 'You stay here, in case she comes back. I'll look for her.'

'All right, my lover.' Her voice easy and indulgent. 'You know she'll be around some-where. What can happen to her here?'

In that moment, Maurice thought he hated the woman. She had no idea of the danger Lucy could be in. He moved as fast as he could down the street, pushing open shop doors, shouting to the people inside, not caring that he looked like some sort of madman. Then there she was. He saw the dark hair and the purple cardigan. She was staring into the window of a jeweller's, lusting no doubt over a silver pendant or a ring with a coloured stone.

'Lucy,' he said. 'Maid, you've got no idea how scared I've been. Don't ever go off like that again.'

The woman turned and smiled. She'd heard the anxiety in his voice but not his exact words. It wasn't Lucy. It was a stranger who looked nothing like her at all.

★ ★ ★

Later, back in his own home, talking to Matthew Venn, Jonathan's man, he couldn't explain what might have happened. 'She was there with me, and then she just disappeared.'

'You're sure Lucy was with you when you started talking to Pam?' Venn was patient. He didn't ask Maurice to hurry, or make him feel bad about what had happened, but Maurice was aware of time passing, the clock ticking. The longer these questions took, the less time there'd be to find Lucy before it got dark.

He tried to focus on the question, to be honest. 'I saw Pam across the road and I hurried over to catch her before she moved on. She hadn't noticed me, you see, until I went over to her. I didn't want to miss her.' He didn't say that he'd always had a bit of a crush on Pam, even when he was married. Nothing said between them, and certainly nothing done, but it had been there all the same. A connection. 'Perhaps I left Lucy behind then. I thought she'd followed me, but she might have been looking at the shops and not seen me go.'

'What would she have done, do you think? If she'd turned around and seen you weren't there?'

'I don't know.' Now Maurice was nearly in tears and struggling to hold himself together. 'I always *have* been there for her.'

'Does she have a mobile phone?'

'Yes, I got her one a while ago. She'd been mithering for one. She loves it, texts me when she gets on the bus on her way home and uses it to keep in touch with some of her pals. But she didn't have it with her today. I told her not to bring it. I told her she could give her full attention to her old dad for a change.'

'Can I see it?'

'Of course. It'll be in her room. I'll fetch it.'

Maurice stood at the bedroom door for a moment before going in. He remembered Lucy chatting away to herself before they'd set out and thought he might lose his mind completely if he didn't get her back soon. He took the phone back to the policeman and handed it over.

'You find her,' he said. 'Just you find her.'

33

Jen Rafferty had been enjoying her time at home with the kids. When they'd been younger she'd found it hard to deal with them after she'd been away at work for a while. She'd thought she *should* be delighted to see them again, but it had never been like that. She knew a good mother would miss her children and love their company, but each time she returned to the house, the noise and the chaos had come as a shock. It had taken her a while to get used to the fights, the rolling around on the floor, the hyper behaviour and disobedience. She'd known they were playing up, punishing her perhaps for her absence, for taking them away from their father. In the end, the children would calm down, become easier to manage again, but those first few hours of renewed contact had been a nightmare. At work she was in control. At home, it had seemed, she had no control at all.

Now, it was easier. If she was honest, it was easier because she didn't see so much of the children. They were more independent. They spent a lot of time in their rooms, sleeping until midday if left to themselves. She wasn't so overwhelmed by their demands. They were better company too. She could share jokes with them; they found the same things funny. She liked them as people as well as loving them because they were her children.

Today she prised them out of bed by ten and drove them to Instow for brunch. A treat. The tiny cafe did the best sausage sandwiches in the world, and the very best coffee. Instow was where the two rivers met and across the wide stretch of water she could see Crow Point, where the dead man had been found. The view gave her a new perspective, not just on the landscape but the case. Although she'd determined to give Ella and Ben her full attention, she found her mind wandering back to that first afternoon of the investigation, to the assumptions they'd made about Walden, the complexities that had since emerged.

It was midday and she'd just arrived home when her phone rang. Matthew.

'You're not going to tell me you want me there yet, boss.' She was still relaxed after the meal, after larking around with her kids. 'I was thinking I'd spend an hour taming my garden before coming in to the station.'

'We've got another missing person. Lucy Braddick. She seems to have disappeared into thin air. Barnstaple high street full of shoppers on a Saturday morning.' There was something close to despair in his voice. 'Maurice is in bits.'

'Where do you need me?' Not joking now.

'I'm with Maurice in Lovacott. I thought it was best to bring him back here. Ross has got a recent photo. Can you join him in the town centre? Someone must have seen her. She'd stand out, be noticed. Talk to shopkeepers and passers-by.'

The kids had already disappeared back to their

respective bedrooms. She shouted up that she had to go in to work. They called back but seemed unbothered.

★   ★   ★

It was lunchtime in the town. Jen ended up walking from home, because she thought it would be quicker and she could look out for Lucy on the way. According to Matthew, Lucy and Maurice had planned to go to the park for ice cream when they'd finished shopping, and if she'd lost sight of her dad, the woman might have continued on her way there alone.

The breeze blew the river into little waves and the smell of mud and saltmarsh came to her across the grass and the freshly dug flower beds. A fusion of the wild and the tamed. Jen thought that summed up this part of Devon. She stood for a moment, looking into the playground where parents were pushing children on swings, or staring at their phones while their offspring amused themselves. That would have been her, she thought. The bad parent. Today it was mostly dads. Maybe they were single fathers, spending time with their kids. Or just thoughtful men, giving the mothers a couple of hours to catch their breath. There must be some thoughtful men in the world.

No Lucy.

Jen walked on faster, taking the path that ran alongside the river. Past the museum and across the road to the high street. She phoned Ross.

'Any news?'

327

'Nothing. Where are you?'

'Just coming into the high street. I checked out Rock Park on the way, but there was no sign of Lucy there.' She was walking so fast that she had to catch her breath.

'I'll meet you.'

She saw him before he noticed her. He was handing out photos, but as if he was in a rush, not taking time to chat to the shoppers. He'd be a better detective if he learned some patience, but she'd probably been the same when she was younger. Needing action. Desperate for progress.

'I've done the high street,' he said. 'A few people recognized her. They'd seen her with her dad, but nobody saw her on her own. And there was no sign of a scuffle.'

'So, what do we think happened?' Jen was remembering a time when Ella was three, just refusing the pushchair. They'd been in a busy shop in Liverpool, and the girl had disappeared, vanished as if she'd been part of a magician's trick. Jen had been frantic, imagining her daughter snatched and terrified, imagining too her husband's reaction to the lack of care. Because it would have been her fault and she'd have to pay. A shop assistant had found the girl in one of the changing rooms, wearing a hat she'd taken from one of the shelves. It was so big that it almost hid her face, she was standing on a chair and staring into the mirror. There'd been a rush of relief, and Jen had been crying and laughing at the same. She'd never told Robbie. It would just have been another excuse for his fury.

Nobody had seen Ella go, although she'd been wearing a bright green dress and she had a mass of red curls. People's attention had been focussed on shopping or on talking to their friends. Now, Jen thought, an elephant could wander down the middle of Barnstaple high street and not everyone would notice.

'I don't know,' Ross said. 'Maybe it was someone she knew, someone she trusted . . . '

'Maybe.' Jen wasn't so sure. She didn't know enough about people with Down's syndrome, but from what Matthew had said, Lucy had been sparky, confident, kind. If someone had asked for her help, maybe she'd have gone with them, even if it had been a stranger. 'Can you check out CCTV for the street? I'll give it one more canvass. I might pick up some people you missed.'

And I'll give them time to think, not make them hurry or panic.

He nodded. She saw him disappear into a bakery, and thought he'd be getting his lunch before going back to the police station. That made her think about Lucy; she was a big woman, who clearly liked her food. Walden had befriended her with sweets when they'd started chatting on the bus. She might have become distracted, for example, by the offer of a free sample of cake or biscuit, lured away from the crowds on the main street.

She walked back up the street, pulling people into conversation about Lucy, describing her clothes, making her real for them. 'You might have seen her around with her dad. She's here most Saturdays. She goes to the day centre at the

Woodyard. A lovely smile. She's gone missing and her dad's in a dreadful state. You can imagine.'

There was only one sighting of Lucy on her own. The owner of a gift shop, just across the street from where Maurice had been chatting to Pam, had seen her.

'She was out on the pavement, looking in at the window display. It is lovely, though I say so myself. I waved to her and she waved back. It was quiet, nobody else in the shop. It's that time of year, isn't it, between Christmas and Easter. There's always a bit of a lull. No, I didn't see her talking to anyone.' The woman was happy to chat. As she'd said, the shop was quiet. She must be bored.

'You didn't see anyone approaching her? Or looking in at the window at the same time as she was?'

The woman thought for a moment. 'She turned away. I think someone tripped on the pavement and she turned around to watch, or to help. I didn't see her after that.'

'Did you see the person who tripped?'

'Not really. Not in any detail. There was just a bit of a crowd suddenly, someone talked about calling an ambulance. You know how it is, when there's a bit of a drama. People start staring. The shop door was open so I could hear a little bit of what was said.'

'You didn't go out to see what was going on?' Because Jen thought this woman would want to see. If she was as bored as she seemed, she'd surely be curious.

'No, I was just on my way to see if I could help when the phone rang at the back. A customer with an order. By the time I came into the shop again, everything was back to normal. The ambulance never turned up, so I suppose the person who fell hadn't really hurt themselves.'

Jen swore in her head, using words that would have made even Ben blush. If the woman had been in a position to see, she would have made a great witness. Jen hoped the incident had been captured on CCTV. At least they'd know where to start looking.

'You must have seen who fell, though? Was it a man or a woman?'

'I'm sorry, I didn't really see. By the time I'd got to the door, people were standing between me and the person lying on the pavement.' She paused. 'I think it was a man. I got a glimpse of jeans and trainers. But really I can't be sure.'

'Was Lucy still there then?'

'Yes! She was there, on the edge of the group, watching. I saw her just before the phone rang.'

'And when you got back into the shop?'

'I told you. Everyone had gone then. Nobody was there.'

Back on the pavement, Jen had more questions for the passers-by. 'Did you see someone fall earlier today? A woman with Down's syndrome helping them up?'

But the incident had happened nearly two hours before and these were new shoppers just passing through. Jen questioned the assistants in the shops nearby. They hadn't seen anyone fall.

In the police station, there was an air of confusion. Vulnerable adults were sometimes targeted by sexual predators, bullies, weak and pathetic people who needed to control. But those victims were usually alone, lonely, known to social services and the police because of their isolation and vulnerability. Christine Shapland and Lucy Braddick were well cared for; they lived with their families. Christine had not been raped or assaulted. There seemed no motive for either kidnap.

Matthew was back in Barnstaple. He'd left Maurice Braddick in the care of a neighbour. Now, he stood in front of the team, trying to make sense of it all. Jen listened from the back.

'We know that Christine Shapland's abductor asked her questions, lots of questions,' Matthew said. 'But that doesn't help us much, because she couldn't understand what he wanted. Or he freaked her out so much that she was too scared to listen properly. Perhaps that tells us he wasn't used to dealing with people with a learning disability. He was impatient.' He paused and Jen saw that he was trying to gather his thoughts. 'We know too that there's a link between the abductions and the Walden murder because Christine was held in the man's flat in Braunton. The flat's sealed off and crawling with CSIs so Lucy won't be taken there. I hope someone's got an idea about what might be going on here, because I don't. And Maurice Braddick, her father, is going through hell.'

He looked out at them, wanting them to know that this was important, more important perhaps than finding Walden's killer.

'There's another connection between this abduction and our murder victim. Walden sat beside Lucy on the bus to Lovacott in the week before he died. I'm still not sure how that might be relevant. Anyone got any ideas?'

Jen stuck up her hand. 'Could Walden have told Lucy something that might implicate the killer in the murder?'

There was a moment of silence and Jen felt the room waiting for the boss's response. They were like kids in a classroom not sure of their friend's answer and unwilling to commit themselves.

'That might work,' Matthew said. 'But why snatch Christine too?'

Another silence. He looked around the room and then continued:

'In the end, motive is less important than finding Lucy. We've got people checking the countryside around Lovacott pond, where Christine was released, but they've found nothing yet. Ross, you've been looking at CCTV covering the high street. Can you help us out here? Give us something to work on?' Jen thought she'd never heard him sound so desperate.

'Nothing yet.'

'I was talking to a shopkeeper,' Jen said. 'She saw Lucy looking in at her window display. Apparently, someone tripped on the pavement. I wonder if that could have been a deliberate diversion. Could Lucy have been taken while everyone else's attention was on the person who'd fallen? Or if it was someone Lucy knew, perhaps she could have been persuaded to help them to a nearby car.'

Matthew nodded. 'Can you see if there's a CCTV recording of the accident, Ross? At least it's somewhere to start.' He paused. 'We need to check the alibis of all the people involved in the investigation — the women in Hope Street, the Salters, Christopher Preece.'

'What about the Marstons, the couple in the toll keeper's cottage?'

'Yeah, them too. I know Gaby Henry was in Barnstaple this morning. I went to see her in the Woodyard about her relationship with Walden. The timing would have been tight but she could have been involved.'

Jen stuck up her hand again. 'I wonder if I should go back and talk to Christine Shapland? She'll have had another night to calm down a bit and she might have some snippets of information that could help. She and Lucy were friends. If Lucy was scared or worried about something, she might know.'

'Yeah,' Matthew said. 'Sure. Good idea.'

This time, he didn't suggest that Jonathan go with her. Jen wondered if he'd heard the muttering around the station. Gossip had been spreading. Word was that Matthew was far too close to the case, even that Jonathan should be considered a suspect. After all, he'd been on the coast when Walden had died and he knew both of the women who'd been abducted. He was right at the heart of the investigation.

34

Matthew sent as many officers as he could spare back into the town, to ask questions and to show Lucy's picture. He told Ross to go with them. The DC had been scanning the CCTV for hours and would have lost concentration. It would need a fresh pair of eyes and someone with more patience than Ross to pick up any detail. He knew he'd have to repair his relationship with the man, but this wasn't the time.

Matthew had already been on the phone to Jonathan. 'Can you think where Lucy might be? I've phoned Rosa's family and they haven't seen her, but is there another friend who lives close to the town centre? If she suddenly found herself alone, Lucy might have looked elsewhere for help.'

He'd called Jonathan for moral support as much as for practical information. He couldn't believe in the coincidence of Lucy disappearing too; he didn't expect her to be at a friend's house waiting to be found. Jonathan had always been there for him, ready with sympathy and encouragement, in the middle of difficult cases. But this time, *he'd* been the person who needed to provide the support. Even over the phone, he could sense Jonathan's shock, his horror.

'This can't be seen as your fault,' Matthew said. 'It had nothing to do with the Woodyard. Lucy was out with her father.'

'It's not about that! She's brilliant! Funny and confident. And I've known her for years.' Only then did Jonathan answer Matthew's question. 'She might go to the Woodyard. That might be her safe place. I'll go there now, get all the staff out. We'll start a search.' He was always better when he had something positive to do.

In contrast, Matthew locked himself in his tiny office and tried to think his way through Lucy's disappearance, to shut out the background noise of his own suspicion and anxiety. This wasn't about him; it was about Lucy Braddick. He couldn't help re-running the events of the previous few days in his mind, though, picking at his guilt like a scab. Had his visit to Lovacott and the Salters the night before triggered Lucy's abduction? The decision to go there had been more about his own ego than the investigation, about setting the ghosts of his childhood to rest. Should he have known that Lucy might be in danger? Then he thought this self-indulgent wallowing in endless possibilities would do no good and he got back on the phone.

Christopher Preece answered immediately. 'Preece.'

'Could you tell me where you were at about eleven this morning?'

'I'm sorry?'

'Another woman with a learning disability has disappeared. I'm asking everyone who had even a tenuous link to Simon Walden or the Woodyard to account for their movements.'

'I was here,' Preece said. 'On my own.'

'You won't mind if I send an officer to look at

336

your premises? Take a statement.' Matthew, who was usually so measured and polite, didn't care now about offending the businessman, Caroline's father.

'Of course not, if you think it'll help.' There was a pause. 'Who is it that's gone missing?'

'Lucy Braddick, the woman whom Simon Walden seems to have befriended in the last days of his life.'

Another silence. 'I'll stay in until your officer gets here,' Preece said. 'And do get in touch if there's anything else I can do.'

Matthew's next call was to Hope Street. There was no reply and he left a brief message. He'd ask Jonathan to check if Gaby was still at the Woodyard, working in her studio. He called Caroline's mobile number. She answered almost immediately, giving her name.

'Could you tell me where you've been this morning?' Matthew realized he must sound officious, abrupt, but he could sense the minutes passing and Maurice's voice still haunted him.

'I've been in St Cuthbert's since about ten.'

'The centre is open at a weekend?'

'I'm not in the centre,' she said. 'I'm with Ed in the church.'

'And you've both been there all morning?'

'Yes. Pretty much. Ed had a couple of meetings with parishioners a while ago and I had a wander into town, but otherwise we've been here in the church.'

'What time were you in Barnstaple?'

'About midday.' She paused. 'What is this all about?'

337

He supposed the more people who knew now, the better. That way there'd be more people looking out for the woman. 'Lucy Braddick, another woman with Down's syndrome, disappeared late this morning from Barnstaple high street. I don't suppose you saw her while you were in town?'

'No,' she said, then immediately, 'Do you think she was abducted like Christine Shapland?'

'I'm not sure.' Because what else could he say?

'Look, if there's anything Ed or I can do . . . I mean, searching or anything, do let us know.' She paused. 'Ed used to help out at the day centre. He's very fond of the people there. I know he'd want to be involved.'

★　★　★

Next phone call was to the toll keeper's cottage. There was no reply and that surprised him. The light had faded now — it was surely too dark for Colin to be birdwatching — and Matthew didn't see the Marstons as a sociable couple. He couldn't imagine them out for dinner with friends, for example, or sharing a few pints with mates in the pub. He tried the mobile number Marston had given him and that went straight to voicemail. He told himself there was nothing sinister about the silence. Of all the people orbiting the Woodyard and this investigation, the Marstons had no motive. Colin might run a natural history course for older students at the Woodyard, might have been consulted once about some legal matter by the board, but he'd never met Simon Walden and Matthew couldn't see how he'd have bumped into Christine or Lucy.

Matthew was still worried about the Salters, wondering if his conversation the evening before might have been the cause of Lucy's disappearance. He tried to run again in his head the one question that seemed to have caused anxiety, but he thought he might have imagined the response. He couldn't see how it might be relevant to Walden's murder, and that, after all, had started the drama.

Then he thought that it would be a mistake to call the Salters anyway. It was clear that Grace had lied about Dennis; she'd certainly lie again to give the man an alibi. He got on the phone to Ross.

'I need you to go to the Salters' house in Lovacott. Take a couple of uniformed officers. Be polite. Super polite and apologetic. We've got absolutely no grounds for a warrant, so you'll need to be persuasive to get in. Blame me. Or make up some vague story about Lucy having been seen in the area. If they let you look round the house, it'll mean she's not there, but you might pick up something useful. Find out what they were doing when Lucy went missing. I'd be very interested to know if they were in Barnstaple at lunchtime.'

'Yeah, boss. Of course.' Matthew could tell he was delighted to be released from the routine of canvassing in the town centre and manning the phone. The earlier moodiness disappeared in a flash. He had no emotional baggage with the

Salters and no reason to fear the encounter.

Matthew longed for release too. He yelled to the remainder of his team that he'd be out for an hour, that they should phone him as soon as there was any information and he headed away towards the town centre.

★   ★   ★

He went to look for Edward and Caroline in the church. On his way, he stood for a moment in the quiet cobbled alley. Lights were coming on in the alms houses beyond. Through an uncurtained window he saw an elderly couple sitting together on a sofa, watching television. The old man turned and gave his wife a peck on a wrinkled cheek. She smiled and took his hand. Matthew thought he'd never seen such affection between his parents, wondered again about Mary Brownscombe, the farmer he'd visited with his father when he'd been a child. He hoped his father had found love there.

There'd been some sort of meeting in the church and the couple were just clearing up, folding chairs. Matthew had bumped into a middle-aged man and three teenagers on his way in but Ed and Caroline were alone now. They hadn't heard him come in and had paused for a moment and were talking.

Matthew stood at the door and looked inside. The Brethren had worshipped in dusty halls and gloomy living rooms. This was a church in the evangelical tradition and here there was colour: banners on the walls, more rainbows and doves,

340

all with a message of peace and redemption, bowls of flowers. At the back in one corner, a box of toys to keep bored children amused during the service. Edward Craven was tall and thin, faintly reptilious; he wore jeans and an open-necked shirt. Matthew would have put him down as a social worker too, if he hadn't known he was a cleric.

Their conversation seemed earnest, important, but Matthew was too far away to hear what they were saying and as soon as he started walking up the nave they heard his footsteps, fell silent and turned to face him.

Caroline started moving towards him. The artificial light in the church reflected from her round glasses, so he couldn't quite see her eyes. 'Inspector. We were just talking about the woman from the Woodyard who was missing. Is there any news?'

Matthew shook his head. 'Do you know her?'

'Not through work, but I've heard Gaby talk about her. Gabs goes down to the day centre once a week to teach art.' She looked back at the tall man, hovering behind her. 'This is Edward Craven, my friend and the curate here. He's been an absolute inspiration behind the mental health project at St Cuthbert's.'

Matthew turned towards him. 'And you volunteer at the Woodyard too?'

'I used to, before I got so involved with everything going on here.' Ed's voice was warm and deep. Matthew thought it was a good preaching voice, though it was hard to imagine the man in the pulpit. He seemed too diffident, too anxious. But then, some shy people made great performers. 'What do you think happened to the woman?'

'We don't know. She has a learning disability. Of course we're worried. Especially as another woman with Down's syndrome went missing last week. It seems *she* might have been abducted.' They were still all standing close to the altar, looking at each other. 'Where were you both between eleven and twelve this morning?'

The couple looked back at him, shocked, and for a moment neither of them spoke. 'You can't think we had anything to do with that.' Caroline sounded horrified.

'We're asking everyone who knew Simon Walden,' Matthew said. 'We think Lucy's disappearance is linked to his murder. They'd become friends.'

'I told you I went into Barnstaple to do some shopping, but that would have been later. I didn't leave here until nearly twelve.' Caroline turned back to her boyfriend. 'Ed was manning the office here. The priests and volunteers do it on a rota and it was his turn.'

Matthew wondered if she'd speak for the man when they were married, because he thought they *would* marry. There was something settled, immovable about the relationship. He saw Caroline as one of those supportive, rather interfering wives, who made their husbands' well-being their lives' work. She'd organize the business of the parish, leaving him to be figurehead.

'I had three appointments and saw five

people,' Edward said. 'A couple planning a wedding. Another booking a baptism and an elderly woman in to talk about her husband's funeral.' He paused. 'There are days when my whole life seems to be about death. I can't even guess how many funerals I take in a year.'

Matthew thought that he too seemed obsessed by the dying and the dead. Perhaps their work wasn't so different.

Caroline looked rather disapproving and Matthew expected her to comment, but she said nothing and just placed her hand on Ed's arm. A gesture of sympathy. Or a warning to be careful what he said.

Matthew turned back to her. 'How long were you in Barnstaple?'

'A couple of hours. I didn't actually buy anything. It was just about keeping out of Ed's way while he was working. We'd arranged to meet up again for a late lunch. I went for a coffee and then I was browsing. Actually, it was a restful way to spend a Saturday morning.'

Matthew returned his attention to the curate. 'You were here when Simon Walden first turned up?'

'Yes. Caroline and I were both here. There'd been a service and he was sitting outside, so drunk that he could hardly stand. The centre was closed then, but we let him in anyway. It was pouring with rain and he said he had nowhere to go.'

'Yet it seems he did have a home. A flat in Braunton.'

'We didn't know that then.'

There was a moment of silence. 'Did you keep in touch with the man?' Matthew asked. Because surely that was what clergymen did — they provided pastoral care.

But Craven shook his head sadly. 'I met Simon a couple of times at Caroline's house in Ilfracombe, but I never saw him again in any kind of professional capacity. Caroline's the trained social worker running the mental health project here at St Cuthbert's. I try to support her of course — she does marvellous work — but most of my energy is taken up with my duties here in the parish.'

Matthew took out a photo of Lucy. 'This is the missing woman. Did you see her at all today? She would have been in Barnstaple at the same time as you.'

Caroline took the image. 'No, I didn't see her today, Inspector. I'm afraid I can't help you.'

35

Jen Rafferty sat in the Shaplands' cottage near the creek and eased her way carefully into a conversation with Christine and her mother. Although it wasn't quite dark outside, Susan had drawn the curtains and switched on the light. A fire burned in the grate again. There was more tea on a tray. No scones, because Jen hadn't been expected. In the weak artificial light, the mould on the ceiling was hardly visible. Everything was warm and welcoming. Except for the subject of conversation.

'Lucy's gone missing,' Jen said. She was sitting where Jonathan had been on the previous visit, close enough to Chrissie to reach out and touch the woman. 'We think she was taken by the same man as you. I know it's the last thing you want to talk about again, but we think you might be able to help us.' A pause. 'I'm going to show you photographs of some men. If you see the one who took you, can you tell me?' She lifted the tea tray from the coffee table and put it on the floor. There was a lace cloth underneath and Jen spread the pictures over that.

She'd tracked down an image of Christopher Preece. It had been taken at the time of the Woodyard opening; he was cutting a gold ribbon and there was a big grin on his face. Jonathan was standing in the background, and Jen had had to look twice before being sure it was him, because he was wearing a suit.

She'd thought it would be impossible to find a picture of Colin Marston, but he'd appeared on the U3A website as a tutor, and she'd printed that out. It had been small, and had blurred as she'd tried to enlarge it, but it was better than nothing. He was in a waxed jacket with a pair of binoculars around his neck.

She'd added a picture of Dennis Salter, as a wild card. She couldn't see how Christine hadn't recognized her uncle, but if he'd disguised himself in some way, perhaps she might be tricked. Then there was Edward Craven, the picture taken from the *North Devon Journal*, looking rather grand in full dog collar and cassock, celebrating the day he'd moved to the parish. Jen couldn't think that there was another man involved in the case, and Christine had been clear that a man had picked her up. If Matthew was right and the abductions were all to do with Simon Walden, one of these people must be holding Lucy. It occurred to her that perhaps she should have thrown a bigger picture of Jonathan Church into the mix, but surely if he'd been the abductor, Christine would have known him, and besides, it would have felt like a betrayal to Matthew.

Jen wished the light was better, less shadowy, but it seemed that Susan was thrifty when it came to the strength of the bulbs she bought. Jen held up each photo in turn for Christine to look at, tilting it to catch the best of the light. Watching Christine looking at the pictures, Jen thought she seemed focussed and concentrated.

346

She'd lost the panic of the previous day.

'Can you help me, Christine? Do you recognize any of these men?'

'That's my uncle Dennis.'

'Yes, it is. Well done.'

Christine beamed at the praise.

Susan shot a look towards Jen. 'What's he doing there?'

Jen smiled. 'I just wanted to see what your daughter's memory for faces was like.'

'She's always been good at pictures.' Susan was appeased.

'Is there anyone here you recognize?'

Susan pointed to Preece. 'He's a big cheese at the Woodyard. Loads of money and on the board. A generous man. Without him, the place wouldn't have been set up.' Her fat finger moved across the table. 'And the vicar came and helped out in the day centre a few times when he first moved down here.' She sniffed. 'I haven't seen him recently, though. You get a lot of that. Do-gooders, thinking they're going to change the lives of our people, then getting bored and moving on to other things.' She looked up. 'Nothing happens quickly with people like Christine and Lucy. You need to be patient to work with them.'

'Anyone else?'

'I don't think so.'

'What about you, Christine? Can you see the man who drove the car that picked you up outside the Woodyard and took you to the flat? The man who asked you all the questions.'

Christine looked again at the pictures and

then she shook her head. She seemed upset that she hadn't been able to help. 'I'm sorry.'

'No need to be sorry, my love. You're doing just great.' Jen paused to choose her words carefully. 'You're a good friend of Lucy's. Did she ever talk to you about another friend? A man called Simon Walden. She met him on the bus some nights on her way home.'

There was silence. Complete silence. The main road was too far away for there to be traffic noise.

'Lucy said she was going to help him,' Christine said. 'In something important.'

'What was that, my love? How was Lucy going to help him?'

Christine shook her head. 'She didn't tell me. She said it was a secret.'

'Lucy didn't give you any idea at all? It might help us to find her.'

Christine looked up. 'She said she was going to help him to save the Woodyard.' She shivered, although the room was very warm.

Susan came up and put her arm around her. 'She's been shivering all day. It must be the shock after all she's been through. Here you are, my lover, let me get you a cardie. We'll keep you cosy.' She pulled a knitted jacket from the back of her chair and wrapped it around her daughter as if it was a blanket.

Jen looked at the cardigan. It was purple. Maurice had said Lucy had been wearing a purple cardigan when she'd gone missing. 'Doesn't Lucy Braddick have a cardigan a bit like this?'

'Yes,' Susan said. 'Exactly the same! We all went on an outing to Plymouth with the Woodyard just before Christmas to do a bit of shopping, and they both got one.'

'Did Christine have it on when she was snatched from the centre?' Jen tried to remember what the woman had been wearing when they'd found her at Lovacott pond. Her clothes had been wet then, patched with mud, almost unrecognizable, but surely she'd been wearing this.

'Yes. I was going to bin it, but Chrissie loves it so much. They said they were like twins, her and Lucy. So, in the end I put it straight in the machine and it came out like new. It's not real wool, see, so no damage in a hottish wash.'

Jen left them sitting together, warm and snug, and went to sit in her car to phone Matthew.

★   ★   ★

'I think it could have been a case of mistaken identity. The car driver had been told to pick up a woman with Down's syndrome wearing a purple cardigan from the centre and got Christine, not Lucy. He said to Christine that he'd been told to give her a lift back to Lovacott. Both women would have been going there.'

'But Christine doesn't look much like Lucy. Lucy's hair is longer.'

'From behind, though, wrapped up in the purple cardigan, it might not be possible to tell them apart. Then Christine was sitting in the back of the car and the driver would just have glimpsed her in the mirror. And once he'd got her to the flat, what could he do? Just say it had been a dreadful mistake and drop her back at the Woodyard where anyone could see him? Perhaps he thought she'd have the same information as Lucy, and he asked his questions anyway.' It was quite dark outside now. No moon. No street lights.

'Then he got frustrated, took her to Lovacott where she was heading originally and dumped her by the pond,' said Matthew. 'I suppose it makes a kind of sense. But that implies that more than one person is involved in this. Someone giving the orders and someone carrying them out.'

'I asked Christine about Lucy's friendship with Walden. Lucy told her that together they were going to save the Woodyard.'

Matthew didn't answer immediately. 'I'm going to withdraw from the case. I should have done that from the beginning. There was always a conflict of interest and the Woodyard is obviously at the heart of it. I'll contact management in the morning. From tomorrow you'll be in charge. Temporarily at least, until they decide what to do next.'

Jen didn't know what to say. She had mixed feelings. She'd never headed up such an important case and it had been her ambition since she'd joined the service. But this was Matthew. A good man and a good detective. 'We'd better crack it tonight then, hadn't we, boss. I'm coming in to the station and I'll see you there.'

36

Ross and Jen arrived back at the station at about the same time. The day had been so full of events that it felt late to Matthew, as if it could be nearly midnight. In fact, Saturday night had just started in Barnstaple and from the police station, he heard music and voices, revellers on their way to the restaurants and bars.

Jonathan phoned. 'We've searched every inch of the Woodyard. No sign of Lucy.'

Matthew wanted to talk to him about what Lucy had said regarding Walden's secret plan to save the centre. *Do you know what this is about? Why does the Woodyard need saving?* But he thought he'd already involved Jonathan too much in the case. Matthew had always seen the point of rules, the need for order. That was why he'd joined the police. The decision had been his own small attempt to save the world from the chaos that he'd felt was about to engulf them all when he lost his faith. Life without the laws of the Brethren had seemed random and without meaning. He couldn't see how every individual following their own path, selfish, weak, could form any kind of decent society. The law provided structure, its own morality. A safety net.

Now, he couldn't pass on information about an ongoing inquiry to someone who might be involved and who was certainly close to people who *were*.

'It's going to be a late night.'

'Don't worry,' Jonathan said. 'Just find her. I'll be waiting for you.'

Ross burst in, swinging the door almost off its hinges. Like a bored teenager, he could never keep his frustration to himself. 'The Salters weren't bloody there. No sign of them. What a waste of a trip.'

'No sign of Lucy either?'

'We went all the way round the house, but there were no lights on. I looked through the downstairs windows, but it was almost dark by then. Impossible to tell if she'd been there.' Ross paused. He knew what Matthew thought about rules too and wasn't sure what the inspector would make of an attempted forced entry, but he continued anyway. 'I couldn't find any way of breaking in. I did check all the doors and windows just in case, but it was impossible. The Salters are very heavy on security. Verging on the paranoid.'

Matthew nodded and on impulse phoned his mother's landline. He still remembered the number from when he'd lived in the house. He was only half surprised when she answered.

'Ah, you're there,' he said. 'I thought there might be a Brethren meeting tonight. Or some sort of get-together. I've been trying to get hold of the Salters, but nobody's home.'

'No,' she said. 'There's nothing like that as far as I know.' Her voice wasn't as sharp as it had been in the past, but she wouldn't give him the satisfaction of asking why he wanted to know. Matthew was grateful for that. He replaced the receiver. His thoughts were wheeling and dipping like the gulls over the estuary, groping for an explanation, feeling that at last he was making sense of what might lie behind Walden's death. He'd never considered pride as one of his sins, but now it occurred to him that Jen might be right. He might crack the case overnight. The thought gave him an unexpected thrill of achievement. Then it occurred to him that Lucy was still missing and that he had little of which to be proud.

Jen arrived just as he replaced the receiver. 'I've told the kids it'll be an overnighter, but that's no excuse for them to have a party. I don't want to go back in the morning to vomit and a bunch of comatose teens in sleeping bags, looking like giant slugs on my front room floor.'

He grinned, grateful for the lift in mood. Her ability to raise his spirits alone made her an invaluable member of the team. He'd brewed coffee in the filter machine and they sat around one of the tables in the big room. Ross joined them.

'I think we're looking at a conspiracy,' Matthew said. 'If Jen's right and Christine was snatched by mistake, at least two people are involved.' He turned to Jen. 'She couldn't identify any of the men in your photos?'

Jen shook her head. 'But the pictures I managed to print off aren't brilliant quality. I don't think Colin Marston's mother would pick him out from the only shot I could find.'

'I've been trying to phone Marston all evening,' Matthew said. 'No reply.'

'I can't see how Marston can be important,' Ross said. 'He doesn't have the same strong link to the Woodyard as the others. He only teaches a weekly course there. Besides, if he'd kidnapped Lucy, I'd have thought he *would* reply to appear less suspicious.'

'He told me he'd offered the board a couple of pieces of informal legal advice.' Matthew remembered the conversation on the shore. He'd thought Marston was being pompous, inflating his own importance, but perhaps he was more caught up in the affairs of the Woodyard than they'd realized. Again, a few strands of the investigation came together in his mind and he thought he could glimpse a motive at least. 'We need to track down Colin and Hilary Marston, and the Salters who seem to have mysteriously and conveniently disappeared too. Can you get the word out? I want them brought in to the station as soon as we find them. We've got their car registrations.'

'As suspects?' Jen sounded shocked.

'Not yet.' Matthew grinned. 'They'll be helping us with our enquiries. Respectable people like them, they'll be glad to help the police.'

Ross got to his feet and stretched. He'd been still for long enough. They were both looking at Matthew for an answer, but his thoughts were too tentative at this stage. If he put them into words, they might disappear altogether.

'Could it be about money?' Jen said. 'We know that Walden had plans for his two hundred grand, but then he sent it to his solicitor for safe keeping instead. We know he'd been planning a big donation to the Woodyard, then thought better of it. Perhaps he'd discovered something dodgy had been going on. The organization at the Woodyard seems a bit chaotic so fraud could have been relatively easy. Preece and Salter are both trustees and they both have a background in finance. Could they be filtering off donated cash or charitable funding for their own use? It does happen with charities. There have been a few cases recently in the press. One guy got away with hundreds of thousands. And it can take years for any crime to come to light. That would fit in with the conspiracy theory.' She looked at Matthew. 'Jonathan wouldn't be aware of that. He manages the place but I guess he has nothing to do with the financial administration.'

Matthew didn't know what to say in reply. He appreciated Jen's kindness. He wanted to tell her that Jonathan was the most honest man he'd ever met, that his husband would work at the Woodyard for nothing to keep it running, that he fretted if he'd thought he'd undertipped a waiter in a mediocre hotel, but until they found Walden's killer, Jonathan would still be an object of suspicion.

'It would be interesting to look at Preece's and Salter's bank accounts. They seem prosperous enough, but they might have had problems with money.'

He was thinking that Preece had provided the deposit for the house in Hope Street. Matthew had gained the impression that the man was trying to buy his daughter's affection. He was probably still subsidizing her lifestyle. Perhaps that, and the guilt-ridden donation to begin the development of the Woodyard, had depleted his savings.

'Let's bring Preece in too. If he hasn't disappeared like the others. We'll interview them separately, see if we can find some inconsistencies in their stories.'

He couldn't imagine what Salter's guilty financial secret might be. It could be related to the Devonshire Building Society, perhaps. Could he have been stealing from them too?

Ross gave an embarrassed little cough. Matthew could see now that he'd been building up to this throughout the conversation, gathering his courage. 'Perhaps we should look at *Jonathan's* bank account too. Just to put you both in the clear in case the press gets hold of the connection.'

Jen jumped in, fighting. 'Is this your idea or Oldham's? Been brown-nosing again, Ross? More cosy chats over a few beers? Hoping for another speedy step up the ladder?'

Matthew raised his hands, a gesture of agreement and peace-making. 'You're quite right, Ross. I'll give the forensic accountants all the details. For Jonathan's accounts and mine. We have to be transparent here. And as all our victims and witnesses seem to be connected to the Woodyard, I've already discussed the conflict of interest with Jen. She'll be taking over the case tomorrow. You'll be reporting to her from first thing in the morning.'

He sent them away then and sat for a moment

in his office. Matthew felt no resentment about the request to disclose his financial affairs, but he wished it had been done differently. The decision had obviously come from Oldham, but filtered through Ross. The DCI had been too idle or too cowardly to ask himself, and that wasn't fair either to Ross or to him. He suspected that Jonathan would find the idea of being a suspect faintly amusing, especially if the motive was supposed to be greed. Money had never mattered much to either of them.

Matthew tried to set office tensions aside and replayed the conversations he'd had with Salter and Preece. Suddenly his perspective shifted. There was something that mattered more to both these men than money too. He wound back the timeline since the opening of the Woodyard to look for a trigger, something that might have led to one murder and two abductions. Then he stood up and made for the door.

'Where are you going, boss?' That was Ross, at his desk. A little subdued, but resentful because he was still here, in the police station, waiting.

'I need to speak to a witness.' He still thought it was too soon to tell the team about his suspicion. There was someone who had far too much to lose.

★   ★   ★

The Rosebank Care Home was two storeys high, purpose-built with a narrow strip of garden in the front. Parking for staff and visitors was at the back, most of the spaces empty now. All but a few rooms were in darkness. It was only nine o'clock but it seemed that most of the residents were already in bed.

The door was locked and he rang the bell. A buzz and a crackly voice through the intercom. 'Who is it?'

'Inspector Venn for Mrs Janet Holsworthy.'

A brief silence. 'You'll find me in the office at the end of the corridor.' The door clicked open and he went in.

Through open bedroom doors, he saw carers in pink tunics helping the last remaining residents still up to prepare for bed. Matthew imagined his father in a place like this — because surely his hospital ward hadn't been very different — and he thought there were worse things than death. One woman was sitting on a commode. He turned away and hurried on before she saw him. Rosa's mother sat in a small office, a plate on the desk in front of her, with a half-eaten sandwich and a banana skin. A mug of coffee in her hand.

'I haven't got long,' she said. 'I'm just on a break.' But it seemed that there was no fight left in her. She waited while he took the chair on the other side of the desk.

'I need to know about Rosa,' he said. 'One man's dead and her friend, Lucy Braddick, is missing.'

She nodded. He thought she was very tired. She must scarcely sleep, working all night and looking after her husband and daughter during the day.

'Why don't you tell me what really happened?

358

Why Rosa doesn't go to the Woodyard any more.'

'You met her,' the woman said. 'That's how she's always been. Affectionate. Loving. She'll hold the hand of a stranger. When she was a girl she'd climb onto the knee of anyone who smiled at her. We tried to teach her that wasn't a good thing to do, that she should sit with her legs together if she was wearing a skirt, that not everyone wanted to be cuddled, but she didn't understand. How could she? She was innocent.'

Matthew didn't speak.

'When the day centre moved to the Woodyard we thought she'd be safe. The same staff went with them. We liked Jonathan. He wasn't so hands-on but he was still in charge.' Another period of silence. 'There was a visitor. Someone who came and took advantage of her. Took advantage of her because she was so trusting.'

'Did Rosa tell you what happened?'

'Not at first. I could tell that something had happened when she came in that afternoon. She said she was feeling poorly, that she needed to stay at home the next day. We thought the move had unsettled her. That it was nothing serious.'

In the distance one of the home's residents started shouting. 'Help! Mummy! Please help me!'

'Do you need to go to her?' Matthew asked.

Janet Holsworthy shook her head. 'That's Eunice. She shouts every night just before she goes to sleep. She'll settle now.'

There was one more scream, low and plaintive, and the home was quiet again.

'When did you realize that Rosa had been abused?'

'I thought a bath might calm her. I saw that her underwear was torn. There were bruises.'

'She'd been raped?'

Janet shrugged. 'She couldn't say in any detail what had happened. She wouldn't know the words. But she'd been assaulted.'

'Why didn't you go to the police? To a doctor?' But Matthew knew the answer. This was delicate, personal. They wouldn't want to tell the story to a stranger. 'You could have told Jonathan. You knew him.' Matthew tried to keep the emotion out of his voice.

'Jonathan wasn't there. He'd been away for three weeks on honeymoon. I went to the big boss. Something had to be done.'

'The big boss?'

'The head of the trustees. Christopher Preece.' She paused. 'I phoned him first. He asked me to his house, he said it would be best to talk there.'

Matthew pictured her standing outside the house by the park, nervous, but expecting sympathy, that something would be done.

'When I got there, it wasn't just him,' Janet said. 'He said it was such a serious allegation that he had to consult his colleagues. There were three of them. Three men.'

'Who else was there?' Matthew could only imagine how intimidating that must have been.

'One was another trustee. Dennis Salter. I hadn't met him before. And there was someone else who they said was their legal advisor.'

Colin Marston. Though what someone who'd

overseen contracts in the car industry might have to do with a criminal case of sexual assault, Matthew couldn't imagine. He'd be there solely to intimidate.

'It must have been frightening for you. Facing those men.'

'It was the word *allegation*. As if I was making it all up. Mr Preece said he couldn't understand how it had happened there at the Woodyard with all the staff around. I told him it had happened in a counselling session. They'd started that when the centre first moved to the Woodyard. One-to-one chats in the small meeting rooms, the users talking about the place, their ideas and hopes for the future.' She looked up at Matthew. 'He asked if I had proof. If I'd been to a doctor or the police. As if I wasn't telling the truth. I told him I couldn't have put Rosa through that. Not yet. That's why I was talking to him, so he could help us through the process. Rosa wouldn't understand without support. She'd get in a state and she wouldn't be able to explain. Imagine her having to go to court!' Another pause. 'But I told him I'd kept the torn knickers. They were stained. I didn't tell him about the skirt, though, and the fact that the skirt was stained too. I kept that. My secret.' She looked up. 'I was thinking about the American president and that scandal with the young girl. It was a skirt that proved *she* was telling the truth. I didn't trust them, you see. There'd be DNA, wouldn't there, on both of them?'

'There would.'

'I don't think they were expecting that I'd have proof.'

'What happened, Janet? Why didn't you pursue it?'

She stared up at him and he saw she was crying. 'Because they bought me off. They gave me money to keep quiet. It was a dreadful time. My husband had just lost his job and there was no cash coming in. We were waiting for the welfare people to sort out his payments. I get attendance allowance for Rosa, but that's nothing, a pittance. We were weeks behind on the rent. And Preece offered me money.'

She shook her head as if she was trying to shake out the memory. 'I knew it was the wrong thing to do, but he was so persuasive. It was as if it wasn't about the money at all. Not really. He said the Woodyard was such a great project and any bad publicity would mean the funding would stop and all those service users would be left without care. He promised to keep the perpetrator away and make sure that he got help. He'd never be allowed to do anything like that again.' A little gasp. 'And then he wrote the cheque. *Buy something nice for Rosa*, he said. *Take her away for a break, a weekend*. It wasn't huge but it was enough to pay back the rent that we owed. It was enough to keep us going.' Another pause. 'That's why I didn't tell you about Rosa when you came looking for Chrissie Shapland. I was still ashamed at taking their money. They told me when I took it that it was a kind of contract. I was promising to keep quiet. To keep the secret.'

'Was Preece the only person to sign the cheque?' Matthew asked. 'Or did Mr Salter sign it too?' If it was a joint signature, it would have come from the Woodyard account, not from Preece's personal bank, and there'd be a record of that. A record that Walden might have come across. None of the office doors in the building were ever locked and Jonathan would never have picked up any discrepancy in the accounts.

'They both signed it.'

Matthew nodded, but still he showed no emotion. 'Has anyone else come along to ask you about Rosa's story? A man called Simon Walden?'

'Is he the man that was killed out at Crow Point?' She seemed shocked.

'That's right. He was a volunteer at the Woodyard. I think he was taking an interest in what happened to Rosa.'

'No,' she said. 'I've never met him.'

Matthew felt a stab of disappointment. His theory, his hope of bringing the investigation to a close, was based on Simon having discovered what had happened to Rosa.

Janet continued: 'The only person from the Woodyard we've seen recently is Lucy Braddick. You know, Rosa's friend.' She looked at him again, her eyes so tired that they looked bruised. 'Did you say she was missing?'

He nodded. 'That's why I'm here, bothering you. We need to find her.'

'It was a couple of weeks ago. The two of them text from time to time, scraps of nonsense. Then Maurice phoned and said Lucy was missing

363

Rosa. Could he bring her round after the Woodyard? They came to tea. It was lovely to catch up and the girls got on as well as they always had. They disappeared upstairs and we didn't see them until it was time for me to go to work.'

Matthew thought for a moment. 'Could Lucy have taken the skirt with her? Because I think Rosa must have told her what happened. Perhaps just after the abuse took place. Perhaps Lucy saw that Rosa was upset.' And if Lucy had confided in Walden, he might have asked her to help him find evidence. This could have been his great campaign, the secret that they shared.

'I don't know! The skirt was in a plastic bag in my wardrobe.' Janet was thinking. 'I haven't checked if it's there. Not recently.' A pause. 'The girls were in my room, though, that day. I heard their footsteps through the ceiling and I shouted up to them not to be cheeky monkeys. I thought they were trying on my clothes. Rosa likes to do that. To dress up in my things, my high-heeled shoes. She comes down with her face plastered with make-up.' She looked at Matthew. 'Shall I phone my husband and ask him to check?'

'If it's not too difficult for him.'

'He'll be upstairs now anyway, getting ready for bed.'

Matthew sat quite still and tried not to listen to the conversation, tried not to allow emotion to cloud his judgement. He only looked at the woman when she clicked off her mobile.

'The skirt's gone,' she said. 'He's looked everywhere.'

'Did Lucy have a bag with her when she came to visit?'

'Yes,' Janet said. 'A shoulder bag. Maurice said she should leave it with him when she went upstairs, but she took it with her.'

And she hid the skirt in it and carried it to the Woodyard to give to Walden. And even when Chrissie went missing and Walden died, she kept her promise. She kept her secret.

'Thank you,' Matthew said. 'Thank you.'

She put her mug on her plate and looked at her watch. 'I should go,' she said. 'My break was over five minutes ago.'

'Who was it, Janet? Who abused your daughter?'

There was a moment. He thought she still might refuse to tell him. 'It was the clergyman.' She stood up. 'The young curate. Of all the people you'd think you should trust, it would be a man of God.'

37

Matthew was surprised, when he returned to the police station, to find that only forty minutes had passed. It still felt as if time was stretching, allowing him the chance to recover Lucy. Giving him hope that he'd find her well and alive.

Ross was in the police station, waiting for him. 'We've only got Preece so far. Jen's with him. She hasn't started on him yet, she was holding him in the interview room until you got back. No sign of Salter or Marston or their vehicles. We haven't been out to Marston's place yet, though.'

'Leave that for now.' Matthew didn't want Marston scared off until he'd worked out the details of the case in his own mind; he certainly didn't want to send a patrol car out, siren blaring. 'Let's see what Preece has to say for himself. He might know where Lucy is. Even if he wasn't involved in the abduction, he was a part of the original conspiracy.' He described his conversation with Janet Holsworthy.

'Why would they do that? Cover up the sexual assault on a vulnerable woman?' Ross looked sick.

'Because their reputations are dependent on the success of the Woodyard. Because they're powerful, entitled men and they could. And then the cover-up became more toxic than the original assault. They were all involved and they

366

all had a lot to lose, but Preece is Caroline's father and Caroline is Craven's girlfriend. Perhaps he was protecting her reputation too.'

'Should we get Craven in?'

'Yes. Let's lean on him about Lucy Braddick. The rest can wait until morning.'

★   ★   ★

Christopher Preece looked unflustered, but he'd done tricky business deals in the past and he'd be used to presenting a cool face to the world. Jen sat opposite him, waiting. If she'd been hoping to ratchet up the tension with her silent presence, it seemed that she'd failed.

'We know about Rosa Holsworthy.' Matthew had just come into the room and was still standing.

'I'm sorry?'

'We know that you paid off her parents to stop them pressing criminal charges against one of your volunteers.'

'Ah,' Preece said. He gave his slow, politician's smile. 'I'm afraid that's not quite how I remember it.'

'How do you remember it?'

'The woman's parents were reluctant to put their daughter through the anxiety of a trial. There'd be the issue of consent. As I understand it, Rosa had the reputation within the day centre of being a little . . . ' he paused ' . . . promiscuous.'

'She's a woman with a learning disability and she was assaulted by an adult whom she trusted, whom her parents trusted, in what they considered to be a place of safety.' Matthew felt himself grow angry. The tension that had been building all day was turning to fury.

Preece looked up at him and affected surprise. 'I'd have thought you'd be as unwilling as we were to have any complaint made public. That you'd be grateful for the position we took. Your husband also holds a position of authority within the establishment.'

'Although he was away at the time and was never consulted.' Matthew forced himself to stay calm. Preece was playing games. Trying to wind him up. 'Lucy Braddick, another of the day centre users, went missing this afternoon. Do you have any idea where she might be? We're extremely concerned.'

'I'm afraid I can't help you, Inspector.' The man leaned back in his chair. His arms were folded.

Matthew took a seat next to Jen Rafferty. 'Your daughter supports your work at the Woodyard. Did you tell Caroline about the assault on Rosa? Or did she already know? Did she ask you to make the scandal involving her boyfriend go away?'

'No! Of course not.' He seemed a little rattled now. 'It was a management decision. Nothing to do with her.'

'Do you think she would have approved of the way the matter was handled?' Matthew thought he could play dirty too.

There was a moment of silence. 'Possibly not, Inspector. But Caroline is young and idealistic.

She probably doesn't understand that if news of what happened became public knowledge, especially if there was a court case concerning Craven, all public and most private funding for St Cuthbert's mental health centre would dry up. He's a curate at the church that sponsors her work. She'd be without a job. And her friend Gaby would find herself unemployed too, because the incident happened at the Woodyard Centre and that's dependent on charitable donations too.'

Matthew leaned forward across the table. His voice was clipped and precise. 'You do realize that if you'd dealt with Mrs Holsworthy's complaint appropriately at the time, Simon Walden would still be alive? Two women would have been saved the trauma of abduction? Events have run out of control, Mr Preece. They're still running out of control and I hold you responsible. Please think about that.' A pause. 'Now, is there anything more you can tell me?'

He thought he might have got through to the man. There was a moment of silence. Then Preece spoke again.

'I'm very sorry, Inspector. I'm afraid I can't help you.'

Matthew left the room. He needed to clear his head, to get fresh air, space to think. He stood outside for a moment. On the wooded mound of Castle Hill, against the background noise of Saturday night partying, someone was playing the guitar. The sound, plaintive, floated across the concrete towards him.

★ ★ ★

Back in the open-plan office there was still no news of the Salters or the Marstons. Ross looked up from his desk. 'They've got Craven, though. They're bringing him in now.' His phone rang. Ross picked it up.

'It's probably Maurice,' Matthew said. 'He's desperate. He was phoning all afternoon when I was here.'

Ross spoke briefly, a few words of thanks, then replaced the receiver. Matthew could tell from the man's face and from the overheard conversation that Maurice hadn't been the caller, that this was important.

'There's been a 999 call,' Ross said. 'The woman who rang gave her name as Lucy. No other name and she rang off before the emergency handler could take more details. She didn't even have a chance to say what service she wanted. But the guy in the call centre had seen all the publicity about the missing woman. He thought we should know.'

Matthew was thinking that when all this was over he'd track that man down and send him a bottle of very good Scotch.

'He must have a record of the phone number.'

'Yes. It was a landline and he's already found the name and address.'

'Come on, Ross! Is it someone known to us?' For the second time that day Matthew wanted to strangle the man for holding back information.

'Colin Marston,' Ross said. 'Toll keeper's cottage.'

38

They pulled Jen out of the interview room, and left Preece alone with a uniformed officer. Matthew thought they'd need a woman with them. On the drive to the coast, he was swamped with guilt, and couldn't escape thoughts of the mistakes he'd made earlier in the day. He should have sent a team out to the toll keeper's cottage earlier. He'd been misled, obsessed with the Salters. The cottage was close to where Walden had died and it should have been an obvious place to look.

He was overwhelmed with admiration for Lucy too. Somehow, she'd managed to get to a phone and to call 999. He thought she must have been interrupted; he hoped she'd cut the call herself, that her captors hadn't realized what she was doing. If they had, it would be unlikely that she'd still be in the cottage.

Ross was driving. He was in an unmarked car, no lights, no siren, but taking them down the narrow roads like a maniac. In other circumstances Matthew would have told him not to be so ridiculous, but now, in his head, he was urging him on to more speed. At the toll gate they slowed down.

'Go through,' Matthew said. He slipped Ross some coins. 'Park near my house. They won't be so suspicious then. We haven't given Preece any opportunity to make a phone call so they might not realize we're after them. Jonathan and I have visitors all the time. We can walk back.'

The curtains in the cottage were drawn. The Marstons' car was still there. It was possible that the couple were still in the building. That Lucy was there too. At Spindrift, all the lights were on and Jonathan's vehicle was in the drive. Matthew thought how good it would be to be in the house, just the two of them, in the long room by the fire, this nightmare over.

The detectives walked back towards the toll gate in silence, using the torches they'd brought from the station until their eyes got used to the gloom. An owl, flying low over the marsh, was caught in the beam. At the cottage, Matthew sent Ross to the back door and then rang the bell. No reply. There was a crack in the curtains and he looked into the front room. It was much as it had been when they'd visited on the day of Walden's death. A bit cluttered. Books and files on the shelves. A couple of dirty mugs on the low table. Nobody inside this time, though. He rang the bell again, but harder, leaning on the button. There was still no reply and, leaving Jen at the front door, he walked around the rest of the house, trying to look inside whenever he came to a window. Ross was still waiting at the back door.

'This frame is completely rotten.' His voice was so low that Matthew had to bend towards him to hear. 'We'll have no problem forcing an entrance if we need to.'

All the other curtains were shut tight and Matthew made his way back to Jen. She was peering through into the living room and waved him towards the gap in the curtains. 'Look. Wasn't Lucy wearing that when she went missing?'

Across the threadbare armchair was thrown a purple cardigan.

He led her to the back of the house and to Ross, who was still waiting for them, pacing, impatient for action.

'She's definitely been in there.' Jen's voice was high-pitched, panicky.

Ross put his shoulder to the door. There was the creak of splintered wood and it fell inside, almost intact.

Matthew pulled the door out of the way.

'Hello! Police!'

The back door led straight into the kitchen. The kettle was warm but not hot. Dirty plates on the draining board. In the bin the remains of takeaway fish and chips.

Jen had moved through to the living room and was looking at the cardigan. She showed Matthew the label of the cheap high street chain where Susan had said they'd been shopping in Plymouth. 'I'm sure this is Lucy's.'

On the hall table there was a phone, a landline. Matthew pressed the redial button and got through to emergency services. 'That confirms that she made the call from here.' He shouted up the stairs: 'Hello, Lucy.' Silence.

Matthew went up. He told the others to stay where they were; he'd already be contaminating any possible scene. There was a narrow landing, with a bathroom ahead. A stained enamel bath. Surely a man who'd been a lawyer would be able to afford better accommodation than this. Perhaps Marston had conned them all, including the Woodyard board, and lied about his qualifications and experience. Or had the pull of the wildlife on the marsh really been the big draw?

Every muscle felt tense, and his heart was racing. He wondered if this was the onset of an anxiety attack. He'd suffered from them when he first went to Bristol as a student but hadn't had one for years. He wasn't sure what he was expecting to find in the upstairs rooms. Another stabbing perhaps. Blood. He thought he wouldn't know how to tell Maurice if anything had happened to his daughter, found himself groping already for the words to explain. For a story. The bathroom was empty. A search team would come in later, but now he just wanted to find Lucy, to get her back to her father.

He pushed open one of the bedroom doors. A spare room, barely furnished with a single bed and clothes rail. Still no sign of the woman. Nowhere to hide a body. The last bedroom obviously belonged to the Marstons — Colin's clothes were neatly folded on a chair, Hilary's thrown on the floor. He pulled back the duvet, but there was no blood-soaked mattress, no Lucy. He was hit by relief and an overwhelming sense of anticlimax. In the ceiling of the landing, there was a small plyboard hatch that would lead into the loft, but Matthew could tell that Lucy was too big and too physically unfit to get through it. He shouted down to the others:

'She's not here.'

They gathered in the cramped hall.

'What do we think?' This was Jen. 'That they caught her ringing out to the emergency services and realized they had to get her out of the house? They'd know we'd be on our way. Their car's here, so how did they move her? Taxi? Did they get someone to come and give them a lift?'

'Maybe.' But Matthew wasn't sure the Marstons would have waited for someone to drive from the town. They were city people and they'd expect an immediate police response. 'Or maybe they just walked her out. They hoped we'd find nobody at home. They might not have realized she'd given her name or the call-handler would be bright enough to pass the message on to us. They could be hiding, waiting for us to go away again, so they can bring her back. Marston knows the marsh and the shore. He'd be aware of the places to hide her.'

★　★　★

They separated. Jen and Ross went inland, following the road that ran along the marsh. That was the more likely place for the couple to have taken Lucy. She would find it hard to walk quickly over soft sand, and they'd want her to move quickly. Matthew headed to the shore towards Crow Point. That was his territory. He thought he'd know it as well as Marston. It was where Simon Walden had been found dead.

There was a half-moon, covered most of the time by cloud, misty, hardly giving any light. Matthew climbed the bank of dunes. Home lay to his right, brightly lit. He thought he could smell woodsmoke. Jonathan would have lit the log burner, would be waiting, restless and anxious. On the far bank of the river, a string of lights marked Instow, and beyond the mouth of the Torridge more lights: Bideford and Appledore. The map of his patch.

The tide had been low when they'd left Barnstaple but it had turned now and was on its way in, the water inching its way up the shore. He could make out the thin line of foam, white against a grey beach, where the waves were breaking, but little else. He checked his phone to make sure he had signal, that Jen and Ross would be able to call as soon as they had news.

He was starting to think that this was fruitless and he should already have called in more officers through headquarters and the coastguard rescue team. This search was going to take more than three people. Behind him, he heard a rustle in the dunes. Shifting sand. Some small animal sliding home with its prey. Then a heavier step. Ross and Jen had already walked all the way to the road perhaps, and had come to join him here on the shore. Or maybe they'd found Lucy, but there was no phone signal where they were, so they'd come to tell him. He turned to call to them, though he thought they should be able to see his silhouette on the ridge of the dunes, even in this light. But before he could shout there was another sound, then a sharp pain. Then everything went black.

39

Jen moved along the dark lane, only aware of Ross because she could hear his footsteps. She'd never lived in a place without street lights, without the background white noise of traffic, and wondered how Matthew and Jonathan could bear the silence. It made her panicky, so stressed that she could feel her heart racing. She'd hated playing hide-and-seek as a child, the tension of waiting in some dark corner to be caught, and now her imagination was running wild; she pictured Lucy in the dark, terrified, at the mercy of strangers.

To hold on to a shred of control, she let fire at Ross. 'What is it about you and Oldham? Why do you end up doing his dirty work?'

They were walking each side of the narrow road away from the toll gate towards Braunton, occasionally shining the light from the torches into the ditches. Shouting Lucy's name. Hearing their voices echo away into the empty space.

'My dad worked with him. They both joined the force as cadets.'

'Your dad was a cop?' Jen had never heard about that. Ross didn't speak much about his family. Only about the gorgeous Melanie.

'He didn't stick it out for long. He couldn't hack it, ended up working for Routledge. You know, the store in town? He ran the menswear department.' Ross spoke as if that was something to be ashamed of.

Jen nodded. Routledge had been still running, just, when she'd moved to Barnstaple, but times had been hard for retail since the recession, and it had long gone.

'Joe Oldham was still a mate, though, even after Dad left the force, still around. I think he bailed them out when Dad lost his job at Routledge. He was more like an uncle. When I was a kid, we went on holiday with him and his wife Maureen every year. They couldn't have children.' He stopped to shout for Lucy. Still no reply. No sound at all. Jen wanted to fill the silence, but she knew there was more to come. 'I had more in common with Joe than I did with my dad — he encouraged me to apply for the police, joined me up to the rugby club — and there were times when I wished I was *his* son. I thought there was more I could be proud of.'

'So, when he asked for favours you didn't think you could refuse?' Jen felt almost sorry for him.

'Yeah, something like that.' A pause. 'Now I don't know how to get out of it.'

Jen thought of Oldham, red-faced, smelling of booze from his drinking the night before, starting to lose it. 'I don't think he'll be in the force for very much longer.'

There was the sound of an engine behind them. The noise split the silence, shocking, making the panic return. A car must have been parked right off the road, hidden by a spinney of trees, and now it tore down the lane behind them, going so fast that they had to scramble out of the way. In the dark and at that speed, she had no idea of the colour, let alone the make, of the vehicle.

Jen pressed her phone to call Matthew. She had signal but there was no reply. 'I think we should go back. See if the boss is okay. That wasn't some courting couple.'

She started running back along the track. They'd gone further than she'd thought and she soon got out of breath and needed to walk. Ross overtook her and she heard his running footsteps disappear into the distance until they faded to silence. She had another moment of panic, felt smothered by the dark so she could hardly breathe. Then she must have turned a slight bend in the road because there were lights ahead of her, a long way off, but providing somewhere to head for. Comfort. Spindrift, Matthew's home. She passed the toll keeper's cottage and continued towards the dunes and the beach, more confident now that she knew where she was. She'd be able to navigate her way from here.

There was no sign of Ross. He must have left the road already, taken the same path as Matthew over the sandhills towards the shore. Just as well that one of them was fit. She turned off the road and began the scramble to the ridge of dunes, needing to stop again when she reached the top to catch her breath. Looking down at the beach, all she could see was a flashing buoy somewhere in the distance. Then the brown cloud cleared and briefly the beach was flooded with moonlight. She saw something far below the high-water mark, close to the incoming tide. No colour. The light wasn't sufficiently strong to make out more than a shape. A heap of discarded clothes, perhaps, or some washed-up debris from a passing ship. It could be a weird sculpture. Something Gaby Henry might have put together from found objects, a twisted piece of driftwood covered by seaweed. Ross was standing there and he was shouting.

She wasn't a sporty woman. She'd never seen the appeal of Lycra and the gym, but now she ran. The strong moonlight had disappeared again, and the object she'd seen from the dunes was no more than a grey shadow, marginally darker than the flat sand that surrounded it. Ross was still shouting and she could hear the desperation in his voice.

40

Matthew woke to a bright light, pain and cold. He couldn't scream because his mouth wouldn't open. Later he thought that had, at least, provided him with a tatter of dignity. He couldn't yell with pain or whimper like a child. It gave him time to pull himself together. There was noise too. Somebody shouting. A voice he recognized. Ross. Then the tape was pulled from his mouth. More pain. Ross shouted again and Matthew had recovered enough by then to realize the man was shouting to Jen. 'It's the boss!'

Ross put his arm around Matthew's back and pulled him into a sitting position, cut the tape that was binding his hands.

'Lucy?' Matthew could hear Maurice Braddick's voice in his head, recriminating. *So, they managed to save you. What about my girl?*

'Alive.'

'Where?'

'Here, on the beach. Not far from you.'

'For God's sake, see to her first.' Matthew was pleased that he'd managed to shout.

'Jen's already with her. She wasn't far behind me. And you were unconscious. I thought you might be dead.' Ross sounded very young, as if he'd been crying. He repeated the words. 'I thought you were dead.' He cut the tape that had been tied around Matthew's ankles and at the

381

same time the clouds parted again. Matthew held on to Ross and pulled himself onto his feet. For a moment he stood with his hand on the DC's arm. 'Thanks,' he said. 'Great work.'

He saw that he'd been lying on the sand, and about two metres away Lucy was being helped by Jen. The woman had been gagged and tied too. Matthew walked unsteadily towards her, and in the spotlight of Jen's torch, saw her in small glimpses: a trainer, turned on one side, covered in sand. An arm, soft and fleshy, very white against the shadowy shore. An eye, open, then blinking in the torchlight, alive. Lucy had been lying helpless on her side. Even a fit person would be unable to move in that position, and she was unfit, cold and scared. Jen was pulling away the parcel tape that was wound around her mouth and her head. Lucy winced at the pain as strands of her hair caught in it.

He shone the torch onto his own face so she could see who he was. There were tears rolling down her cheeks, but she gave a grin, defiant and brave. The water was only metres from them now, sliding up the beach, a gentle and secret killer. If she'd been there an hour longer, Matthew thought, Lucy Braddick would have drowned. *And if Ross hadn't found us, I would have drowned too.*

Jen untied Lucy's hands and feet. Ross took off his coat and wrapped it around her. Together they helped her walk a little way up the beach, until she was safely away from the tide. Her legs gave way again and she collapsed onto the sand.

'You'll need to call an ambulance.' Matthew

had the worst headache in his life but his mind felt sharp and clear. Focussed. As if he'd OD'd on caffeine and could take on the world. 'Tell them exactly what happened and they'll need a chair or a stretcher to move her. Someone will stay with her and wait for the crew.'

While Ross was making the call, he phoned Jonathan.

'We've found her. On the shore near the house. She's cold and she's been tied up and I want her checked out medically before we start talking to her. Can you come? Stay with her until the ambulance crew gets here? Ross and Jen are here, but I don't want to leave her with strangers. We've moved her up the beach a bit out of the way of the tide, but we'll need help to get her over the bank. I don't want Maurice to see her like this.'

He could hear that Jonathan was already moving. Matthew imagined him grabbing his coat and hurrying out. While he was waiting he made the call to Maurice. The phone was answered immediately. 'Yes?' Hopeful and fearful all at the same time.

'It's all right, Maurice. She's fine.' This wasn't the time to give him any details. 'We're getting her taken to the North Devon District Hospital just to be checked over if you want to meet her there. Jonathan will be with her, and my sergeant Jen Rafferty, so you don't need to worry.' He looked at Lucy, who was sitting on the sand, shivering with shock and cold. 'Can you talk to your dad?'

She stuck up two thumbs and gave him the

same defiant smile. The words came slowly. It was a struggle for her to get them out. Each syllable a small triumph. 'Hello, Dad! Yes, I'm okay. I'll tell you all about it when I see you.' There was a pause. 'Can you buy some chocolate? A Twix and a Kitkat. I'm starving.' She handed the phone back to Matthew. The effort to be brave seemed to have exhausted her and she started crying again.

There was a torchlight in the distance now, coming closer: it would be Jonathan doing the characteristic fast walk that was almost a run. He arrived more quickly than Matthew could have hoped, his arms full, throwing him off balance. There was a waterproof coat, which he put on the sand for them to sit on and a blanket, a flask. 'I had coffee already made.' He was sitting beside Lucy, wrapping the blanket around her on top of Ross's coat.

'I don't like coffee,' she said. She turned her head. Matthew could tell it was painful for her to twist her neck. 'Have you got any biscuits?'

'It just so happens . . . ' And Jonathan pulled a packet from his pocket, like a conjuror.

She munched, almost content, almost enjoying the adventure and the attention now Jonathan was here.

Jonathan looked up, spoke in a whisper to Matthew. 'Who did this? And what happened to you?'

Matthew didn't answer that. 'I'll leave Jen with you. If Lucy speaks about it, will you both make notes? Or even better, take a recording. But no questions yet. An interview on a beach in the middle of the night with a woman in shock wouldn't be admissible in court and I don't want this cocked up.'

They nodded. Matthew looked out again towards the water that still crept slowly up the sand towards them. He thought that with the strength of the tide here, Lucy's body might never have been found. He too might have been dragged out into the channel, still alive, but unable to save himself. Drowning in the dark water, sucked under by the currents. The stuff of his nightmares. 'The ambulance will be here soon. I need to go.' Matthew was already walking away and if Jonathan replied, he didn't hear.

It was Ross who shouted after him. 'Wait! You had concussion. You need to go to the hospital too.'

Matthew stopped and looked back at him. 'No time for that and I'm fine.'

A silence. He thought Ross was going to insist, but he said, 'What do you want me to do?'

'Take the car. I'll pick up Jonathan's from the house. Find the Marstons and the Salters. Bring them into the station as soon as you track them down. Tonight. Don't wait until the morning. Jen was right. This is all about conspiracy. Entitled people more worried about their own reputations than the people in their care, losing any sense of humanity along the way. A kind of collective madness. They're all involved to some degree.' He'd reached the top of the bank and could see the flashing lights of the ambulance.

'Where are you going?'

'To speak to a witness.'

On the track, he stopped to point the ambulance crew in the right direction. The toll keeper's cottage was still in darkness. Matthew took a moment to check that nobody was there then made his way to Spindrift, to his home. There was still the strange clarity that felt almost like a dream. He lifted Jonathan's car keys from the hook in the kitchen. There was a file on the table labelled 'Woodyard Finances'. There was a coffee stain on the cover and the pages were a little dog-eared. Jonathan had obviously had the report for a while and struggled to get to the end of it. But even if he'd read every word, Matthew thought it was unlikely he'd find a record of the sum made out to Janet Holsworthy.

★   ★   ★

It was nearly midnight when he got to twenty Hope Street, but there was still a light showing through the glass panel in the front door. He knocked loudly. As usual, it was Gaby who answered.

'What's happened? Have you found Lucy?'

'Yes,' he said. 'We found her. Is Caroline in?'

'Yeah, we were watching a film.' Gaby led him through to the living room.

It was less than a week since he'd first been here, but the place, colourful, cluttered, student-chic, already seemed familiar. Caroline was on the sofa, legs curled under her. The film end-credits were rolling. He turned back to Gaby. 'Could I speak to Miss Preece on her own, please?'

'Of course.' He saw she was about to make a joke, to ask why he was being so formal and dramatic, but she thought better of it. She gave one last, curious glance at the two, and then she left the room.

Caroline uncurled her legs and sat upright. 'What's this about, Inspector?' She took off her glasses and polished the lenses with the edge of her cardigan, then replaced them. The only sign that she might be nervous.

'You knew that your boyfriend had assaulted a vulnerable woman.' This wasn't a question. Matthew was sure Craven would have told her; he would have left the day centre immediately afterwards, run to her and confessed. That was the relationship they had.

'I don't think assault is the right word.' So, she was prepared to fight. Good. He was in the mood for confrontation.

'What word would you use?'

Silence. At last she spoke. 'He will never do anything like that again.'

'Can you be sure?'

'Yes.' She was confident that she could fix Edward Craven, that she had the power to reform him. Where had that arrogance come from? Her religious faith? A guilty and doting father who'd told his only daughter that she could achieve anything she wanted?

'You did know that Simon Walden had found out what had happened? That he was threatening to go public? He'd been planning to leave a will in the Woodyard's favour, but he changed his mind. He saw that as condoning the cover-up.

And he was consulting a lawyer about the next step to take. He had proof.'

Her face was white. Stony. 'Edward didn't kill Simon.'

'How do you know?'

There was a moment's silence. 'Because Ed was as shocked as I was when he found out Simon was dead. And because he'd have told me. He can be a fool, a bit pathetic, but he doesn't lie.' The eyes behind the round spectacles were almost fanatical. Matthew saw that Edward Craven would be her mission in life. She'd be there, waiting for him when he came out of prison. She thought she could cure him and she'd make sure he was dependent on her forever. Caroline stared up at him. 'What would you do, Inspector, if someone you loved made one stupid mistake? If there was one instant when he lost control? Wouldn't you want to protect him?'

He didn't answer that. He didn't like to think about it. He wasn't quite sure how he'd answer. 'Somebody tried to drown Lucy Braddick tonight.'

'I've told you, Inspector. Ed isn't a killer.' She was rattled, Matthew could tell.

'But I think he could have been a part of her abduction, and he was certainly responsible for the capture of Chrissie Shapland.' Because the men in charge would want him tied into the plan. Edward would be the weak link, the one most likely to break down and talk. They'd have to give him a reason not to confess, make sure he had too much to lose.

Silence again.

'We showed Chrissie his photograph.' Of course, Chrissie hadn't recognized Edward Craven. In the photograph he'd been dressed in a cassock and she would have been looking at the strange clothes, not at the man's face.

'He was scared,' Caroline said. 'They bullied him. They said it was vital to find the evidence Simon had been holding, the evidence that could lead to Edward's arrest. They told him that Lucy was the key to finding it.'

'He'd already assaulted a woman with a learning disability, but they put another in danger.' Perhaps it was the blow to his head, but Matthew felt his mind fizzing with rage, not just about Craven and the person who'd knocked him out on the dune but the group of powerful men who'd been so thoughtless about the results of their actions.

'She wasn't in danger!' Caroline was almost shouting now.

Matthew ignored her and continued talking. 'Edward picked up the wrong woman, though, didn't he?'

She nodded. Matthew thought part of her despised the man's incompetence. She continued quickly: 'He let Christine go, though, and then he phoned the police and pretended to have seen her from the Lovacott bus. He knew that you'd find her.'

After holding her for two nights, scaring her witless and putting her mother through hours of misery.

'And this morning? Did he take Lucy?'

'No! He was in the church office, having meetings with parishioners. Just as he told you. You can check with them.'

'He'll be at the police station now, and he'll be charged with rape and abduction.' Matthew stood up. He wasn't even sure why he'd come to the house in Hope Street. Perhaps because this was where the investigation had started, because he'd felt that Caroline should be forced to take some responsibility for the events that had rolled out. If she'd persuaded her boyfriend to admit to the assault on Rosa immediately after it had happened, a man would still be alive.

'I'll come with you!' She was on her feet too, scrambling for her bag.

'No,' he said. 'I think you've done quite enough damage already. Don't you?'

★ ★ ★

When Matthew returned to the police station, Edward Craven was being interviewed. He'd been held in a cell until Ross and Jen had returned.

'Jen's talking to him now,' Ross said. 'She got a lift from the hospital. Maurice is there and Jonathan's still with Lucy. Apparently, Craven seemed almost pleased to see the arresting officer. Like it was a weight from his mind.'

Or an albatross falling from his neck.

'Is Preece still here?'

'Yes. He's called a fancy solicitor.' Ross paused. 'All these respectable people . . . ' He could scarcely get his head around it. He'd been brought up to believe that respectable people could do no wrong.

'It's the respectable ones who have most to lose. That's why they got tangled up in the conspiracy to hide what happened. If they'd told us about the assault when it happened, the Woodyard would have hit the headlines for a few days and then it would have all been forgotten.'

'It's a bloody shame you and Jonathan were away when Rosa Holsworthy was assaulted.'

'I know.' Because Jonathan wouldn't have cared about the Woodyard's reputation. He'd have been only concerned to protect the people in his care.

A phone rang. Ross answered.

'British Transport Police have picked up the Marstons. They were at St David's station in Exeter, waiting for the first train north. They'll hold them in Exeter overnight.'

'Do we know how they got to Exeter?'

'Taxi, according to the guy I spoke to.'

'We need to talk to the driver, find out what time he picked them up. It's possible that they gave up the use of their house, but I don't see that they can have played any part in the abduction or attempted murder of Lucy Braddick. Marston might have been proud to be consulted in the role of legal advisor, but he wasn't so emotionally involved in the success of the Woodyard that he'd think it was worth killing for. I think Walden's murder so close to their home seriously freaked the couple out. That's why they had such a morbid curiosity about what went on there, why they tried to be so helpful.'

It was two in the morning. Matthew was still in the big office with the remaining members of the team, but he phoned Jonathan. He didn't have the energy to walk to his own office. 'Are you home?'

'Yes, they let Lucy go back to Lovacott with Maurice. Poor chap, the shock nearly killed him. He looked ten years older. But so glad to have his daughter back.' A pause. 'She's looking after him, not the other way around. He seems more of a victim than she does.'

'Go to bed,' Matthew said. 'I won't be done here for hours.'

He'd just clicked off his mobile when the phone on Ross's desk rang again. Ross put his hand over the receiver to pass on the message. 'Gary Luke's in an unmarked car on the square in Lovacott. The Salters have just returned home. They drove round once as if they were checking to see if anyone was watching the house, but they've gone in now. Do you want him to pick them up?'

'Not yet. We'll go and speak to them there and bring them back with us. You come with me, Ross.' He thought he'd fall asleep at the wheel and anyway, he needed someone with him to keep him straight and controlled. He was too close to the Salters to be impartial, too close to losing his temper. 'Tell Luke to stay there, though. I'll doubt they'll be going anywhere else tonight, but just in case.'

41

Jen Rafferty sat opposite Edward Craven in the interview room. It was chilly — the heating must be on a timer at weekends — and she was hungry. She'd offered to get the duty solicitor for Craven, but he'd refused. A uniformed officer she scarcely knew sat beside her. The recorder was running and she'd identified everyone present for the machine.

The curate looked impossibly young, much younger than his real age, which she knew now was twenty-seven. He was wearing jeans and an open-necked shirt, a tweed jacket, and looked, she thought, like a posh Oxbridge student in a nineties time warp. His black shoes were highly polished. Jen supposed he'd wear those for work. He looked as if he'd been crying. She struggled to push away the pity, to think instead of Rosa, confused and hurt, of Janet Holsworthy, who'd been intimidated and humiliated by three powerful men.

'Tell me what happened.' She'd learned from Matthew that open questions worked best with suspects like Craven.

'Jonathan was away on holiday. What he called a honeymoon. He'd decided that the Woodyard day centre clients should have key workers, people they could chat to about any worries. Not the care staff they met every day. In case one of the staff was bullying, being abusive.' He looked up and she saw the blush rise from his neck. He understood the irony in what he was saying. 'Jonathan was Rosa's mentor, but because he was on holiday and I was there on a visit, they suggested that I speak to her instead.'

'I understand.'

'They shouldn't have asked me to do that. They shouldn't have put me in that position. It wasn't what I was trained for.' Still making excuses, making up a story to spread the blame.

Jen felt the pity drain away completely. 'You'd already been DBS checked and you could have refused if you felt uncomfortable in the role. I don't think the Woodyard can take responsibility, do you?' He didn't answer and she continued. 'Where did you meet her?'

'One of the small meeting rooms had been specially chosen for the sessions. It was furnished to be homely, welcoming. A couple of armchairs. Wallpaper. Rosa was already there when I arrived. She smiled and asked me if I was all right. As if I were the client and she were looking after me. I sat on the arm of her chair, because I thought that was what she wanted. That was how it seemed. I couldn't help it. She was so . . . ' he struggled to find the word ' . . . available. She smiled again. It wasn't an innocent smile. It was suggestive. Sexy.' That was clearly not a word he was accustomed to saying. Another excuse. Another justification. Jen forced herself to stay silent. She wanted to put him straight, to yell at him the things she'd never had the courage to tell her husband: *How dare you blame the victim! You were the one with the power. It was nobody's responsibility but your own.* But she imagined her lips zipped shut. Stuck with super-glue. The man would condemn himself with his own words.

Craven was talking again. 'I put my arm around her shoulders. I thought it might calm her.' A pause. 'She was very soft.' He stopped, looked up. 'That sounds as if I'm making excuses. I'm not making excuses.'

Oh, but you are. That's just what you're doing. Still Jen stayed silent.

'I wanted to touch her. And I did. I should have had more control, I know that. And then it was all over. Very quickly. And I felt so ashamed and disgusted. I was crying.' He looked up.

'Did you rape her?'

'I didn't think I had. That wasn't what it felt like. I didn't think I'd hurt her.'

'You did hurt her.'

He nodded, but she still wasn't sure that he accepted his guilt. 'You had sex without consent. We need to be clear about this. That was rape.'

Still he seemed unable to accept the fact of his guilt. 'I told her how sorry I was.'

'What happened next?'

'I tried to explain that it was our secret. I wouldn't tell anyone if she didn't. She just smiled and asked me again if I was all right.'

'And then?'

'I wasn't sure what I should do. I went to find Caroline. She'd just finished a session with a client and we went for a walk along the river. She could see I was upset. I said I'd have to tell my boss, or the bishop. I couldn't dream of being a priest now. I'd have to resign.' He paused. 'There was a cold wind blowing across the water. I remember that. Hail that stung my face. And do you know? Part of me was relieved to be going, to be leaving the priesthood, the parish. Because I don't think I'd make a very good priest. I find it overwhelming. The demands. I'm too confused. Too weak.'

'But Caroline persuaded you?'

'She said it was my duty to stay. I had so much to give.'

And you've always done what Caroline told you.

'She said she'd be strong enough for both of us.'

'So, you carried on with your life and said nothing.'

'Yes!' He looked up at her. 'And I thought she was right. Really, that seemed the brave thing to do. The least easy.'

'When did you know that the incident hadn't just gone away? That Rosa's mother had found out?'

'Christopher Preece asked to see me. He called me to his house. I thought he might call in the police, or at the very least demand my resignation, but he said the work that was happening at the Woodyard was more important than me, more important than my conscience. I had to stay away, never come to the place again, never mention what had happened with Rosa to anyone.' He paused. 'I promised. What else could I do?'

'Did he ask you to stay away from his daughter?'

'No!' That seemed to astonish Craven as much as it did Jen. 'He didn't ask that of me.' A pause. 'He said I made her happy and that was all he'd ever wanted.' A pause. 'I think he liked the power he had over me. He said if I ever did anything to upset her, he'd tell the police.'

'Tell me about the abduction of Christine Shapland.' Jen wondered what the time was and glanced at her watch. Outside it was still quite dark. She wished she'd had the chance to phone the kids before she started the interview; they'd both be well asleep by now.

'That was horrible! A terrible mistake!'

'You picked up the wrong woman.'

'Preece phoned me, told me my actions had come back to haunt me, to haunt the Woodyard. He said Lucy Braddick had proof. There was an item of clothing with semen stains. A skirt. She'd know where it was.' The blush again as if the words were worse than the action of abducting a vulnerable adult. 'He said I should pick up a woman with Down's syndrome, who'd be wearing a purple cardigan. I should say I'd been asked to give her a lift to Lovacott but I was to take her to a flat in Braunton.'

'Who gave you the key to the Braunton flat?'

'Nobody. They said it had been left there, under a slate, next to the door.'

'Go on.'

'I was to ask her to give me the clothes she'd stolen from Rosa, or to tell me where they were, and then I was to let her go. But yes, I got the wrong woman. I couldn't even get that right. She didn't understand the questions I was asking. It was a nightmare! I didn't know I had the wrong woman until I got a phone call. I asked what I should do and they said it was my mess and I should sort it out.'

Jen thought about that. Preece had known that Craven had abused one vulnerable woman, but he'd set him up to be alone with another, in a situation where she'd be scared and powerless. 'Did you touch *her*?'

'No!' The question seemed to horrify him. 'Of course not. I was scared and I just wanted it to be over. I was panicking. I left her in the flat with food and drink. I knew Preece would be angry if I didn't get what he wanted, but it was horrible. Such a mess. I just wanted to run away, but I couldn't do that.' He looked up. It was almost as if he wanted Jen's approval. 'I did the right thing in the end.'

Again, she forced herself not to respond, to keep her voice even. 'You took Christine to Simon Walden's flat. He'd already died by then.' She paused for a beat, looked straight into his eyes. 'Did you kill him?'

'No!' Craven was spluttering in his panic. 'No! I didn't know who the flat belonged to. I was just following orders. I didn't know that Walden had anything to do with Rosa. As far as I knew, he was a homeless man with mental health problems. Someone who'd turned up drunk to the church and whom we'd helped. Someone Caroline had taken pity on.'

Another of her lame ducks. Someone like you.

Jen thought about that. *But really, you had nothing in common with Simon Walden. He was on the side of the angels.*

'Someone searched Walden's flat after you dropped Christine at Lovacott. Was that you?'

'No!' Now he was crying.

Jen couldn't tell if they were tears of fear or frustration. They certainly weren't tears for Simon Walden. 'Where were you this afternoon?'

'I was with Caroline this morning. Then I had a series of meetings with parishioners. People who wanted to organize baptisms and funerals. Their names and phone numbers will be in the office. You can call them, check.'

'And then?'

'Then we spent the afternoon together.' He paused. 'Really, I couldn't go through that again. The stress of picking up the woman and asking questions that she didn't seem to understand. You don't know what it was like. I was on the verge of a breakdown. I still dream about it.'

And I expect she does too.

'Someone tried to kill Lucy Braddick this evening,' Jen said.

'That wasn't me!' He screamed the words and she saw that he was unravelling, that his control and his reason were slipping away. She knew that she should stop the interview, before she pushed him over the edge. She didn't believe that he'd killed Walden or attempted to drown Lucy. He didn't have the courage or the strength to have hit Matthew on the head so hard that he was knocked out. They had his phone and that should give them some idea of his movements.

She looked at her watch. 'Interview terminated at two a.m.' She stood up. She felt unclean, desperate for a shower. Suddenly, she didn't want to be in the same room as him.

He looked at her, suddenly calm. 'You hate me. Now everyone will hate me.'

She didn't know what to say, then remembered a form of words used by one of the nuns who'd taught her. 'I don't hate you. I hate what you've done and what it led to.'

She left the room and didn't look back.

42

On the way to Lovacott, Matthew was still wired, fizzing. It was the end of the case, the shock of survival. There was no light at the front of the grand house on the square at Lovacott, but when Matthew leaned on the bell and Dennis Salter answered the door, he was fully clothed.

'I expect you're surprised to see me,' Matthew said. 'I should be dead.'

'I'm sorry, but I don't know what you're talking about.' Imperious. Dennis had always put on a good show. If Matthew was alive, he must know that Lucy would be safe too. Did Salter think she'd be so cowed she wouldn't speak? Or that the authorities would take no notice of the evidence of a woman with a learning disability? And it had been so dark on the beach, he'd know Matthew wouldn't have been able to identify the man who'd hit him, that he'd have no proof.

'You're up late,' he said.

'I've been visiting the sick.'

'The same brother you had to take to A&E on the evening that Chrissie went missing?'

'I've explained that Chrissie's abduction had nothing to do with me. Really, Matthew, this is verging on harassment. Have you seen the time? As you say, it's very late and I need my bed.'

'We know that you didn't abduct Chrissie. That's one reason for the visit. To explain what happened.'

Dennis looked at him warily. 'I'm sure an apology could have waited until a reasonable hour.'

'This is serious.' Matthew felt his temper rip, pulled apart like threads on a torn piece of cloth. 'I need to speak to you and to Grace.'

'You can't speak to Grace. She's been in bed for hours.'

'Don't lie to me, Dennis.' He knew he was yelling but now he didn't care. 'We've been watching the house. We know you both arrived home forty-five minutes ago. Now are you going to let me and my colleague in, or shall I continue shouting so we wake all the neighbours?'

Dennis Salter stood aside and let them in. Grace was standing at the bottom of the stairs watching.

'Shall we all go into the kitchen?' Matthew said. Taking charge. Taking over their territory. 'We'll be more comfortable there and this might take a while. This time of night we could probably all use some coffee to stay awake.' He pushed ahead of Dennis and through to the back of the house. It was as he remembered: a table covered with a green oilcloth, a couple of easy chairs and at the other end the kitchen proper with a stove and sink. The window was curtained, but he knew it looked out over a small walled garden, with a gate into an alley beyond. He sat at the table and nodded for Dennis and Grace to take the armchairs. Occasionally, after meetings, his father and Dennis Salter had drunk small tots of whisky here. His father had liked Salter, admired him; they'd been friends. That idea made Matthew feel ill. 'Stick the kettle on, Ross.'

He waited until the instant coffee had been made before speaking again. 'I see you're both wearing slippers. Very sensible to change as soon as you get into the house. I'm always trying to persuade Jonathan — my husband Jonathan — that would be a good habit to get into. Very Scandinavian.' He knew he was rambling and wondered if that was the result of his blow to the head. A pause and a sip of seriously dreadful coffee. 'My constable needs to see the shoes you were wearing when you arrived home this evening. Don't move. He'll find them himself, if you tell him where they're likely to be.'

Dennis and Grace shot a look at each other and Matthew knew that they'd been on the beach, tying up Lucy Braddick, dragging her below the tideline in the hope that she'd drown. There would be sand in the treads of their shoes, even if they'd wiped them carefully before coming into the house. He wondered briefly what his mother would make of that when the news got out, if it would dent in the slightest her faith in the Brethren. Or had she always guessed that Salter was a tyrant and a bully but been too frightened of upsetting the group to speak out? Had her loyalty to the Brethren been more important than anything he might have done? Ross left the room without waiting for them to speak.

'Someone tried to kill me tonight,' Matthew said.

'And you think that was me? Really, Matthew,

I think you must be mad. Your mother said that the stress of university made you ill. It seems this investigation has been too much for you too.' Salter gave a strange little laugh.

Matthew, who had never had a violent impulse in his life, pictured himself punching Salter; he imagined the dull crunch of his fist on bone and skin, the blood and the shards of bone protruding from the man's face. But in that moment, he saw that was exactly what Salter wanted. He wanted to make Matthew crazy. Who would believe the allegations of a violent psychotic and a woman with Down's syndrome? Was that how he'd controlled Grace all her life? With the threat that people would think she was mad if she spoke out against him?

'Let me tell you a story.' Matthew kept his voice even. The impulse to violence had passed, but he still felt charged, light-headed, that he had the power of the story-teller, the preacher. The couple in front of him gave him their full attention; they were hooked. 'Once upon a time a good man arrived in Barnstaple. He was sad and lost and thought he'd found salvation when he moved in with two young women. One was his project worker and one worked at the Woodyard Centre. He'd been weighed down by guilt because he'd killed a child in a road accident, but he started to turn his life around. He started to suspect that an abuse had taken place in the Woodyard. Perhaps he overheard a conversation between the perpetrator and his girlfriend when he first turned up at the church and they thought he was too drunk to understand what they were saying. Perhaps all his information came from the woman with Down's syndrome he befriended in the Wood-yard cafe.' He looked up. 'This is a true story, so you must tell me where I go wrong.'

He was aware of Ross coming back into the room. He held a pair of women's trainers in one hand and men's walking boots in the other. He slipped them into a large evidence bag and took off his gloves. He gave a brief nod to show there was sand on the soles. The Salters were still staring at Matthew, almost entranced, waiting for him to continue.

'Simon Walden carried out his own investigations. Nobody took much notice of him. Who was he? A homeless alcoholic, who'd made a mess of his life. But he wanted to do something important, to make things right. What would you call that, Dennis? Atonement? A need for redemption?' He looked at Salter, but still there was no response.

'In the weeks before his death, Simon started to travel here, to Lovacott on the bus. At first, I thought that was to give him a chance to chat to Lucy. He'd recruited her to help him, because she was a friend of Rosa Holsworthy, the victim in the assault. And I'm sure they did chat through plans. But that wasn't why he was making the trip. Each evening he'd get off the bus and sit in the pub over the square from here. The Golden Fleece. The landlady thought he was in love, waiting for a woman. And each evening he'd be disappointed when the woman failed to show and he'd just get the bus back to

Barnstaple.' Matthew saw that Ross was giving him his full attention too. Some of this story was new to *him*.

'And Simon *was* waiting for a woman. But not for a lover.' He paused and turned to Grace. 'How did he even know you existed?'

'Oh, Dennis talks about me,' Grace said. There was an edge to her voice. 'I'm part of the reason he's so admired. The devoted wife at home. The wife with mental health problems he has to take care of. I'm part of the story.'

'How did you first meet?'

'He came here,' she said, 'when he knew Dennis was at a trustees meeting.'

Dennis stared into the room; his face showed no emotion at all.

'And he asked for your help, didn't he, Grace? He didn't realize how cruel Dennis could be, how controlling he was. He treated you like a strong woman, able to make your own decisions. He thought that once you knew what was going on, that Preece and Dennis had covered up the sexual assault of a vulnerable woman, you'd be ready to act.'

'I said I couldn't tell him anything,' Grace said. 'That there was nothing I could do.'

'But he didn't give up, did he? He said he'd be in The Fleece every evening until you were ready to talk to him. And the week before he died, you plucked up enough courage to go over there. Did you tell him what you knew?'

'We went for a walk,' she said. 'Out to the pond where you found Chrissie; it still felt like winter then, just before the good weather came.

406

There was thin ice on the water. Frost on the trees.' She paused. 'I couldn't be seen talking to him in the pub. Someone would tell Dennis. They think so highly of him here in Lovacott. They think he's a great man, a kind man.' Again she allowed emotion, a sneer, into her voice.

'And you told Simon what you knew?'

She nodded. 'I told him.' She paused. 'Simon *was* a good man. He wanted to do the right thing.'

'Did Dennis find out that you'd spoken to him? Is that why Simon Walden had to die?'

There was a silence. No traffic outside. No birdsong. Then Dennis's voice, affable and persuasive as always. 'You can't trust what Grace says, Matthew. You know that. She's always been emotionally frail and given to strange fancies.'

'I told Dennis,' Grace said. 'He was here when I came back and he wanted to know where I'd been. I can't lie to him. He knows when I'm not telling the truth. I don't have my own life any more. He said I'd done a wicked thing, telling him our business. The man could wreck all the great work at the Woodyard. If he died, it would be a form of sacrifice. It would serve the greater good.'

'I didn't kill Simon Walden.' Dennis was still confident and easy. 'You know that, Matthew. I was celebrating your father's life at his funeral. In front of your mother and many of their friends. I spent all morning with your mother. I felt that she needed my support.' A pause. 'As you weren't there to give it. In different circumstances, if you were a more attentive son, you might have been at the service to vouch for me.'

Matthew didn't say that he *had* been there, at the chapel of rest, at least, and that he'd said goodbye to his father in his own way. 'But you didn't need to kill Simon Walden, did you, Dennis? You just had to let Grace know that it would be convenient if he died. As she said, you control her. Like a puppet-master. Like the king who let it be known that he wanted Thomas Becket killed in Canterbury, you set up the train of events that led to murder without getting your hands dirty yourself. Because your wife doesn't have her own life any more. She hasn't for years. She's so terrified of you that she'll do whatever you want.' Matthew turned to the woman, his voice gentle. 'What did you do, Grace? How did it work?'

She turned away from her husband and started speaking. 'Simon had given me his mobile number. I called him and told him that I'd found something that would incriminate the trustees. A copy of the cheque they'd given to Rosa's mother. We arranged to meet.'

'Why did you choose Crow Point?'

'I used to go there with my parents. They had a little boat that they kept at Instow. We had picnics there when I was a girl. I thought it would be a good place to die. I would like to die there, listening to the wind and the waves.'

'How did you get there?'

'I drove there in Dennis's car. He'd got a lift to the funeral with a friend. I can drive, although I seldom do these days. I'm a capable woman.' A

408

pause. 'I *was* a capable woman.'

'What about Christine? That was the day before she was snatched so she was here with you. She wasn't at the Woodyard that day.'

'I left her at home, watching television.' Grace's voice was very calm. 'She was happy enough and I knew it wouldn't take long. I'd be back before Dennis was home.'

'So, you drove to Braunton. What happened next?'

'I didn't drive down the toll road,' Grace said. 'Dennis had become friendly with a couple who lived in the cottage there and I thought they might recognize the car. I parked at the other side of the point, the seaward side, behind the dunes at Braunton Burrows, and I walked from there. Simon was waiting for me. I saw him in the distance. He was looking out.' She lifted her head. 'I think Dennis is right and I'm mad. I must be mad.'

Matthew pictured her, lanky and awkward, with her scarecrow straw hair and her staring eyes, walking over the sand towards the man she was going to kill.

'I knew nothing of this.' Dennis spoke for the first time since Matthew had begun his story. His voice was as Matthew remembered from his childhood. Deep and rich. The sound of God. 'Of course I wasn't pleased that Grace had gone behind my back to speak to Walden about our affairs, but I didn't threaten her. It's ridiculous to suggest that I asked her to kill him.'

Grace ignored him. It was as if he hadn't spoken. 'I'd brought a knife with me; it was in

409

my bag. An ordinary kitchen knife. I sharpened it before I left home. I wanted it over quickly.' She looked up at Matthew. 'It was over quickly. He had no idea what was happening.'

'And when it was over, what did you take from Simon's body?'

'Anything that might identify him. His phone and his wallet. A letter with his address on. An address in Braunton.' Grace looked up. 'You see, Matthew, I was thinking quite clearly at that point. Perhaps I wasn't mad after all. There can be no excuse.'

'Did you take a key from Simon's body?'

'Yes, there was a key. I brought it home. I haven't seen it since.'

'What did you do then?' Matthew felt suddenly relaxed, almost disengaged. This was almost over. Soon he'd be back at the house on the shore with Jonathan. They'd lie in their bed and watch the sun come up over the marsh.

'I drove the car back here. I arrived just before Dennis. I told him what I'd done.'

'What did Dennis say?' Matthew tried to picture that. Grace opening the door for her husband, sand on her shoes, blood on her hands. The meeting in the dark hall, the explanation. And all the time Christine Shapland had been in the kitchen at the back of the house, watching television. Had the man been pleased? Or horrified?

'He said that we should pray.'

There was another silence, deep and dense. Matthew couldn't bring himself to ask what they'd prayed for. Forgiveness? Walden's soul? Or that they wouldn't be found out?

410

'Where have you been this evening?' Matthew made the words conversational, a polite enquiry to cover his anger.

'We were out to dinner with friends.' Dennis would take over now. This was dangerous for him. In Lucy Braddick's attempted murder he was at least as involved as his wife and he would have constructed a story. Perhaps he'd convinced himself in part that it was true. But then Matthew had blundered in, climbing the dune. He would have found Lucy if the clouds had parted to let the moonlight through. But this wasn't about *him*.

'Which friends?'

'Colin and Hilary Marston. You might know them. You're almost neighbours. They're newcomers to the area, but Colin has become a valuable part of the Woodyard.'

Matthew nodded. It was too soon to tell him that the Marstons had been picked up in Exeter, and though they might have let him use their house, Salter couldn't implicate them in the attempted murders. That could wait for a formal interview.

'Your car was seen, driving off at speed, from a parking spot behind a bank of trees. Not long after I was assaulted. Can you explain that?'

A pause. Was Salter starting to realize that he wouldn't be able to escape this time, that his power and his charm would no longer be enough? 'There must be a mistake, Matthew. That wasn't us.'

'And during the day? Have you been into Barnstaple at all?'

411

Dennis paused. He wasn't sure how much Matthew knew. He wouldn't want to be caught out in a direct lie.

Matthew continued. 'You'll be aware of course that most of the streets in the town are covered by CCTV.'

'We often go into Barnstaple to do some shopping on a Saturday.'

'Lucy Braddick was snatched from the high street. She was there with her father and she wandered away from him for a moment. Someone caused a diversion by pretending to fall.' He paused. 'Someone wearing jeans and trainers like those belonging to your wife.'

Dennis was still considering his answer when Matthew continued. He was tired now and these were just word games. He knew what had happened. Salter wouldn't have managed to abduct Lucy on his own. He must have persuaded Grace to help him, and as always, she'd done his bidding. 'Did you see Lucy and Maurice in the town and take your chance? Or did you know they'd be there? Because that's what they do most Saturdays and you must know them. You've lived for years in the same village.'

Dennis stared ahead. In a neighbouring garden a dog barked.

'How did you get the Marstons to help you?' Matthew was in full flow now. Nothing would stop him. 'Did you promise Colin a seat on the board at the Woodyard? The post of paid administrator? Because you never approved of Jonathan, did you? Or did you give them some

412

story about Lucy being a danger to herself? Or tell them that *she'd* killed Simon Walden? They'd believe anything of a woman with Down's syndrome. Whatever the excuse, they let you use their house to hold her.'

This time Dennis did respond. He stood up, his arms folded, and looked down at Matthew. His face was very white and a nerve throbbed in his neck. He was struggling to hold things together. Matthew thought that for all his life he'd been obeyed. He'd basked in the adoration of his congregation and he'd bullied into submission the people he couldn't persuade to love him. Even now, he couldn't believe that Matthew was standing up to him.

'This is highly irregular. You can't talk to me like this in my own home and without a solicitor present. Making wild accusations. It's the middle of the night.'

Matthew stood too. 'You're quite right, Mr Salter. We need to do this at the police station and under caution. Detective Constable May will read you both your rights. You're being arrested for the attempted murder of Lucy Braddick and the murder of Simon Walden. Ross, call the police van to take them in. No reason why the neighbours shouldn't know what's happening at this point. They'll read about it in the *Journal* soon enough.'

* * *

When they arrived back at the station, Jen was still there, and suddenly, Joe Oldham ambled in.

413

It was so unusual for him to be around after hours that Matthew wondered if the concussion was hitting him at last, that the boss was an hallucination.

'I hear it's all over,' Oldham said. 'Good work, everyone. I'm off to my bed now and we'll catch up tomorrow.' He took a half-bottle of whisky and three plastic tumblers from his briefcase, set them on the table, then wandered out again, a confused and amiable bear lost in the forest.

They gathered in Matthew's office, with a small tot of the whisky each. Jen perched on his desk and Ross leaning against the door. All of them, it seemed, too tired to bear their own weight.

'You should have gone home,' Matthew said to Jen.

She shook her head. 'I wanted to see it through to the end. To see you bring them in. We've got enough, haven't we, to convict?'

'The Salters and Craven, certainly. Lucy still had Rosa's skirt hidden in a drawer in her bedroom. Maurice found it this evening. I'm not sure about Preece and the Marstons. They could say that what they did in covering up the assault on Rosa Holsworthy wasn't criminal. I'm sure they'll argue that they believed they were acting in Rosa's best interests and in the interests of the Woodyard.'

Ross shifted his feet. 'Do you think Walden did the right thing, stirring it up? If he'd left it alone, he'd still be alive and Lucy and Chrissie wouldn't have been put through that trauma.'

Jen turned on him, red hair flying. 'Is that

414

what you really think? Just cover it up and it'll go away? That's what the men at the Woodyard thought. Are you one of them?'

'No,' Ross said. 'No. But he was obsessed with it, wasn't he, with the story of Rosa, and I'm not quite sure why. He had a new life. A beautiful woman. He was making friends. He'd get a job as a chef somewhere in the season if he was as good a cook as everyone makes out. I'm not sure why he let that obsession take over his life.'

'Because he knew it was important for the truth to be told.' Jen turned back to the room. 'And because of the guilt he'd carried round with him since he killed the child in the road accident. I looked into the incident again. It was something his ex-wife said when she was talking to us about it. *A child like that. So helpless.* And the ambiguous response of the parents when they learned of Walden's death.' She paused. 'The child had brain damage. She was severely learning disabled and she only had months to live. It was personal for him. He was already obsessed.'

43

When Matthew arrived home, it was morning. A still, spring day. Jonathan had stayed up, waiting for him as he'd promised, but he was asleep in the rocking chair in the living room, the fire out and the curtains drawn. There was a glass on the floor beside him, but otherwise the house was tidy, the kitchen clear. Jonathan didn't mind mess, but he knew Matthew hated coming home to it.

Matthew drew the curtains and let in the light. Jonathan stirred. He looked up at Matthew. 'Is it over?'

'Yes,' Matthew said. 'It's over.'

'I was thinking we might visit my parents later,' Jonathan said. 'Get away from the coast for a bit. Have a walk on the moor.'

'Blow away the cobwebs.' Matthew kept his voice light. Jonathan seldom made the trip to the farm and when he did, they were duty calls: birthdays and the run up to Christmas.

'Build some bridges,' Jonathan said. 'Seeing Maurice and Lucy together I thought I should make more effort.'

Matthew knew what was coming next and got in first. 'Perhaps I should invite my mother to Sunday lunch some day.'

'It seems like the right time to ask her.'

There was a moment of silence. Outside the waves broke on the shore and the gulls cried.

416

We do hope that you have enjoyed reading this large print book.

Did you know that all of our titles are available for purchase?

We publish a wide range of high quality large print books including:
**Romances, Mysteries, Classics
General Fiction
Non Fiction and Westerns**

Special interest titles available in large print are:
**The Little Oxford Dictionary
Music Book
Song Book
Hymn Book
Service Book**

Also available from us courtesy of Oxford University Press:
**Young Readers' Dictionary
(large print edition)
Young Readers' Thesaurus
(large print edition)**

For further information or a free brochure, please contact us at:
**Ulverscroft Large Print Books Ltd.,
The Green, Bradgate Road, Anstey,
Leicester, LE7 7FU, England.
Tel:** (00 44) 0116 236 4325
Fax: (00 44) 0116 234 0205

Other titles published by Ulverscroft:

THIN AIR

Ann Cleeves

A group of old university friends leaves the bright lights of London and travels to Unst, Shetland's most northerly island, to celebrate the marriage of a friend. But late on the night of the wedding party, one of them, Eleanor, disappears — apparently into thin air. Soon her body is discovered, lying in a small loch close to the cliff edge, and Detectives Jimmy Perez and Willow Reeves are dispatched to investigate. Before she went missing, Eleanor claimed to have seen the ghost of a local child who drowned in the 1920s. Jimmy and Willow are convinced that there's more to Eleanor's death than they first thought. Is there a secret that lies behind the myth — one so shocking that someone would kill many years later to protect it?

THE MOTH CATCHER

Ann Cleeves

Life seems perfect in Valley Farm, a quiet community in Northumberland. Then a shocking discovery shatters the silence. The owners of a big country house have employed a house-sitter, a young ecologist named Patrick, to look after the place while they're away. But Patrick is found dead by the side of the lane into the valley — a beautiful, lonely place to die. DI Vera Stanhope arrives on the scene with her colleagues, and when they search the attic of the house, where Patrick has a flat, she finds a second body. All the two victims have in common is a fascination with moths. As Vera is drawn into the claustrophobic world of this increasingly strange community, she realises that there may be deadly secrets trapped here . . .

COLD EARTH

Ann Cleeves

In the dark days of a Shetland winter, torrential rain triggers a landslide that crosses the main Lerwick-Sumburgh road and sweeps down to the sea. At the burial of his old friend Magnus Tait, Jimmy Perez watches the flood of mud and peaty water smash through a croft house in its path. Everyone thinks the croft is uninhabited, but in the wreckage he finds the body of a dark-haired woman wearing a red silk dress. In his mind she shares his Mediterranean ancestry, and soon he becomes obsessed with tracing her identity. Then it emerges that she was already dead before the landslide hit the house. Perez knows he must find out who she was, and how she died.